To Ed   11-5-04

'Tis a dull road indeed, that has
no turns. I hope you enjoy the
journey of The Auld Sod.'
                              Best wishes
                                Dave

THE AULD SOD

Had we but a day to spend,
At nothing more than being friends,
What better place could e'er we be,
Than on the auld sod, set hard by the sea?

Out we'll go midst gorse and heather,
Braced for wind and foul weather,
It's fairways only, lad, you'll say,
Greens too, mate, no shots astray.

And when, too soon, our day is done,
Eighteen battles waged and won.
Last putts fall, and like the light,
Scores will fade, but ne'er the fight.

In the gloam, a piper stands,
Echoes drone 'cross dunes of sand.
It's a glass we'll hoist, a dram or two,
For all the shots struck straight and true.

Well done, lad, a match well-played,
No quarter asked, none giv'n 'way.
And nothing's so grand, we both will agree
As the splendid auld sod, set hard by the sea.

~ From the memoirs of Angus MacKenzie ~

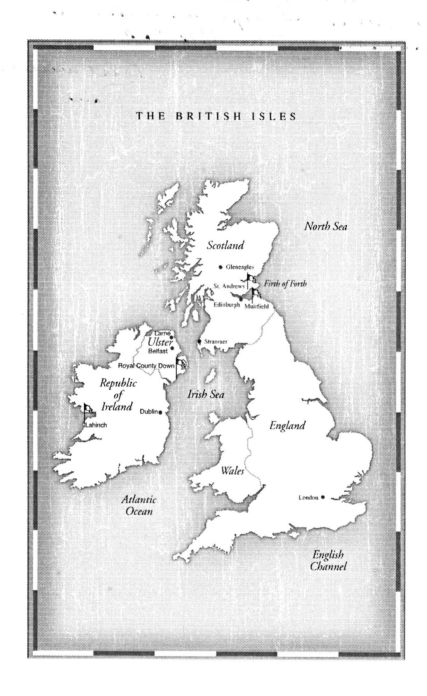

THE BRITISH ISLES

North Sea

Scotland

● Gleneagles

St. Andrews
Firth of Forth

Edinburgh Muirfield

Larne
Ulster
Belfast ●

Royal County Down

● Stranraer

Republic
of
Ireland

Dublin ●

Irish Sea

England

● Lahinch

Wales

Atlantic
Ocean

London ●

English
Channel

THE AULD SOD

A Novel

David Edson

iUniverse, Inc.
New York Lincoln Shanghai

The Auld Sod
A Novel

All Rights Reserved © 2004 by David Edson

iUniverse, Inc.

For information address:
iUniverse
2021 Pine Lake Road, Suite 100
Lincoln, NE 68512
www.iuniverse.com

ISBN: 0-595-32518-1 (pbk)
ISBN: 0-595-66623-X (cloth)

Printed in the United States of America

For My Father

ACKNOWLEDGMENTS

*T*he term *acknowledgment* falls far short of the gratitude deserved by those who supported my quest to capture the spirit of ***The Auld Sod.*** In truth, no tribute can measure up to the selflessness of family and friends who rally behind the selfish pursuits of others. This was their gift to me. Their thoughtful consideration and indulgence of my passion for this novel will always be my fondest memory of the journey.

Above all, it was the encouragement of my wife, Debby, that allowed me to explore the outer reaches of my imagination, and her loving patience that allowed me to press on.

No attribution would be complete without a wink and a nod to my daughters, Shannon and Lauren, and my mother, Eloise. They, too, were unwavering in their support during times it would have been easier to just throw in the towel.

A special thanks to Dr. Louis Attebery, whose early edits helped shape the story; to Dr. David Kelly, whose later edits helped shape the style; and to my assistant, Michele Vela, whose insight helped shape the artwork and the format.

I am most grateful to Graeme Baxter for allowing the use of his incredible rendering of The Road Hole on Old Course at St Andrews for the cover, and for his paintings of The Swilcan Bridge, Muirfield, Royal County Down, and Lahinch, to introduce each of the four parts of the story. Graeme's work brings to life the soul of the grand linksland of the British Isles.

And, finally, to all the friends who took the time to read *The Auld Sod* at various stages, and to provide honest criticism and comforting praise, I am forever indebted.

Bill Hay; Scott Pasley; Jim Smith; Jim Curran; Andy Gerlicher; Bill Stanwood; Mike Bideganeta; Steve Lydiatt; Don and Geridee Farley; Dan and Merritt Wilson; John and Connie Bachman; Craig Bachman; Mr. and Mrs. Jimmy Gabrielsen; Bob Maloney; Carolyn Walker; Joe Quirk; Marv French; Bruce and Linda Cadwell; Ray Davis; Kathy Burney; Kathleen Lewis; Harve Menkens; Dick Estey; and Joe and Carol McAndrew.

PROLOGUE

▼

*A*ngus stood his clubs against the rail outside *The Cleek and Brassie* and stepped through the open doorway, his tweeds still glistening from the cloudburst that had cornered him on the inward nine. He shrugged out of his jacket and grabbed the collar with both hands, shaking off beads of rain before draping it over the coat rack to dry. In one swift motion, he removed his cap and swiped it across his thigh, spraying even more mist into the air. With the flick of his wrist, he spun the cap onto a hook next to his jacket and turned to join the revelry in the pub, which, by now, was alive with golfers replaying their rounds and repairing divots to their egos with whatever tonic they had deemed suitable for the task.

"Yer lookin' a bit bedraggled, Angus," called a familiar voice from behind the bar. "Off our gemme, today, were we?" The brogue of Malcom Campbell sounded more from the west of Scotland than that common to these parts . . . more Ayrshire than East Lothian.

"I've had my fill of golf," Angus replied, shuffling over to his permanent slot at the end of the bar. "Stand me the Talisker if you please, Campy."

"Needin' somethin' with a wee more bite to it tonight, eh lad?" Campbell said, using a bar towel to dry the inside of a tumbler before tipping a generous pour of the single malt for his friend. He paused to allow Angus a taste of his scotch. "Never known you to give in to the rain, Angus."

"Oh, it's not the weather, Malcom. I'm just tired of playin' bogey golf."

"Aye, there was a time we could make all the bogeys we wanted using a single club," Campbell replied. "Any club in the bag, at that."

"These days, I'm hard-pressed to scuff out a par, let alone a birdie, car-ryin' fourteen of the blasted bats in my arsenal."

"Maybe yer clubs remind you of all the shots you've mishit. Why don't you trade 'em for some new equipment?"

"It's a poor workman that blames his tools, Campy. There's nothing wrong with my clubs a better swing wouldn't fix."

Malcom moved over to a slate board, chalk in hand, poised to enter a score for Angus on a grid that displayed the names of eight men down the left-hand column and the number of weeks until The Open Championship across the top.

"What number do I post, Angus?" he asked.

"WD," replied Angus.

"WD, my arse," Campbell growled. "You know the rules . . . if you dunna post a score ev'ry week, from now 'til The Open, ye canna win the jug. You'll nae be withdrawin' from this tarnamint, lad . . . not on my watch."

"I'm not competing this year, Campy. Scratch my name from the field. I don't need any reminders of how I once could play . . . but can't anymore."

"Don't be comin' into my pub feelin' all sorry fer yerself, Angus MacKenzie," Campbell shot back. "If you think anyone cares about yer gowf scores, you've got yer head in the gorse. It's the pleasure of yer com-pany we're lookin' for. You scratch from the tarnamint, and I'll scratch yer name off that jug," he said, pointing to the trophy across the room.

On the mantle above the fireplace sat an exact replica of the claret jug awarded by The Royal & Ancient Golf Club of St. Andrews to their *cham-pion golfer of the year*. For over two decades now, it had been a tradition at *The Cleek and Brassie* to compete for bragging rights at the pub. To win, and to have one's name engraved on the claret jug was, in its own way, every bit as important to these men of Gullane as it was to the profession-als who pursued golfing immortality in the world's oldest championship, The British Open. While the quality of play might not measure up, the pride, and the striving, and the friendships, surely did.

It wasn't just the sad state of his golf that had put him in a foul mood. This had been coming on for quite some time. Angus was feeling old and alone. And, to make matters worse, he was embarrassed now by his childishness. These days, writing, and tippling, and little else, held his interest when weather closed in. Oh, there had been a time, not so long ago, when he would have ignored the elements and headed out for a quick nine. A good stretch of the legs, and the feel of club in hand, once rescued him from the doldrums. But now, he shuddered at the mere thought of getting wet, and was dismayed at how freely he had settled for more sedentary ways. Of late, he found it far more agreeable to slip into his post at the end of the bar and bend elbows with his mates, give ear to their light-hearted slander, and return a jab or two of his own. Whenever the rain gave way to a tolerable mist, he was off to the pub in search of camaraderie, that rare gift only friends can provide.

With a storm lurking off the Firth, and his malaise in full bloom, today seemed an odd time for Angus to resume his golf. He hadn't played in weeks, and seemed not to care. Then again, not once in twenty years had he missed the opening day of the annual tournament. And, to be perfectly honest, the work on his novel this morning had produced nothing of value, raising the prospect of a long afternoon before the day's first drink would be poured . . . reason enough to repair to the links. Odds were still in favour of Angus filling his cups before the sun fell beneath the yardarm.

If his expectations were modest, the results were nil. With bogeys on each of the first seven holes, he was tempted to pick up and go home . . . the easy way out, seeing as how his cottage sat a mere stone's throw from the seventh green. Instead, he carried on, and, in the end, was able to scrape together enough game to salvage two unsightly pars. As luck would have it, of course, one of his triumphs came on the eighteenth . . . a fitting end to a perfectly fitful day . . . golf's cruel way of tantalizing its patrons . . . dispensing just an ounce of pleasure to disguise its cruelty . . . luring them back for another round of pain and torture.

"Well, Angus. I need a number," Campbell persisted.

"88."

"A *MacTarnahan*," Malcom trilled, as he entered a pair of eights into the space beside Angus' name. Eighty-eight was the jersey number of Tommy MacTarnahan, the legendary right winger for the Edinburgh Lions of the Scottish Rugby Federation in the 1940s. Campy had a label for any score, mostly the retired numbers of oldtime ruggers. But, the goal was to shoot the temperature. Anyone shooting the temperature was sure to earn medalist honors, inasmuch as the mercury in Scotland, even in summer, was seldom over par.

"Y' canna win the jug, Angus, if y' dunna get around in fewer strokes," Campy added, winking at the other golfers who lined the bar with their swill of choice in hand.

"The last time I looked, my name was etched on the jug three times," Angus countered. "I seem to recall seeing Malcom Campbell on it but once."

"Aye, but here I am, a poor, one-legged man, competing against blokes with two healthy limbs. I should be getting' strokes from the field to make up for for this handicap of mine."

It was during the Second World War, while fighting the Huns in North Africa at El Alamein, that Malcom's right leg had been blown to smithereens by a mortar shell. Yet, he was one of those indomitable characters who seemed to find redemption in suffering, a rare soul who could turn grief into gratitude, if not outright joy. Considering the battalions of men who had forfeited life to secure that godforsaken spit of sand from the Axis, Malcom reasoned his own loss of limb was but a token sacrifice to the cause. Why, no less than Churchill himself had paid homage to the veterans of El Alamein by claiming; *Before El Alamein we never won a battle, and after it . . . we never lost one.*

"You're too proud to accept strokes from anyone," Angus replied. "You'd sooner gimp your way around and lose, than grovel for strokes, even from the best players."

Malcom had been fitted for a prosthesis, but wore it only to play golf. He preferred to move about the pub using a hickory-shafted brassie with deep grooves carved into its persimmon head from the constant pressure of his fingers. The athlete in him was evident yet, as his stump swung rhythmically beside the splendid old cane.

"I'll give y' that, Angus. Gowf is nothing more than compensatin' for weaknesses. Missing a leg keeps my head steady. If I don't, I'll fall on my arse. There's a lot worse things than being shy a leg."

Angus enjoyed wiling away the hours with Malcom, reminiscing and swapping lies. He wondered, though, just how much of his pleasure should be attributed to the soothing balm of scotch whiskey poured non-stop by his friend. He'd seen many a good man broken by the bottle and worried that he, too, might become just another old sot, lost in his misery, abetted by an all-too-willing barkeep. So, when they rehashed the past, only the most pleasing of memories were allowed . . . no space in their album for remorse. Memories, after all, were their armor to fend off the trials of old age, and, at the end of the battle, the pillows into which they would softly settle and cushion the final few blows.

His earliest memories of *The Cleek and Brassie* were as a lad, sitting outside on a bench while his father had gone in for a dram or two. Back then, the conversations meant nothing to Angus, just the rants of old men about wars and derring-do in places off the far edges of the map, exploits and locales well beyond his comprehension. He could still recall the voices drifting over the transom, conveying sentiments of honor, commemorating an era when Great Britain was the world's most powerful and relevant nation. It never occurred to Angus that he might someday become one of those relics seated at the bar, mired in the past, for he had always seen himself as that lad on the bench, looking to the future. Yet, here he was, listening in rapt attention to rants of Malcom Campbell.

"What'll it be tonight, Angus? Gowf . . . literature . . . politics?" Campy asked, tipping another shot of Talisker into the empty glass in front of his friend.

Reluctant as Angus was to discuss his golf game, he was even more tight-lipped about his writing. It was a subject that would be off limits, at least until after the third pour. And they made a point of almost never discussing politics. Even the closest of friends could get out of sorts over politics. Beyond that, there was really only one topic to be avoided . . . Muirfield.

Thirty years had passed since Angus had received his invitation from The Honourable Company of Edinburgh Golfers to become a member of their distinguished order. He was flattered, of course. Only men of distinction were asked to join The Company, and even then, the honour was reserved for those of impeccable credentials and breeding. The offer had come shortly after his treatise, *Golf in Modern Society*, had been published, and he saw the overture as a validation of his work.

Angus, though, had never been much of a joiner. He had little interest in climbing the rungs of the social ladder, and intended to politely decline. Not that he didn't fit into this elite circle, for Angus was accomplished in his own right, a well-read, and gracious man who could go toe to toe with any blue-blood. He did, however, lack pedigree and the knack for pretense . . . attributes which, if not required, were, among the privileged, ever-present. Simply put, he preferred plain folk.

While scholarly debate was not standard fare at *The Cleek and Brassie*, Angus could always count on a spirited discussion with men like Campy, whose insights gained clarity in direct proportion to the amount of single malt they consumed. For someone whose entire career had been spent in the midst of self-styled intellectuals, Angus felt very much at ease with this lot. The uncommon wisdom of these quite common men was credential more dear than a diploma in science or law or literature, and *infinitely* more valuable than an aristocratic title.

Angus was at odds with himself . . . on the one hand, loyal to Malcom and his mates at the pub, and on the other, seduced by the prospect of playing golf on his favourite links course. In the end, he joined the club, reasoning he could enjoy both the golf at Muirfield and the camaraderie of *The Cleek and Brassie*. His friends felt betrayed. They saw his choice as an act of snobbery, and none more so than Malcom Campbell. He let Angus know how he felt, and never mentioned it again. As the years passed, if Malcom harbored any ill feelings about Muirfield, he kept them well-hidden.

When they talked of golf, it was a conversation of connoisseurs, as if the topic were rare wine or fine food. They would begin with a critique of the art of clubmaking through the years, then rank the great courses they had played. Always mindful of the game's venerable lore, they would contrast the styles of golf's legendary characters and recount the most notable matches and shots they had witnessed through the years. The tales were often repetitive, but never grew dull, as, night after night, these clever wags would delight *The Cleek's* constituents with an endless array of fact and fiction.

Angus believed golf replicated the stages of life. For young men, he would say, the game is an outlet for competitive passions, a means to prove one's worth. Midlife, it becomes a social medium, a vehicle through which to fraternize with like-minded friends. And, in the twilight of our days, it is something of a trusted confidant, as familiar and comfortable as a pair of old slippers. Rare is the sport, he would continue, played in groups, yet offering serene introspection.

When no mates were at the ready, Angus was content to roam the course as if in a realm all his own, just a man and his clubs versus the links and its elements. In life, as in golf, Angus had always played it as he found it, until lately, when the black dog of melancholia had begun to nip at his heels, and he, in turn, had begun to nip at the bottle. For a man late in his seasons, it was a bit like invoking winter rules, just a wee nudge to improve his lie.

Malcom's view of the game took a slightly different slant. Golf demands our best, he would maintain. Nothing less will do. It is meant to be an examination of skill and emotion, always and forever. Unfair conditions are part of the bargain, whether in life or in golf. No preferred lies.

Even in his present state, Campbell fancied himself a scratch player, refusing charity from opponents. Unlike Angus, he cast nary a glance at who he once had been, looking instead toward the player he might become, defying the very existence of a handicap. Old Man Par was the standard . . . always and forever. It was a mark he achieved more often than not.

From their favourite table along the west wall, Angus and his mates could look out onto the links of Gullane No. 1, and take in the first tee and eighteenth green. During the occasional lull in conversation, heads would turn toward the window to observe a loop just beginning or one coming to an end. Invariably, compliments would ripple through the pub noting a drive struck solidly or a putt well-holed. And, without fail, an equal measure of ridicule would find its way around the room to underscore the embarrassing lip-out or the tee ball gone awry.

"How's the novel coming, Angus?" asked Campy, refilling his tumbler for the third time.

"The usual difficulties . . . overwritten and disconnected. On balance . . . a cartload of odds and ends."

Writing, for Angus, had become more pastime than calling, done to reflect rather than report. Nearly fifty years a journalist, he had moved into retirement and found it vacant. While relieved to no longer be slave to the news, and pleased to be rid of those dreaded deadlines, his urge to write had not passed quietly. To be perfectly frank, however, it should have come as no surprise when his leap from reporter to novelist fell short. There was no reason to believe he would ever become as fluent with fiction as he had been with fact. His grasp of syntax was helpful, of course, but with little skill in devising plot or in developing characters, and unpracticed in the art of dialogue or narrative voice, a novel had proven elusive.

In defense of his shortcomings, Angus would offer up the old saw that, "*Writing is merely a labour of love.*"

Campbell was not as charitable. Self-appointed critic of all half-arsed endeavours, he would simply sneer and call it *crrrap*. "Clichés," he carped, "have no place in literature . . . and there's nothing so trite as the tale that begins in the midst of a storm." He was referring, of course, to his friend's fondness for using weather as the backdrop for the opening scene.

Beyond this good-natured give and take, Angus saw writing as a process, not unlike solving a vast crossword puzzle. Besides, what did Campy know? *His* writing was limited to scrawling out the daily bill of fare on a chalkboard. No, a bit more focus, a dab of inspiration, a ration of hard work, and, perhaps, a novel might emerge. Angus would have done well, however, to remember that inspiration is fickle . . . a muse, coming in fits and starts. And, while the muse may, from time to time, take up temporary residence in the bottle, seldom does he call it home. It was becoming frightfully clear that Angus would be better-served putting pen to paper prior to his daily excursions to pub, long before the whiskey could subdue his senses.

*   *   *

Sometime around eleven, just before the heavens spat out a liberal dose of hell, Angus stumbled home from *The Cleek and Brassie*, intending to rewrite some of his jottings from earlier in the day, only to find them strewn across the room, a paper trail of countless failed edits. If only he'd had his wits about him, he might have put the cottage in order. Doors would have been latched, and shutters fastened. Instead, they were clapping out a calypso to the wind. Deep in his cups and stone deaf to the rage outside, Angus had begun a slow surrender, and so, too, had the fire, leaving the kitchen exposed to icy blasts streaming down the flue. Sheets of stationery were being whisked about, and near the hearth lay a collection of handwritten notes, crumpled into wads and tossed haphazardly toward the dying embers.

In no mood to tidy up, and in no condition to wordsmith, he somehow managed to cobble together a paragraph describing the storm, ever faithful to the notion that tales set in the British Isles must always depict the elements. With his mind in a muddle, and eyes glazing over, Angus strained to proofread his latest drivel.

That afternoon, a squall formed over the Firth. To those on shore, it seemed harmless enough amid bright blue skies, more likely to retreat into the North Sea than race toward land. Then, at dusk, breezes freshened and changed direction, clouds blackened and began to boil, gathering strength for an all-out blow. And, by midnight, stocked with water and charged with electricity, a thunderhead swept across Gullane Hill, detonating an artillery of lightning bolts, and shredding the air with shrapnel-like rain.

This effort soon went for naught, as it, too, was wadded and pitched into the pile of rejects. Discouraged by the lack of fresh ideas, and fending off the sedative effects of alcohol, Angus turned from prose to poetry, hoping to clear the fog. Just a few simple lines, perhaps, something to help focus his thoughts. But, as was so often the case during these late-night sessions, he was barely able to scratch out the odd stanza or two before slipping off into oblivion. Though he looked to be in pain, slouched in his chair, face flattened to the table, the drone of his snoring suggested little concern for comfort. All that remained of his recent work were dozens of drafts, cast to the wind, save one, a single sheet of verse, wedged between his cheek and the table, soaked with the spittle that was drooling from the corner of his mouth.

*   *   *

At first light, the storm eased, not that it mattered to Bobby. He took great pleasure from delivering the news on time, even in foul weather. Cycling over cobbled streets and slinging newspapers at darkened houses offered a certain sense of accomplishment. What fine sport it was to hit every porch without breaking any windows or depositing his wares into the shrubbery. He didn't even mind leaving the comfort of bed before sunrise. But, as with those who had covered the route before him, he cringed at the thought of his final delivery . . . the dreadful climb up Gullane Hill . . . soggy grasses soaking every inch of clothing . . . sand clinging to every dampened crease . . . not to mention the chill to his bones. All this, and the spectre of old man MacKenzie, had caused others to abandon the route after a few jaunts up the Hill. But Bobby Fenwick was determined not to be among them.

He pedaled hard beside Gullane Golf Links, the hush of dawn broken only by the hum of tires over rain-slickened stones. Dead ahead loomed a majestic mountain of sand, its thickets of gorse populated by sheep and rabbits and an ancient Scotsman. Leaning his bike against the stone wall at the end of the lane, Bobby stuffed the last of the newspapers inside his mackintosh. His mates had cautioned that MacKenzie could just as easily have his papers delivered by post but, instead, took great pleasure in watching the Hill break their spirit. To them, it was some sort of fiendish character examination devised by a doddering recluse to gauge the mettle of today's youth against that of his own mildewed times. And, they had counseled Bobby the crusty old bastard was not worth the effort.

Tugging his cap snug to his brow, young Fenwick stared up at the faint light atop the hill, shielding his eyes from a veil of mist blown in off the Firth. He shuddered beneath his wind-breaker, wondering why MacKenzie had to have his newspapers so early . . . and not just *The Scotsman*, he muttered, but the *London Times*, and the *Irish Independent*.

No sooner had he begun his ascent than the grade began to grow steeper, turning sharply around the face of an embankment before vanishing into a tangle of fescue and marram. Bobby nestled into the shelter of a sandy blowout and studied the seaside grasses just ahead, hanging limp and sodden, a writhing snarl through which only a machete could hack out a trail. Then, scuttling crab-like, beneath the canopy of sedge, he lurched back into open ground, wheezing in the half-light of morning, trying to imagine what MacKenzie did with so much bloody news.

Cloaked in shadows, he peeked inside his mack to make sure his cargo had been protected from the damp. Further ahead and much higher, Bobby could just make out the summit and the outline of a cottage tucked into the hillside. Knee-deep in sand and grass, he braced for his final assault on the Hill over one last stretch of dunes that pitched and rolled before him like surf in a storm. If this much news was needed, he mumbled, slogging between the hillocks, why couldn't MacKenzie at least wait 'til dawn to take delivery?

When, at last, he reached the cottage, Bobby was surprised to find the old man absent from his usual station. Most days, he could be found teetering on his rocker, protected from the elements by a screened-in porch. More than once, Bobby had sensed MacKenzie watching him climb, taking full measure of his efforts as he thrashed his way up the hill. Just last month, he overheard Malcom Campbell outside *The Cleek and Brassie* laying odds that young Fenwick would give in to the weather and early hours as had all the others after a month or so of hill duty. But, to Bobby's delight, MacKenzie had replied, this youngster wasn't at all like the others. Lugging newspapers to a secluded cottage in the dead of night was more than enough to deter most children, Angus told Campbell . . . but not Bobby . . . he had the grit. According to Angus, this mere jot of twelve was more than a match for the windswept dunes of Gullane Hill. And so, despite his reputation as a cranky old Scot, Angus MacKenzie had, by his own words, revealed himself to be less the curmudgeon, more the gentleman.

Today, there was a light in the kitchen, but no sign of the old man. Though he now knew Angus only pretended the role of a grouch, Bobby stood trembling on the top step, fearful he'd kept Mr. MacKenzie waiting for his precious news. Young Fenwick cracked open the screen door and tiptoed across the porch. As he peered into the kitchen, the breath was sucked from his lungs by the sight of a lifeless body hunched over the table. Bobby suddenly wished he could take back every unkindness he had ever said or thought about the old man.

"Mr. MacKenzie, sir?" he whispered, gently nudging the elbow of the slumping figure, hoping for some sign of life.

"Angus, please . . . wake up!" he cried. His voice had grown louder, more urgent.

Peering over the old man's shoulder at the sheet of paper stuck to his face, Bobby gently removed it and began to read. Not exactly sure what was meant, he guessed the words must have been written by Angus before he had . . . well . . . Bobby couldn't think about that just now. He jostled MacKenzie's shoulder, trying to make sense of it all.

Flaccid flesh does crease and fold,
Too long lived in, growing old.
Dare endure this steep decline,
And comes again that ageless pine,
Though not for things now and here,
Rather, deeds of yesteryear.
Gone, the roar of carpe diem,
Fetch instead . . . what might have been.

Rain reigns, welcome worn,
Plays the warden, dripping scorn.
Solitude, once the preference,
Seems now, a prison sentence.
Maudlin mood exacts its toll,
For it is he who robs the soul.
And of this cellmate do beware,
Wretch, felon . . . alias Despair.

Mr. MacKenzie must be sad, he thought. But he was too young to make a connection between these feelings and death. At this point in his life, Bobby knew only of hope, not despair.

"You can't die now," his voice trembled. "Get up . . . please! Don't you be quitin'! You've got more writin' to do!"

"Unnhh," came a groan from beneath the heap. Angus slowly lifted his head and shoulders as if bearing the weight of Atlas.

"Bobby? What are you doing here?"

"I brought your papers, Mr. MacKenzie," the lad replied in relief. "You must'a fell asleep at the table last night."

"Campbell," he mumbled, remembering his night of bonding with his mates at *The Cleek*. "Too much Talisker," he moaned, recalling his unsteady climb to the cottage.

"Bobby, I hoped you'd never see me in such a state. A man my age ought to set a better example."

"Oh, you're a fine example, sir," said Bobby. "I'm just glad you're not dead."

"So am I, lad," sighed Angus, though given his current condition, death had its appeal.

The pounding between his ears raised doubt as to whether the therapeutic effects of whiskey in the eve were worth the excruciating invoice of the morn. Angus handed Bobby a fiver and thanked him for caring. Young folks nowadays seemed to show less regard for their elders than in his time. To him, respect was a quality that seldom improved with age. Either one had it early in life, or one did not. This Fenwick fellow had it.

And to Bobby, the real purpose of his trek up Gullane Hill was not to receive Mr. MacKenzie's generosity, but to gain his approval. His opinion mattered. And today's encounter had shown Bobby this was not some crotchety old recluse taking pleasure in the adversity of others. He was just lonely.

Angus watched the boy bounce down the hill through spangles of sunlight until, again, he was merely a speck, head bobbing above the marram like a buoy in the harbour. Then, he was gone, consumed by sand and grass and mist. Angus retreated to the warmth of the kitchen, reflecting on the intemperance of last night, wishing he could swap his fatigue for a bit of that youthful vitality.

*   *   *

Angus spread the newspapers onto the table and massaged his temples, vowing to curb his use of alcohol. The prescriptions of Malcom Campbell, he had deduced, were far less noxious if taken in smaller dosages, and carried fewer side effects when restricted to medicinal use. The teapot trilled the arrival of Earl Grey, his favoured remedy, and Angus poured a steaming cup, adding a dollop of honey to appease the throb behind his eyes.

He opened the *London Times* to a headline proclaiming ominously . . . *CAR BOMB KILLS LORD DUNTHORPE.* It was yet another violent incident in England signaling a renewed state of unrest. Buried within the text, the article conceded no evidence could be found of IRA involvement, but the inference was clear . . . who else could be responsible? The *Times* reported the Irish Republican Army, led by its political arm, Sinn Fein, had been trying for several months to force new elections in Ulster, its latest attempt to install a coalition government in Belfast. These efforts, it said, had gained little traction, opposed in parliament by an unlikely alliance of liberals and conservatives, strange bedfellows, whose rallying cry was Remember 1916. Against this inflammatory backdrop, tensions had mounted, and threats had been made. Initially, there were minor disturbances and acts of vandalism. Then, a series of random attacks on public property had been reported. And now this, a prominent member of parliament . . . murdered.

Frowning, Angus slurped his tea and folded the *Times*. This resumption of bad blood was all too familiar, all part of a debilitating cycle. Irish Catholics would demand concessions to their political status in Northern Ireland, and the Brits would refuse. The IRA would resort to terror in an effort to gain recognition of its demands, and England would retaliate, using even greater force in reprisal. The hostilities would escalate until one side could no longer stand the bloodshed. Then, a truce would be put in place until the cycle could begin anew. Angus had observed this course of conduct for half a century and found it senseless.

Surely there must be better news elsewhere. He opened *The Scotsman* to the banner: *LORD DUNTHORPE DEAD; IRA SUSPECTED.* The story by leading journalist, Gordon Strand, all but tried, convicted, and condemned the IRA to the gallows. It pulled no punches in laying blame on the Irish for using terrorism to gain political leverage. As far as it went, Angus didn't quarrel with Strand's point of view, he simply thought it superficial. By his way of thinking, one should never go so far as to murder an elected official in order to achieve political gain. He did, however, endorse a policy by which public servants would be marched en masse to the woodshed to have their backsides reddened . . . just enough of the strap to unseat their dogma. To Angus, it seemed the press devoted too little space and even less thought to writing about the root cause of Irish troubles. If only a bit more insight could be shared as to how Ireland and England had gotten into this malignant orbit, perhaps some meaningful dialogue might ensue, and a solution be forged on the anvil of fact, far removed from the bellows of emotion.

Angus grimaced at his own hyperbole, weary of investing this much thought into matters of the public domain. He preferred light reading, but today, for no good reason, he had altered his schedule. It was not his practice to start with the front page, with its entirely-too-depressing accounts of current events. Of course, the obituaries weren't exactly uplifting either. But at least the names he read there were mostly contemporaries, people who, like him, had lived full lives, unlike those on page one, that, all too often, had met a tragic end. Generally, he would begin with the *Irish Independent.* The news from Dublin seemed more eclectic, less staid than the London or Edinburgh slant. Eventually, though, he would get around to reading all three papers, because a newsman must be balanced. He was, after all, still a newsman at heart.

Angus resumed his routine by opening the *Independent* to section three, the obituaries. He couldn't remember precisely when this ritual had begun, but knew it wasn't some morbid preoccupation with dying that caused him to turn there first, each day. It was more an acceptance, a resignation, he supposed, that death was gaining ground on what remained of his life. Angus had grown accustomed to keeping up with friends and acquaintances by reading the death notices.

A fresh cup of tea and a slice of burnt toast were arranged to one side as Angus began to study the alphabetized columns. He wasn't looking for anyone in particular, but fully expected to find someone he knew had passed on. Dunking the toast, he observed, as usual, that some of the accounts were quite elaborate, lengthy descriptions of the deceased's life work, virtual biographies of those favoured few whose endeavours had been deemed newsworthy by some editor. And, as he had also come to expect, other notices were brief, containing scant detail, mere footnotes of lives that would now cease without so much as a trace of public acclaim. Angus had begun to think today he might be spared the grief of another lost colleague when, there it was, near the bottom of the page. He inhaled sharply and read.

> *Riley Padraig O'Neill, age 77. Born March 17, 1898; died May 4, 1975. Renowned Irish amateur golfer. Services May 8, 1975, St. Theresa's Chapel, Lahinch, Ireland.*

Angus folded the paper and slumped in his chair, inflating his cheeks in a slow exhale. Riley's life had been distilled to just four words, not even a complete sentence. Though he knew well that newspapers are frugal with space, Angus thought it sad a life this full had been deemed a footnote. Not a word had been written about Riley's role in the struggle for an Irish republic. Oh, indeed, he had been a fine golfer, but that was a mere scrap of his identity. Riley had been an Irishman in a perilous time, a time when true Irishmen put their dreams of a free and united Ireland above personal safety. This was a life, perhaps too complex to be condensed into an obituary. For a man whose beliefs had been shaped by the epic myths and poetic romance and traditions of Eire, a simple epitaph might have been more suitable. In a word, Riley O'Neill was a Gael.

Angus stepped to the kitchen cupboard and removed a half-empty fifth of Bushmill's. Tipping a splash into his teacup, he hoisted it skyward out of respect for Riley's presumably heaven-bound spirit and murmured . . .

> *May the Lord hold you in the hollow of His hand, Riley O'Neill*
> *and not close His fist too tightly.*

Angus downed the dram and felt a sudden emptiness. He had cherished Riley's friendship, but could not remember ever telling him. Surely theirs had been a bond requiring no reassurance. Sentiment seemed of little use to someone prepared each day to forfeit life. After all, hadn't Riley believed there could be no greater glory than to lie dead at an early age for Ireland? He must have known the esteem he commanded. If not, he had long out-lived its importance. Either way, there was no time to rue the past. It was already Thursday. To reach Lahinch in time for a Saturday service, he'd have to catch the next train from Gullane.

*   *   *

Angus slid his suitcase from the top shelf of the closet. The well-trav-elled leather was plastered with decals from Istanbul to Morocco, Madrid to Berlin, a colorful patchwork of exotic destinations, revealing the tours of a correspondent. He turned to examine his once smart but now tired wardrobe. In addition to the usual tweeds and worsteds, he selected his Muirfield blazer and Lahinch tie. Draped over a hanger near the back of the closet, Angus noticed his highlander's kilt, a MacKenzie clan tartan of forest green and navy blue, cross-checked in crimson. This proud Gaelic garment that centuries ago had graced ancient battlefields was now rele-gated to weddings and funerals. He took special care in folding it into one of the zippered dividers.

When he had finished packing, Angus noticed his old canvas golf bag propped in a corner, the heads of a dozen forgotten friends peering at him from above its round opening. Swatting dust from these relics with a tat-tered towel, the memories of countless rounds he and Riley had played together began to cloud up in his mind like the tiny particles that had just taken flight. He would bring them.

Angus arranged his luggage on the front steps of the cottage and gazed across the Firth. The sturdy limestone structure he had rescued long ago from decades of disrepair stood lovingly restored to its original charm. Only an hour from Edinburgh, it had been a refuge from the stir of the city and, in old age, his sanctuary. Angus paused to slip into the comfort of his rocker, the weathered rails creaking against the porch as he turned to take in the broad vista of this magnificent corner of his beloved Scotland. A shroud of morning mist had given way to bright sunshine and, across the moors, he could see the heaving contours of Muirfield, fairways like fingers, reaching in every direction from the splendid Tudor clubhouse standing watch over stately grounds. As Angus embarked on this final pilgrimage to honor his friend, it seemed only fitting the place of their first meeting would be in full view.

Beyond Muirfield lay the Firth of Forth, a broad estuary forming a harbour at the mouth of the River Forth before spilling into the North Sea. On days more clear than this, his view stretched across the Firth to the coastline of Fife, hallowed home of St. Andrews, once the cradle and now kingdom to the game of golf. And further south, the seagulls were flocking to Bass Rock, the headstone of North Berwick, sentinel to Scotland's eastern shore. He tacked a short note to the screen door informing young Bobby he'd be away for awhile and to hold his newspapers.

When the cab arrived, and the luggage was loaded, Angus hardly noticed. Even the driver's request for a destination was met by a vacant, barely audible, directive to Gullane Station. Speeding off, the years little more than a blur, Angus began to ponder a life that, with Riley's passing, was now barren of those he loved most. Decades removed from his last trip to Lahinch, Angus seemed to recall it taking the better part of two days by train and ferry. As he traced the route in his mind, the emotion of Riley's death began to wash over him and, with more than half a century of friendship and rivalry to sort out, he was grateful for the long trip ahead.

PART I

▼

MUIRFIELD

Chapter 1

*T*he whistle today seemed more melancholy, a wail really, as if to mourn the end of a journey rather than signal its beginning. The train began its slow roll through Gullane, and Angus settled into his cabin, staring out at the countryside streaming by . . . a tranquil setting of seaside hamlets from a bygone era . . . small, quaint villages, resisting the advance of urban haste, holding fast their rural charm. Again, the whistle wailed, and again came the twinge of remorse Angus felt whenever he heard its plaintive cry, for it meant leaving home. Now that death had become his only occasion to travel, he wondered, would his own passing receive this same shrill lament?

Angus glanced at the faded canvas bag, and the hickory-shafted clubs, rusted from years of neglect. Standing them in the corner of his compartment, he removed the mashie and gripped it firmly, as if preparing to play a shot. He noticed the smooth leather wrap had been worn slick, and the whipping that held the forged iron club head to the wooden shaft had begun to unravel. He reached into the side pocket for an emery cloth and began to scour corrosion off the clubface, soon restoring much of its original cast.

In time, Angus lost interest, distracted by thoughts of Riley and events that had shaped their lives. Slipping the club back into the bag, he began to survey the cabin. Reminiscent of the Orient Express, a train on which he had once journeyed from Paris to Athens, this was luxury defined, harkening back to an age when travel by rail was more opulent, less austere.

Angus loosened the curtain stays to darken the compartment, and plumped the down-filled pillows, admiring the handsome finishes. Panels of mahogany were inlaid with cherry, and the fixtures were meticulously fitted with brass. Elaborate jacquards had been cleverly coupled with plaids and paisleys to envelope the room in a sumptuous tableau of greens and blues and burgundies. And, on a panel above the dressing table hung an exquisite rendition of the Edinburgh skyline, painted by an impressionist whose signature, *Van something or other*, was illegible.

He turned open the register knob to allow steam to rise, and the aroma of graceful aging flooded the air like the inside of an oaken wine cask. The comfort of the cabin and the train's gentle sway, drew him onto the inviting softness of the berth, where he stretched and yawned, gazing at the bagful of clubs as if they somehow held the lost treasures of his youth, and soon, he was adrift in the Spring of 1921.

*   *   *

"MacKenzie!" shouted the caddie master as Angus scrambled to his feet. "Y'll be packin' Sir Thomas' clubs this marnin'. He's solo."

"Yessir, Mr. Blaine."

"Get t' the farrst tee, lad! Th' grrreat man's rrarrin' t' gae!" Blaine roared.

Nodding, but saying nothing, Angus raced up the short path from the caddie shed, bolted past the starter's booth, and skidded to a halt just inches from a particularly large man whose head was lowered as he fumbled with his waterproofs.

"Ahh . . . there you are, lad," said the hulk, his distinctive face emerging from the shadow of his cap. Angus' eyes were drawn at once to a jagged scar extending from just beneath his left eye to the corner of his mouth, a red welt that resembled a permanent teardrop sliding down his cheek.

"Thomas Forgan," the man blared.

"Angus MacKenzie, sir. I'll be your caddie today."

"You're not one of the regular caddies," scoffed Forgan.

"No sir," whispered Angus, looking about to see if anyone was within earshot. "I'm much better than the regulars."

"Impertinent sort, aren't you?"

"No sir. I've seen their work."

"Let's get on with it then," the big man harrumphed. "It's not getting any drier and, God knows, I'm not getting any younger."

The fairways of Dunvegan sprawled across the hills west of Edinburgh like tentacles of an octopus. As with most exclusive clubs, one did not apply for membership. This was a realm to be entered by invitation only, an opportunity conferred upon those wealthy few whose means exceeded their appetite for extravagance. The Dunvegan Golfing Society traced its beginnings to 1761, when a collection of well-heeled Edinburghers commissioned Willie Park, Sr. to lay out the first nine holes. A multiple winner The Open Championship, golf's most coveted prize, Park had responded by designing a sporty little course on the outskirts of the city.

Dunvegan was but one of many clubs enjoyed by Sir Thomas Forgan. As publisher of *The Scotsman*, Edinburgh's most prominent newspaper, he was privileged to hold memberships in such august organisations as The Royal and Ancient Golf Club of St. Andrews and The Honourable Company of Edinburgh Golfers at Muirfield. But for reasons known only to him, Forgan seldom played either course, electing to utilize both clubs purely on matters of business or politics. When he did play, it was usually at Dunvegan . . . alone.

Chatter around the caddie shed portrayed Forgan as aloof, a man who refused to cultivate casual acquaintances. Having dabbled in competitive golf as a young man, he was said now to find recreational play tedious, and people in general, boring. A single digit handicapper most of his life, Forgan had begun to suffer the harmful effects of advancing age, causing his golf scores to rise . . . a development, the caddies noted, that Sir Thomas Forgan dealt with by quite often flouting the rules.

Low scoring seemed unlikely on a day that had deteriorated from mist to sleet. It was more an occasion to stretch the legs and to clear the mind of office clutter. Yet, true to his boast, Angus had ably advised the big man on his club selections and had cleverly detected the correct putting lines. For his part, Sir Thomas had executed his shots far better than in recent memory and, as far as Angus could tell, the man had broken no rules. And so, in the icy rain, they had reached the final tee with an improbable score of three over for the day. Par at the last would give Forgan a 74 . . . his personal best at Dunvegan.

"Where'd you learn to caddie, MacKenzie?"

Though Angus had caddied since the age of ten, he sensed Forgan might be impressed by more distinguished credentials. "From playin' the game, sir. I'm on the University team."

"Are you now?" Forgan replied, drying his hands on the last unsoaked corner of his towel. "When do you graduate?"

"Later this month, sir."

"And what're you studying, lad?"

"Journalism, sir," replied Angus, pleased at the turn the conversation had taken.

"Well, if I get this score to the clubhouse, you're in for a tidy sum."

"I'd prefer a position at *The Scotsman*, sir . . . if one's available, that is," Angus ventured, staring steadily at Forgan.

"Let's get this round to the clubhouse first," replied Sir Thomas, squinting down the final fairway through heavy rain, "then we'll discuss business."

Another precise drive at the last left Forgan a second of 143 metres to the green. From a slightly uphill lie, and with a stubborn breeze off his left cheek, Angus handed Sir Thomas the mashie, knowing this shot would play a good bit longer than it measured. But, for the first time in the round, Forgan overruled his caddie, selecting the mashie niblick instead. And, though it might have been more than adequate firepower under normal conditions, this club seemed less than was needed now. Forgan laid into the ball with a strapping blow, but wind and rain and elevation conspired to detain its flight at 138 metres, just far enough to reach the front bunker, where it dove into the embankment and plugged.

Peering through the deluge, Angus could see that the ball had buried, and bogey would likely be the best Forgan could manage. Sir Thomas' shoulders slumped, and the look in his eyes was a psychologist's dream, an eerie fusion of disappointment and rage and disgust. Forgan stomped off into the torrent well-ahead of his caddie, their unique bond based on mutual success now broken by this fit of pique.

Reaching the top of the rise, Angus circled around the far side of the hazard to retrieve a rake while Forgan climbed the brow of the bunker, presumably to inspect his lie. With Angus turned away, Forgan planted his right foot onto the soggy lip at precisely the point where the ball was lodged. Suddenly, like the pit of an overripe peach, the ball spurted from under the crease and rolled to the bottom of the bunker. When Angus turned back, he was astonished to see that Sir Thomas no longer faced a predicament, and instead had a simple shot from a level lie to save par. But was it for par? How had the ball gotten from its buried lie to this safe spot?

Forgan splashed to within a few feet of the hole and sank the putt for a round of 74. Or was it 75? What score would Forgan record?

The words of Duncan McDevitt, his old caddiemaster at North Berwick, came drifting back . . ." *They's two types o' gowfers, Angus, them what plays the ball as she lies, and them what don't. If ye ever get stuck loopin' fer the wrong sort, drop the bugger's clubs, and quit 'im on the spot.*"

A keen judge of human nature, McDevitt had gone on that day to describe for Angus his theory on golfers who believed themselves above the rules . . . an attitude of entitlement he called it. Having enjoyed success in other aspects of life, he claimed such men saw mastery over the game as their privilege, earned or not. The misfortunes so often encountered in golf were simply not to be endured by them. Sharp dealing was commonplace in business and politics. Why should golf be any different? After all, it was merely a game.

McDevitt spat. *"Merely a game, me arse,"* he had scoffed, *"gowf's the window to a man's character."*

Which type was Forgan? He had gone through the inward nine without a blemish on his card. And, though not enough club, his approach to the last had been struck perfectly. So, either he had taken the view that he didn't deserve a plugged lie and was entitled to improve his position, or the ball had come free from the bunker's soft sand on its own. Angus wondered which of these traits would be registered on the card.

The storm intensified as if in protest. Lightning crackled nearby, and thunder echoed across the course. Cuffing Angus on the shoulder triumphantly, the publisher invited his young caddie into the men's grill for post-round refreshments. While Angus viewed the invitation as a job interview, Sir Thomas saw the lad's presence more as useful corroboration to any members who might doubt his score.

With clubs cleaned and stored, Angus struggled to tidy his clothes in the dank caddie quarters . . . to no avail. The deluge that had dogged him all afternoon now caused his shoes to squeak at every step and the cheaply-woven wool of his jacket to take on the foul odor and disheveled appearance of the sheep from which it had been shorn. Angus had advanced well beyond wet to sodden.

Once inside the clubhouse, Angus was overwhelmed by the sheer vastness of this gothic manor. Better suited for the Scottish highlands, it boasted walls of burled walnut and chandeliers of cut glass. The granite fireplaces were spacious enough to accommodate the stags whose antlered heads hung above the mantles. With tapestries depicting the exploits of Scotland's ancient warriors, William Wallace and Robert Roy MacGregor, draped from its massive oaken beams, the place reeked of tradition and old money.

Angus sneaked into the lounge through the servant's entrance to find Sir Thomas soothing the shrill protests of the Club Secretary, Mr. Derrick Oldham. A disapproving glance from this high-strung official told Angus his place was outside in the custody of the caddie master rather than inside hobnobbing with the members. Sir Thomas spotted Angus, and motioned him to a table where the day's card was prominently displayed for all to view. As Angus settled into the leather lounge chair, he saw that a 74 had been recorded.

Placated for now by the five pound note Forgan had tucked discretely into his vest pocket, Oldham once again shot contempt toward Angus and slunk off to the safety of his office, where, no doubt, he would plot the removal of this waterlogged intruder. Sir Thomas strode across the room, dressed to the nines. The sight of the publisher having swapped his damp togs for such finery gave Angus even more discomfort as the steady dripping from his own dreary clothes began to form a puddle around his shoes.

"What'll you have, lad?" asked Sir Thomas, gesturing for the bar steward.

"Talisker, sir," replied Angus, needing something strong enough to combat his uneasiness and the numbingly damp day.

"Two Taliskers, Hadley," Sir Thomas barked to the barman. Then he narrowed his stare toward Angus and asked in deep, intimidating tones, "so you want to work for my newspaper, do you?"

"Oh, yes sir," replied Angus hopefully, adding, "I've always admired the way *The Scotsman* presents the news."

The single malts arrived, neat, in crystal tumblers, along with Hadley's own sneer, a reasonable facsimile of the one Oldham had offered.

"Slai'nte," Sir Thomas saluted. "To your health."

"Aye, slai'nte," Angus replied as they charged glasses. "The Irish have it right, don't they?" he continued, absently endorsing this Gaelic toast which ranked one's well-being ahead of one's wealth.

"Hardly anything the Irish do is right!" Sir Thomas corrected sharply. "They're a feckless lot, full of toasts because they're always drunk."

Angus tugged nervously at his collar and smoothed the sleeves of his rumpled jacket. Already uncomfortable in so grand a setting, he wanted no part of an ethnic debate with his powerful host. This imposing edifice and its illustrious members were reason enough for Angus to shrink. Even the hired help had looked down their noses at him. He quickly reasoned it best not to take issue with this affront to his mother's stock. No time to rise to the defense of the Irish. And so, in awkward silence, they sat sipping and swirling the amber liquid.

"The fact is, lad, you've caught me at an opportune time. We have an opening at the paper for an apprentice reporter, and you've shown plenty of spunk today. Just the sort of spirit we need. If you can write as well as you caddie, better still, if you can write as well as you pry your way into places you don't belong, then you're *Scotsman* material."

Angus was relieved that Forgan's mood had lightened. For now, at least, the topic of the feckless Irish was abandoned.

"Oh I'm a good writer, sir," Angus boasted in youthful self-promotion.

"And by that, Mr. MacKenzie, am I to assume you are also able to write well?" the publisher asked, staring through Angus to see if he would recognize his grammatical faux pas.

The young man's shoulders slumped, and his face flushed. "Th . . that's what I meant sir. Given the opportunity, I assure you I will be able to correctly distinguish between good and well."

"Oh, undoubtedly," Sir Thomas allowed, as if unconvinced. "And that, I suppose, will be all well and good. In any event, I'm as interested in your golfing ability as I am your writing skills. If you're able to play top calibre golf, we'll see that you compete in all the important amateur events. You may even get to cover some of them for the paper. Tell you what, if it fits your schedule, you may begin with us June 1st."

Angus was flabbergasted. Despite the idle slip of his tongue, he hadn't sabotaged his chances. He made a mental note to be more careful. He was about to become a newsman, and newsmen must be accurate. Under Sir Thomas Forgan's patronage, he would be able to pursue his passion for golf and get paid to chronicle the game. His mind was racing in contemplation of the possibilities when it occurred to him to acknowledge the offer and to inquire about the pay. He thought better of it. Forget the pay. You're lucky to have gotten the job. You'll get paid if you do good work . . . or was it . . . if you work well? If your work is of high quality . . . if . . .

"Well, MacKenzie, what do you say?" asked the publisher, growing more impatient by the moment.

"Er . . . thank you, Sir Forgan . . . uhh . . . Your Eminence . . . er . . ." stammered Angus, finally extricating himself from the demons of syntax.

"Mr. Forgan will do," Forgan laughed, cutting Angus off mid-reply, "or, Sir Thomas, if you wish to observe protocol."

"Thank you, Mr. Forgan, sir," gushed Angus, still unable to fathom his good fortune.

"Hmmm, yes . . .," Sir Thomas mumbled in the manner of an important man whose attention span has reached its outer limits. Glancing at his pocket watch, he exclaimed, "My, my, just look at the time! I'd best be getting on. It's been a most pleasant day, MacKenzie. We'll see you on the first of June. By the way, the position pays fifty quid monthly to start."

"Yessir, Mr. Forgan! Thank you sir. And, oh, that was a grand game of golf you played today, sir!" Angus was at his ingratiating best as he gulped down the last of the scotch and pumped Sir Thomas' huge right hand with both of his.

Forgan departed the lounge, and Angus watched him pause at each table to solicit the congratulations of his fellow Dunvegan members, some of whom accommodated him, though none with sincerity.

It truly had been a fine round, hadn't it . . . a phenomenal score on such a dreadful day? Why couldn't Angus just accept the outcome? Forgan's ball must not have imbedded in the bunker. Surely, it had come loose on its own. What other explanation was possible? What could be gained from posting an incorrect score? Angus was certain he'd be better off not knowing.

Chapter 2

*T*he days until graduation seemed to drag on endlessly. Angus spent much of these final few weeks at the University searching for just the right quarters from which to embark upon the next phase of his life. To his surprise, a flat on Abercromby Place unexpectedly became available. Consisting of three rooms on the second floor of an Edwardian townhouse, the apartment overlooked the secluded gardens of Queen Street Park, which, curiously, were sunken some four metres below street level. Located on Edinburgh's north side, his new quarters were a fifteen minute trolley ride from the offices of *The Scotsman* in the old town district, and placed Angus within walking distance of the city's most interesting sights.

To live and to work in Edinburgh had been his dream since boyhood. The son of Alex MacKenzie, a Scottish fisherman, and Nettie Neel, an Irish seamstress, Angus was an only child with a modest upbringing. Indulgences were rare for the MacKenzies of North Berwick at the eastern tip of Scotland, and so, when Angus first laid eyes on this center of culture, this Athens of the North, it brought to mind the words of Robert Louis Stevenson that . . . *Edinburgh is what Paris ought to be.*

From an early age, his father had insisted Angus work hard. If a young man is to get on in this world, Alexander MacKenzie would say, he must earn his way. Not that Angus needed any encouragement to persevere. North Berwick was full of tenacious Scots whose beliefs were shaped by Protestant preachings of the will of man as the main determinant of success. And his father's philosophy came as much from personal experience as from any abiding Presbyterian faith. In fact, the clan MacKenzie were highland Scots. Their roots were Gaelic, and their religion, Catholic. But centuries of parry and thrust between Protestant reformers and the

Catholic church had resulted in widespread conversion to Protestantism by many Gaels, including the MacKenzies of North Berwick. Alex had come to embrace the notion of self-determination espoused by the Presbytery, because it squared with his own view of man's place in the universe. Though he had married an Irish Catholic, Alex had little patience for the ceremony of her faith. And so, on the rare occasion when he did attend church, it was at the Presbyterian kirk where services were short and simple.

Each morning before dawn, Angus would go with his father to cut bait until Alex sailed into the North Sea in search of cod. Afterwards, he would race home to scrub the smell of fish from his hands and change into a fresh white shirt and plus fours. His mother would pack his lunch, and remind him of his place among elders, and admonish him to disregard any foul words those *gowfers* might utter. Nettie, it seemed, had a new piece of advice each day, an adage or two to guide his ways, the product, he imagined, of an overactive Catholic conscience. Then, it was off to the caddie shed and the links of North Berwick to be first in the queue for an early morning loop.

Winters in Scotland were dreary, and toting golf bags in the slop was as arduous as fishing the North Sea. But when the long summer days arrived, the life of a caddie was glorious, and Angus was eager to spend entire days on the links. It was not uncommon to go four times 'round before the sun could settle behind the Lammermuirs. Fascinated by the game and its traditions, the links of North Berwick became his own private observatory of human behaviour.

He watched as certain so-called gentlemen would bend the rules in order to gain an advantage over their opponents. And he took careful note of how the peaks and valleys of emotion could affect play just as surely as the humps and hollows of terrain. It was clear the game of golf involved a good deal more than keeping one's head down and maintaining a straight left arm.

Though little more than a rank beginner, Angus had the unexpected good fortune to be drawn from a lottery to loop for the great Harry Vardon in a match against the other prominent golfers of the day, James Braid and

J. H. Taylor. It was during this outing that Angus discovered the qualifications of a top player . . . follow the rules to the letter . . . keep your emotions in check . . . and trust in your swing . . . lessons unfortunately lost on some of the entitled members.

Quite unexpectedly, after young MacKenzie helped Vardon pinpoint the correct line to the sixteenth, North Berwick's celebrated Redan hole, the great man took Angus aside to show him the over-lapping grip he claimed was indispensable to fine golf. And, from that moment on, it was the game of golf that held Angus in its grip.

*   *   *

Just as Alex declared perspiration as the path to personal achievement, Nettie was equally insistent that Angus pursue a formal education. When fishing kept his father at sea for days at a time, his mother would take him to Edinburgh or St. Andrews for a tour of the universities. It was there she revealed to her son the traditions of her Irish childhood, sharing with him the many tales of heroism and romance that had been passed down through her family. Nettie was proud of her Gaelic upbringing and, despite Alex's Presbyterian ways, never completely abandoned her Catholic rites. Oh, she might accompany her husband to the kirk out of respect for family unity, but never would she give up saying the rosary, or attending mass every Sunday night, or, each week, quietly confessing her sins to Father Hannigan at St. Michael's Chapel in North Berwick.

Just as important though, was Nettie's grasp of the pain that could be inflicted by religious bigotry. To illustrate how cruel the struggles between Protestants and Catholics during the Reformation had become, she often took Angus to the martyr's tower at St. Andrews. There, engraved into this granite obelisk, were the names of the heretics who had been burned at the stake for their resistance to the Catholic church in the sixteenth century. It was then, Angus first realized the hypocrisy of religion and, though already skeptical of those who would brandish the rites of faith as symbols of their devotion, he pledged to his mother a life of tolerance for the beliefs of others.

Angus attended North Berwick Commons, pursuing a curriculum woefully deficient in the fine arts. But, while these academic footings may not have offered the advantages of an Eton, or the rigor of a Harrow, Angus applied himself. He more than made up for his lack of classical instruction by reading . . . not the sort of reading one does just to get by, but the heavy lifting shouldered by a truly inquisitive student driven to understand his subjects in depth. And, in the striving, he achieved top marks and earned a scholarship to the prestigious University of Edinburgh.

Angus excelled in school, and was keen on athletic pursuits such as rugby. By his fourth year, however, he was judged too slow to become a top-notch rugger, and turned exclusively to golf. In the manner of his parents, Angus understood the merit of hard work and made the most of his limited physical talents to not only make the university team, but to become its captain. Eager now, to test the lessons of academic theory and the self-discipline of sport against the more exacting demands of a career, off he went to work for *The Scotsman*.

*   *   *

During his first days on the job, the newspaper's managing editor introduced Angus to his new colleagues, rushing him through each of the departments in an accelerated training exercise. A rotund, fiftyish man, his bald pate ringed with friar-like fuzz, Hamish MacClanahan was a wellspring of knowledge about *The Scotsman's* history, its people, and its political leanings. Hamish could be seen everywhere, ink-stained sleeves rolled up to his elbows, and wire-rimmed glasses perched on the crown of his round, pink head.

To Angus, this affable fellow became the perfect mentor, closely observing his work, yet granting him leeway to suffer the mistakes of a novice and, above all, showing the patience and tolerance that allowed him to learn from his lapses. As the weeks passed, and the relationship between master and apprentice grew more comfortable, Angus soon felt at ease to ask Hamish for advice on a wide range of topics. Sir Thomas Forgan was, of course, at the top of his list.

"What can you tell me about Mr. Forgan?" Angus asked Hamish one day over lunch.

"Sir Thomas Forgan . . . M.P.," Hamish replied, thoughtfully. "Well, he's one man I wouldn't want to cross."

This squared with his own first impressions, but Angus wanted more. "M.P.? So, he's a Member of Parliament as well as a knight?"

"Not a knight, a baronet. He's the 14th Baronet of Colby in County Down, Ireland, a rather modest title by noble standards, but hereditary, with a formal designation of 'Sir'. And yes, he was elected just last year to represent the East Lothian district of Scotland."

Getting right to the nub of his concern, Angus asked, "Any idea why he has such a hard spot for the Irish?"

"I should think it's the same for Forgan as for most Protestants in Ireland . . . centuries of hatred stoked by fear and distrust of the Pope's power. I'm sure you'd hear similar misgivings from a Catholic about the Protestants."

"But he strikes me as an Englishman, rather than a member of the Irish gentry."

"We all become Englishmen over time, I suppose," Hamish replied in a high-pitched chuckle that caused his ample midriff to quake. "Isn't that their grand design?"

"How did he come by his title?"

"Forgan is a Scottish name. His family was among the lowland Scots who were part of the English plantation of Ulster in northern Ireland during the 1600's. My guess is that his ancestors demonstrated exceptional loyalty to the Crown and were rewarded with title and a good bit of land."

Inspecting the contents of his second sandwich, Hamish lifted a corner of the top slice and sprinkled its multiple layers with a generous application of salt.

"Unlike the native Irish Catholics who were Anglophobes, the Scottish emigrants were usually Protestants, and equally keen Anglophiles," he replied. "So, Sir Thomas Forgan is one of those unusual cases . . . Scottish lineage . . . born an Irishman . . . bred an Englishman. *He* probably does-n't even know where his true allegiance lies."

"Well, he seems to have great contempt for the Irish. Given the fact his fortune stems in no small part from Ireland . . . it's just not right."

"Careful, lad. Don't be too quick to judge. And I wouldn't joust with him over the Irish!"

"I just want to understand who I'm working for."

"A powerful man with lots of friends in high places. He can reward you . . . or ruin you."

"Ah, but power wears well on those who use it wisely, and pinches those who don't. By the way, how'd he get that nasty scar on his face?"

"Listen, Angus, we're not dealing with some case study from your college ethics text! This, my good man, is real life. Rarely do the almighty receive their due . . . and pity the poor souls who've fallen victim to their sword. Take care that your ideals don't get in the way of clear thinking. As for the scar, who knows . . . a childhood accident, perhaps?"

He lied. Hamish knew precisely how Forgan had gotten the scar, but had chosen not to tell Angus. It was a simple omission, a white lie, meant to shelter his new protégé from the truth. Hamish hadn't calculated this deception, it had just come out, as if his subconscious had instructed him not to entangle this young innocent in such an unseemly state of affairs.

*   *   *

Those early days at *The Scotsman* were some of Angus' most memorable. He diligently applied himself to the task of honing his writing skills, yet there was ample time to practice golf and to immerse himself in the rich diversity of Edinburgh. Angus threw his heart into describing weddings and funerals and petty crimes, and covered even the most mundane sporting events with boundless enthusiasm. But it was after hours in the watering holes of Edinburgh's veteran newsmen that Angus soon discovered he could learn more from listening to these well-oiled voices of his craft than by writing obituaries.

On days when news was scarce, Hamish would dispatch his young charge to another journalistic workshop, the wharves of Edinburgh. From pickpockets to sailors, prostitutes to stevedores, this part of the city was teeming with an odd assortment of characters who managed to survive in a milieu quite apart from the mainstream. Largely ignored by polite society, an element of danger seemed ever-present in this dockside culture, and its allure drew Angus in. These rough and tumble eccentrics of the quay provided articles of human interest on slow days, and a source of anecdotes that, later in life, he would fashion into a collection of short stories, *The Lost Souls of Edinburgh.*

Still, it was the game of golf that interested him most. A diversion growing in popularity, golf had become an important topic of journalism, tailor-made for Angus. On its surface, the game might seem silly, especially to the uninformed. Yet beneath this simple façade, he knew it to be endlessly complex. Merely applying clubface to ball, as one would hammer to nail, was challenge enough. But, as Angus would hasten to point out, in order to achieve any measure of success, a player is asked to repeat, time and again, this sophisticated task of hand-to-eye coordination. And, once a level of proficiency in ball-striking is reached, then to do so in all conditions . . . wind and rain and uneven lies . . . becomes the next, more advanced, assignment.

If further consternation were required, one need look no further than the game within a game . . . the subtle intricacies of chipping and putting. The power that enables a player to cover long distances from the tee must inevitably be augmented, once the green is reached, by a deft touch. But executing each of these skills in the heat of battle, Angus maintained, adds a dimension of difficulty that may be consistently overcome only by those so talented as the game's reigning triumvirate . . . Vardon and Taylor and Braid.

This, he had always said, defined golf . . . enjoyed by many, but mastered by few, an exercise in mental discipline as well as emotional control, allowing those less physically gifted to compete on equal footing with the strong. So central was this concept to the game, no less than the venerable Royal Troon had taken for its club motto, the Latin . . . *Tam Arte Quam Marte . . . as much by skill as by strength* . Angus was quick to observe that, from all who wish to conquer it, golf insists any such dominance, if ever achieved, shall be fleeting. In this game of infinite contradictions, he saw a metaphor of life's drama and angst, and was eager to use his new position to impart its lessons.

But could he attract the non-golfer as well as those who played the game? After all, *The Scotsman* had hired him to build an audience, a broad-based readership, more than a cult following. He doubted few would be as passionate about the game as the diehards who lived and breathed it. What universal truths were to be gleaned from this ridiculous pastime? Well, for starters, surely anyone would be able to recognize the code on which golf is based, the notion of honor as prerequisite, requiring all deceit be checked at the first tee . . . no bigotry . . . no misbehaviour . . . just courtesy and respect. If only the world outside the fairways subscribed to such views, what a world it might be.

*   *   *

In time, Hamish saw in Angus a more capable writer than most of the journeymen on his staff and directed him to research an event the editor hoped would launch the young reporter's career as a journalist . . . The British Isles Cup. This championship, in which the best players of England, Scotland, and Ireland would vie for the unofficial title of top amateur golfer in the United Kingdom, was to be contested later that June at Muirfield Golf Links in Gullane. With the date of the tournament drawing near, Angus was summoned to Sir Thomas Forgan's offices on the Royal Mile near Edinburgh Castle.

Though, at first, eager to meet with Sir Thomas, once inside this lavish suite, Angus was seized by sweaty-palmed anxiety. His heart was palpitating with worry over the reprimand he expected to receive for mediocre coverage of Colin McTweed's death. Admittedly, his obituary of the Balmoral Hotel's long-time manager had been substandard. But surely Forgan would understand his interest in the unexplained disappearance of Florris Finch, the pier's most popular madam. Piecing together bits of information about this concierge of carnal delights, Angus had found evidence of foul play. Fascinating stuff, to be sure . . . much more so than McTweed's obituary . . . but as excuses went, this one needed work.

Getting caught up in the investigation had proven a distraction, and had caused the cub reporter to bestow upon the admirable Mr. McTweed a less than adequate tribute. He wondered, would such short shrift now cost his job?

By the time Forgan's shapely young assistant announced the publisher would see him, Angus was barely able to stand. Wobbling toward the massive double doors, he stepped unsteadily across the parquet threshold onto an ornate Persian rug, and was still refining his explanation for the McTweed gaffe when Forgan's booming baritone broke his train of thought.

"MacKenzie, you've got your first assignment!" the big man bellowed. "The British Isles Cup at Muirfield . . . you'll be reporting and competing!"

The publisher looked the supreme capitalist in a heavily starched shirt, its winged collar framing his ample jowls, and its French cuffs monogrammed with the initials TCF. Forgan was thickset but robust for a man in his fifties who had been denied few of life's pleasures. A snowy mane streamed backward from his widow's peak and, wedged imperiously into his right eye was a gold-rimmed monocle, presumably meant to draw attention from the unsightly scar on the opposite side of his face. The crowning touch was a pinstripe suit of navy blue, and a regimental tie of burgundy and silver, each hand-tailored from silk on Jermyn Street, at the center of London's fashion district.

Sir Thomas tilted backward in an enormous leather chair, his shoes and spats gleaming as brightly as the mahogany desk onto which they had been placed and, from this seat of high command, he drew deeply on a cigar befitting a man of his stature. The room was swathed in an asphyxiating curtain of smoke and power.

Angus stammered, a thank you and asked, "Wh . . . When do I depart?"

"In due time, my boy. Let us first find our bearings," replied Sir Thomas, removing his feet from the desk and coming to full height. "I've been giving some thought to your role as both participant and reporter. A bit awkward, don't you agree?"

Not waiting for a reply, Sir Thomas pressed on. "Let me get straight to point, Angus. Do you mind going underground on this assignment? I mean do the work-up for someone else's by-line?" Forgan had predetermined the answer, but allowed Angus the courtesy of his own response.

"And relinquish all public credit for my writing, sir?" bleated Angus.

The young reporter was dressed as if next up on the first tee, his grey tweed plus fours suitably complemented by argyle stockings of scarlet and black. The early beginnings of a paunch filled his neatly-pressed white cotton shirt around the fourth and fifth buttons, and the hint of a double chin folded over the collar above a checkered bow tie.

"Precisely, my boy. After all, it pays the same."

"Surely you know it's not the pay, sir. A writer lives for his work to be recognized."

"There will be time for all that," Forgan patronized. "For now, it's best you report on the *QT*."

Angus resisted the urge to sulk, determined to accept the assignment and all of its conditions in the best of spirits. Despite a propensity for bulkiness, he had a pleasing, if plain, face. Thick red hair flowed from a point high on his forehead in a series of small rivulets, and a bushy moustache seemed to explode from beneath his nose like an over-used broom. With eyebrows to match, Angus needed a fairly large head to accommodate his profusion of hair and, for a man of average size, he had one.

"Now, let's discuss logistics. Here's your train ticket to Gullane," Forgan said, handing Angus a small folder. "I've arranged lodging at the country home of my colleague, Lord Ashley. Greywalls, I think he calls it. Splendid place . . . gardens and such . . . and Muirfield is ten paces from the library. Yes, you'll be most comfortable there. Oh, and here's twenty quid to cover incidentals. Wire for more, if needed."

"Aye, sir. Of course, sir," Angus replied.

For all his jocularity, Forgan's mood turned suddenly somber. "You realize, Angus, the British Isles Cup is not just any championship," he said icily, absent any recent good humour.

"Indeed, sir," Angus piped back, anxious to be on his way.

"Last month, while you were graduating from the University, a squad of upstart American amateurs beat our best lads in an informal match down at Hoylake," Forgan muttered, his already-loud voice gaining decibels.

"The notion of biennial matches between Great Britain and America is on firm footing with the Royal & Ancient and with the United States Golf Association, under George Herbert Walker's leadership. In fact, it's being dubbed The Walker Cup in his honor."

Forgan sucked the stubby remnant of his cigar and explained. "The British Isles Cup will be one of the qualifying events to determine who will represent Great Britain next year when the Walker Cup officially commences. I've been named to chair the R & A's selection committee."

"Congratulations, sir," said Angus, noting the self-regard that had begun to swell in his new boss.

"We mustn't lose to the Yanks!" Forgan growled. "I will not abide losing . . . at anything . . . to anyone!"

Rising from the chair so as to further intimidate, the great man blared the words with such contempt there could be no mistaking the significance he assigned to victory or the ends to which he might go to achieve it.

"Aye, sirrr," Angus replied with a surge of his native Scottish burr that seemed to surface whenever he got his patriotic hackles up. "We'll crrrush the bastarrrds!"

"That's the spirrrit, lad!" Forgan mimicked, overlaying his own bit of acquired brogue.

Irish born and London bred, transplanted to Edinburgh by the choices afforded position and wealth, Forgan was clearly no fool. He understood the value of being a Scotsman in the land of Scots. With a voracious taste for the finer things in life and an insatiable thirst for power, he had adapted well to the customs and colloquialisms of this country he now considered his own. His capacity to take up the Scottish ways, coupled with business acumen second to none, had enabled him to expand an already wide sphere of influence, and to amass a fortune few could rival.

The roster of Forgan's residences read like Sotheby's list of addresses for the rich and famous that had been featured in a recent edition of *British Living*. A flat in London . . . the country manor outside St. Andrews . . . a villa in Portugal . . . an Edinburgh brownstone . . . and, of course, the family estate in Ireland, assured Sir Thomas of a lifestyle that had progressed well beyond excess to ostentatious. Only the finest French vintages graced his wine cellar, and his cigars were imported from Havana by Dunhill's of London. With a wardrobe cut from Italian silk, and garages reserved for Bentleys and Duesenbergs, Forgan was awash in material treasures.

But, it was from his collection of memberships at the most prestigious of private clubs that Forgan gained his greatest satisfaction. Using title and affluence as his entree, he had gained access to the high chambers of power in Britain and, once within this exclusive province, he was determined to become its most influential inhabitant. Outwardly, he had all the trappings of a charmed life, and a captivating manner with which to beguile even the most sophisticated audience. Sir Thomas was one of those men who seemed to have everything, including an unmitigated gall to proclaim; not only are his riches well-deserved, they are, in fact, wholly insufficient.

And yet, something was missing. Where was the pleasing warmth that accompanies those who are surely genuine? Where was the disarming sincerity that, in the possession of uncommonly great men, places everyone at ease? Where was the light, sparkling like diamonds from the man blessed with true integrity, that irresistible brilliance, exposing as fake the zirconian glitter so often flashed by those whose real stock in trade is deceit? Was Forgan to be trusted? Angus wondered.

"Off with you, then," said Sir Thomas, rising from behind his desk and draping his arm around Angus' shoulder. "And best of luck to you in the Cup."

"Aye, sir," Angus replied uneasily. "I won't let you down, sir."

"Oh you may be certain of that, Mr. MacKenzie," Forgan replied with the smug look of a man accustomed to getting his way.

Angus back-stepped out of the baroque doors that stood as sentries to this citadel of luxury, stealing one last glance at his new employer, sizing up Sir Thomas Forgan's shiny veneer for that telltale crack.

Chapter 3

*A*ngus was greeted at Gullane Station by Lord Ashley's valet, an octogenarian named Horace Maxwell. Unaccustomed to such lavish attention, and judging Maxwell far too frail for strenuous labor, the young journalist insisted on stowing his own luggage in the boot of the Vauxhall. Minutes after leaving the station, the black sedan began slowing to make its approach into the pea-graveled driveway of Greywalls, and the classic lines of the main house came into view. With garden walls extending like open arms on either side of a center mall lined in lavender, the country estate bade visitors welcome. At the end of the drive, the automobile came crunching to a halt in a turnabout that curved gently up to an arched main door. As he took in the elegance of Greywalls, Angus found it odd the stones were mottled, exhibiting more warmth of brown than the foreboding of grey suggested by the estate's moniker.

With Lord Ashley away on business for the remainder of the week, Angus was shown by Horace to his quarters on the second floor above the library. A cozy room, replete with antiques, it featured a four-poster bed and, to one side, on the nightstand, sat a porcelain wash basin with matching pitcher. Angus crossed to the window and flung open the leaded-glass panes to reveal an unobstructed view of Muirfield's gentle terrain extending to the Firth of Forth. It was his first glimpse of a scene that in later years would provide great comfort. With lush bent grass greens flanked by sinister-looking sand chasms, and parched ribbons of fairway bracketed by the reddish-brown of marram grasses gone to seed, this was quintessential linksland.

From his elevated vantage point, Angus observed how Muirfield linked the sea with the more arable land beyond. This sand-blown expanse surely must have been considered barren for agricultural purposes, if not wasteland altogether. Yet, it was ideally suited for golf. With closely-cropped fescues and rangy sea sedge taking root to form nature's fairways and rough, and hummocky hollows providing just enough unevenness to invoke trepidation for each shot, this was a golfer's Mecca.

On the train ride to Gullane, Angus had sifted through various historical accounts of The Honourable Company of Edinburgh Golfers, as much out of personal interest as in preparation for his assignment. He found it fascinating that The Company had been formed in 1744 at Leith, a small fishing village situated five miles from the outskirts of Edinburgh. Unbeknownst to Angus, it had begun as an organisation of professional gentlemen seeking refuge from the strains of trade and commerce. As the city prospered, the original five hole layout, Leith Links, had predictably fallen victim to urban progress, and The Company moved in 1836 to Musselburgh, some fifteen miles away. But in time, it too became overcrowed, prompting relocation to its present site in 1891.

Angus knew that Old Tom Morris, widely regarded as the patriarch of modern golf and the dean of early golf course architecture, had been chosen to lay out the original eighteen holes, but Morris' original work had been recently refined by two other highly acclaimed designers, Harry Colt and Tom Simpson. Something lost and something gained in the name of progress, he supposed.

*   *   *

The kitchen staff at Greywalls had prepared an afternoon snack of cucumber and cream cheese sandwiches with crusts neatly removed. A platter stacked high with the petite morsels was placed on the sideboard in a narrow hallway near the door leading out to the golf course. A pitcher of lemonade and another of tea sat next to a bowl of apples and apricots. At the far end of the bureau stood a vase of freshly-cut white roses, lending an air of formality to an otherwise ordinary buffet. Angus poured himself a glass filled half with lemonade, and half with tea. He devoured three of the dainty sandwiches, and stuffed an apple into his pants pocket. Gulping down the murky mixture of tea and lemonade, he headed out to the storied links of Muirfield, refreshed.

Angus had asked Horace not to bother with his clubs, yet here they were, deposited in the bag stand next to Muirfield's clubhouse. Arriving two days prior to the tournament, the young newsman had planned to gather details for his article but, more importantly, had hoped to arrange a practice round. Angus introduced himself to the starter as a contestant in the British Isles Cup and was told he could play away at his leisure. If he was looking for a game, the starter added, a Mr. Riley O'Neill from the Irish Golfing Union, was on the premises.

Angus shouldered his bag and headed toward the practice ground to warm up before playing. Finding the area deserted, he picked a spot near the left side and began to stretch by hooking both elbows over the shaft of a club, slowly pivoting around the axis formed by hips and legs. Well-limbered, Angus tugged open the drawstring of his shag bag and emptied forty or so practice balls onto the turf. A few chips and half-swing pitches were just what he needed to retrain hand and eye to ball and to regain his feel. Angus settled into his usual routine, swinging the niblick, followed in order by the mashie, the cleek, and the spoon. Working methodically through the bag, he practiced shaping each shot to fit any condition that might arise. As his confidence grew, Angus was down to the last few balls and in good form. It was now time to hit that most obstinate of all clubs . . . the driver.

"Will y' be hittin' the rest of those rascals?" asked a gravelly voice from behind Angus in a tone that implied he wanted to hit the remaining balls himself.

Startled by the intrusion, Angus whirled to find a slender young man leaning against his clubs, legs crossed at the ankles, a hand-rolled cigarette drooping from the center of his mouth. As the stranger pinched the half-smoked butt between thumb and forefinger, his upper lip curled back to reveal a perfect set of teeth and the semblance of a smile. Black, deep-set eyes, scrutinizing but friendly, stared out from the handsome face. His slicked-back hair, black as soot and prematurely grey at the temples, was made even more resplendent by a heavy application of tonic. The intruder could have passed for a star of silent screen.

"You've found yer rhythm for t'day, lad," said the stranger in a pleasing sing-song lilt distinct to certain Irishmen. "You'll only upset the balance of power if you keep at it."

Though not yet thirty, the fine features of his face were already marred by crow's feet at the corners of his eyes and mouth. Ill-fitting plus fours cascaded over a pair of argyle stockings, seen peeking out from above unpolished golf spikes. Oddly, a brass plate had been cobbled onto the toe of his right shoe to combat the incessant abrasion of a golfer's follow-through, while a thorough scuffing prevailed elsewhere. A dingy shirt, more yellow than white, was frayed at the cuffs and collar and, out of its placket, sprouted a greenish tie, loosely knotted and tucked between the second and third buttons. Angus examined this curious ensemble and found himself gawking at the tie's insignia which, of all things, appeared to be a goat.

The stranger thrust his powerful right hand toward Angus and spoke in a voice the product of too many cigarettes . . . "R. P. O'Neill, Lahinch . . . Riley, to me mates."

"Angus MacKenzie, *Edinburra*," replied Angus, stressing the Scottish pronunciation. He plunged his hand into O'Neill's broad mitt only to find his fingers would barely stretch across the man's palm. He was now helplessly confined in a bone-crushing grip.

"Please, hit the rest of these," Angus offered, stepping aside to allow O'Neill to the tee. He pointed to the balls with his left hand and clenched the right one, attempting to restore feeling to his fingers.

In a dramatic flourish, as a swashbuckler might unsheathe sword from scabbard, O'Neill pulled mashie from bag and stepped toward the tee. From a narrow stance, the club was drawn back to just past waist high, as if to hit a three-quarter knockdown shot. Suddenly, the leverage of those great hands and wrists, coupled with perfect timing, conspired to send the ball shrieking off the clubface like a banshee. It whistled through a stiff headwind in a low, drawing trajectory, coming to rest some 180 metres away. Angus blinked in disbelief.

"That'll do," O'Neill crowed, retrieving the smoldering cigarette he had tossed aside to play the shot. "Wouldn't want to upset the balance of power, now would we?" he chortled, winking at Angus. "Will y' be wantin' a game this afternoon, lad?"

"I'd be pleased to join you, Mr. O'Neill," Angus answered stiffly, astounded by what he had just witnessed.

"Mr. O'Neill's me Pap! . . . least I think he is. You can call me R. P., or Riley . . . or you'll be playin' alone."

"And what does the 'P' stand for?"

"Parrboosterr," Riley trilled, smiling impishly.

"Parbuster?! Not bloody likely!"

"Aye, 'tisn't," agreed Riley, still wearing his silly smile. "But you might think otherwise when we finish."

Striding side by each toward the first tee, Riley paused to let this last jab take effect. Then, as if to ease Angus' obvious discomfort, he whispered, "'P's for Padraig . . . I swear . . . 'tis."

"I think I'll just call you Riley," replied Angus, leaning his golf bag against the bench, and surveying Muirfield's formidable first hole.

"Give y' two a side for a pint o' Guinness," Riley said, removing the cover from his driver.

Angus stared at it, dumbfounded. An aluminum clubhead with a brine-cured leather insert and ram's horn flange was attached with red whipping to the end of a ring hickory shaft. He had never seen a club like this.

"Who made that?!" asked Angus.

"James Braddell, Belfast," Riley replied, proudly holding the clubhead closer so Angus could see the maker's name, J. Braddell, stamped on the crown. "How 'bout yers?"

"Tom Auchterlonie, St. Andrews," Angus said, pulling his driver from the bag. He held it up for Riley to see a darkly lacquered persimmon head, attached to the hickory shaft with black whipping.

"I play to scratch," Angus said, returning to the terms of their bet. "I only get shots from the professionals, and never more than one or two."

"You're not playin' any blasted *pru* t'day!" admonished Riley. "Take the cushion while you can, lad, cuz Ol' Parbooster won't be offerin' it again!"

"We'll play straight up," Angus insisted. "You have the honor. Play away."

"Have it yer way, y' stubborn Scot," Riley muttered, bending to tee up the well-worn Slazenger he had pressed into yet another tour of duty.

Riley assumed his narrow stance with the graceful, dance-like movements that so often adorn the athlete. Then, without so much as a glance toward his intended target, he took the club back to its familiar waist-high position and, displaying an air of confidence other golfers can sense, split the fairway with a rocket that landed at 250 metres.

Visibly shaken, Angus stared out at the thin strip of sun-baked fescue turning lazily to the right before vanishing abruptly from view. A daunting opener of over 430 metres, the first featured a bunker that yawned insidiously at the left corner of the dogleg, and opposite beckoned an ocean of knee-high marram. In his mind's eye, the fairway had narrowed to a sliver. Angus fidgeted to gain his alignment. He milked the handle of his driver, as tension, the traitor of all golf swings, crept into his hands and arms.

Angus snatched the club away from the ball in an uncontrolled spasm and, at that moment, the die had been cast . . . an accident waiting to happen. No personal heroics could alter the outcome. Just prior to impact, that decisive moment of truth, Angus was reduced to lunging his right shoulder through the hitting zone in some frantic attempt to salvage the wreckage. The result was a low hook that failed to rise above head high, darting like a frightened hare into the steeply revetted sand coffin at fairway's bend.

Angus slung his bag over his shoulder in disgust and stomped off toward the bunker in irate silence, determined to recover from this inauspicious start. A study in contrasts, Riley sat on the bench calmly hand-rolling another cigarette, the first of a dozen or so he would manufacture during the round.

The young Scot's dappled complexion of red and brown was now aflame in purple as he marched down the fairway muttering a stern lecture. He scolded himself for not savoring the moment, and he denounced all those misinformed articles about Muirfield that had painted various incomplete images of the course. But, for that matter, no written word could have prepared him to play here. Not even the beatitudes of golf's poet laureate, Bernard Darwin, had done justice to this divine linksland. Lofty as his visions had been, they were no match for actually walking this hallowed turf. It was tight and bristly, crunching beneath his spikes, demanding that shots be clipped cleanly from its fescue. Like Wimbledon to those whose sport is tennis, there simply was no surface better-suited to a golfer than the terra firma of Muirfield. Play the game as it is meant to be played, it shouted. No slipshod strokes allowed . . . only square clubfaces and shallow divots. Angus supposed God had sculpted this ground for mere mortals to test their human frailties. But you needn't genuflect at the first sign of adversity, lad. *Come on, MacKenzie*, he urged, *you're in the arena . . . stand your ground . . . be a gladiator.*

It worked, or something did. That ghastly drive off the first tee seemed to calm his nerves and sharpen his focus. Angus rappelled down the sheer face of the bunker, castigating the evil architect and his wicked band of workman who had revetted brick upon sod brick to form this earthen stockade. Staring into fifty tiers of turf as if they were prison bars, he somehow blasted from this dungeon to within 75 metres of the green. *They have yet to build the bunker that can hold my Dreadnaught niblick*, he bragged inwardly, pleased at having bent its loft from a standard 45 to an unheard of 52 degrees. He quickly reconsidered, knowing full well he was whistling past the graveyard. These tombs had been dug for those careless enough to get in and too foolish to take the cautious way out. Only a reprieve from the gods of golf had spared him a sentence of hard labor in this chamber of horrors. To forego contrition was to tempt fate. Next time, the powers that be might not look so favorably upon the impenitent. Best to give thanks and move quietly on.

After skipping his third shot to 20 feet, Angus cleverly engineered a putt with as many bends as the road to Dundee. Riley, on the other hand, nearly holed his second for an eagle when he rifled a mashie directly over the flag. But, with a straight-in six footer for birdie, the Irishman lipped it out. Quite unexpectedly, the hole had been halved in par . . . a snapshot of the *grand auld gemme* itself.

*   *   *

"Where do you hail from, MacKenzie?" Riley asked as they strolled down the eighth fairway.

Other than the occasional '*you're away*' and '*nice shot*', the two men to this point had tended to their own games, intent on making any adjustments that might be needed.

"I was reared in the village of North Berwick, twelve kilometers, or so, that way," Angus replied, pointing due east. "Quite different from Edinburgh."

"Aye, after leavin' the quiet of Lahinch for the lights of Dublin, I know something of city rot."

"And just what rot is that?"

"Well, Mum wanted better schoolin' for me, so off to Dublin I went. Found it the center of higher larnin', sure enough, but also the seat of ev'ry social ill known to man. You can see more foul deeds in one Dublin eve than you'd find in a decade of country livin'."

"I know what you mean," Angus replied, reflecting on the squalid conditions of Edinburgh's wharves.

"Where'd you get yer schoolin'?" asked Riley.

"University of Edinburgh. And you?"

"St. Edna's School for Boys, just outside Dublin. Have you landed a job yet, lad?"

"I work for *The Scotsman* . . . you know, the newspaper. And you?"

"A bit o' this, and some o' that. Anything to put a punt or two in me pocket. Bein' a university man, you might know something of the Irish situation," Riley added warily. And then, in a low whisper, "me real work is to get the Brits out of Eire."

"I read about the Easter Rising of 1916," said Angus. "Seems to have ended badly for a lot of Irish. Surely you weren't one of the conspirators."

"I was there, and by God I'm still standin'. '16 was just the beginnin'. One day, the English'll get what's comin' to 'em."

"From what I've read, the Brits have the Irish rebels well in hand," Angus said, after holing another ten-footer for par on the eighth. "By the way, how'd you manage to get into this event, with a war going on?"

"Lied through me teeth, I did . . . professed to be an Ulster unionist," replied Riley, as he cracked another letter-perfect drive down the ninth. "Besides, there's a cease-fire while we mull over the treaty."

"So, are you here to spy on the Brits, or play golf?" Angus joked, laying up well short of the green.

Riley lashed a spoon past the stone wall that formed a claustrophobic boundary to the left of the ninth fairway, and as his ball trickled onto the green some 245 metres away, he roared, "I'll be doin' a bit o' both, lad!"

*   *   *

Few words were spoken during the remainder of the afternoon as they returned to fine-tuning their games. Oh, Riley dropped in an occasional slur about the Brits, but Angus let them slide, not much interested in talking politics. The play of both men followed the pattern of the first hole. Riley's exceptional driving and brilliant iron play yielded birdie opportunities that he repeatedly squandered, while Angus' scrappy short game rescued par from the most unlikely predicaments. The manner by which they each had managed to equal the card was quite different, with Riley reaching every green in regulation, but taking thirty-four putts. And Angus, while hitting just six greens, had needed but twenty-three short strokes. Though their methods belied the numbers, the two were deadlocked nonetheless.

Whipping out the J. Braddell in an obvious show of frustration, Riley sputtered, "You're a blasted wizard at gettin' up and down from the crrrap, y' are, MacKenzie!"

"And you're a bloody genius from tee to green, O'Neill!"

"Aye, but I've nothin' to show for it."

"There you go, seein' the glass half-empty. For the love of God, man, you're level par, and damn lucky to be tied with me!"

"Luck me arse! 'Tis just like a Prod to think ev'rything a Fenn does is luck! And what would you be knowin' about the love o' God . . . not much, I'd wager."

"What's come over you!? I was just givin' you a dose of your own sharp tongue. Didn't mean to stir up hard feelings."

"Don't be foockin' with me, MacKenzie. Y' think I don't know the score here? It's been good of you to play a practice loop when no one else is around, but I doubt you'll be as sociable when the Brits show up."

Angus was stunned. Hamish had forewarned him certain members of Ireland's Golfing Union were likely to speak out on the Irish troubles, and that interesting copy might be made of their enthusiasm. Even though Riley had talked politics earlier, this mention of religion using a crude Irish euphemism for Protestants, came as a complete surprise to Angus, especially on the golf course, where any discussion of personal matters was strongly discouraged by the game's unwritten etiquette. Playful barbs had been freely exchanged during their match, but they were good-natured banter, common among golfers who enjoy each other's company and respect each other's game, not the sort of biting remarks that would arouse anger. Tempted to ignore the outburst, Angus turned instead to a reporter's technique, urging Riley to reveal its origins.

"And just what, pray tell, is a Fenn?"

"As if y' didn't know," Riley scoffed.

"Can't say I've ever heard the term."

"Lotta good yer university larnin's done you." Riley derided. "Fenn's shart for Fenian. Irish Catholics in the fight for a free and united Irish republic, are the Fenns," explained the little Irishman, his chest swelling like a banty rooster.

"What got your blood rushing in that direction?"

"Argh . . . the imbalance of power! You wouldn't want your Scotland split into separate countries by the Brits, now would you, lad?!"

"Of course not. But here we were playing a friendly round of golf, and all of a sudden you're attacking my religion, and, for all I know, making it a battle for Ireland's freedom."

"I s'pose you're right, Angus. Politics and religion are best discussed over a pint. But I was curious as to which way you lean on Ireland's troubles. Here I am, a poor Fenn surrounded by Brits and Prods. I need to know who to trust."

"I can see where you might be uneasy in the company of the English or the Scots, all of whom are most likely Prods, er, Protestants. But I'm just here to play golf. No need to pick a fight with me."

"Ireland's dear to me soul, she is. And, for all I know, it's *you* that's doin' the spyin'! Can't be too careful about who I call me mate."

"Aye . . . you've made that quite clear! That, and your exclusive relationship with The Lord God Himself!"

Perturbed, but resolute, Riley turned to face the 18th fairway. The dim light of dusk cast long shadows across the links, and the wind howled furiously in their faces. As he had all afternoon, Riley bludgeoned the ball with a perfectly-timed center strike, propelling it through the gale as if through a vacuum. It came to rest within a niblick of the green on this 400 metre hole.

Reminded that the match was still in doubt, and determined to finish the round with his best golf, Angus finally caught one flush on the face, cracking by far his longest drive of the day, yet a full fifty metres short of Riley's. After nipping a mashie under stubborn gusts to the middle of the green, Angus edged closer to watch the cocky Irishman.

With his usual nonchalance, Riley played a low, hooking shot. And, when the ball flew utterly unaffected by the wind to four feet of the flag, the Scot's advantage of hitting first had proven useless yet again.

Angus surveyed his putt of thirty feet as if The Open Championship itself was at stake, then calmly rolled his Dunlop over a troublesome knob and into the hole for a closing birdie. As with most putts that afternoon, he knew it was in the moment the ball left the putter-face. It was a brilliant display of finesse, capping off a round of one under par 70, as preposterous as it was pleasing. Angus had just experienced one of those rare and wonderful days when that great equalizer, the putter, had shaved at least a dozen shots off his score.

"Argh!" Riley groaned. "A fine plate of haggis, that!"

"Aye, the cruel agony of a timely putt," Angus teased.

"You won't be concedin' this wee one, then?" Riley asked with more than ounce of whining in his tone.

"Not likely. You've missed half a dozen already. You're due to make one though. Takes merely the blink of an eye to brush it in."

"Don't be remindin' me," Riley bristled. "The cup's beginnin' to look the size of a keyhole."

Hastily addressing his four-footer in the manner of a golfer who has lost all confidence, Riley's wobbly stroke sent his Slazenger veering weakly to the right of the hole . . . a pathetic attempt that hadn't even come close. The disappointing par gave him a round of 71 . . . one back of Angus.

Raking the ball back to the position of his first putt, he repeated the attempt. This time, as he rolled it resolutely into the back of the cup, Riley managed a wry smile and mumbled . . . "Ah, you're a grand shadow boxer, y' are, Riley O'Neill. When are you goin' to make a putt when it counts? You're the Parbooster today, Angus. Upset the balance of power, y' did."

"I was lucky and you know it. How do I know you didn't miss that tiddler on purpose?"

"I'd never do such a thing! There's nothin' more impartant than beatin' the Scots."

"Unless it's beatin' the Brits!"

"Now you're onto somethin', MacKenzie! Come on then, I'll stand you that Guinness."

Chapter 4

The two rivals propped their clubs against the bag stand, squinting through twin images of twilight, the original drooping low on the horizon, fiery hues setting the sky ablaze, and its likeness, a mere reflection off the slate roof of Muirfield, somehow shone even brighter. But, then, it had been one of those days that made their entire being shine more brightly.

The warmth of the June sun had dueled to a standstill with a persistent breeze off the Firth, and their faces, flushed by the elements, registered the skirmish. Mssrs. Slazenger and Dunlop had been cleverly maneuvered over firm, fast turf, out of the grasp of heather and gorse, and their scorecard recorded the memorable journey. Most dear, however, was the friendship that had been forged from the day's competition, and their lives would forever chronicle the encounter.

Angus had won today's contest and, while proud to have beaten such an accomplished foe, it wasn't the victory that pleased him most, it was the companionship, knowing he and Riley had given their all, and could now socialize in grace and mutual respect. It was the consummate gift of a gentleman's game.

Sadly, their perfect day was about be marred by a dose of life's harsh realities. As the two men entered the grille, they were greeted by a society more thrifty with its privileges than a Scot with his money. Muirfield had made an exception to its *members only* policy so that contestants might partake of post-round libations. Yet the faces of the club's constituents, glaring at Angus and Riley as though they were common poachers, made it known this concession had been made grudgingly. Unlike many of their fellow competitors, these two played public golf, and it showed. Belittled but unbowed by this clubby set, they were proud to be standard bearers for the masses.

Dusk settled over the grounds and contestants from the three golfing unions began to congregate in the bar. Angus and Riley worked their way through the boisterous crowd to a table near the large bay window. From there, they had a panoramic view of the links and the sea and a somewhat secluded spot in which to recount their round.

"May I be of sarrvice, gentlemen?" asked the bar steward in a muddled highland brogue.

"Coupla' pints o' Guinness if you've got it, guv'ner," said Riley, digging into both pockets for spare change.

"Please sarr, there's nae charrge," the barman protested. "One tug each, compliments of the Rrroyal & Ancient."

"No offense guv'ner, but we lowly Irish don't take handouts from the Brits," Riley insisted, handing the man several coins.

"Rrroight you are, laddie," the waiter replied, winking as he slipped the change into his trousers.

Twin glasses of black ale with heavy tan foam overflowing the brims were delivered by the palsy-handed steward. In a series of carefully-timed tremors, he stood the stouts in front of the wind-whipped golfers without spilling a drop, then placed a generous platter of stilton cheese and soda wafers in the center of the table.

"Let me know if I can be of furrtherr sarrvice, gents," he said, turning to assist the next table.

"Slai'nte," Riley saluted, hoisting the over-flowing pint of molasses-colored ale toward Angus.

"Slai'nte," replied Angus, charging his glass into Riley's with a sense of ease not felt during the same toast he'd shared with Sir Thomas Forgan.

"Tell me more about the Fenns," urged Angus, taking a long swig of the dense liquid.

"Hoosh," Riley warned, spewing Guinness from his nostrils. "The place is crawlin' with Brits. Wait'll they thin out."

"Well . . . what did you think of the course?" asked Angus, quickly changing the subject.

"Ah, she's a beaut', ain't she now," Riley gurgled through his ale. "Maybe the best I've played."

"A grand place. Nothing contrived. Every shot, natural," Angus added, mentally retracing the links.

"Not like me home course of Lahinch," said Riley. "She's a test, she is, but all blind, all the time."

"What is it they say? A shot is only blind once?"

"Aye, and don't take me wrong. Lahinch is a crackin' good spot to larn the game, and a lovely links to play as a regular, but this here's an enchantin' layout. Don't be showin' up here with warts on your game, 'cause this ol' lass'll find 'em and lay 'em bare for all the world to see."

"I read where Old Tom Morris laid out both courses," Angus offered, retrieving a tidbit from his limited knowledge of golf course architecture.

"That he did. The master 'imself! And two more diff'rent links you canna imagine. Lahinch is like the Irish; quirky, and full of the leprechaun, requirin' more than a bit o' luck for a good score. Muirfield's like the Scots; grim and sober. Only guts 'n grit will return a low card here."

"You're obsessed with our differences, O'Neill!"

"Me country's about to be split in two by our diff'rences!" barked Riley.

Most of the bar had now cleared, as contestants and members began to seat themselves in the main dining room. With the wary eye of a soldier on reconnaissance, Riley glanced about the room, giving the patrons a thorough once-over and judging them harmless enough. Both were eager to share their views on religion and politics, and Angus ordered another round of Guinness along with ham sandwiches and chips and vinegar. All was neatly arranged on a fresh linen tablecloth as the men resumed their dialogue on Ireland's troubles.

"How did you know I'm a Protestant?" asked Angus.

"Y' fit the type now, don't you?" replied Riley. "Earnest and hard workin', ye are. I could tell that by the way you play the gemme o' gowf."

"You can't berate a man for trying hard."

"Noo, y' can't. I was just givin' you our view of the enterprisin' Scots. The Brits shipped a passel of Prods into Ireland long ago, and damned if they didn't enterprise us native Irish outta our land!"

"Well, I enterprised you out of the match today, too. Are we going to fight over that, the way Fenns and Prods fight over religion in Ireland!?"

"Argh! Sorry 'bout that nonsense on the course. I was just tryin' to get under your thin Scottish skin . . . findin' out which side yer on. But, stubborn *and* clever y' are."

"Seems to me, you're the one with thin skin!" Angus argued. "But I'm still confused on how the Irish Catholics came to be called Fenns."

"Mmmm," Riley mumbled unintelligibly through a mouth filled with food. "Well . . . did you have any heroes whemmmm . . . you were growin' up, Angus?"

"Only my parents. They sacrificed every personal comfort to send me to the university."

"Aye, sure. Mum and Pap doted on me as well. But what about heroes from your Scottish heritage?"

"If you mean men like Robert the Bruce, or William Wallace, I know their importance in the annals of our nation's struggles, but I don't worship them."

"Well, in me homeland of Eire, there's a grand history of warriors who've fought British tyranny over the ages. Their tales were told to me ev'ry night as a wee lad. Maybe you've heard of Finn mac Cumhhail."

"Finn MacCool?" replied Angus between bites. "The subject of Irish fairytales?"

"That's the English version of the man, but Finn was real all right," replied Riley, furrows forming on his brow. "Centuries ago, the Irish had their clans, and their kings, just like the Scots. Fenians, led by MacCool, were professional soldiers. Roamed over all of Ireland, they did, in service of the kings."

"Mercenaries, then. Paid to protect the clan chieftains."

"In a manner of speakin', lad, they were . . . true enough."

"Whatever became of these ancient Fenians?" Angus asked, certain his proud Irish acquaintance would continue this fairy tale in all its glory.

"Well, the clans and the Fenns were conquered by the Brits, with help from the Scottish Prods. And with their defeat, we Irish lost our Gaelic birthright."

"Let's see if I understand all this. The Fenians of today are out to restore the Gaelic culture and unite the people of Ireland in a free republic."

"Couldn'a said it better meself. Since I was knee-high to a donkey, I've been roused to follow in the footsteps of the Fenians of old and help rid Eire of the Brits and their henchmen, the Scottish Prods. So, I joined Sinn Fein, a modern version of the Fenians."

"And just what does Sinn Fein mean?" Angus had an idea, but was curious to learn more from an Irishman.

"Gaelic for *'ourselves alone'*."

"I take it you're a member."

"Aye, involved in the politics of Sinn Fein, I am, and active in the fightin' through the Irish Republican Army."

"So the Irish Catholics are claiming the Gaelic culture as their own, are they?"

"And why wouldn't we now?"

"Well, we Scots are Gaels too, you know," challenged Angus. "Once, we were Catholic as well . . . at least 'til the Reformation. The Scottish Prods have lived for centuries in Ireland, so why aren't they just as Irish and just as Gaelic as you Catholics?"

Angus had overstated his case, curious to see how Riley would react. A descendant of the clan MacKenzie, Angus was well aware the Scottish Protestants that had emigrated to Ireland were not at all Gaelic but mostly lowland Scots whose forebears had been Angles and Saxons and Picts and Normans. It was the highland Scots who, like the MacKenzies, were of Gaelic stock. And it was the highlanders' own blood-stained defiance of British rule that bore closer resemblance to Ireland's struggle. Many a MacKenzie had died at the Battle of Culloden in 1746, the last futile attempt to restore a Catholic, Bonnie Prince Charlie, to the English throne. Angus' great-grandfather, Baird MacKenzie, clan chieftan at the time, had fallen at Culloden, run through on the bayonet of a Royal Scots Fusilier, another Scot turned Brit.

This inglorious defeat on the moors of Inverness, very near the links of Royal Dornoch, brought to a close an otherwise glorious era. Chieftains soon betrayed their subjects in the name of profit. The braes, once home to clansmen, were soon inhabited by sheep and cattle. Weapons were banned, as was the wearin' of the kilt. Members of the clan not in line to become chieftains fled to find work in the lowlands. And now, despite centuries of an ancestry melded into British culture, Angus felt a certain kinship for Riley and his Gaelic Fenns. Their blood-lines were more alike than not, cut from the same bolt of tartan, so to speak.

Another tale for another time, perhaps, but a reminder, nonetheless, that it was not so farfetched to think they might have some distant relative in common. Angus' mother, Nettie, was an O'Neill whose family had dropped the *'O'* and anglicised the name to *'Neel'* to avoid persecution by England. These ceaseless witch hunts by the Brits had caused many a respectable Irish family to seek refuge in an English name, only to suffer the wrath of Gaelic brethren who cried shame at the defection. Doubtful such cowardly links to a shared past would endear him to Riley, Angus chose not to mention it. Riley was sure to see treason as the motive for surrender. Angus might believe that a Gael once, is a Gael forever, but he was equally certain that his friend would not. To Riley, the proof was in the deed, each and every day. By his reckoning, even the least bit of sedition could render any Irish unworthy of being considered a Gael. But rather than debate the finer points of ethnicity, Riley turned to their most obvious differences, those widened by time and sharpened by attitudes.

"Arghh! The Reformation! That's where it started. T'wasn't enough to kill off the clans and take our land. The bastards tried to stamp out our religion. Besides, the Scots have no int'rest in speakin' the native tongue, or in followin' the Gaelic customs. They'd rather be English!"

"You'd have all the Prods deported to Scotland, then?!"

"Ah, if t'were as simple as that, we'd be dancin' a jig in the streets of Dublin and Belfast!"

Riley now set off into a wildly one-sided rendition of the tormented Gaels of Eire. Some of the tales were familiar, told to Angus as a child by Nettie. But as the wee man spoke, it was obvious this topic was his alone. Employing an odd mixture of passionate rhetoric and grim instruction, his delivery called to mind the fire and brimstone of a missionary laced with the sobriety of a judge. These oral archives were the lifeblood of Gaelic culture, prideful heirlooms passed on from generation to generation, romantic reflections of a tragic past by which the Gael is defined. And, in turn, these myths and half-truths and unsettling hard facts had begun to define O'Neill.

A millennium or so ago, he explained, the Clan Ui' Naill had been royalty, held in highest regard by all men. At a time when only the fierce survived, they held by force much of the land in northern Eire, the Ulster of today. For centuries, the clans were successful in repelling such barbarous invaders as the Vikings and the Normans. But in time, as England gained a foot-hold, the chieftains and their Gaelic followers grew vulnerable.

Angus could picture Riley seated before the same smudgy peat fire that had burned in the cottages of the Ui' Naill for eons while his father repeated the miseries he had heard from his father before him until they became part of Riley's personal ethos. A shrillness crept into Riley's lilt as he recounted how hatred had become a way of life between Irish and English. Catechism had taught him to bear up under the suffering, but any urge to turn the other cheek had long since given way to deep-seated resentment toward the Prods, a rancor too strong for even faith to conquer, a loathing subsumed by Gaelic lore. It had become Riley's own personal poison, a toxin so lethal it might have been labeled with skull and crossbones.

He pointed to the Rebellion of 1641 in Ulster as a flash-point for the Catholics who went on a bloody rampage against Protestants in a sort of blind rage toward British barbarism. Though Riley downplayed Gaelic guilt in this event, Angus knew from the other side of the looking-glass that England had recorded 1641 far differently. It was commonplace to point to these savage slayings as proof of the Pope's conspiracy to destroy Protestantism. And, it provided an excuse for further reprisal and land-grabbing . . . not that one was needed.

In fact, 1641 brought onto the heads of the Irish rebels the wrath of Britain's High Protector of Protestantism, Oliver Cromwell. And this, according to Riley, had cemented, forever, the division between Prods and Fenns, a rift between the haves and have nots. He speculated, only half-jokingly, that this infamous date had been carved into the headboards of all Prod beds so it was their first thought each morning, and last memory each night.

Riley continued to hand-pick fragments of history for Angus' benefit, taking him through the aftermath of the Battle of Boyne in 1690, when William of Orange retained the English throne by defeating the Catholic troops of his challenger, James II. It was yet another tragic incident, driving ever deeper the wedge of mistrust between Catholic Gael and Protestant *Gall*, the Gaelic word for foreigner. And, with the marching season of the Orange Lodges less than a month off, 1690 was an especially disturbing event for Riley and the rest of Catholic Ireland. He explained to Angus how Ulster in July would bring with it a steady stream of epithets against the Pope, performed to drums and patriotic songs regaling the victorious armies of Orange.

Though his jaw was now tightly clenched, Riley was determined to tell the rest of the Gaelic story according to O'Neill. It was in the eighteenth century, he explained, that the Penal Laws began to further erode the influence of the Catholic church. Priests were hanged . . . a great uncle, Father Eoin O'Neill, among the victims. Mass was observed at great risk, and then, only in the secrecy of secluded glens. Bounties were paid to informers, fellow Irishmen so desperate they would betray their own to the Brits for a price. Under the shadow of this threat, many Catholics were driven to abandon their faith. But, like water eroding rock, the Penal Laws widened the chasm between Ulster and England, dire straits indeed, arousing Prod and Fenn alike to question the balance of power.

And, by 1798, the republican views of that great and learned Irish Protestant, Wolfe Tone, began to bond these warring religious sects to their Irish roots, by suggesting a higher social good might come from co-operation rather than conflict. Tone pointed out how Protestants would deny Catholics access to schools, then complain of their ignorance . . . they would persecute the Catholic religion, then denounce as conspiracy their secret conventions with priests. Having foreclosed every means of improvement, Prods would then dismiss Fenns as unworthy of liberty. This polarity, said Riley, spawned discontent from Gall and Gael alike, infusing just enough unity to spark a movement to oust England from

Ulster. It was a hopeful sign to most Fenns that Ulster Prods were ready to leave behind their Englishness, or their Scottishness, and become Irish.

But when the rebellion failed, the price was dear. Tears welled up in Riley's eyes as he described the heads of rebels impaled on spikes for public display, among them his great-grandfather, Seamus O'Neill. As penance, the Brits ushered in the Act of Union, abolishing the Irish parliament, and shelving Catholic emancipation for thirty years. Ireland's future would now revert to an uglier past.

Riley gave a heart-wrenching account of the Great Famine in the mid-1800's, and England's indifference to the suffering of Ireland. The Irish populace, he said, went in three directions . . . *them that died . . . them that wished they'd died . . . and them that sailed to America.* As he recited the roll call of relatives that had fallen into each of these camps, his voice carried with it their collective resentment toward the English.

Riley could offer no explanation for all the failed attempts to unify Ireland, just a shrug and a nod toward the *Fates*, a comfortless and despairing acceptance of a quest that had been star-crossed. But centuries of discontent led to a belief that England, or *John Bull*, as it was called by the Irish, wouldn't leave Ireland unless his toes were trod upon. And this was a topic on which Riley was at his patriotic best.

Only nineteen when he completed his study at St. Edna's School for Boys, Riley had enlisted in the Irish Volunteers led by Padraic Pearse. This was the first of many occasions that Riley would speak of Pearse, his mentor, and headmaster of St. Edna's, and his pride was palpable. Though crushed in their attempt at ousting England in 1916, Riley described Pearse and his cohorts as poet warriors, noting the stirring oratory and tragic martyrdom that had begun to galvanize Irish public opinion around the idea of an Ireland, free and undivided. In just these past two years, the steady stream of violence visited by the IRA onto prominent British leaders and their venerable institutions had caused England to consider ceding home rule to Ireland. By the time Riley had completed his short course, Angus was dizzy with Irish history. But the lesson wasn't over just yet.

"This is our last, best chance," Riley blared. "The very future of our country's at stake! They'll split Ireland into North and South, with the six

Ulster counties under direct British rule. The twenty-six counties in the South'll have a sep'rate government called the Irish Free State."

"And what if the Irish voters don't accept the terms?"

"Back to war with the Brits, I 'spect. No Sinn Feiner wants to swear allegiance to the Crown, and none of us want the partition. But we're not too keen on goin' back to fightin' the Brits, either."

"Sounds like you're damned if you do, and damned if you don't. Might be easier to deport the Prods."

"Too late for that, I'm afraid," Riley replied, not at all interested in Angus' humor. "No, the Prods can stay, if they'll just accept one Irish government."

"So, Sinn Fein's aim is to have a single government controlled by the Irish Catholics who hold a vast majority in the south. You say trust us. But you don't trust the Prods!"

"And why not!? We're the real Irish . . . Gaels from the farst o' time. I'm descended from the great clan king, Ui' Naill of Tyrone!"

"Then the fight is to reclaim your throne! You're no better than the Brits."

"The fight is to bring all the Irish together in a united purpose, with north and south treated alike! And that includes the Scottish Prods . . . if they'd rather be Irish than British."

"I gather the Irish leadership is not opposed to using violence to accomplish their goal."

"As Padraic Pearse, would say . . . *Better is a short life with honour, than a long life with dishonour.*"

Reaching into his pocket, Riley began shuffling through photographs tucked in the lining of his wallet until he located the one of a man dressed in the long black robe of a professor and pince nez glasses. He shoved it toward Angus. Pearse had a feral quality, a gaze that struck Angus as just the sort of wild-eyed stare a bona fide radical might project. Beyond that, quite ordinary. Nothing to suggest this was a man who could inspire an insurrection against anyone, least of all the omnipotent British empire.

"So that's Padraic Pearse," Angus said politely. "Doesn't look like the sort of fellow who'd be moved by the ancient legend of Finn MacCool."

"MacCool was a man of action. So was Pearse!"

"But isn't his adage of a short life with honor just perpetuating the romantic myth of MacCool, and reinforcing the notion that all the ancient wrongs require retaliation?"

"I'll try t' overlook your slap at me heroes, Pearse and MacCool! We tried to negotiate with the Brits, and look what it got us, a nation divided!"

"You're befuddled, man! On the one hand, you're ready to accept the partition and the oath of loyalty, and build on this first step. And on the other, you still want war with the Brits. You can't have it both ways. The leaders of Ireland have as many political voices as Scotland's got sheep. You've got to start singing from the same hymnal."

"Ain't as simple as you're tryin' to make it, Angus. If a majority in Ireland accepts the partition and the oath of loyalty, then the minority is likely to set off an Irish civil war. And if we don't accept the terms, we'll be back at war with the Brits. I'd sooner be damned for killin' Brits . . . than be damned for killin' me own Gaelic brothers."

"It's getting late," said Angus, sensing the futility of this debate and the desperation of the Irish plight. He glanced up at the clock. "I'd best be checking my room and stowing my things. Where are you staying, Riley?"

"I'm at the Golf Hotel in Gullane," he said, accenting the first syllable of the nearby town as would a local so it came out *Gill'n.* "How 'bout you?", he belched as he drained the last of his Guinness.

"Greywalls," Angus replied sheepishly.

"I should'a known you'd be puttin' in with the Brits," goaded Riley.

"I'm not putting in with anyone. It's just convenient."

"I heard it's full of Brits, and I want the lowdown on all of 'em," joked Riley, slapping Angus on the back as they left the men's grill.

"What are your plans for tomorrow?"

"Workin' on me putting stroke. I saw you doing somethin' today I want to try."

"Oh, and what was that?"

"Keepin' me head still and me hands quiet."

"That would help. You might also shorten your stroke and accelerate through the ball."

"Whoa, lad! A feeble mind can only deal with one or two ideas at a time!"

"I'll see you here on the practice green, then?"

"No, I'll work on it over at Gullane. I like to collect me thoughts alone before a tarnament. See you Tarsd'y."

"You won't be attending the banquet?" Angus asked in surprise, referring to the pre-tournament dinner scheduled for Wednesday evening.

"Noo, it's just a bunch of stiffs tryin' to impress each other."

Realizing the futility in trying to persuade Riley to attend, Angus sighed and said, "Alright then, be well."

"Steer clear of the Brits, now," cautioned Riley, slinging his clubs over his shoulder.

"G'night," Angus called from the shadows.

Angus entered the rear door of Greywalls to the clamor of loud voices and laughter coming from the study. He eased down the hallway to avoid being discovered by what was sure to be a room full of English golfers. As he reached the foot of the stairs, he tiptoed past the door to escape formal introductions.

Chapter 5

*A*ngus was awakened by a faint echo. Click . . . pause . . . click . . . pause. Repetitive and evenly paced, it reminded him of an unhurried metronome yet somehow seemed altogether different. He sat up, straining to identify the sound, and it stopped. Rising, half-asleep, Angus shuffled to the open window and squinted out at the thin red ribbon of morning through sand-encrusted eyes. Drawing back from the distant horizon to the golf course below and rubbing away the night's gritty deposits, he could just make out the silhouette of a golfer on the practice ground. The sound resumed.

Although the flight of the ball was not visible, Angus listened with an ear keenly attuned to the sound of a shot struck well . . . the whoosh of a club speeding toward impact . . . the click of metal against gutta percha . . . the inimitable hiss vanishing into unlit sky. Like the musician who is able to identify perfect pitch and timbre, Angus could determine the quality of each shot merely by its resonance, and at a distance of fifty metres, he had-n't heard a single note from any of the instruments in the shadow's ensemble that sounded even remotely off key.

The mere thought of practicing golf in the dark struck Angus as peculiar. Dressing hurriedly, he bounded down the stairs three at a clip. Exiting Greywalls onto Muirfield's links, dawn was upon him, the scent of sea salt latent in the moist morning air. As Angus strolled to the practice tee, hands in pockets, feigning disinterest, the image slowly came into focus. It was obvious this was no ordinary golfer. Tall and slender, with a long, lazy swing to match build and demeanor, the silhouette's precise yet effortless movements were turning out golf shots that would have impressed even one as discerning as Riley O'Neill.

Then, as if the air were swarming with insects, a low hum began to fill the pause between clicks. Hmmm . . . click . . . hmmm . . . click. Darkness receded, and some twenty metres off the end of the practice tee, Angus could make out a mound. On closer inspection, Angus could see the mound was a man, sitting cross-legged on the grass. From turban to kaftan, he was clad all in black and facing east toward the breaking dawn, hands resting on knees, thumbs and middle fingers touching to form circles. Drawing on his vague recollection of Far Eastern cultures, Angus realized the man was deep in some stage of meditation and, judging from the humming sounds that emanated from his direction, must be in the midst of a mantra. Angus glanced at the golfer and back again at the mound. Bewildered, he could not stop staring.

"May I help you?" asked the lanky golfer, neither looking up at Angus, or deviating from his routine.

"Oh," gasped Angus, moving closer, "Good morning."

"Are you getting anything useful?" asked the young man in an unctuous tone and distinctly British accent.

"I . . I . . I wasn't spying."

"Of course not."

"Angus MacKenzie." Angus offered, extending his hand.

A painfully long pause that bordered on rudeness was followed by a response delivered with the smug air of superiority, "Collier . . . Colby . . . Ames."

Cradling MacKenzie's hand effeminately, Ames looked down his beak-like nose through round spectacles framed in tortoise shell. With the pleats of his linen slacks pressed to razor sharpness, and a pink, long-sleeved shirt of the finest Egyptian cotton, it was evident that Ames was as familiar with high style as he was with golf.

"Well, I'd best let you get on with your practice," said Angus, sensing the Brit had no use for him. Then, as if to engage the dark mound in conversation, Angus glanced his way, but the humming only intensified and showed no sign of abating.

"Yes. You should," Ames said in blunt monotone, turning back to the cluster of balls. "You're not playing in the championship, are you?"

Above the vee of his ivory-hued sweater vest was a Cambridge club tie of robin egg blue. The blonde hair was center-parted, and the uncooperative cowlicks on each side were plastered in pomade to make them behave. Lurking beneath the fair locks was an angular face punctuated by piercing green eyes.

"Yes . . . I am," Angus replied in a tone of inadequacy, knowing he didn't have the pedigree of Ames, whose trophies included nearly every amateur title worth winning.

"Well, then," Ames said dismissively, implying Angus' own response had revealed his lack of qualifications for an event such as this, and that he was, indeed, out of his element. Conversation over.

Angus recognized the brush-off and rather than offer some pitiful defense of his game, he pivoted on his heel and strode briskly back toward Greywalls. Click . . . pause . . . click . . . pause. The echo of club striking ball again grew faint as he reached the back door.

*   *   *

The dining room was crowded with hungry young men and the inviting aroma of freshly cooked food. A buffet of waffles, scrambled eggs, and ham had been laid out on the long dining table. Side dishes of stewed tomatoes, sautéed mushrooms, smoked herring, and lox were placed in sterling chafing dishes on the sideboard. Alongside, coffee sat steaming in a brass urn, and juices filled a dozen crystal pitchers. Angus stocked his plate with a spoonful of eggs and a slab of ham, and noticed Jamie Ferguson, the youngest member of the English Golfing Union, sitting alone next to a window that overlooked the garden. The pudgy seventeen year old prodigy was busily filling his freckled cheeks with waffles as Angus approached.

"Angus MacKenzie. Edinburgh. Mind if I join you?"

"Er . . . I guess not," said a startled Ferguson, hurriedly searching the room to determine whether any British colleagues might object to his fraternizing with a Scot. "James Ferguson. Sandwich, England," he said, rising to shake Angus' hand. "Friends call me Jamie."

"Sandwich. Isn't Royal St. George's located in Sandwich?"

"Why yes! My home course! You've played there?"

"No. But I've heard only good things about the course. After all, it is on The Open rotation."

"You simply must play there sometime. Collier says it's his favorite course in the British Isles."

"Collier Ames?"

"Indeed, yes. Do you know Collier?"

"We just met. He was out practicing before dawn."

"That's Collier. He practices with more purpose than any golfer I know. And it shows in his results. He's simply unbeatable!"

"Is he now? And what makes you so certain?"

"Well, there is renewed interest in amateur golf now that the Walker Cup is becoming a reality. We've seen a marked rise in number of outstanding players in Great Britain, and Collier has beaten all of them. The resolve of the English Golfing Union is unequaled now that Sir . . ." Ferguson stopped mid-sentence and appeared to choke on a chunk of sausage. He backpedaled. "Amateur golf is on the rise in England."

Angus tried unsuccessfully to steer their conversation back to the topic of just who was behind the revival of British amateur golf. But Jamie Ferguson's lips were now sealed, as if he had suddenly realized it might be considered inappropriate to reveal the name of *Sir Someone* to an outsider. Instead, as Ferguson chattered on about the golfing prowess of Collier Colby Ames, Angus found it necessary to divert their discussion to less annoying topics, such as the unusually warm weather, or the kaleidoscopic colors in the garden, or the merits of the new Haskell golf ball . . . anything but Ames. He even considered asking the young Brit about the mysterious other man on the practice ground with Ames, but thought better of it. Only half-hearing Ferguson's prattle now, Angus' subconscious had slipped reflectively back to Collier . . . Colby . . . Ames . . . and Colby, County Down.

*   *   *

When, at last, he escaped the effusive Mr. Ferguson, Angus strolled into Gullane to dispatch a telegram to *The Scotsman*. The story of the tournament had been his discovery of the obscure Irishman, Riley O'Neill, as a leading contender. Angus felt obliged to inform his employer of the scoop that presumably had eluded competing newspapers. By winning most of the events leading up to the British Isles Cup, Collier Ames had received the lion's share of coverage from publications like the *London Times*. And while this attention of the press was well-deserved, Angus had a hunch about Riley's chances. Besides, as Hamish had counseled, there would be plenty of grist in an article about an Irishman during these times of political unrest in Ireland. He intended to see his story through.

Angus bypassed the telegraph office and went directly to the Golf Hotel to see if Riley was in. When the clerk informed him no Riley O'Neill was registered, a now-puzzled Angus postponed the telegram and headed instead to Gullane Golf Links. Quickly covering the few blocks from the hotel to the first tee, he approached the starter's hut in hopes of finding Riley.

"Top o' the mornin' to you, sir," said Angus to the starter, whose name, Wm. C. Stanwood, was printed in block letters above the tiny cubicle.

"Aye, and the remainder o' the day to you, laddie!"

The white wooden structure sat snugly beside Gullane No. 1's first tee, its steeply pitched roof sporting a fresh coat of British racing green, and on the peak rested a tarnished weather vane whose once gleaming copper patina had long since turned chalky. The hut was crammed with golf paraphernalia. In addition to balls and tees and scorecards, a golfer could obtain from Mr. Stanwood anything required to ward off the one constant in Scotland . . . inclement weather.

"Have you seen an Irishman named Riley O'Neill this morning?" asked Angus.

"'bout this high?" Stanwood deadpanned, holding his hand five and a half feet off the ground. "Wearin' too-big knickers and a brass-toed shoe?"

"That'd be him."

"Came down here last night 'bout ha' past dark to practice his puttin'. 'Spect he just slept in one o' the bunkers up by the first green. Called it his

Gowf Hotel, 'e did! The Irish travel on the cheap, y' know. And, last night bein' a fine, dry ev'nin', he was prob'ly up at the peep o' day playin' a quick loop."

*   *   *

The moist chill of a Scottish morn intruded, unchecked, into Riley's joints. Though dawn had not yet broken, he unwrapped himself from the leather golf bag that had served as his overnight sleeping companion and stood, stretching, in the bunker beside the first green. Tossing a few golf balls onto the dewy grass and stabbing them toward the cup, he soon tired of the tedious nuances of putting and headed to the tee to do what he liked best . . . hit the J. Braddell.

Riley's boyhood had been filled with golf played in the faint flicker of daybreak. If lessons at St. Theresa's and Yeats by the peat fire had been his sacrament, then nightly stories of Culchulain and Finn Mac Cumhhail had been his sustenance. But it was golf in dawn's hopeful light that had become Riley's religion, and the golf course of Lahinch, his chapel. It was there he had sorted out his feelings of the forces at work in Ireland. It was there he had resolved to attend St. Edna's and study at the knee of Padraic Pearse, the master of Gaelic revival. It was there, in the solitude of golf's cathedral, his passion for a free and united Ireland had been born.

Today, Gullane would be no different than Lahinch. In this temple of eighteen altars, an invocation could be heard with each thwack of the ball and, with each clink, as it fell into the cup, a benediction. Immersed in quiet seclusion, the links of Gullane No. 1 led Riley to the top of its heralded hill where, cheeks flushed by breeze, he once again turned inward, sorting out the feelings of an Irishman stifled by British rule. He agonized over the sentiments he had so strenuously expressed in the outburst aimed at Angus during their practice round. It could not have been helped. The crusader lives to convert the nonbeliever. Angus was just such a skeptic. Perhaps Riley had been a bit abrupt in his approach, but his point had been made. If you were going to be the friend of Riley O'Neill, you must at least be willing to examine the plight of Ireland through Irish eyes. Angus had met the test head on and seemed worthy of Riley's trust.

"Is that him just now, teein' up at the last?" asked Stanwood.

Angus stared across the first fairway to the eighteenth tee a few hundred metres away. The slight, dark-haired figure preparing to drive his ball looked to be Riley. As he swung, Angus knew at once it was his new Irish acquaintance. With an arc so swift it was no more than a blur, the ball was sent bounding between two fairway bunkers and onto the front apron of the green, some three hundred metres from the tee. As much delight as Angus took from watching the Irishman play, the sight of Riley, sauntering down the fairway, wearing the irrepressible grin of an incurable optimist, served as proof the wee man enjoyed it even more.

"The lad enjoys life's simple pleasures, and keeps me in stiches," said Stanwood. "That's why 'e gets to sleep on me gowf course and play for gratis."

"Things *are* lively when Riley's around," conceded Angus, striding over to Gullane's eighteenth green.

"Playing golf for lodging is a professional's game!" Angus yelled to Riley as the little Irishman strutted jauntily toward the green, golf clubs secured to his back by the crooks of both elbows. "You may be jeopardizing your amateur status, O'Neill!"

"Better that, than sleepin' at Greywalls!"

Meeting greenside, the two men clasped hands, and Angus watched as Riley chipped to within inches then tapped in for his birdie. It was a round of 67, completed in under two hours.

Angus noticed sand particles clinging to the back of Riley's greasy black hair and still others enmeshed in his sweater. Crystals that had stuck stubbornly to the seat of his pants from a night of being bunkered, now refused to be dislodged, even during this brisk round of golf. The tweed glistened in the morning sun as if woven with threads of mica.

"Seriously, Riley, why didn't you say you needed a room last night?"

"I didn't. The '*golf hotel*' was grand. Besides, I'd sooner sleep in a boonker, than next to a Brit . . . 'specially if the host is Lord Barrington Ashley."

O'Neill combed the sand from his suety hair and wiped it on his trousers to remove any grains stuck between the tines.

"Listen, Riley, I met our chief competition this morning," Angus said excitedly.

"We met our competition yesterday," Riley shot back, "and her name is Muirfield."

"Oh, I know we should just worry about the course, but this chap Collier Ames . . ."

"I know all about Ames," Riley interrupted. "Travels with some sort of mystic . . . a Pakistani, I hear . . . named Rawahli something or other . . . supposedly part psychic, part hypnotist. But you can be sure, he's all phony."

"What do you mean?"

"Ames pretends this bloke is some sort of golf guru, possessing mystical powers that give him exclusive access to the inner secrets of the game, you know, the ability to close off those negative thoughts that get in the way of our best golf."

"But you're not buying it."

"Not for a minute. This high priest from the East is nothing more than a shill . . . a ploy by Ames to get inside the skull of his opponents."

"I get it. You start worrying about the Pakistani, and you forget to play your own game."

"Aye, lad, lookin' for an edge, he is . . . the way Brits do."

"But what if there is something to this hypnotism business?"

"I'll hypnotize the miserable bastard . . . show him the business end of my J. Braddell, I will. He'll be in a trance, alright."

"Well, on that high note, I'm going to wire a telegram to the paper," said Angus, "then I'm headed back to Muirfield for some practice. Care to join me?"

"I like it here better. No airs. Just regular folk like Mr. Stanwood there," Riley said, pointing to the starter's hut.

Walking toward the telegraph office, Angus glanced back at Riley and waved. The spirited little Irishman was practicing his woeful putting stroke with an even more disfigured stance than the one he had employed during yesterday's practice round. Still mystified by the contrast between Riley's ball-striking and his putting, Angus penned a brief telegram . . .

> *R.P. O'Neill posted 71 in practice round. Should have been 65. Prepared to write feature article. Please advise. AM.*

Angus waited while the clerk clacked out the message on his key, then headed back to Greywalls. A crew of volunteers had hoisted flags of the three countries up masts located in front of the Muirfield clubhouse. The scene reminded Angus just how provincial the world could be in rural Scotland, far from the strife of Ireland. Here flew the Irish Tricolor, its green stripe emblematic of the Gaelic Catholics, its orange stripe representing the Protestants of William of Orange, and its white stripe symbolizing peace and trust between the two. Next to the tricolor, unfurled the flag of Scotland with its field of royal blue and white cross of St. Andrews. And beyond it fluttered the Union Jack, purporting to unite England, Scotland, Ireland, and Wales under the crosses of St. George, St. Andrews, and St. Patrick. To the uninformed, all within the Empire seemed well.

Angus spent the day practicing his short game and watching the other contestants arrive and depart the first tee for their practice rounds. He observed all shapes and sizes of golfers who displayed all makes and models of golf swings. They shared one common ingredient, the ability to propel the ball great distances on a straight line. What he could not ascertain from either their appearance or their swings, however, was their resolve, that indefinable quality which separates the proficient from the pretender . . . champion from charlatan.

*   *   *

As the day wore on, Angus was practicing his chipping and putting when the Club Secretary, John X. P. Morrisette, handed him an urgent telegram from the offices of *The Scotsman*. Tearing open the envelope, Angus read . . .

No articles on the Irish! The story is Collier Ames. TCF

A far different Sir Thomas Forgan was beginning to emerge. The *hale fellow, well-met* persona Sir Thomas drew forth whenever he courted favor was being overshadowed by the darker, more Machiavellian, character Angus had briefly glimpsed during their encounters at the publisher's office and at Dunvegan.

Crumpling the telegram, he stuffed it into his pocket. Hamish had warned that a writer and his editor may have conflicting slants on a story but, more to the point, a publisher's opinion could override either. Forgan's predisposition toward the *feckless* Irish was becoming all too apparent to Angus. Perhaps he should write two stories, one featuring Riley, and the other, Ames. But in truth, he argued with himself, the story was about both. Unfair as it seemed, there was little doubt Sir Thomas was bent on playing up the Brit at the expense of the Irishman. Even as an apprentice, Angus could see his notion of a press which engages in unbiased reporting amounted to little more than the naiveté of an idealist. Angus decided to trust his instincts and write an article contrasting the two competitors. If the effort fell short of Forgan's expectations, or his prejudices, so be it.

*   *   *

The opening banquet was conducted in the grand ballroom of the Muirfield clubhouse. It was a magnificent setting, elegantly appointed for the occasion, and the event featured a menu and wine list to be rivaled only in the finest restaurants of London. Angus found he had been assigned to a table comprised of four Brits, two Irishmen, a fellow Scot, and Collier Ames. From the moment Angus was seated, Ames began to preside over the conversation as if he were Chief Justice of the Exchequer. The Englishman could not have been more overbearing had he been clad in a crimson robe and fitted with a powdered wig.

"You should have seen my shot on the fourth . . . within inches of an ace! And the look of panic on the face of the poor sap paired with me . . . why, he was utterly undone!"

"What score do you think will qualify tomorrow, Collier?" asked one of his fellow Englishmen.

The tournament called for a 36 hole medal round on Thursday. The field of seventy would be cut to the low eight qualifiers for match play, with quarterfinals to be played Friday morning and semi-finals in the afternoon. The final, contested over 36 holes on Saturday, made for a grueling format designed to identify the player best able to withstand the rigors of both medal and match play. Only golfers who displayed consistently fine form and unwavering emotional control stood a chance under such a thorough examination.

"I should think 150 will qualify for match play," Collier replied. "The course is quite firm for this time of year and promises to become even more swift in this damnable heat."

"How did you score today, Collier?" asked a colleague.

"69. But I missed several makeable putts," Ames preened.

"Who're the favorites? Besides yourself, I mean," chimed Angus, wondering if Collier would even acknowledge there were other contestants in the field.

"Oh, I don't know, really," his tone lacquered with boredom. "MacKenzie, isn't it?" he continued, barely tolerant of Angus. "I expect some of our lads from Cambridge to show well. Larry Dirleton, or perhaps even you, Somersby," Ames said smarmily to Robert Somersby, a Cambridge man seated to his left.

"Reports have it, you posted a fine card MacKenzie," he continued. "Over your head, perhaps? And your Irish cohort, O'Neill, what of his game?"

"Oh, he's a much better golfer than me."

"*I*," Collier corrected in a tone dipped in disdain. "He's a much better golfer than *I* . . . not me. In any event, I see O'Neill saw fit not to grace us with his presence. Hardly Walker Cup behavior, even if he is an able player"

"He's a bit out of sorts," said Angus, still blushing from the grammar lesson he had received from Ames. He now wondered what had come over him to make excuses for someone he hardly knew.

"Oh I'm quite certain he's ill," sneered Ames. "Sick to death he doesn't measure up to a proper Englishman . . . or even a Scot," he added, revealing his notion of the social pecking order in the United Kingdom. His sarcasm drew high-pitched cackles from his British cronies.

"Yes, he'd be most uncomfortable here, I'm sure of it. Do the Irish even use utensils while dining?" he asked pointedly, raising more laughter.

The two Irishmen seated at the table, Mick Callahan and Sean O'Sullivan, were both Prods from County Down. Ames had surmised these burly Ulstermen would place their religion, and their loyalty to the Crown, in higher stead than Ireland. After all, hadn't Ulster done just that for centuries? He was mistaken. Tonight, their Irishness was offended. As they slid back their chairs and invited Collier and his Cambridge chums outside for a more spirited discussion, Angus saw the evening headed toward disaster and interceded to avert an incident.

"I'm sure you weren't serious about the utensils, were you, Collier," Angus urged diplomatically, hoping Ames would exercise some much-needed British tact.

"Of course, not," sputtered Ames, as if on cue. He glanced warily at the two beefy Irishmen preparing to remove their jackets.

"I was trying to crack wise, and can see now that my remarks were misguided. Please, gentlemen, accept my deepest apologies."

Callahan and O'Sullivan eyed one another as though assessing the sincerity in Collier's tone. Neither was convinced Ames had meant what he said, but were even less interested in making a scene. The apology had been sufficiently audible for all to hear and, whether or not genuine, they resolved to accept this feeble offering and finish the evening with decorum.

"All right, Ames," snorted Callahan in a clipped British accent common to Ulster, "we accept. But don't start thinking all subjects of the Crown are anything like you. We don't condone your airs of superiority. Best keep them in check."

"Right-o, old boy," Ames smirked. "I'll just do that."

*   *   *

The contestants were eager to adjourn for brandy and to check tomorrow's pairings, when Lord Atwater, a high-ranking official of the Royal & Ancient, stepped to the podium for closing remarks. Reciting the particulars of play for the championship, he covered the local ground rules, ad nauseum. Yawns filled the room as Atwater lapsed into a monotonous soliloquy on amateurism and other lofty ideals. With heads sagging listlessly and eyes rolling in disbelief, the audience suddenly became alert and attentive as Lord Atwater moved on to a discussion of the Walker Cup.

The dapper old aristocrat explained why the Cup was destined to become the most prestigious amateur event in the world of golf, and how perfectly grand it would be for Great Britain to prevail. After describing its format in abundant detail, he concluded the evening's festivities by outlining the selection criteria that would be used by the Royal & Ancient to select the team for Great Britain. To the surprise of no one, social status was given parity with golfing ability and sportsmanship.

Mercifully, the speech ended, and many of the contestants repaired to the bar for nightcaps. Against his better judgment and the pre-tournament counsel of Hamish MacClanahan, Angus vigorously partook of the vintage champagne being poured from bottomless, dust-coated magnums. Somehow he managed enough presence of mind to note the pairing of A. A. MacKenzie and R. P. O'Neill and C. C. Ames in the 7:36 a.m. tee time, but it was well past midnight when Angus and the last of the revelers vacated the bar.

Chapter 6

*S*till groggy from the effects of last night's bubbly, Angus was searching for his putting touch when the starter's call pierced the morning calm.

"Next on the tee, frrom Edinburra, Scotland . . . Misterrr Angus MacKenzie!"

With hammers clanging away at his skull, Angus was pleased to be paired with the best players in the field, and delighted to get out early, before the wind got up. The cacophony inside his head proved a useful diversion from the anxiety of the day's first shot as Angus slashed at the ball in an unbridled frenzy, zipping it down the fairway to within twenty metres of Ames and O'Neill. The performance drew a smattering of applause from other competitors gathered near the first tee to watch the featured threesome begin their round. The accolades of his peers, however modest, were just what he needed to bolster his ego. But could he match them shot for shot? Angus had good reason to wonder.

The greens were softened by a membrane of morning dew, and the wind scarcely whispered. As a result, Muirfield dispensed none of its usual ferociousness. Conditions favored low scoring, but none materialized. As if sensing her own vulnerability due to the benign elements, Muirfield deployed a second line of defense, the uncanny ability to make each shot feel awkward and uncertain, introducing just enough doubt to keep even the most skillful of golfers off balance.

Angus seized the early lead with an unlikely 72 that included three chip-in birdies. He was closely followed by Collier, whose 74 was marred by an out-of-bounds on the ninth. Riley, whose putting stroke had begun to resemble an old woman sweeping her stoop, settled for a 75. Walking off the eighteenth green, shaking hands, and signing scorecards, the breezes had begun to freshen, and the day was growing hot. The afternoon round promised to be far more challenging, as greens and fairways were certain to wither beneath wind and sun.

A luncheon of assorted cold cuts, cheeses, and breads was neatly arranged in the clubhouse dining room. For the more adventurous, there were trays of mashed potatoes, slabs of highland beef, and mounds of Yorkshire pudding. And, to ensure everyone was well-fortified for the remainder of the day, a tantalizing selection of desserts was arranged on a carousel in the center of the room.

Nursing a stomach unsettled from the stress of competition and last night's overindulgence, Angus was unable to eat a full portion. He assembled half a ham and cheddar sandwich and went outside to eat alone near the practice green, leaving Riley and Collier to lunch together. Their surprisingly gracious behavior toward each other during the morning round had given Angus no reason to think attitudes might change. Besides, he lacked the energy to officiate their differences.

Riley piled his plate with mounds of mashed potatoes and huge slabs of roast beef, and ordered a pint of Guinness. Collier chose a cutlet of ham, no bread or cheese, and prepared a steaming pot of chamomile tea. In a complete departure from his characteristic aloofness, Ames joined Riley at a table near the bay window and was first to break the silence.

"Nice round, O'Neill." The words were squeezed from his throat in a low croak, as if the life had been wrung from each before its release.

"Aye, and y' did well yourself, Ames," Riley chirped.

"I could have done without that spot of bother on the wretched ninth," whined Collier.

"Ahh, there's the game o' golf for you. Fickle, she is."

"And that is precisely the difference between you and me, O'Neill. You think the game is whimsical, and I believe it is all a matter of will and control."

"Aye," said Riley, and with an edge well-sharpened on the whetstone of Irish discontent, growled, "we Irish know all about the will of the Brits, and how you control our lives with it."

The tone of Ames' voice had charged the hackles on Riley's neck and he could feel a rush of blood. It was a familiar sensation, one he experienced whenever fear or anger were on the rise. He knew all too well the consequences of this surge of adrenaline left unchecked.

"If England hadn't taken control of Ireland, it would have been France or Spain or some other country with a stronger resolve than the Irish," Ames continued. "It is preferable, wouldn't you agree, to be part of an English-speaking realm?"

Riley felt a tautness invade his arms and face. The clenched fists and constricted jaw were a common prelude to assault, and now they began to command the moment. Until this encounter with Ames, nothing had aroused his urge to do battle quite like his experience in the Easter Rising. Separated from his unit of Irish Volunteers as they stormed Dublin Castle, Riley was cornered by a British Coldstream Guard. Even now, he could feel the icy steel of the rifle barrel on his neck, placing him at the mercy of the Brit. But it was the soldier's voice, shrill and nasal and insolent, quite Ames-like, warning he'd shoot at the slightest movement, that caused Riley to recoil. With one knee braced against the cobblestones, his left arm had swiped the gun barrel off his neck while his right fist came off the deck with the speed of his J. Braddell through impact and buried into the man's solar plexus. With the Brit doubled over from the blow, Riley head-butted his enemy to the ground and, in one swift move, somersaulted the length of his frame, pinning the man's shoulders under his knees. The mere memory of hand to hand combat under life-threatening circumstances was enough to sober Riley, if only for a moment. Reluctantly, he returned to the conversation with only slightly less rancor.

"No people have been so mistreated as the Irish under English rule," attacked Riley, the singsong of his lilt rising and falling like an aria. "You took our land and tried to force feed us your customs and your religion. If you'd leave us be, we'd . . . we'd . . . still be speakin' Gaelic!"

"And if you wouldn't resist so strenuously, we might show more pity," said Collier, defending the Crown's party line. "Why not accept things as they are, the way you do in golf?"

It must have been the utter helplessness in those Coldstream eyes that interceded in this bout with Ames. On that fateful Easter Sunday in 1916,

Riley had grasped the Brit's helmet with both hands and cinched the chin-strap tightly around his throat, tearing loose the man's right ear in the process. Using his knees on the Englishman's shoulders for leverage, and with those huge hands tightening the garrote, he choked all life from the man. It seemed to take forever. The gurgle from his throat, the tongue lolling from his mouth, the strength ebbing from his body, were all grue-some reminders . . . but death seeped out through the eyes. Riley was for-ever transformed by the terror in those bulging eyes. Oh, he might again fire his rifle at the enemy from long range, but this incident was so much more personal. Taking another man's life with his bare hands would either become his modus operandi in dealing with conflict, or it would become a governor, a conscience to be invoked whenever passion turned to rage. Ames had provided the ultimate test of which it would be, and Riley was barely able to draw back from the urge to throttle him.

"Never in bloooody Hell!" boomed Riley, springing to his feet and top-pling his chair in the process. "What happens in golf is natural. There's nothin' natural 'bout tearin' a country in two, the way the Brits have torn Eire. You won't hear the end of the Irish 'til we get a united repooblic!" Riley threatened, tipping over his chair as he storming out.

Angus witnessed the confrontation from his spot beneath an apple tree and hurried over to see if a mediator might be needed.

"The Brit got me hackles up!" Riley seethed.

"That much I could see. Listen Riley, we're off in half an hour. You'd better go hit a few balls and try to calm down."

"I can't be bothered by his kind. I'll just beat the bejaysus out of him on the links!"

"Now you're onto somethin'," Angus said guardedly, wondering if Riley was referring to the golf or, whether he had in mind something a bit more serious.

*   *   *

That afternoon, Muirfield revealed its true character. A two-club wind blew stiffly out of the north, crossing from right to left on the first hole.

When all three players missed the green and failed to save par, the battle was joined. The shrewd routing of holes at Muirfield links set up its subtle defenses. Going out, the golfers faced nine holes configured clockwise around the perimeter of the course. Coming in, they were met by nine set to the interior, returning to the clubhouse counter-clockwise. As a result, the course demanded the player to adapt to the ever-changing direction of the wind. It was a stern, straight-forward challenge that defiantly declared . . . *ask no quarter, for none shall be given.*

Not surprisingly, while Riley and Collier raised their games to meet the elements, Angus was spent. Having summoned all his skill and energy to hold the morning lead, shots were dropped at the first, seventh, tenth, and two more at the sixteenth, leaving him five adrift of par as they reached the last. Going out, he had been joy-riding in a Bentley. Coming home, the Bentley was a bucket of bolts in a wheelbarrow, and Angus, a crash victim strapped to a gurney.

The double bogey Collier had suffered at the ninth in the morning round was trumped by an eagle there in the afternoon. With just the blemish at the opener and pars on the remainder of his card, he was one under for his round, two over on the day.

After his bogey at the first, Riley had played flawlessly. As if by divine intervention, he managed to coax in short birdie putts at five, nine, twelve, and seventeen, to stand three under for the afternoon, one over for the day.

Suddenly, from behind a sand dune, in a sort of spectral stealth, appeared Rawahli. His entrance was so unexpected, so inconspicuous, it was as if somehow he had been present all day. This appearance in person seemed merely incidental to the metaphysical being . . . except for the eyes. Angus had not seen the man's face full on until now, and those eyes were otherworldly . . . indigo . . . a shade so bright one was commanded to lock onto them. They were a penetrating blue, set against a white, brighter than a polar icecap, and eerily etched in red, as if recently emerged from a desert sandstorm. Above his forehead, in the center of the turban, was a sapphire of slightly darker blue, creating the appearance of a third eye. And, from around his neck, on a leather thong, hung a talisman, a yellowish amulet that he rolled between the tips of his long, brown fingers while murmuring a series of unintelligible phrases. Clouds crossed overhead, casting a variegated light over his features, rendering him alternately Pakistani then Moorish . . . Persian then Arabic. He might have been any of these extractions, or none of them.

Riley glanced uneasily in the direction of Rawahli, then glared angrily at Ames. For all his usual cockiness, it was clear to Angus, as Riley prepared to drive on the eighteenth, that the Irishman was shaken. Despite his avowed skepticism of the powers of Ames' man, the mere presence of this curious fellow had changed the karma of the moment. The unthinkable crept into Riley's head. From the dark recesses of his mind, where latent and, at times, unwelcome ideas are granted a voice, came whispering; *a birdie will close out Ames for medalist.* Riley fought to regain his focus. He backed away. He hadn't consciously summoned this distraction. So, why had it come? He'd been sailing along on his own quiet sea of serenity, that inner sanctum which, for a golfer to be at his best, is utterly void of thought. How had this unwanted notion gained access to his senses? A spell? His subconscious run amok?

Mental detours on the golf course were for undisciplined players, those who are easily distracted, not for Riley O'Neill. Until now, never would he have fallen prey to such a diversion. But this was the subliminal at work, insidiously crowding out matters at hand, insisting that he imagine the conclusion of the round, and the Brit's inevitable dismay at losing to a *mere* Irishman. It was irrepressible and, given root, a force against which conscious intellect would be no match. Now without compass or sextant or starlit night, Riley sailed on in seas less calm.

O'Neill assaulted the ball maniacally, somehow catching it on the leather insert of the J. Braddell, sending a lightning bolt down the left side. Solidly struck, but slightly wayward, it landed atop a swale bisecting the fairway at about 240 metres and careened off misshapen knob toward a thicket of gorse. From the tee, the players could see the ball would be difficult to find and impossible to play. Like the curtain of fog that lifts without warning, Rawahli vanished.

Ever the opportunist, Ames took careful note of Riley's dilemma and played safely, choosing his spoon for control on a hole which, downwind, would play shorter than usual. A sensible shot, it rode the tailwind to the center of the fairway some 150 metres from the green.

Still reeling from his afternoon of uninspired play, Angus was now consumed by an overwhelming urge to take full advantage of the favorable breeze. Alas, the tension which often attends a harder-than-normal swing, found its way into his tee shot, causing him to come over the top of the ball. Flaring weakly, high and to the right, it was devoured by the ravenous mouth of a bunker, revetted as if to repel a division of German panzers.

Riley ended the day disastrously. Taking an unplayable lie from the gorse, he dropped into a whorl of marram, then barely managed to gouge the ball from the whins to the edge of the fairway. After pitching to forty feet, his effort to save double bogey became a harrowing adventure that culminated in the unlikely holing of a slippery ten footer. Riley's nightmarish ending to an otherwise exemplary round revealed a putting stroke so grotesque, that anyone with the courage to watch would have wept. Given the circumstances, it had been a miraculous six. The round of 70, coupled with an opening 75, put Riley in at 145.

Angus limped home, blasting his sand shot backwards out of the bunker, then blading a mashie to the front of the green some sixty feet from the cup. With his mind immersed in a fog as thick as the haar that rolls in off the Firth in winter, he batted the ball thrice. It couldn't really be considered a three-putt inasmuch as the act of putting implies elements of thoughtfulness and technique clearly absent from this abysmal finish. The 78, added to his morning score of 72, gave Angus 150 for the day. He had already begun the painful replaying of his afternoon collapse, which was sure to place him perilously close to the projected cut line.

Ames enrolled his playing companions in yet another tutorial on course management. As if he had authored a textbook on the subject, he carefully lofted a niblick to the center of the green and meticulously two-putted for par. A final round 70, together with 74 in the morning, put him in at 144. Ames had secured medalist honors and top seeding for match play.

"Well, O'Neill, you gave way to the game's whimsy like a good Irishman," Ames crowed, shaking hands, not out of grace, but because obliged to do so by the traditions of the game.

"Aye, and you willed your way to victory," Riley replied bitterly. He somehow managed to resist the urge to crush the Brit's dishrag hand in his powerful grip.

"And you, MacKenzie," clucked Ames, "collapsed like the Irish economy during the potato famine."

"Nothing to be proud of, but not as shameful as the Brits turning their backs on the suffering of the Irish during the famine," countered Angus, choosing to ignore Ames' outstretched hand rather than endure another limp handshake.

"An Irish sympathizer! Listen MacKenzie, the famine spared the poor bastards who died a lifetime of hell. I'd say we did them a favor. The dead avoided the misery of squalor."

Angus could see wrath rising in Riley's face like foam on Guinness. Stepping quickly between the two, he escorted Riley from the green where they were greeted at the scorer's table by Lord Atwater. With his usual fastidiousness, this fine old fellow inspected the card to ensure it had been properly attested by all. The mere presence of the noble Atwater seemed to cast a sheet of calm over what otherwise might have deteriorated into a scene much like the one Angus had mediated the previous night.

With dozens of Muirfield members looking on, the inevitable oohs and aahs of praise and disappointment arose from the spectators as scores began to be posted on the wall of the caddie shed. Angus felt queasy. The double bogey at the last may have been his undoing. Though he was anxious to see how the rest of the field had fared, Riley convinced him a good, stiff drink would be the best tonic.

"Two Lagavulins, guv'ner," Riley ordered from the bar steward, hoping a peaty Islay single malt might provide Angus with the roaring crescendo to his day that his golf had not.

"Thanks, Riley. Uisge beatha."

"Uisge beatha," said Riley, repeating the Gaelic toast that celebrated whiskey as the *'water of life'*. He inhaled the humid scent of salt and peat and smoke.

"Ames was right, I folded like pleats in a kilt."

"Yer too hard on yourself, lad. You stopped bein' Angus out there, and tried to be me, or Ames. That ain't your game, lad. You've got to play your game and shut out what others are doin'."

"I'm hard put to be me, when you and Ames are hitting every shot pure, and I'm scraping it around."

"'Tis numbers, not postcards, laddie. The sooner you figure that out, the sooner you'll win."

"But you and Ames have a certain style."

"Aye, style and tuppence 'll buy you tea and scones. Be yourself, and you can win. Try to be me, or Ames, and yer sure t' lose. Take your choice. Now, let's go see if the others bungled it as badly as you."

*   *   *

They studied the scoreboard carefully. The possibilities were clear. With six scores already posted lower than Angus' 150, only two players remained on the course with a chance to catch him. Robert Somersby, who had fashioned an unexpected 73 in the morning, seemed certain to make the cut. As Angus and Riley joined the other contestants surrounding the green to witness the suspenseful finish, the Cambridge man crouched over a short putt for 76 and calmly tapped in to qualify. Now, only Lawrence Dirleton could prevent Angus from joining the elite field.

In the final threesome of the day, Dirleton paced the fairway. He puffed nervously on what remained of his cigarette. He changed clubs. He tossed a pinch of fescue skyward to gauge the wind. Again, he changed clubs. Needing par to match a morning round of 75 and force a playoff with Angus, Direlton seemed determined to wring from the moment all the drama that he could. When he got around to playing his approach to the green, it was indifferent at best, checking up some forty feet away. Ironically, the same indecipherable undulations which had conspired to produce Angus' three-putt, now lay directly between Dirleton and the cup. The swales that Angus had cursed only an hour earlier were now his best friends. A Dirleton reprise of his own stumble was not out of the question. Of course Angus wasn't wishing his opponent any bad luck . . . he was merely rooting for the swales.

Dirleton examined the putt from every possible angle in an effort to calculate the incalculable. He stood frozen over the putt for a such a ridiculously long time that murmurs of derision began to rumble through the gallery. When at long last he swatted the ball, it was done with what seemed to be far too much force. Scuttling over the humps, it was dead on line and gathering speed as it hit the back of the cup. Catapulting high into the air, the ball hovered mid-flight, and with it, Angus' aspirations for further play. Spinning to earth, it momentarily came to rest on the lip of the cup, together with his dreams. Then, as the ball toppled those few fateful inches into the hole, his heart sank with it. Angus had been ousted.

Chapter 7

"There's no justice to the game of golf, Angus," Riley patronized, as they sat in the men's grille nursing a repeat of the pungent single malt, and recounting the many opportunities Angus had failed to seize.

"Golf is all *too* just," Angus rejoined. "You said Muirfield would expose a golfer's warts. Well, she found all of mine this afternoon."

"Aye," said Riley, nodding. "And you'll be all the better for it next time."

"I suppose," said a disconsolate Angus, "but I wanted a shot at Ames tomorrow."

"You'll get your turn," Riley comforted. "Yer a damn fine player, y' are."

"If I could just drive the ball, maybe I could compete with you and Ames."

"If it's better drivin' y' want, watch the best players. They always deliver the club to the ball the same way every time," replied Riley. "You don't."

"What do you mean!?" Angus demanded. "I've got a pretty decent swing."

"Looks better'n most," said Riley. "But looks ain't impartant. No, lad, y' release the hands early. Sign of a golfer tryin' to control the outcome. The driver's a powerful tool, she is, and requires a strappin' swing. I'll take ugly over pretty, if it gets the club square to the ball every time."

"When I swing hard, I lose accuracy."

"Yer not prepared to swing hard, lad. You've got rigor mortis of the wrists and that wee tilt of yours is a poor excuse for a turn."

"So what should I be doing to improve?"

"Imagine yer cloutin' the ball into the Firth, instead of squeezin' it into a bushel basket. Tryin' to be too fine is a recipe for tension, and tension is the devil's workshop for a golfer. It puts a tether on power. And when the heat is on, it causes the swing to get sharter and sharter until there's nothin' left but wishful thinkin'."

"You're right, Riley," Angus replied, as the day's distress began to recede against the therapeutic qualities of the scotch. "I spent most of today hopin' I could get in with a good score, instead of playing aggressively, one shot at a time."

"For me, there's nothin' quite like standing over a drive and knowin' exactly where she's goin'," said Riley. "But you must get the same feelin' when you putt. Yer short game's as good as any I've seen. Ev'ry putt looks like it's goin' in."

"Chipping and putting are the only way I can compete. I give up too much distance off the tee to play with the best."

"I don't see any place on the scorecard to measure how far you drive it. Seems to me the game asks only how many times you strike the ball . . . not how hard . . . or from where."

"I just think the driver sets up low scoring."

"Aye, but if you can't close the deal with the putter, par could care less. You don't give your short game enough credit, lad. I'd give anything to putt like you."

"Quit worrying about the prospect of missing, and you'll make more putts," offered Angus.

"And, if you drive your ball without givin' a bloody shite where it goes, you'll get more distance!"

They laughed, having just given each other identical bits of advice on different aspects of the game, and in so doing, they revealed another of golf's subtleties. Unyielding as par can be as a standard of excellence, the avenues to reach it are as many and varied as the players giving chase. And, while the great ones complain of the shortcomings in their game and long for the abilities of others, par is forever indifferent, offering both comfort and distress . . . uniquely friend and foe.

"As you said yesterday, Angus, we should see the glass half full instead of half empty," said Riley.

"Easier said than done, Riley." He wanted to ask Riley what had come over him on the eighteenth tee. Had Rawahli called up a curse? Angus decided now was not the time to broach the subject. If he wanted to avoid another flare-up, it was best not to ruffle the Irishman. "How do you see the rest of the tournament playing out?"

"Oh, I'm not much good at divinin' the future."

"But you know all the players strengths and weaknesses."

"Best to let fate have her way," he replied. "Then again, I guess a peek at the brackets would do no mortal harm."

Angus rushed into the men's locker room to retrieve the pairings sheet for the quarterfinals. Freshly typed copies were being distributed to a group of Muirfield members by Captain Morrisette's dour assistant, Mr. Scofield, who was now scowling Presbyterian disapproval as these wealthy patricians noisily placed their bets. It was a scene one might experience anywhere sport is played and men are passionate about the outcome. Seldom is it enough to simply root for one's favourite player, especially for those who have the extra bob or two to wager. Bragging rights are fine for some, but for these men to be considered sporting blokes by their peers, they had to back their talk with cash. It was time to put up or shut up.

1921 BRITISH ISLES CUP QUARTERFINALISTS

C. C. Ames
    vs.   ———————
L. A. Dirleton

        ———————

J.T. Wilson
    vs.   ———————
M. W. Callahan

                CHAMPION

R. P. O'Neill
    vs.   ———————
R. D. Somersby

        ———————

J. W. Ferguson
    vs.   ———————
Wm. D. Sayers

The overwhelming favorite in the early action was Ames, even money to win the three matches necessary to secure the trophy. The young phenom, Jamie Ferguson, was a surprisingly strong backup choice on the basis of his solid third place finish in the medal play rounds. And the Irishmen, O'Neill and Callahan, were being given no chance whatsoever.

Riley and Angus studied the brackets intently and carried on a running commentary about the talents of the finalists. Absent any direct knowledge of a player's ability, they shared what they had read, or what had been rumored. It was a formidable field by any measure, and Angus longed to see his name on the sheet. Why hadn't he played safely on the eighteenth . . . like the disagreeable, but oh so disciplined, Collier Ames?

"I won't be lookin' past anyone," Riley mumbled, shaking his head in deference to the competition.

"I see Ames, Callahan, you, and Sayers advancing. And you and Ames in the final."

"Ferguson will take Sayers," opined Riley, referring to the oldest and youngest players in the field. "Ferguson's fearless, and won't be put off by Sayers," Riley said, alluding to the fifty year old's reputation for gamesmanship. "Besides, over 36 holes always take the young legs."

"And the other matches?"

"You're on the mark, but I won't be lookin' past Ferguson. And Ames better not be lookin' past Callahan. So what'll you be doin' tomorrow, Angus? Now that you've botched your chances."

"Watching the tournament like the rest of the duffers, I suppose. And writing my article to set up the finals."

"What article?"

"I told you during our practice round that I work for *The Scotsman*. Have you forgotten?"

"I didn't realize you were a reporter," Riley said coolly. It was obvious he was trying to weigh the import of Angus' position at the newspaper. "I thought maybe you were a typesetter, or the copy boy. Now I see why you befriended me, to get material for your blasted British rag."

"I did no such thing. We met purely by chance, and I wasn't looking for a scoop." He had edited his response to suit him.

"I'll be int'rested to see what you write. We Irish usually get the short end of the story in Great Britain."

"Well, I promise to be fair. And for what it's worth, I want to wish you luck tomorrow," Angus replied, finishing his scotch and extending his hand.

"According to Ames, luck's got nothin' to do with it," said Riley, icily. "Will and control are all that matter."

"Don't believe everything Ames says. We all need our fair share of luck to win."

"I'll tell you what luck is, Angus MacKenzie. Luck is an Irishman bein' allowed to compete at all!"

"No need to jump down my throat! I was just bein' a friend. Too bad you think all Brits and Scots are against you."

"It's just that ev'ry time I think of Ames, I'm reminded of the past four hundred foockin' years of British tyranny!"

"There you go rattling sabres again. I've got no axe to grind in the fight between England and Ireland. Besides, you can't keep bashin' every Brit and every Scottish Prod you meet, just for their nationality and their religion. There's a limit to that *'ourselves alone'* attitude. You'll need some help if you're to get your republic in peace."

"Who said anything about peace? Maybe you should help Ireland grind her axe. Keep that in mind when you write your blasted article."

"Maybe I will," said Angus rolling his eyes in exasperation. "But keep this in mind, Riley O'Neill, luck resides at the corner of preparation and persistence."

"Well, if it's practice that's needed, then I've got about as much chance of beatin' Ames as the Irish have of negotiating a fair treaty with the Brits. You know how he prepares."

"And you know that your game doesn't improve with practice. You're already prepared. You don't need the perfect technique. You're after that perfect feel. Just go out and play your game, and quit trying to be like Ames . . . unless, of course, you plan to practice in the dark!"

Riley finally gave in to Angus' joking and replied with a chortle, "Maybe this wee leprechaun can throw a shillelagh into the will of Ames and bust up his control."

"That's the spirrit, lad. Go out and crrrush the bastarrd!"

*   *   *

The Saturday edition of *The Scotsman* lay folded on the front step of Greywalls. Rising before any staff had stirred, Angus took the newspaper into the library and placed it on the table by the sofa, anxious to see what had happened to the article he had submitted. He poured hot water into a china teapot and dunked a sieve spoon of Earl Grey. Squeezing a wedge of lemon into the tea, he sat sipping for several minutes in the softness of a wing chair, eyeing the paper. When he finally summoned the courage to open it, he was shocked to find his story the front page lead.

ENGLAND vs. IRELAND FOR THE CUP

by Angus MacKenzie

Golf is a mirror. How one behaves on the golf course is a reflection of character. At this year's British Isles Cup, contested on Muirfield Golf Links, the stage has been set for one of the game's great dramas. Collier Ames of Cambridge, England, and Riley O'Neill of Lahinch, Ireland, have reached the finals of the tournament by demonstrating, over 72 arduous holes, that, as golfers, they are incomparable, and as rivals, incorrigible. So diverse are their backgrounds, that the match we witness may be as much about ideology as it is about sport.

What does the mirror reveal about these two adversaries? Ames captured medalist honors by posting 144 over the 36 hole qualifier. And, just as Muirfield will expose a golfer's frailties by constantly examining his ability to control the golf ball under difficult conditions, so too, did Collier Ames administer such an inquest of his opponents' will. Playing flawlessly, Ames revealed no weaknesses, and granted opponents no glimmer of hope, crushing

Dirleton 6 and 5 in the quarters, and besting Callahan in the semis, 4 and 3. The Englishman is doggedly resolute. Nothing can pry loose the jaws of this pit bull once his teeth are sunken into the pant leg of an opponent.

O'Neill, runner-up in the medal qualifier at 145, was, by contrast, less clinical on his path to the finals, yet every bit as impressive. With emotions prominently displayed on his sleeve, and a style that is quite unconventional, there is no denying his skill. Outwardly, O'Neill exhibits a disposition that rises and falls like the barometer in April. Accepting the caprice of golf, but never succumbing to it, both of O'Neill's matches see-sawed, with a 3 and 2 ousting of Somersby, and a 1 up thriller over Ferguson. The Irishman seems to court the excitement of a close contest, showing flashes of brilliance, but opening his spigot of talent only at those times it has become absolutely necessary.

Saturday's 36 hole final will begin a 8:00 a.m., and may portend the battles fought of late between England and Ireland over Home Rule. A calculating Ames versus an impassioned O'Neill has all the markings of a David Lloyd George versus Michael Collins debate, or, if one is so inclined, a reprise of the ancient wars between the two countries. Unlike those battles of yore, however, tomorrow's siege begins and ends on even footing. These lonely combatants, armed only with the weapons of golf and their own resourcefulness, will determine the outcome within the well-defined constraints of the game. No cunning . . . no deception . . . no reinforcements . . . just golf, to determine who holds the balance of power.

Angus was stunned. Not only had Sir Thomas run his original piece unedited, he had run it under Angus' by-line. At first, he was elated, then uneasy, as he began to reflect upon the impact this might have on his standing in the intimate circle of amateur golf. But, as he placed the paper onto the table, Angus caught the headline of another article just beneath the fold.

Written by Arthur Simpson, a highly-regarded veteran newsman assigned to the political scene in the British Isles, the article announced . . . *IRA THREATENS MEMBERS OF PARLIAMENT*. Angus skimmed the column.

England's Prime Minister, David Lloyd George, had appointed a panel from the House of Lords to arbitrate the Irish demands for a Free State. One member, Lord Barrington Ashley of the East Lothian district of Scotland had been particularly outspoken in his support of partitioning Ireland into North and South. The Protestant Unionists in Ulster, Ashley contended, would be cannon fodder for the Catholic Nationalists in the South if not protected by the Crown.

These remarks, made at a public appearance in Belfast, had received a sharp riposte from Sinn Fein and the Irish Republican Army in the person of Michael Collins. The article quoted Collins in Dublin as calling for the head of Lord Ashley, and all the other British aristocrats who knew nothing of what was best for Ireland. Simpson's piece stopped short of predicting an outbreak of violence by the IRA, but only just short.

Given Lord Ashley's stature in British government, Riley's reluctance to lodge at Greywalls now seemed quite understandable. Angus strode briskly toward the practice ground to locate the Irishman.

*   *   *

"'aven't seen the wee man this marnin'," said the starter, Jack Byrne, closing his right nostril with his thumb and blowing snot to the turf from the left. "'spect he's o'er at Gill'n practicin' the new puttin' stroke I showed 'im. Prob'ly be here just in time t' tee off. He's not much on consortin' with the Brrits y' know."

"Oh, I know, Mr. Byrne . . . all too well," said Angus, stepping with care as he retreated. "Thanks."

Angus hurried back to the men's grille and found Collier handicapping the match for a crowd of fellow Englishmen who were sipping tea and devouring a plate of croissants slathered with black currant jam.

"Looks like a black day for the Irish," crowed Ames, predicting O'Neill would fall. "It will be a modern day Reformation . . . the second coming of Cromwell," he said, referring loudly to Oliver Cromwell, Lord Protector of the English, whose notorious slaughter of Irish Catholics in the 1640's was well-documented.

"Quite an article this morning, MacKenzie," Ames cackled. "Bit of an Irish bias, don't you think?

"No," replied Angus, "just the facts."

"And just what sort of deception is perpetrated by the journalist who competes in the event he's covering? God only knows what story you might invent if you were in the finals. And what, pray tell, qualifies you to comment on the politics of England or Ireland?"

"I report only what I observe to be the truth."

"Any trouble, Angus?" Riley asked as he entered the grill.

"No, I'm holding my own. Thanks."

"You gave a good account of the tarnament. You've even got me int'rested in how it all turns out."

"Then you're not put off by my article?" asked Angus, as he and Riley edged toward the bay window, putting some much-needed distance between themselves and the Brits.

"And why should I be? You seem to have your facts straight. I am wonderin', though, how you can keep up the playin' and the writin'. Seems something's got to give. Wouldn't be fair to the lads for you to do both . . . 'specially if you're going to start commentin' on politics."

"I'm sure you're right. It was foolish of me to think I could do both."

"If you've got to choose between your golf and your writin', I'd give the writin' a go. Yuv got a way of gettin' at the truth, Angus. You seem int'rested in saying what's right."

"Thanks Riley, but I thought Arthur Simpson's column this morning gave the Irish equal time."

"Equal time me arse! Simpson just told th' world what a violent man Michael Collins is. If something happens to Lord Ashley, you can be sure Collins and the IRA will be blamed."

"Why should anything happen to Lord Ashley?"

"Oh, I don't know, shite happens," he replied, then quickly changed the subject back to Angus. "Consider this, lad, the world's full up with amateur golfers, but it'll never have enough fair-minded jarnalists."

*   *   *

Saturday dawned under a mantle of fog so dense a search light was needed to find the fairway. Conditions hadn't improved by the time the starter called Ames and O'Neill to the first tee. Angus sized up the gallery and sensed a decidedly pro-British crowd. Only mild regard was being shown for the Irish dark horse. Angus squinted through the gauze and noticed a familiar figure standing to the right side of the tee. As he maneuvered through the gallery toward the shadowy hulk, Angus suddenly realized that Sir Thomas Forgan had joined the proceedings.

"Good morning, Mr. Forgan," Angus offered timidly.

"Oh, good morning, MacKenzie," the publisher replied with that air of indifference to which underlings are often subjected by men of supposed consequence. "Should be a crackerjack."

"Aye, and what brings you out, sir?"

"The match, of course. And I'm to preside over the closing ceremony, as well. You know, furnish a few choice words of wisdom . . . and announce the selections to the Walker Cup team."

"You mean those who qualify as a result of their performance here?"

"All of the men who've qualified from their fine play here, and, of course, we already know who else has made the team."

"Based on other competitions?"

"That, and general comportment . . . and, of course, social standing. By the way, MacKenzie, fine article in today's edition. Bang-up first effort."

"Thank you, sir. But I expected to see someone else's name under the banner, and anticipated some changes to the text."

"Yes, well, I considered the whole business and decided you're a better writer than you are a golfer. By publishing the article with your by-line, I can force a decision. The golfing fraternity won't look kindly on your competing against them, and then writing about them. Clumsy arrangement at best. I guess the choice is yours; competitive golf, or serious journalism."

Angus was as offended by this snub to his golfing ability as he was flattered by the praise of his writing. It had occurred to him that, despite a commendable showing, he might be over-matched at this level of competition. Reluctantly, he had begun to think more seriously about journalism, which meant playing golf purely for recreation. In due course, Angus might have come to this very conclusion, but would preferred to have done so on his own. He resented Forgan's ultimatum, and he glowered.

"I guess there is only one choice . . ."

"Well done, lad. You won't regret it."

Angus wasn't so sure. "What about the text of my article?" he asked, wondering if he had misconstrued Forgan's telegram.

"On the whole, quite unbalanced . . . slanted in its suggestion of British imperialism, and more than a bit sympathetic to the Irish. These thoughts, however supported, belong on the editorial page."

"But you ran it on the front page!"

"Ah yes, a prominent display that will serve to deflect any criticism I might receive for not selecting any Irish for the Walker Cup."

Angus felt weak. "No Irish? But what about Riley O'Neill?"

"Fine golfer . . . rebel activist . . . social misfit. Not at all the sort we want to represent Great Britain. And, there's a nasty bit of evidence that casts doubt on his amateur status."

"What do you mean?!"

"It seems he received that J. Braddell driver of his as a gratuity."

Forgan lit a Cuban.

"And that disqualifies him as an amateur?" Angus was growing more shrill.

"Lesser offenses have caused forfeiture of one's amateur standing." Sir Thomas was lecturing now and exhaling smoke into Angus' face.

"With all due respect, sir, it seems to me the committee is going out of its way to see our team is free of any Irish!" Angus was indignant now and coughing through a veil of smoke.

"The Irish know the rules. Let them comply like the rest."

"Would you feel similarly if Collier Ames was found to be outside these pristine standards?!"

The air suddenly was filled with Forgan's silent rage. Recoiling, the publisher sputtered, "What are you insinuating!?"

"Er . . . nothing," replied Angus, beating a hasty retreat from his accusation. "I would just hope the rules are being applied evenhandedly."

"The committee is beyond reproach!" Sir Thomas blared, glancing sideways at several members of the gallery who had overheard his outburst. "If you persist in this behavior, MacKenzie", he seethed, emitting a low hiss between clenched teeth, "I'll be forced to reconsider your employment."

Angus now realized he had violated Hamish's cardinal rule by allowing his principles to outrun his common sense. He quickly reviewed the facts. Riley *had* revealed a rebellious side. Even though Angus harbored suspicions from his chat with Jamie Ferguson that Sir Someone might be Sir Thomas, and though he believed it more than mere coincidence that Colby was Ames' middle name, and the name of Forgan's estate, he really knew nothing of either man's behaviour. So, any suggestions to the effect that Ames or anyone else may have violated the rules of amateurism were not only baseless, they were irresponsible.

"My apologies, sir. I was just reacting to what strikes me as unfair treatment of the Irish."

"Steer clear of matters that are none of your concern, MacKenzie, and we will get along famously," Forgan snorted, satisfied he had cowed his young associate into submission. "Rest assured, I know what's fair for the Irish."

*   *   *

The match was as epic as the history of Ireland itself. Neither Ames or O'Neill complained of the conditions, but those in the gallery wondered aloud whether a match played in fog this thick might as well be played at midnight. The first two holes were completed in par, and entirely without the benefit of vision. Skies like these demanded clairvoyant sharpness and expert feel. Only players this gifted, in one with themselves and their swings, could have found fairways and greens knowing the slightest detour would result in a lost ball.

The sun burned through, and O'Neill began a display that had the gallery mumbling in disbelief. Riley unveiled his entire repertoire. Launching drives of unimaginable distances and fashioning iron shots of every conceivable shape, he was in complete command of his game. Low, hard hooks . . . high, soft fades . . . crisp knockdowns . . . sharply spinning pitches . . . command seemed woefully inadequate to describe O'Neill's play. Nonpareil came closer. The Irishman may not have invented the game but, on this occasion, took it to heights previously unseen.

Ames was not the equal of O'Neill in any category except, of course, putting. In watching his play over the past few days, Angus had observed Riley's obvious discomfort on Muirfield's slick contours. It was as though he believed real golf involved only shot-making. To him, putting was an obligatory inconvenience. If only Angus could have putted for Riley, they might have closed out Ames, 10 and 9. It was not to be.

O'Neill's erratic play on the greens kept Ames in the contest, allowing him to extend it to extra holes. And just as Angus had presaged in his article, Collier clung stubbornly to the Irishman's pantleg all afternoon, holing putt after lengthy putt to save par, while Riley convulsed over tiddler after clinching tiddler. Early in the match, Ames had conceded O'Neill's superior play from tee to green, at least for today. But rather than fall victim to the brilliance of Riley's skillful exhibition, he kept his eye on the one thing that mattered . . . scoring. If only he could scrape together enough good shots to stay close, then maybe, just maybe, he could pull off the unexpected . . . that one shot which, when played at the just right moment, renders meaningless an opponent's more aesthetic performance.

Angus could sense the outcome . . . too many chances cast aside by Riley like petals of a daisy. As putt after putt failed to fall, the wee man became more resigned to a fate dictated by fallen petals. Muirfield loves me . . . she loves me not . . .

In fairness, O'Neill's dilemma was due as much to the endless number of putts Ames seemed to will into the hole as to his own inept short strokes. The Brit was engaged in amazing feats of prestidigitation. As if by sleight of hand, he was able to control the path of the ball. Ames had been clutching so tightly to those coattails for such a long time, a lesser competitor might have forgotten the match and tended to his bloodied fingertips, or ministered to his bruised ego. Not Ames. He simply would not give up. Angus was beginning to think there may, indeed, be something to this mantra of will and control.

By the time the players reached the par three fourth, their 40th hole of the day, Angus was busily condensing his notes of the match. When he looked up, he caught sight of a black turban above the gallery. The winds of change descended over the battle. The demeanor of the players was transformed. Collier, on the defensive all day, now laced his mashie on a tight, hooking trajectory to combat a pernicious left-to-right cross-wind and, when the ball settled only inches from the pin, the actual putting of it became a mere formality. The Pakistani again had appeared at a crucial moment in the match, the fates had been altered, and he had vanished. Riley had been one-upped by Ames.

"Well Ames, you beat me fair and square."

"Pity about those tedious little putts, O"Neill."

"Aye, me wretched putter let me down, she did."

"Details, details. Just like an Irishman to ignore the bothersome fine print. Ask poor Michael Collins about the fine print he overlooked in his treaty negotiations. Your careless-ness on the greens gave me a victory . . . but his oversight in the office of David Lloyd George will split Ireland in two."

The Englishman's incessant carping had stretched O'Neill's fibers of self-restraint to their limits. Collier's words conjured in Riley's mind an ancient and bloody carnage . . . thousands of Irish heads severed from their owners, skewered onto Cromwellian pikestaffs, and paraded about the countryside as a deterrent to the rebellious Catholics of Ireland. Ames had intended, of course, to invoke anguish of a different sort, the British proposal of December 1920, which would result in the partition of Ireland into north and south . . . less violent perhaps, but to an Irishman, every bit as painful. The popular view was that David Lloyd George had hoodwinked the Irish negotiators into accepting a nation divided, and many Irish had laid the blame at the feet of Michael Collins. Riley did not. He blamed British deceit, and the duplicitous leadership of one Eamon de Valera.

The way Riley saw it was that, even though Collins had been involved as one the principal negotiators, de Valera, then President of Ireland, had hedged his bets by staying in Dublin during the negotiations. If Collins and the others had brought home a republic, he could have claimed credit. If they brought home anything less, he would be able to denounce their actions. He did the latter. Despite criticism from every corner, Collins remained an heroic figure to most Gaels, especially Riley, who had served under his command in the Irish Republican Army.

Riley tried his best to remain composed in the face of the Brit's onslaught. But, like cat gut that snaps when strung too tightly on the racquet, the cords of his temperament could no longer contain his rage. Not about to let this English blowhard besmirch Ireland or its heroes, Riley clenched his fists into sledgehammers, snapped, and came unraveled.

Standing in the center of the 4th green, the impetuous little Irishman became airborne to compensate for his eight inch height disadvantage and landed a sweeping right hook to Ames' jaw, crumpling him to his knees like a heron whose spindly legs had failed. He was poised to lay Ames out with a left cross, when Sir Thomas Forgan raced onto the green and intercepted Riley's punch mid-flight. By the time Angus reached his side, Riley was being unceremoniously ushered from the grounds.

"Sorry for the disturbance, Angus, but I'd had a gutful of the Brit. I had to shut his gob."

"Couldn't have done it better myself! But I'm afraid this sort of behavior will require three or four *Our Fathers* and at least half a dozen *Hail Marys*." Angus joked, trying to ease the strain of the moment.

"As if y' Prods know anything about penance!" Riley snorted, hurriedly unknotting his Lahinch tie while the authorities bustled him toward the gate.

"Listen Angus, I want you to have me cravat," he said, as the local constable steered him toward the front gate. "You've proven to be a real friend. You always give as good as you get . . . in golf, and in friendship."

"I'm honored, Riley," Angus replied.

"If we never meet again, you'll have this to remember me. The goats are the mascots of Lahinch. They're always on the course, and give great comfort to the golfers by predictin' the rain."

"It's the perfect memento, Riley," Angus said, proudly cradling the tie in one hand and patting the Irishman on the shoulder with the other. "But I won't be needing any reminders of who you are. You're as ornery as an old goat and every bit as predictable as the rain in Ireland!"

Chapter 8

*A*ngus retrieved his golf clubs from the caddie shed, and was packing them to his room at Greywalls when he spotted Mick Callahan standing outside the rear door of the clubhouse enjoying a cigar. Leaning his clubs against the stone wall that divided the two properties, he ambled over for a word with the big Ulsterman.

"Thought I'd better make sure you don't burn the place down before tonight's closing ceremonies, Mick," Angus said, laughing loudly.

"Ssshhh," Mick admonished, holding a forefinger to pursed lips and brandishing his cigar toward the second floor above him. "Forgan's finagling up there," he whispered.

Through the open window, Mick and Angus could see the animated shadows of several men. Their voices rose, then receded, as emotions ebbed and flowed in the room. The unmistakable foghorn baritone of Sir Thomas Forgan dominated the discussion.

"Now see here, Atwater," boomed Forgan, "I won't stand for any Irish on the Walker Cup team."

"I agree that we have sufficient grounds to exclude O'Neill from the squad, Thomas," replied Lord Atwater, "but I find absolutely no cause to do the same in Michael Callahan's case. After all, he was a semifinalist here, and gave Collier Ames a spirited match. He is clearly one of our best players."

"I have it from a most credible source that Callahan is not loyal to the Crown," snarled Forgan. "Oh, he's of Scottish descent, and was reared in a right reverent Presbyterian family, but his sympathies lie with the Irish nationalist rebels. We can't have his kind taking center stage at the Walker Cup. It just wouldn't do, to give the Yanks the impression we can't control our own subjects."

"But we can't summarily ban all Irish from the Walker Cup," Lord Dumbarton interjected. "The young men who have earned the right to play, should be selected. To exclude them for political reasons, or for social bias, runs contrary to the canons of fair play on which the Royal & Ancient is founded."

"Until the Irish accept their place in the world, they will continue to receive their comeuppance," Forgan blared. "The only compromise I will tolerate is the naming of Callahan as an alternate. If questions are raised, I have ample evidence that his behavior is at odds with the standards of a more civilized society. Furthermore, Dumbarton, must I remind you of that unfortunate dalliance in the Cotswolds?"

Lord Dumbarton went stone silent. All eyes in the room were cast in his direction. This was not the sort of behavior one would expect from a gentleman, but then, Thomas Forgan was no gentleman. To him, money and position might well ensure desired results, but the leverage of a personal indiscretion was more reliable. He used *The Scotsman's* resources to compile dossiers on each his colleagues for use at just the right time . . . which was whenever he wanted his way. One of Forgan's investigators had gotten wind of Dumbarton's occasional trysts in the country with Lady Ashley, and the escapade, complete with photographs, had been added to the poor chap's folder. The entire committee knew they, too, were subjects of Forgan's profiles, and that any indelicacies would be similarly recorded for his use. Never had so voluble a group been so thoroughly quieted. Men whose skill in the art of parliamentary debate was so keen no opponent was safe from the bite of their arguments, now looked as if they'd had their incisors removed . . . sans anesthesia.

Angus leaned against a trash bin, accidentally knocking off its lid. The sound of metal against stone echoed like cymbals in the stillness of the night. Heavy footsteps reverberated across the hardwood floor above them, and the leonine head of Sir Thomas Forgan appeared in the open window, sending Mick and Angus scrambling through the doorway into the safety of the locker room.

"I'm not sure why we should bother to attend the closing ceremonies," Mick growled in disgust. "It's clear to me Forgan plans to make the Walker Cup the private domain of the English."

"It *is* disappointing to see politics and prejudice spill over into an idea so grand as the Walker Cup," said Angus. "The object is to bring people of differing persuasions closer together, not distance them further. I am curious though, to see just how Forgan handles the awards ceremony."

"Angus, the hypocrisy of this man knows no bounds," snarled Mick.

*   *   *

Muirfield's ballroom was crowded with tuxedoed gentlemen mingling in the haze that billowed from cigars and pipes and cigarettes. Liquor flowed freely and conversations were rife with off-color humor, lending an aura of bacchanalia to the occasion. Captain Morrisette served as master of ceremonies. After thanking the staff and the volunteers, he introduced the esteemed members of the Royal & Ancient Golf Club and The Honourable Company of Edinburgh Golfers who had deigned to attend an event with such a wide assortment of station and breeding. After he had droned through a far-too-flattering account of Forgan's role in the world of golf, Morrisette yielded to the publisher, whose pretentiousness enshrouded the dais like the cloud of smoke suffocating the room.

"Gentlemen," Sir Thomas began. "It is indeed a privilege and a pleasure to stand before you this evening as the Chairman of the Walker Cup Selection Committee. As you are aware, the Walker Cup has been established as a competition between the foremost amateur golfers from the United Kingdom and the United States of America. It will be contested year to commemorate the good will and friendship and mutual aid between our countries, and every other year as an emblem of the peace that was won at such a dear cost in the Great War."

"Honor . . . integrity . . . trust. These are the hallmarks of true friendship, and the tenets upon which the game of golf is founded. Golf celebrates the amateur who displays these qualities, one who is drawn to the game for the sheer pleasure of playing, rather than for financial reward. So too, do we, the Royal & Ancient Golf Club of St. Andrews, as stewards of the game, celebrate the amateur, and the merit of social grace. For it is a shameful civilization that stifles the advance of culture and dignity and refinement."

"Therefore, with due consideration of these principles, and the skill of these lads on the links, it is the privilege of the Royal & Ancient to name twelve individuals and two alternates to the 1922 Walker Cup team. Please step forward as your name is called so that each of you may receive your engraved invitation."

"The first recipient is, of course, our team's stalwart, Mr. Collier Ames. Mr. Ames is the very embodiment of the high standards on which our grand game was founded. There is simply no one who measures up to the skill with which he plays, or the grace he exhibits. For those of you who may not yet be clear as to what sort of person the R & A is seeking to represent Great Britain in the Walker Cup, look no further than Mr. Ames, for surely, he embodies everything amateur golf is meant to be."

Collier Ames climbed to the dais and stood next to Sir Thomas, his purplish-green jaw swollen shut. No boastful smile . . . no smug acceptance speech . . . no condescending remarks toward the Irish. Riley's fists had momentarily silenced his arrogance.

"In addition to Mr. Ames, the following gentlemen have earned positions on next year's Walker Cup team. Mr. Dirleton; Mr. Wilson; Mr. Somersby; Mr. Ferguson; and Mr. Sayers."

All non-Irish quarterfinalists. Angus smirked at the choice of Sayers. The crusty Scot from Carnoustie probably thought a social grace was something to be recited before supper.

"The final six positions belong to players who were the top finishers in this year's major amateur events. Gentlemen, please come forward as I call your name: Mr. Massey; Mr. Glaston; Mr. Whitney; Mr. Avondale; Mr. MacPherson; and Mr. Chastain."

All English, thought Angus. All members of the Oxford & Cambridge Golfing Society. It would seem society was the underlying theme to the selection process.

"Finally, the alternates," Sir Thomas continued. "Mr. Callahan and Mr. MacKenzie."

"And that, gentlemen, concludes the ceremony. Thank you for your for attention and your fine play. Congratulations, and good night."

*　　　　*　　　　*

The crowd dispersed amid boisterous conversations, with many of the contestants drifting into the bar for final farewells and late-night libations. Angus sidled up to Mick, hunched over the end of the bar, nursing a double shot of Jameson's.

"Well done, Mick," said Angus, placing his hand on Callahan's shoulder, "and well-deserved."

"I won't accept their invitation to be a damned alternate!" Mick shot back. "They're just paying lip service to the pretext of fair play. Don't you see, Angus, the whole slate is English. Forgan is waging his own personal war against the Irish!"

"It *is* sad to see the British conjuring up yet another forum in which to strut their social superiority . . . sort of like peacocks in a menagerie of us barnyard animals," said Angus, as he removed the envelope containing his embossed Walker Cup alternate's invitation from inside his tuxedo jacket.

While Mick continued to rail against the politics of Sir Thomas Forgan, Angus slowly raised and lowered the envelope in the palm of his hand as if to weigh its contents. Heavier than expected, he slid his thumb under the sealed flap and removed the invitation along with five, crisp ten pound notes.

"What's that?!" exclaimed Mick staring at the small stack of bills Angus now placed on the bar in front of them.

"I have no idea," replied an astonished Angus. "My salary at *The Scotsman* is fifty quid per month, but I expected to be paid by cheque or bank draft, not in pound notes."

At the far end of the bar, Collier Ames, Lawrence Dirleton, and Robert Somersby were all gleefully unsealing their envelopes and stuffing money into their wallets. Mick quickly opened his envelope to find it contained only his invitation.

"I guess I'm not on the payroll!"

"Trust me, Mick, I am not being paid to play golf."

"What other explanation can there be for the fact only you and your British cohorts received a nice little stipend in your envelopes?"

"I'm not quite sure, but I intend to find out. Listen, Mick, it's been a long week, I think I'll call it a night."

"Not me. I plan to soak up as much formaldehyde as they'll serve," Mick replied, hoisting his empty glass toward the bar steward, a gentle reminder he was in need of a refill.

*   *   *

On Monday, Angus arrived earlier than usual at the offices of *The Scotsman* hoping to talk with Hamish. The round man was nowhere in sight. But with copy for the front page already laid out, and Hamish's apron folded over the back of his chair, it was obvious he must be nearby. While he waited for the editor to return to his morning work, Angus read the news. The headline proclaimed; *LORD ASHLEY LOST AT SEA!*

Arthur Simpson reported the ferry from Belfast to Stranraer had capsized in the Irish Sea while crossing late the previous night. Seven passengers had been lost, all of them British citizens, among them, Lord Barrington Ashley. As Riley had predicted, the IRA, under the direction of Michael Collins, headed the list of suspects. But there had been no explosion, and fourteen other passengers and crew members had made their way to the safety of a lifeboat. Nonetheless, based on the remarks of Lord Ashley in Belfast the previous day, and Collins' response in Dublin, the official position of *The Scotsman* was to blame the matter on the IRA. It was a troubling coincidence, to be sure. But Angus remembered strong winds had been forecast for the west coast of Scotland on Sunday. He wondered if Simpson had bothered to research whether a storm might have swamped the ferry.

"Well, Angus, you've had quite a week!" Hamish chirped, as he entered the room and donned his apron.

"Aye," Angus replied, "the tournament was grand . . . except for the outcome, and the Walker Cup selections."

"Yes, I suppose the best man didn't win. But were you truly surprised by who was named to the team?"

"Not in the least, now that I'm beginning to understand the politics of it all. As the Brits would say, the selection process was not exactly *cricket.*"

"How so?"

"Mick Callahan and I overheard Mr. Forgan blackballing any Irish from the team. And there's a closeness between Forgan and Collier Ames that seems most irregular."

"How would their *closeness* taint the selection process?"

"Well, for starters, it gives the appearance of collusion to exclude qualified players from the Walker Cup team."

"Hold on there, laddie. Conspiracy is a serious charge to level at the publisher of this newspaper. You'd better get your facts straight before you march off in that dangerous direction."

"Hamish, you know a great deal about Sir Thomas. And you know damn well I'm onto something. Surely, there must be something more you can share. Come on man, out with it."

Hamish now wished he didn't know so much about Sir Thomas Forgan. It was one thing to have been a confidant on certain personal matters of Forgan's choosing, but quite another to have access to all of the most intimate details of the man's life. Nearly ten years had passed since he had entered Forgan's office during one of the publisher's many excursions to London on matters of Parliament. MacClanahan had mistaken a leatherbound volume of private memoirs for the journal of editorial ideas Forgan had asked him to review while he was away. It was an honest-enough oversight at first, but Hamish soon realized that, fascinating as it had been to learn of Forgan's peccadilloes, he should immediately have stopped reading. By the time he had finished, Hamish was privy to m of Sir Thomas Forgan's darkest secrets.

"You must promise to use caution, Angus," said Hamish.

"You can trust me."

"I think you're far too rash to be discrete, but I can see Forgan has begun to use his power unfairly. Something must be done. And, since you're determined to see this crusade through to the end, you may as well know what I know."

Before commencing, Hamish moved the completed tray of type to the next table and replaced it with a blank tray. In a moment of reflection, he asked almost rhetorically: "Where to begin? Well, as a young man, Thomas Collier Forgan set off for Cambridge to receive a proper education and the lessons of social refinement."

"Hold on, Hamish. The *'C'* in TCF stands for Collier?!"

"Indeed it does, and a *'collier'* is a coal miner, which is what the Forgans were originally, before the English transplanted them and thousands of other Scots to Ulster and gave them Irish land. But if we keep digressing, you'll miss the real story," he said, continuing to set type.

"Sorry, Hamish, I was struck by the coincidence of the name Collier. Please, go on."

"Patience, lad. I'm coming to that. When Forgan graduated, he returned to the family estate in County Down. While training to assume the duties of governing his demense, he became enamored with one of the estate's Irish servants."

"Was she Catholic or Protestant?"

"Good heavens, does it matter?"

"Well, I find it fascinating how, in their own land, the Gaels seem to end up serving the Galls."

"This *Catholic* servant was a lovely lass whose family, the Monahans, had owned much of the land comprising the Baronetcy of Colby before it was confiscated by the English and given to the Forgans."

He paused momentarily and deleted a few words from the copy before continuing. "Thomas Forgan had employed his considerable charms in an effort to capture the heart of Sinead Monahan. A handsome man and wealthy, it never occurred to him a lowly Irish lass might want something more . . . true love, for instance."

Hamish paused again to wipe his hands, looking into the eager eyes of his young reporter. He remembered that gaze, that obsession for the truth. All reporters worth their salt had it. Ten years ago, Hamish had it. Forgan's journal had drawn him in, but titillating as it was, Hamish knew it had been scrubbed of the gory details. As a reporter, new to *The Scotsman*, Hamish had felt the same wave of uneasiness about Forgan's character that Angus described today. Deep in debt and sole provider for a young family of six, Hamish couldn't afford to lose his job. If Sir Thomas Forgan was not to be trusted, then no position was safe. He quickly reasoned that job security depended on information. And so, as any capable reporter would, Hamish merely followed the journal's lead to its source . . . Newcastle, County Down.

"Sinead was as revolted by Thomas Forgan as he was smitten by her," Hamish continued. "She snubbed his advances at every turn. And, in turn, he became frustrated, then morose, and finally, enraged. After all, how could this lowly wench refuse his charms? In his view, the Forgans had saved the Monahans from a life of poverty. In time, her vulnerability gave way to his power and brought about, let's just call it a shameful union."

"Shameful union?! Which is shorthand for what, Hamish? Forced marriage? Rape? What, exactly?!"

"Marriage? No. Rape? Well . . . most assuredly the fruits of power that have been harvested for centuries by those who have no remorse over placing the disadvantaged under their dominion," Hamish said, wiping his hands on the blackened apron.

"If Forgan had his way with Sinead Monahan against her will, it's rape! Soft-peddling it as acceptable because it's been practiced for ages doesn't make it any less criminal."

Angus had a point. Maybe Hamish had grown too accepting of Forgan. After all, the publisher hadn't been convicted of a crime. It was easier for Hamish to remain in the employment of Forgan if he could somehow pigeonhole this incident into the context of what, for centuries, had been a way of life. As excuses go, this one was weak by any standard, but Hamish needed his job. To go around thinking of Forgan as a felon, simply wouldn't do. In order to work beside Thomas Forgan, he had to rationalize the man's wrongdoings. On the other hand, he had leverage, the kind of leverage Forgan often used against others. Knowing the truth about Forgan meant power. His job was secure. It was time to share the evidence.

Hamish walked over to his cubby of an office, pushed aside stacks of copy, and knelt next to a small, metal filing cabinet. He pulled a tiny key from his vest pocket and unlocked the top drawer. Retrieving an official-looking document, it was folded in thirds, wrapped in heavy green stock, and bound tightly in the center with a leather strap. Hamish untied the strap and unfolded the document, placing it onto the table in front of Angus. The caption read: ***Inquiry into the Assault of Thomas Collier Forgan.*** It was dated June 22, 1894, and carried the official seal of the Constabulary of Newcastle, County Down.

"Where did you get this?" asked Angus.

"Reporters always find a way to the truth, right Angus?"

"And when it comes to Forgan, just what is the truth?"

"Read for yourself."

"Given the Forgan influence in County Down, I'd have thought any damning records would have been sealed."

"Oh, they were sealed. But I'm always amazed by what can be made public for a price. Such valuable information, so very cheap."

"Bribery seems out of character for you, Hamish."

"Just a nudge, lad. The pump must be primed."

Angus read page one. It began with the questioning of Dr. Malachay Chase by Constable Hugo Halifax. Angus soon learned that Dr. Chase had been summoned to Colby on the morning of June 22, 1894 to tend to an injured Thomas Forgan. With Ulster on the cusp of the marching season, Chase alerted the authorities, worried that the IRA may have been active in Colby. The doctor found young Forgan's face an open wound, a deep gash cleaving his cheek from eye to mouth. Chards of glass glistened in a stream of blood dripping from his chin. Sixty-two stitches later, the wound had been sutured.

Angus skipped through the remainder of the doctor's account until he reached the exchange between Thomas Forgan and Halifax. Forgan's version of the prior evening's events centered on the ungrateful Sinead

Monahan. He blathered on about how he had lavished his generosity and affection on the woman, only to be rewarded for his kindness by the crack of a wine bottle across the cheek. The filthy trollop, he now called her, had caught him off guard in the cellar and laid him low with a bottle of port.

A cunning lass, and dangerous, she was . . . like all the Irish, Halifax added gratuitously. It was the constable who now fed Forgan his lines. Never turn your back on the Irish, he sniped, or it's a knife they'll stick in it. On and on he went about the black-hearted Gaels and, beneath the words, Angus could feel the hatred. This was no even-handed inquest seeking the truth. Halifax was building a case of assault against Sinead.

It was not until Forgan and Halifax had filled the record with all the character flaws of the Irish that Sinead Laurel Monahan was allowed to speak. But, even against the contempt that wove its way through the Halifax line of questioning, Sinead's version rang true. Through all the bullying and the scoffing and the leering, she held fast. She may well have wept as she told the story, thought Angus, but he could detect not the slightest quiver in the written word.

Sinead told of a self-absorbed Forgan, lusting after her like a ram in the rut. When his charm failed, he resorted to his power. She had seen the change come over Forgan. He had begun to taunt and demean her in the presence of family and friends. And, more worrisome to Sinead was his way of trying to isolate her from the safety of others.

Angus was ill-prepared for her detailed account of the horrors she had endured. On the eve of June 21st, the Forgans were hosting their annual Summer Solstice gala for much of the Irish ascendancy. Colby Manor was astir with pomp and circumstance, the landed gentry making merry in an orgy of food and drink and song. Sinead devoted a good bit of her statement to the degradation she and her family suffered in service of this so-called aristocracy. Her tone was resentful to such a degree that Halifax had pressed for detail, seeking a motive for her assault. Her sole assignment that night was to keep the wine glasses full. Prior to her many trips to the wine cellar, Sinead would mark the location of Forgan, fearful he might follow. Several visits to the cellar had gone without incident until just past midnight, when the revelry was at its peak.

At that late hour, Sinead explained, she was rushed. The wine was flowing freely, and guests were impatient. She hadn't noticed Forgan was no longer seated in his usual wing chair facing the fireplace. The booming voice she thought was Forgan's turned out to be that of Ian Forrester, a blow-hard in his own right. As she entered the stone cavern, fifteen feet below the kitchen, the heavy iron door closed and latched behind her.

Hamish locked onto Angus' stare. His eyes were wide with alarm. Sinead's voice was still quite controlled, and her words unequivocal. She painted a picture of a beast stalking its prey.

"Such a strappin' man, he was . . . not to be denied. I screamed, but the words stuck in my throat. He bound me with his arms. I couldn't breathe. I struggled, but had no strength. He laid me face-first over a wine cask and tore off me bloomers, and . . . from behind . . . he . . ."

Her words trailed off, the reporter recorded a slight pause while Sinead took a few moments to compose herself before continuing.

"His full weight was on me, and wheezin' like the divil, he was, a vicious animal with no cares but his own. In front of me was a rack of empty wine bottles. With him bent on finishin', I grabbed a bottle by the neck and swung it backward over my shoulder as hard as I could into his face. Reelin' from the blow, he slipped out of me, blood spurtin' from his head. With his pants around his ankles, he was in no condition to give chase, was he now? So I heaved open the door and ran up the stairs."

Angus was nauseous. This graphic description of the most despicable behaviour imaginable, was more than he had bargained for. He had seen enough of Forgan's character to know he was capable of practically anything. But rape? Unimaginable.

"See here, lass," Halifax interceded, *"smearin' Mr. Forgan is a dangerous tack. 'Tis an honourable family whose good name you slander."*

"And what of my good name, sir?"

"You'll find your name drug through the pigsty, if you tell that story in court with not a shred of evidence," spat Halifax.

"I'll have evidence aplenty in nine months, sir. The honourable Mr. Forgan's seed is sproutin' in me belly."

"You don't know that, you Irish whore!" Forgan protested.

"And that, sir, is but one of your many failings. You have no idea what a woman knows. A babe it'll be . . . in nine months . . . mark my words."

*   *   *

"Nothing in the transcript about charges being filed," sighed Angus.

"No charges were filed. Halifax had three choices. Believe Forgan, and arrest Sinead Monahan for assault. Believe Sinead, and arrest Forgan for rape. Or, do nothing."

"But a crime had been committed!" Angus protested.

"And which crime is that, lad?"

"Rape. Of course."

"Surely you're not that naïve, Angus. A Protestant like Forgan was not going to be charged with the rape of an Irish Catholic. Not in Ulster. Not with the Forgan family wealth."

"Cozy it up anyway you like. It's still rape."

"I won't quibble with you about how to characterize the act, but labeling it one way or another won't change the outcome."

"What outcome?"

"Nine months later, Sinead did, indeed, give birth." Hamish removed his apron and turned to face Angus. "All her choices were equally unpleasant. Sinead found Forgan contemptible, and would never have considered marriage, even as a means to legitimize her offspring. The atonement she would have had to endure from the Church, however, for birthing a bastard child, was unbearable."

"But she could have left the Church."

"And be condemned to purgatory and eternal damnation? No, she couldn't leave the Church. And, abortion was no choice. Not only was it unsafe, the Church had assigned even greater guilt to abortion than to bearing a child out of wedlock."

"So Sinead brought the child to birth."

"That she did, lad. But even more difficult was her decision to give the child up for adoption. Forgan took the boy to London, where he located the Ames, Sinclair and Millicent, a middle-class couple, eager to adopt a son. Sir Thomas never returned to Colby Manor," he said, wiping his hands on the apron before folding it.

"Ames?! Collier . . . Colby . . . Ames!"

"Right again, lad. Sir Thomas imposed a few conditions before parting with the boy. He was to be named Collier Colby. And the stipend Forgan offered them was to be used for the lad's formal education at the finest schools."

"Curious fellow, Thomas Forgan. Even in discarding his own flesh and blood he had to impose his will, and be in control. But how did Sinead Monahan deal with all of this."

"Some stories do end well, Angus. Sinead had Padraig O'Neill to take her mind off Forgan. I learned from a relative that Sinead married O'Neill, and left Colby for County Clare and the village of Lahinch."

"O'Neill of Lahinch! Good God, man . . . you don't mean . . ."

Hamish could see the wheels churning as Angus began to add up the facts.

"Riley must be their son!" His calculations were correct as far as they had taken him. Just one final equation. "But, then . . . Collier Ames and Riley O'Neill . . . are . . ."

"Half brothers," Hamish said, impatiently completing the unfinished algorithm.

"Remarkable. Just bloody remarkable."

"I trust the behaviour of Forgan and Ames now makes sense."

"Sense? Hardly. But I'm beginning to understand the context. Whatever animosity Sir Thomas feels toward Sinead is obviously being played out against Riley."

"So it would seem. In any event, it's clear that Forgan's hostility toward Riley is more than a random act of an Ulster Protestant directed at an Irish Catholic. It also seems to me Collier is being manipulated to achieve Forgan's ends."

"And just what are Forgan's ends?"

"He couldn't possess Sinead as he possesses all things in life, so he aims to visit as much pain and suffering on her and the O'Neills as possible . . . the misguided acts of a man with vast power and no redeeming cause."

"Do either Riley or Collier know they share a mother?"

"I assume only Sinead and Sir Thomas know."

"I wouldn't assume anything. We know, don't we."

"Yes, but we're sworn to secrecy . . . aren't we? Angus? Aren't we?" he growled, looking down his nose.

"Oh . . yes, of course. Listen, Hamish, it's rumored Forgan is maneuvering to have Riley banned from golf as punishment for the incident at Muirfield."

"But Riley was provoked by Collier."

"Provoked or not, being barred for life from competitive golf seems damned oppressive."

"Ah, but the British are well-studied in the art of oppression, aren't they?"

"But the Irish are becoming less willing victims."

"Please be cautious in how you use the information I've shared with you, Angus. Sir Thomas is a most cunning fellow. He could care less who he harms."

"Or whose allegiance he tries to buy!"

"Whatever do you mean?"

"This is what I mean!" Angus replied angrily, removing the five, ten pound notes from his wallet and placing them on the table between them. "I think Sir Thomas Forgan is paying several amateurs to play golf. These were in my Walker Cup envelope, and I don't intend to be one of his toadies!"

"If you think those notes came from Mr. Forgan, you're mistaken, Angus. I thought you might be short of funds, so I arranged for an advance against your monthly salary. I asked Sir Thomas to deliver it to you in Gullane. Apparently, he just placed the money into your Walker Cup envelope. It'll be reconciled to your payroll account at the end of the month. No, if anyone is being paid to play golf, Forgan is doing it out of his own pocket, not from the coffers of *The Scotsman*."

"So you do suspect him! Even without a criminal record, one thing is obvious . . . our Mr. Forgan is not the paragon of virtue he publicly professes to be."

"I know a good many things about Forgan's behavior, and I've shared too much of what I know, Angus. You need to reflect on all you've seen, and decide for yourself what to do."

"You mean decide whether to work for a man I don't respect? Cheat . . . blackmailer . . . rapist . . . I'll need no more than the blink of an eye to do that."

There, he'd said it. Angus had been coming to grips with the truth from the moment of their first meeting. Oh, Sir Thomas Forgan was a captivating character to be sure, one of those men who panders his charm so effectively, the unsuspecting risk becoming infatuated. Angus had been no exception. But in the end, his choice was clear. The skepticism inherited from his father had served him well. Alexander MacKenzie would have dismissed Forgan as *just no damn good*. Old Duncan McDevitt would have insisted he quit the man who doesn't play the ball as it lies. Any temptation Angus may have felt to fall into league with Sir Thomas Forgan was about to be rinsed harmlessly away by the most valuable of human traits . . . good judgment.

"Aye, lad. I have too much of my life invested in this place to stand on principle. But you're young and able and deserve an employer who inspires rather than corrupts."

"You're right, Hamish. I'll never be able to work with Forgan knowing what I now know. I'll have my written resignation on your desk within the hour."

"I think you're making a wise choice, Angus. Selfishly, I'd like you to stay, because you're going to be a fine reporter. But you need a fresh start. I know the publisher over at the Sentinel, Adair Campbell. He's a gentlemen and always in need of capable help. I'll arrange for you to meet him."

Angus was relieved but saddened by this exchange with Hamish. How did someone of such integrity find himself trapped in the duplicitous web of a man like Forgan? If only Hamish had been publisher of *The Scotsman*. To spend his career in the company of one as capable and caring as him was all Angus had ever wished.

"Thank you, Hamish . . . for everything."

"You're making the right choice, Angus," said Hamish.

"Let's plan to meet each month for lunch and ale. I'll call when I get settled."

"I'd like that. I want to keep up on your progress. Good luck, lad. And God speed."

As Angus reached the doorway, he turned and stared at Hamish. The editor had again donned his apron and was fiddling over sections of type with short, pudgy fingers.

"By the way, Hamish, you might want to check the weather conditions on the Irish Sea last night before you run the article on Lord Ashley's disappearance."

"Already did. Sixty knots out of the northeast. Just the sort of blow that'd take a ferry under. Forgan told me to run the piece as is . . . wants feelings raw against the Irish."

Angus shook his head and turned away, hand in the air . . . a farewell to Hamish . . . but not a goodbye.

Chapter 9

The train lurched into Waverly Station, and Angus was awakened by the clatter of its couplings. Though he had slept for only an hour, it seemed much longer. Through a gap in the curtains he could see lights on the station platform, an early warning that dusk had descended in Edinburgh. Angus swung his legs over the edge of the berth and paused to collect his thoughts. He rose and hobbled into the lavatory to wash for dinner. The reflection in the mirror revealed all seventy-five of his years. The hair, now chalky white, had thinned on top to a few wisps, sprouting into a generous canopy over his ears and around the back of his head. The moustache, more ivory than white, had been allowed to droop over his mouth like whiskers on a walrus. The face had become a comfortable expanse of folded flesh, covered with fawnlike splotches. Only the eyes retained the traces of youth. Though they could just as easily have been dimmed by the desolation of life's hardships, through it all, his eyes had remained clear and bright and full of hope.

He brushed the stains on his teeth and splashed his face with cool water, taking care not to dampen his shirt or the goats on his Lahinch tie. The remnants of his muse were still fresh in his mind as he sat on the edge of the berth tying his shoes. Reaching into his overnighter, he located a scrap of paper still bearing the cobwebbed creases of the crumpling Riley had given it fifty years earlier. The letter, postmarked July 10, 1921, St. Andrews, Scotland, bore the official emblem of the Royal & Ancient Golf Club. Angus carefully unfolded the fragile stationery so as to not damage it further and began to read.

Dear Mr. O'Neill:

It has come to our attention that on June 20ᵗʰ past, you committed a most ungentlemanly act while competing in the British Isles Cup at Muirfield Golf links. This despicable deed, which surely must be considered criminal assault, was directed toward Mr. Collier Ames of Cambridge, England, and occurred at an event conducted under the auspices of the Royal & Ancient Golf Club. It is, therefore, a matter subject to our review and dominion.

As you are well aware, one's standing in amateur golf may be suspended as a result of behaviour deemed detrimental to the game. Upon thorough deliberation of the circumstances surrounding this most contemptible act, it has been determined that your actions were so egregious as to warrant banishment from amateur golf for the remainder of your life.

We are, however, inclined toward leniency, and therefore, have elected to lessen your penalty to a term of ten years, which began June 1, 1921. Additionally, should you choose to submit written apologies to Mr. Collier Ames, and to the Royal & Ancient Golf Club, the term of your disbarment may be further reduced to five years.

Most regrettably,

Sir Thomas Forgan, M. P.
Chairman, Rules Committee

The penalty seemed as severe now as when originally meted out. Angus thought back to the talk he'd had with Riley in Edinburgh soon after the letter arrived.

"Riley, you can't stand for this! Collier's behavior was every bit as reprehensible as yours. We ought to petition the R & A for a hearing to present all the evidence of his unsportsmanlike conduct."

"It's kind of you to stand up for me, Angus, but a civil war is brewin' between the Irish people over the treaty. Seems I'll be needed to help sort it out."

"But you'll be out of amateur competition for at least five years."

"Aye," Riley sighed, "hopin' to make the Walker Cup team, I was, and play the best Yank, Bobby Jones. Guess he'll just have to wait for Ol' Parrrbooster."

"Riley, there's something else you need to know about Forgan and Ames," Angus had said, wishing to cleanse his conscience of the secret Hamish had shared with him.

"Me Mum already exposed the scoundrels to me."

"So you know they may be out to do more harm than banning you from amateur golf."

"Aye, and they'll be settin' foot in Eire at their own peril, now won't they, lad!"

Angus returned the letter to the safety of the suitcase and finished dressing for dinner. As he left his compartment, he found the aisle barricaded by a porter struggling to open the adjoining cabin. At the man's feet were two large suitcases and a battered brown leather golf bag containing several hickory shafted clubs, circa 1920. Embossed on the side of the golf bag were the initials *MDC*. Though nearly obscured by the constant chafing they had received, the bag and its initials were familiar to Angus. Lumbering down the corridor behind the porter was the outline of a huge man whose shoulders touched each wall as he swayed from side to side. Angus knew at once who it was.

"Mick," exclaimed Angus. "Mick Callahan."

"MacKenzie! Is that you?" boomed the broad Irishman.

"Aye, 'tis. And where would you be goin' with these antiques?" asked Angus in his best imitation of Riley's Irish lilt, grasping the strap of the leather golf bag and holding it up to Callahan's barrel chest.

"Why Riley's funeral, of course. As are you, judging from that Lahinch tie you're wearing."

"I'm glad to see someone from the early days attending the services. The notice came rather late."

"We may be surprised at who comes to Lahinch. Anyway, yes, I did bring my dear old sticks. Nothing reminds me of Riley like they do."

"Aye, mine are with me as well. I was just headed to the dining car for a refreshment and dinner. Would you care to join me? We'll be underway to Stranraer in a few minutes."

"Let me get settled and I'll be down shortly."

"We have much to discuss," said Angus.

"That we do, Angus" sighed Mick. "We've let the years get away."

PART II

▼

ST. ANDREWS

Chapter 1

*E*scorted to his table by a tuxedo-clad waiter, Angus marveled at the man's dexterity, as above his right shoulder, on the fingertips of a white-gloved hand, rested a sterling tray, a pitcher of water, and two freshly-poured martinis. MacKenzie realigned his silverware and stared blankly out the window, savoring the tart crispness of gin flavored with a hint of vermouth. The train rumbled out of Edinburgh bound for Stranraer, a bustling seaport village situated across the narrow waist of Scotland. Angus examined the schedule and checked his watch, comparing the time of arrival against a delayed departure, calculating whether the lost time could be made up. He sighed, knowing travel by train seldom made for restful sleep. It would, however, provide much-needed time for reflection. And now, he had someone with whom to reminisce.

Mick Callahan filled the entrance of the dining car and Angus motioned to him. Rising to shake hands, Angus noticed how kind the years had been to his big Scotch-Irish colleague. At seventy-eight, he seemed younger, his face having been spared the ravages of time and too much drink. The nose was a bit misshapen, florid as a rosebud, but its oddly out-of-place effect was softened by a neatly-trimmed, silver moustache, the perfect match to an impeccably-coiffed head of hair. Mick was athletically built, sort of in the shape of Scotland itself, with shoulders broad as a cricket bat, and a waist less than half that width. When he looked at Angus with delft blue eyes, the kindness shone through, as would light from a stained-glass window.

"Ordered you a martini," said Angus. "I seem to recall your fondness for gin."

"And what a delightful memory you have," Mick replied, pausing to admire the pristine clarity of the liquid. "It's one of my favourite preservatives. Well, Angus, we might have been paying our respects to Riley on any number of occasions during the past fifty years."

"You're quite right, Mick . . . here's to Riley," he said, lifting his glass to toast their friend.

"To Riley," Mick repeated from beneath his own raised glass.

"He was always prepared to die for his convictions. But tell me, Mick, how did you and the other Protestants feel during the years Riley and his IRA cohorts were targeting Ulster?"

Mick winced. It had been a bone of contention between him and Riley for as long as they had been friends. Though he was Protestant, Mick didn't share the anti-Catholic sentiments of the Order of Orange. He tried to play peacemaker and extract from Riley a promise not to partake in any IRA reprisals in Ulster. But this was a matter well beyond friendship. Riley could not agree.

"I've never subscribed to the notion that ancient grievances between people should be continually resurrected. It obstructs any chance for healing."

Using thumb and forefinger, Mick tweezed the toothpick and examined the olive. Tapping it against the rim of the glass, he slid the garnish between his teeth, taking care no gin was lost on its way to his mouth.

"Besides," he continued, "Riley knew the real enemy was not the Protestants in Northern Ireland, but the British Parliament. Oh, the transplanted Scottish Prods served as a lightning rod, of course, but the thunderbolt has always been the English."

"And the IRA, I suppose, is the eye of the storm."

"The whole matter leaves me queasy," Mick admitted. "I guess it takes someone like Riley to fight a battle for freedom that seems so unattainable. I still marvel at his spirit. Time and adversity have a way of wearing down lesser men."

"He once told me there were times when the Prods were prepared to join the Fenns to remove the Brits from Ireland."

"Rubbish! If you're referring to Wolfe Tone, that was generations ago. Those times are too far removed from the consciousness of both sides to matter today. Riley was like most other Irish Gaels. They have trouble letting go of the past."

"It's not just Fenns who won't let go of the past. Every July, the Prods don their orange sashes and beat their oversized drums and vilify the Pope to celebrate their conquering hero, William of Orange. No one can forget, much less forgive, so long as these rites continue."

Angus used his napkin to sop up the drops of gin that had escaped the confines of the martini glass during his state of agitation.

"I thought for a moment I was listening to Riley himself! You're every bit as excitable, Angus. But let's not forget, old boy, the Catholics do their part to escalate the bad blood."

"One can hardly blame the Catholics for canonizing their martyrs in the face of the Order of Orange. How long can they be expected to allow their noses to be rubbed in age-old defeats?"

"Listen to us," sighed Mick. "We sound just like Ulster, each blaming the other's bigotry, and not conceding our own. Mutual trust is the one element needed to unite Ireland. And it will never happen with leaders who cling to the memories of the old wrongs and glorify them in their speeches."

"After so many lost opportunities to build trust, the fabric of compromise seems frayed beyond repair."

"Sadly so," agreed Mick, "but Riley never lost his faith in the cause, right to the end."

"I wonder why a bona fide leader hasn't emerged?"

"Politicians lack your moral compass, Angus. Any chance for compromise between gets lost in their rhetoric."

"Leaders on both sides have fanned the flames of fear and resentment through the years, but reconciliation must begin somewhere. The violence must end someday."

"Ahh, violence. There's the rub. That brave vanguard of the Easter Rising . . . Pearse and Connolley, and the others, misjudged the opposition. They were too willing to use violence as a cornerstone of the cause. The one tactic England will not tolerate is violence. It offends their so-called sense of fair play. Ghandi's non-violent fasting won their admiration and freedom for India. You know . . . pip pip, old sport. Here's to the chap who takes the high road. The Brits admire that."

"Michael Collins might have succeeded. It's a shame he never got the chance to bring the Irish together."

"The entire history of Anglo-Irish relations is shameful, Angus, but these fellows were more victims of circumstance than of their own short-comings. All were capable men engaged in a fight that could not be won by will or genius."

"Surely Riley and the others didn't struggle in vain, Mick."

"It all depends upon your definition of futility, I suppose. If you adopt the pragmatist's view, then some progress has been made toward the ideal of a republic. But, if you see events as a revolutionary, then the revolution, to date, has failed, because a truly united republic does not yet exist."

Mick paused to remove a cigar from the leather pouch inside his jacket and planted it firmly into his cheek. He offered one to Angus who politely deferred.

"You should try one, Angus. Churchill had it right, you know, *smoking cigars is like falling in love; first you're attracted to its shape; you stay with it for its flavour; and you must never, never, let the flame go out.*"

"It's the mouthful of ashes in the morning that makes me wonder if they're worth the bother," replied Angus.

"Not unlike some love affairs, I suppose. Listen, Angus, you have all the markings of a pragmatist, yet seem dissatisfied with the progress of the Irish. Riley, the revolutionary, was pleased with how far the country had come."

"If you think Riley must have been at peace because he wasn't killed by a British bullet, or didn't spend his last days rotting in a British prison, you're wrong. I think he desperately wanted to see a free and united Irish republic in his lifetime. He just ran out of time, and in the end, resigned himself to the way things are . . . as old men do."

"Let's go dine and talk of better days," said Mick.

"Or, at least of days when we were young," Angus sighed, "and believed we could make a difference."

Chapter 2

*R*ocking from side to side in its rail bed, the train rolled through the Scottish lowlands toward Glasgow. In the comfortable silence that follows a satisfying meal, they gazed at the moonlit fields rushing past, their faces reflecting off the window pane. Mick cut the tip off his cigar, lolling it from cheek to cheek, with no intent of smoking. Angus sloshed the brandy in his snifter with little urge to sip. They were more acquaintances than friends, but that evening long ago in Muirfield, when Mick and Collier Ames locked horns over the virtues of the Irish, and Angus had served as mediator, carried with it a mutual respect which now reached the level of kinship. Both men were deeply appreciative of those few shared moments in their pasts and were eager to recall the best of times.

"Do you still practice law, Mick?" Angus asked, recalling their talk of careers in 1921.

"Not for years. I gave it up to pursue my real passion."

"Which is . . .?"

"Golf," he replied, continuing his simulated smoking.

"Just golf? No work?"

The thought was sacrilege to an enterprising Scotsman.

"Golf is my work and my escape."

A learned man but not one given to detail, Mick, for once, provided more than the bare facts. His training in the law dictated direct, concise answers. It must have been the inflection in his voice and the depth of his discussion that gave Angus pause. His account of years spent playing all the classic courses around the globe resonated in Angus just as it would in any golfer with a dream to test his game against the best layouts. As Mick made known his love for the grand traditions of the game, Angus could hear the purist speaking. The big man always had been a crack golfer, but Angus knew nothing of his interest in the art of course construction. Touring the great venues, and rubbing shoulders with the legendary designers of fairways and greens was what Mick had always wanted.

"What was it that caused you to toss in the law for golf?" asked Angus.

"At some point," Mick replied, "time spent doing what one truly enjoys is real wealth. For me, as for most, the sooner I got about doing just that, the better."

"But surely there was a turning point."

"The Old Course at St. Andrews. Whether it's the traditions you're after, or the golf, The Old Course is where you'll find it. There's a timelessness to St. Andrews that gets into your blood."

The rhapsodies of St. Andrews now commandeered the conversation. Even at his advanced age, Mick admitted to raising goose flesh whenever he played there. Each time, to him, seemed like the first time. Continuing the lecture, he described the allure of the *auld sod*.

"The Old Course just evolved . . . no architect . . . unless you count rabbits and sheep and God. Well, maybe a nip here and a tuck there from Old Tom Morris, keeper of the greens at the old girl for decades," he joked, professing amazement that a course this perfect just happened.

"Still, it's mother nature," he continued, "that's what the great ones, Ross, Mackenzie, and Tillinghast, understood better than others. Most designers can't resist playing God. They try to defend par with all manner of gimmicks. But, the great ones take only what the land provides, find within it one true route, and fashion a challenge for golfers of all abilities. To me, that's a gift few designers possess."

"To be honest, Mick, I've heard golfers criticize The Old Course for its random bunkering, and all those irregular swales. Shots seem to be rewarded or penalized unfairly . . . whimsically, some would say."

"Everyone is entitled to an opinion," Mick replied. "If the debate isn't raging, then the course must be boring. But those who complain about St. Andrews, haven't played there enough. Besides, much of golf *is* whimsy."

"Maybe The Old Course is outdated, Mick. I agree the marginal shot should be penalized, but maybe time has passed her by."

"Not as long as golf is played, my friend. Oh, I'm sure many think St. Andrews is unfair. But golf isn't meant to be fair. It's an examination of skill and emotion. One must play the Old Course time and again to appreciate its subtleties. Each hole provides options the designers of today only dream they could create."

Mick deposited his cigar in the ashtray and moved it into the center of the table to simulate an imaginary bunker. Then, he slid Angus' brandy snifter over to replicate a make-believe green, and began to explain the genius of The Old Course.

"The bunkering at St. Andrews *is* unconventional," he conceded. "They tend to come into play on the line a golfer wants to take . . . right down the center of the fairway."

Sounding very much like a golf course architect, he admonished, "Nowhere is it written that the direct line must be made available to the player."

He extended his arm to the right of the ashtray and began to reveal his next principle using, as case in point, the 4th hole, known as Ginger Beer, for the refreshments that once were served from a hut alongside the fairway.

"At four hundred metres, the accomplished player ought to take the aggressive line. But, with only a sliver of safety down the right side, most golfers, skilled or not, tend to bail out."

Mick arranged a napkin to the right of his arm to emulate the supposed constrictions of gorse. To add to his hypothetical player's dilemma, Mick used his silverware to create an imaginary out-of-bounds, should the dangerous path to the right of the ashtray be chosen. This aggressive line, he explained, leads to the most favourable angle into the green.

He then placed his arm to the left of the ashtray, to show how much more room was available to the safe side.

"The player who chooses safety faces a far more difficult approach. These are the options that make The Old Course great."

"Riley always said The Old Course required a careful plan before each shot is struck, just like a chess game. In fact, he would always walk the course in reverse, just to plot his attack."

"Not many courses were difficult for Riley, but I don't recall him ever planning anything, or knowing the first thing about chess for that matter. When he was playing his best, though, he could thread it through a knot-hole and stop it on your kitchen table, skills not found in any chess master."

"I think it must have been the prospect of the British Isles Cup being held at The Old Course in 1926 that caused him to write those letters of apology to Collier Ames and the R & A."

"Undoubtedly. I think he would have abandoned golf forever, rather than dignify the crap they threw at him. But, how he loved to play The Old Course, and how he wanted to make the Walker Cup team."

"But being away from the game for five years, I wondered whether he could compete."

"He always had such a simple, repetitive swing, just like the hinge of a door. I never doubted he'd be as good from tee to green. And, anything would have been an improvement on that pathetic putting of his."

"I still have the letter he wrote the Royal & Ancient."

Angus fumbled with the lapel of his blazer, reaching inside to retrieve the yellowed scrap of paper held together at the center fold by scotch tape, and passed it across the table. Mick placed half-lens bifocals onto the end of his bulbous nose while continuing to shift the unlit cigar between his cheeks. Gently unfolding the letter onto the linen tablecloth, he noted its date of March 17, 1926, St. Patrick's Day, and read aloud.

To the Esteemed Gentlemen of the Royal & Ancient Golf Club of St. Andrews:

Nearly five years ago, I was involved in an unfortunate incident during play in the British Isles Cup conducted at Muirfield Golf Links. At the conclusion of my match with Mr. Collier Ames, Esq., I struck him squarely on the face with my fist. As punishment, your distinguished organisation exercised its prerogative to suspend my amateur golfing privileges for a period of ten years.

*Through your good graces, however, I was offered reinstate-
ment after five years if letters of apology were sent to the afore-
mentioned Mr. Ames, and to your honourable membership.
The five year term is scheduled to expire on June 1 of this year.*

*Please allow me to express my most sincere regret for the
abominable behaviour I displayed at Muirfield. You may rest
assured that nothing so untoward shall ever recur if I am permitted to resume my pursuit of amateur golf. My most sincere
wish is that I be allowed to compete in the British Isles Cup at
The Old Course in St. Andrews on June 15-18 of this year.*

*Your favourable disposition of this plea for clemency is an act
of generosity for which I would be humbly and forever grateful.*

Most respectfully,

Riley P. O'Neill

"He showed the R & A much more contrition than I thought him
capable," said Mick with a knowing smile.

"Nothing less would do," replied Angus. "But the tone of the letter isn't
Riley's. It sounds too lawyerly. Did you write it for him, Mick?"

"Yes," Mick confessed. "But even as positively regretful as we made him
sound, he was nearly denied reinstatement. I think it was Lord
Dumbarton who cast the deciding vote in his favor, against the vigorous
opposition of Sir Thomas Forgan."

"It *was* Dumbarton who came to Riley's rescue. I later learned the
details of the committee's debate."

"From one of the participants?"

"No. From the scribe of the meeting."

"And who might that have been?"

"Sarah Delano Shiells . . . my wife."

Angus held his snifter by the stem, slowly turning it in the dim light of
the dining car, the bronze liquid glowing against the darkness of night.
Sensing Angus' discomfort with this chapter of his past, Mick sat patiently,

studying the reflections in the window, wondering what should be said. Angus was adrift once again. St. Andrews . . . how marvelous the place had been. He allowed himself yet another visit to the *auld grey toun.*

Chapter 3

*D*own Granny Clark's Wynd and beyond a white rail fence lay acres of sacred ground . . . the first and eighteenth fairways of The Old Course at St. Andrews. Riley and Angus stood behind the railing on that damp June afternoon in 1926, admiring the Valley of Sin that swooped cavernously beneath the face of the finishing hole. They took in the Swilcan Burn meandering across the broad fairways, and gazed in awe at the ancient Swilcan Bridge arching over it. As would anyone who loved the game, they were consumed by the splendor of it all. With the Royal & Ancient club-house rising majestically from behind the green, and hotels and shops to one side, the place possessed both an intimate and communal quality. Nowhere else is the casual observer granted a window into the soul of golf like the one on the railing around the right flank and to the rear of number eighteen at The Old Course.

"Great t' be back on the auld sod, Angus. I can't wait t' play again, even if my game's not up to scratch."

"You must've played *some* golf these past few years, Riley. Surely you're not too far off form."

"Didn't touch a club 'til last week."

"What!? Nobody loves the game more than you . . . except me . . . and, maybe Collier Ames."

"I hate t' think of all the practice Ames has put in these past five years," Riley said, grimacing.

"Well, all you need is that feel, Riley. I'll bet you give the boys a hell of a run for the trophy this week, practice or no practice. But five years without a club in your hands? Come on, it's Angus your talkin' to, not some cockney rube."

"I'd never put up an excuse for poor play, 'cuz each of us is keeper of our own game. But the years since '21 have been hell unvarnished for the Irish, Angus. Civil war saw to that."

Angus could see that Riley was serious. The furrows of his well-creased brow grew even deeper as he reflected on all that had happened since Muirfield. There had been no time for golf shots while rifle shots were being fired. He found it comforting to be here at St. Andrews with his Scottish friend, away from the troubles of Ireland. But he'd sooner forget the past few years than describe the ordeal. Then again, maybe talking about his experience was just what he needed. And, as always, he was curious to learn where Angus stood on the troubles of Ireland.

A slim majority of Irish had ratified the Treaty of 1921, Riley explained, and Ireland was split into North and South. As he had predicted, the de Valera-led minority couldn't stomach two Irelands or the oath of loyalty to the Crown. These hardliners turned to all the old blather like, *death before dishonor,* and *a republic for all of Ireland, or no republic at all.* They ridiculed Michael Collins, who argued this was merely the first step in a long process of attaining a free and united Ireland. So deep was the resentment and the blame, it took very little effort for the minority to prod Ireland into civil war . . . a war that, in Riley's opinion, could easily have been avoided had de Valera been less concerned with his own legacy and a bit more interested in the legacy of Ireland.

As they talked, half a dozen foursomes played through the eighteenth with nary a birdie to show for their efforts. Riley dissected their methods, pointing out the need to stay beneath the hole, but out of the Valley of Sin. He told Angus how he intended to attack this deceptive little gem, and saw no reason the eighteenth shouldn't be birdied with ease. In fact, with a good tailwind, he noted, the green would be well within range of the J. Braddell.

Riley offered his opinion on how the whole mess had begun to spiral out of control at the treaty negotiations. It was there, he believed, that the seeds of civil war had been sown. Acting out of some misguided sense of intrigue, de Valera had stayed in Dublin during the talks, sending Collins and Arthur Griffith and others to London like lambs to the slaughter.

Yes, what everyone said about Lloyd George bamboozling Arthur Griffith was true. The crafty Welshman had pursued his quarry like a lion stalking a warthog. He hadn't singled out Griffith for his lack of intelligence, rather, for his honesty. He knew Arthur could be cornered by appealing to his integrity. Riley conceded the Irish contingent may have been distracted by Lloyd George's background. But did they really think the Welshman's Celtic heritage might produce sympathy for a fellow Gael's plight? If they had been that naïve, they deserved to be fooled. Time would reveal the Welsh lion was concerned with the one thing that matters to all men of high position . . . the preservation of power.

In any event, Lloyd George's cunningly circular logic began with what seemed a trivial detail. During months of negotiations, Riley explained, many trial balloons of compromise had been floated. Naturally, the Protestants wanted Ulster to be split apart from the south of Ireland and to remain under British rule. They feared reprisal from a Catholic-controlled Irish Parliament. And, understandably, the pro-republican contingent from Dublin wanted the whole of Ireland to remain intact . . . no partition. So, the British decided on a ruse that has worked since the beginning of time. As only Riley could tell it, the Brits proposed to slip in just a bit of the partition and, if no one liked it, they promised to take it right out.

The ploy with Griffith proved simple, but elegant. Lloyd George started with the suggestion that they create a Boundary Commission, designed to ensure that any border would be fair. It was a concept buried in an avalanche of innocuous propositions, wrapped in a morass of harmless proposals. Apparently, thinking a Boundary Commission seemed innocent enough, Griffith agreed to the proposal. The jaws of the lion were about to snap shut.

Lloyd George informed Griffith you can't have a Boundary Commission without a boundary . . . and you can't have a boundary without a partition. So, by agreeing to a Boundary Commission, Griffith had *de facto*, agreed to partition. Standing alone, his logic was unassailable. Griffith politely protested he had been taken out of context, but was told a deal was a deal. Lloyd George promised war in three days if the treaty wasn't signed.

"The bastards!" Angus interrupted. "Political blackmail!"

"Aye" countered Riley, "just a continuation of the past four hundred foockin' years. When will we larn, you can't out-Brit the British. Again we tried, and again, we lost."

"But the rest of the Irish delegates were under no obligation to sign the treaty," Angus protested.

"No, and we'll never know if the Brits were bluffing war. But even Collins knew we couldn't fight on, and win."

Riley wasn't quite finished with his theory regarding de Valera. As aide-de-camp to Mick Collins, Riley had seen de Valera's draft of an alternate plan. Under its provisions, the government of the Irish Free State would have come from an election intended to include all people of Ireland, North and South. But, in return, Ireland would have recognized the King of England as head of State. So, this oath of loyalty to the Crown that the minority loathed enough to set off a civil war among their Irish brothers was, at least in draft form, acceptable to their leader, Eammon de Valera. The alternative proposal, which may well have been agreeable to the Brits, never saw the light of day. For the next year, Ireland devoured her own children.

"I witnessed plenty of tragedy during our war," said Riley, "but the worst of it was when Ireland tarned its back on Mick Collins."

"They shot him in the head for his troubles," said Angus.

"Aye, a sad day for Eire," sighed Riley, shaking his head. "On his way home to County Cork, he was. Should've been there when the cowards waylaid him. Might've been better to go out with Mick, than to muddle along with Dev."

"But, at one time, Collins was a hardliner just like the men who assassinated him."

"The thing about Mick was progress. He changed over time to believe in a more peaceful approach."

"You must have been a Collins man, because I still remember you saying you'd sooner kill Brits than your own Irish brothers."

"I trusted Mick. And, in the end, we had no choice but to try and enforce the treaty, even though it came down to killing family. We had to accept the treaty . . . warts and all."

"Seems it was no-win, either way."

"I've killed Brits in the name of the republic, and now I've killed Irish in the name of the republic," sighed Riley. "Take it from someone who knows, killin' won't bring us a republic."

"Thank God your civil war is finally over."

"Ah, but the war ain't over, Angus. 'Tis just a bit more civil. If Mick Collins could see that change must come from within, I'm damn sure the rest of the hardliners can too."

"But what about the northern Protestants? If they don't join in the cause by voting the Brits out of Ulster, the partition will be forever."

"Nothing's forever, Angus. The farst time we met, you told me we'd be needin' some Prods on our side. I've come full circle to your way of thinking. We won't get there by killin' everybody."

*   *   *

Angus and Riley leaned against the rail, watching, as several golfers faltered in their attempts to avoid the Valley of Sin, and smiled in sympathy, as still others floundered in their efforts to master the severely sloped eighteenth green perched above it. They imagined all the ghosts of golf's past who, with varying degrees of success, had confronted these same tasks. Though tempted to spend the rest of the day on the rail observing foursome after foursome negotiate the caprice of this finishing hole, the deadline for registration would soon close.

The two men made their way to the Royal & Ancient and, as they crossed the threshold of golf's venerable home, were struck full in the face by the traditions of the game oozing from its mortises. This historic shrine was steeped in the spirit of the game's founding fathers, with trophies and memorabilia of age-old competitions lining the walls. The men stood in the entryway for a moment, transfixed. Then, caps held reverently at their waists, and heads bowed as if in a chapel, they shuffled over to the receptionist's desk where a Scotsman with reddish-orange in his mutton-chops and the tartan of the Black Watch in his tie, pulled them up short.

"Wherrre may I dirrrect y' two dandies?"

"We're here for the tarnament!" chirped Riley.

"Are y' now? And a hunderrrd more just like y'."

"Y' mean the hunderd hopin' fer second place?" Riley said.

"Doorrr t' yer left," he sighed, shaking his head. "Sarah'll take yer nemes."

Angus slipped through the doorway ahead of Riley and felt the air rush from his chest as if he'd been struck in the solar plexus. But unlike that sickening sensation one feels when the blow is inflicted by a man's fist, this breathlessness was bliss, as if a faint gasp had been forced from him by the soft heel of a woman's palm.

This vision of elegance at the registration table just had to be Sarah. Her suit of fine linen was a style made popular by film starlets of the day, yet infinitely more flattering on her. Angus was quite certain beauty so rare could not have been concealed by even the most modest attire. He stared in silent wonder, consumed by her scent, wafting sweetly about, leaving him light-headed and weak-kneed. Riley, however, was not so subtle.

"Jaysus, Mary, and Jooseph. I've never seen a lass so lovely as you, Miss!"

Flushing, Sarah asked, "Are you gentlemen here to register?"

She sat Emily Post erect in a straight-backed chair, legs crossed gracefully at the ankles and tucked fetchingly to one side.

"Aye! We're here to win the tarnament. Where's the farst tee, and what's the cooorse record? Riley boomed.

"I'm Angus MacKenzie, from Edinburgh," Angus interjected.

"Sarah Shiells, London. Pleased to meet you."

She smiled at both men in a way that each felt it was meant for him alone.

"Riley O'Neill, Lahinch. And the pleasure's all ours."

"Mr. O'Neill, the first tee is straight out that window," she said pointing down the wide fairway, "and the course record is 69, held by Mr. John Ball."

"Ah, you know your gowf, lass. Do y' play the game?"

As Riley spoke, Sarah's slender fingers fussed nervously with a whalebone barette that held in place the soft, black tendrils of her hair. To the inattentive, this primping may have seemed a playful flirtation. The tell, however, was in her eyes. Sarah was drawn to the Irishman, and her eyes said the words. Angus saw it and suddenly felt cast in the role of an extra.

"I've never played golf Mr. O'Neill, but I'm willing to give it a try. By the way, I prefer *Sarah*."

"Aye, sure . . . Sarah 'twill be . . . ever more. And please, call me Riley. Mr. O'Neill is me pap."

"And you, Mr. MacKenzie," she asked, melting Angus with her smile, "are you here to win the championship?"

"It's Angus, please," he said, beaming at the attention, yet distracted by her presence.

Where were the words to describe Sarah? None seemed worthy. Words were his stock in trade, but the superlatives one might invoke to capture the essence of sunsets and landscapes simply would not do. Though blessed with time-honored beauty, Sarah's radiance shone more from the inside out. Had she not been so pleasing to the eye, would Angus have been attracted to her? To a young man accustomed to judging beauty by its outer version, it was hard to say. One thing was certain, however, he was caught in her aura, that innate capacity to make all men feel genuinely important. No, it wasn't just that she made him feel important, she conferred upon him a unique significance, a quality that could not be contrived. Either one had it, or one did not. With a grace transcending the physical, it was the unseen that commanded the moment. Sarah's beauty, alluring as it was, simply could not meet the measure of her soul.

"Yes, of course I'll be trying. But I have no illusions of winning against the likes of Riley."

"Sounds like you've already talked yourself out of contention, Mr. MacKenzie."

Angus saw her smile fade as he conceded center stage to O'Neill.

"I play golf for the love of the game, not to win tournaments."

"Then why register?"

"He'd sooner write than play," said Riley, slipping in his tuppence before Angus could answer. He knew when to upstage.

"You're a writer?"

"Journalist for the *Edinburgh Sentinel*."

"Do you know Sir Thomas Forgan?" Sarah asked, her right eyebrow arching ever so slightly.

"Why yes. I once worked for him at *The Scotsman*. But how do you know Mr. Forgan?"

"He's chairman of the rules committee and the Walker Cup selection committee for the Royal & Ancient Golf Club. I serve as stenographer for both."

"Did you take the notes when they discussed me reinstatement?" asked Riley.

"I recorded every word of the debate," she said, the crimson returning to her cheeks.

"I'd like to know what was said about me," Riley urged.

"I'm sworn to secrecy. But if you come to the ceilidh tonight at St. Andrews University, I might be able to provide you with a hint. Bright lads like you should be able to fill in the blanks."

"We'll be there, won't we Angus? . . . Angus?" waving a fleshy hand in front of Angus' glazed stare.

Blinking rapidly, Angus refocused on Mick across the table.

"I'm sorry Mick. I was revisiting the past."

"That was obvious. It's one thing to be captivated by The Old Course, but quite another to be smitten by a beautiful lass."

"Sarah was so . . ." Again, words had failed him. "She was . . . just . . . so . . ."

"Perfect?"

"Yes . . . quite."

"I've gathered as much. But what happened at St. Andrews, Angus?" asked Mick.

"Everything worthwhile," said Angus, "and, at the same time, awkward."

"Do you want to talk about it?"

"I've kept those days locked up forever. Maybe it would help to talk about them."

"If it's too painful, you needn't open old wounds."

A confirmed bachelor, one would never have suspected Mick of understanding the fairer sex. Yet he had always been able to trace the best and worst of times in people's lives to affairs of the heart.

"It's painful, but glorious, too. Maybe the telling will help me welcome the joy of those times, instead of wallowing in the gloom as I have all these years."

"I'd best get one of those," said Mick pointing to Angus' brandy snifter. "Sounds like we may be here awhile."

"And another for me," nodded Angus. "I'll be needing some fortification to tell the story. For so long it's been easier to think of the events at St. Andrews as a dream."

Chapter 4

Midnight passed, and the maitre d' asked if they might accept service in the lounge while the dining area was set up for breakfast. Mick and Angus moved down the narrow corridor to the smoking car and settled onto a sofa that appeared to have been salvaged from early in the Victorian era, its brocaded fabric severely scorched from decades of fallen ashes.

Never again would there be a time like Queen Victoria's, Angus thought, eyeing the sofa. When this grand old matriarch of the British Isles died in 1901, the Empire over whose rise she had reigned for some sixty-five years began to die with her. Bit by bit, this realm, on which once the sun never set, began to wane. But, as chinks in British armor were revealed in far off places like India and Africa, England tightened her grip on the Emerald Isle, fearful, Angus supposed, of losing one of the few remaining jewels in her crown. After all, Eire was merely a stone's throw away. Who did these Celtic bastards think they were? Defy the monarchy? Indeed! What rot! These Irish wolfhounds must be brought to heel, and made to obey at any cost. The canines mustn't be allowed to rule the kennel, and we, your masters, shall parcel out the pedigrees.

With snifters in hand, Mick lit his now well-soaked cigar, and Angus resumed his story.

"Have you ever been to a Scottish ceilidh, Mick?"

"Yes, but it must be more than fifty years ago now. I couldn't have been more than twenty at the time. The word 'ceilidh' doesn't look much like 'kaylee', does it? As with most Gaelic, our English phonetics aren't very helpful."

"I'm sure the young folks of today would find them silly, but we enjoyed the traditions of our highland ancestors."

"I suppose the youngsters don't dress up in kilts and such. But I'll wager the food and the drink and the music are just as plentiful."

"The music's a bit different. There's more noise than melody in today's tunes."

"Something lost and something gained. Usually more is lost in the name of progress than is gained. But you're right Angus, the old melodies seem sweeter and more innocent than those we hear now . . . just like the times."

"There used to be nothing more inspiring than a highland fling with a spirited lass."

"Sounds like there was plenty of inspiration at the ceilidh you and Riley and Sarah attended in St. Andrews."

"Inspiring for some . . . disappointing for others. It was apparent from the beginning that Sarah and Riley were taken with each other."

"But I thought it was you and Sarah who were married!"

"It wasn't quite so simple as that, Mick. My feelings for Sarah were dear from the moment we met, but her first love was Riley. We danced and ate and drank well into the wee hours at the ceilidh. Then, Riley and Sarah grew . . . well . . . restless. They disappeared and, from that moment on, were inseparable."

Angus had neglected to tell Mick the whole truth. He conveniently failed to mention he'd had his chance. Many soft airs and romantic ballads were mingled that night with the lively jigs and reels. Sarah had chosen a simple Scottish air to share with him. When she had taken his hand and squeezed it, why hadn't he squeezed hers back? When her cheek had brushed against his, why had he not pulled her close? That the melody would forever run through his head, brought Angus both pain and pleasure. That Sarah had offered her hand to Angus before Riley had reached for hers, would leave him forever perplexed. Was she just being polite? How typical of him to sti-fle that moment, for it had been *the moment*. So much promise . . . so much at stake. Angus had danced the first dance, but Riley had seized the moment.

Seeing the anguish rising in his friend's face, Mick conveniently changed the subject. "I recall you and Riley squared off in the semifinal match."

"We did, indeed" replied Angus, returning from the ceilidh. "It was part of the pain . . . competing against my friend who was as taken with Sarah as I . . . and she cheering him, not me."

"I followed you around The Old Course that day," Mick remembered, swatting at a cloud of smoke. "Seems to me, you had the better of Riley for most of it."

"Ah, we had a grand match."

Mick settled back, cigar tucked in cheek, hands curled around his snifter, a most willing listener. There were times when it took all of his patience to sit through other golfers' accounts of rounds that had been particularly important to them. Angus was not that sort. No braggart was he. He knew the game. Besides, St. Andrews has significance to all who have been there.

Angus deployed the ashtray and brandy snifter to serve as green and bunker just as Mick had done earlier.

"With his length off the tee," he began, "Riley could attack the course, taking all the tight, risky, lines down the right side of the course."

"And you couldn't hit it out of your shadow," laughed Mick, "so your only play was to the generous landing areas down the left side," he said gesturing to the wide side of the table.

"Yes, but I avoided those pesky pot bunkers in the centers of the fairways," Angus replied, refusing to dignify the jab Mick had made at his lack of power.

"Aye, and left poor angles to the plateau greens. But, somehow, you managed to maneuver miles of putts over the hummocks and hollows," Mick added, gesticulating with both arms, as if describing the route a roller coaster might take.

"And, as usual, Riley twitched and quivered over his short strokes."

"You were even fours going to the Road Hole," Mick said with the deference of one who understood the magnitude of such a feat.

"We were a stroke better than fours," Angus corrected, "but the wind got up on the inward nine. It favored Riley's length."

Angus thought to himself how he had done that day what he did best . . . manage his game. Throughout the match, he had reminded himself of the options offered short hitters by The Old Course. On *Long*, the par five 14th, with Riley able to skirt the nasty cluster of bunkers they call the Beardies, Angus knew O'Neill would be able to carry Hell Bunker in two, leaving a short pitch to the green.

Angus smiled now, as he recalled how he had ignored Riley's advantage and stayed within himself, playing wide left, toward the 5th fairway, into the Elysian Fields. From there, his second went wide right, leaving an awkward third of 150 metres. Seeing the hole cut on a rise near the front apron, he played through the green and left an easy chip back up the hill for a saving par. And Riley, though close to the green in two, had only a tiny shelf for a target. Too short would leave him under the brow in front of the green. Too long would leave a difficult birdie putt. Long was the place to miss. He came up short. At that point Riley had no choice but to put his next shot well past. Two more from forty feet meant six.

Angus had always believed their play on *Long* that afternoon was the very essence of The Old Course. She can be subdued, but only with care . . . *Tam Arte Quam Marte*. He had learned early on that storming the citadel can bring absolute victory or utter defeat. It was his own conservative play that found par when Riley's distance could not, a result which confirmed his abiding philosophy to always play safe, whether at golf, or business, or personal relationships.

"Your flanking maneuver on the 14th brought the match back to all square," said Mick. "But what happened at the The Road Hole, the 17th?"

"I had the honor. The wind was now three clubs into us. As you know, five is a good score on seventeen, even on a soft day. The railway sheds are nasty for my low drives, so, I wanted to go left, lay up short, and take my chances on getting up and down for par, or bogey at worst. With his length, I knew Riley could easily reach in two, but he also brought double bogey into the mix."

Angus began to fidget uneasily, leaning forward as if something about this episode caused him discomfort.

"I addressed the ball and spotted Sarah in the gallery. She had been rooting for Riley to that point in the match, so I'm still not sure why I bothered to glance her way, but I did."

The brackish air of St. Andrews returned to his nostrils, and the old railway sheds loomed in his memory as if he were once again on the 17th tee. A gathering storm sent most of the gallery racing for cover, but Sarah had stayed, and he and Riley both had been keenly aware of her presence. It hadn't been just a golf competition that day, they were vying for Sarah's love, a prize worthy of their best efforts but unlikely to be settled by the outcome of an event so trivial as a golf match.

"Our eyes met. I hadn't expected such a sensitive smile. I took it to be encouragement rather than sympathy. It was as though she was saying, *I know you can do this.* I was distracted. Instead of concentrating on my tee shot, I was thinking of Sarah . . . and dead topped it."

Angus grew red with embarrassment thinking of the moment. How could Sarah have been interested in him? Being incapable of separating his adolescent emotions from the task at hand was sort of like being unable to wink and twiddle his thumbs at the same time. Only the clumsy were saddled with this impediment. Compared to Riley, he felt a mere boy, not worthy of any woman's attention, especially Sarah's. In his haze, he could hear Mick comment on his inept display and was drawn back from his dream.

"You could have skulled it to the left for the love of God! Then, bogey might have been in the cards. But missing it behind the railway shed assured you of a double . . . or worse."

"Aye," replied Angus, winking as he twiddled his thumbs, "but you must admit, Riley never backed off and played close to the vest. We'll never know if he'd have made a birdie had I been in contention for par, but his three, under those conditions, may have been the best ever."

That pretty well summed up his view of Riley. The Irishman was always in the moment, seldom digressing from the matter at hand. If he was playing golf, he played golf. If he was courting Sarah, he courted Sarah. If he fought for Ireland, he fought for Ireland. Unlike Angus, Riley stayed on task. The exception was Collier Ames and his man, Rawahli. Muirfield was the one time Angus had seen Riley distracted on the golf course. Those two had gotten to him at Muirfield. Only then, had he seen Riley waver from the business of the day. Sarah might never get Riley O'Neill's attention on the golf course. But she had the interest of Angus MacKenzie wherever and whenever she wanted.

"After blistering a drive into that gale, he had 180 metres to the green," said Mick. "I know because after the match I paced it off."

"I'll never forget the way he turned down the toe of his cleek so the ball stayed low. It didn't rise above knee high as it skittered up the raised elbow fronting the green, well to the right of that abyss they call the Road Hole Bunker."

"I've never seen a ball fly so low, and still have that much spin. Otherwise, it would have raced over the slope behind the green and onto that infernal road where all the locals walk."

"Instead, it caught the crook of the elbow and funneled down toward the left side of the putting surface. When it came to rest, damned if he hadn't laid it stone dead to the pin tucked just behind the Road Hole Bunker."

"You still weren't closed out, Angus. A lot can happen on the last. It seems so simple, but it can be treacherous, especially in a wind like the one blowing that day."

"I came close to pulling off the impossible," Angus replied.

"Riley hit that scalding hook of his up to the edge of the Valley of Sin. And you sort of skied your drive."

"I had 132 metres to the pin. I know, because I was right beside the divot I had taken from the same spot in the morning quarterfinal round. From there I ran a knockdown mashie niblick through the Valley of Sin to twenty-five feet above the cup."

"Riley again tried to be too fine with his shot. His ball came to rest just under the hole, then trickled back into that aptly-named basin where all misjudged approaches go to pay penance."

"Committed the *cardinal sin*, you might say," joked Angus.

"Riley was off the green, but you were still away. And when your wicked downhiller went in for a three, I thought you'd squared the match. I was headed to the first tee for a playoff."

"You weren't alone, Mick. I'd never seen anyone hole a shot from the Valley of Sin. Merely two-putting from more than six feet below the putting surface can be a minor miracle. Being such a terrible putter, Riley seemed to have conceded the hole, and was just going through the motions before heading to the first tee."

"How many times have we made putts when we weren't really trying? It's usually when we think we *should* make a putt that our nerve ends get lively. Riley was nonchalant about the outcome. He had that inner calm, rolled it up the slope, over the brow, and into the cup . . . like a rat down a drainpipe."

"Beaten again by the tough little monkey . . . but I won something far better that day."

"What was that?"

"Riley's respect. He told me once, at Muirfield, I gave as good as I got. But this time he said it during a competition. Who could ask for more?"

"High praise, indeed, for someone so easily distracted," Mick said, laughing. "But after finding the luck to beat you, everyone thought it was an omen, and figured Riley would go on to beat Collier Ames in the final and avenge his loss at Muirfield."

"I think Riley wanted to win too badly in the final. Everything in golf that mattered to him was at stake. A victory in the British Isles Cup would have validated him as the game's top amateur. A berth on the Walker Cup team would surely follow, along with a match against Bobby Jones. And, of course, there was the prospect of revenge against Forgan and Ames."

"I refuse to believe Riley O'Neill would ever let the pressure of competition get to him."

"I wouldn't say he choked against Ames. He was just tight at crucial points in the match, didn't make enough putts, as usual, and once again allowed Ames to stay close. In the end, Collier pulled off another heroic shot to dash Riley's chances."

"The shot he holed from the Road Hole bunker was not just heroic . . . more like Homeric! You could empty your shag bag into that coffin and not get one ball within ten feet of the cup. But the one time it counted, Ames was perfect."

"You know, Mick, I've always wanted to ask you about that shot. I remember seeing Collier's manservant, Rawahli, standing on the Swilcan

Bridge when Ames holed out. You don't think he had any special power over Collier's shots do you?"

"Frankly, I've never thought of it 'til now. But no doubt that shot clinched the match . . . a two shot swing. What seemed a certain bogey became a birdie, leaving Riley's par meaningless. When they halved the last, the title, once again, belonged to Ames."

"It just seems to me, Rawahli always showed up when the match between Collier and Riley hung in the balance. And the outcome always tilted toward Ames after he made his appearance."

"I never believed in that mystical mumble jumble . . . neither did Riley. There were lots of coincidences though . . . maybe too many, thinking back on it."

"Oh, I know Riley scoffed at the notion of any curse, but I saw the look in his eyes whenever the Pakistani, or whatever he was, showed up. He seemed less sure of himself, and Collier became even more confident."

"Whatever the cause, confidence, or lack thereof, is the secret of golf. In any event, Riley should have won, so he could have played in the Walker Cup."

"He might have been kept off the team anyway."

"What do you mean?"

"At the ceilidh, Sarah told us of the discussions among the members of the rules committee concerning Riley's reinstatement into competitive golf. Apparently, Sir Thomas had insisted on keeping Riley out of golf for the full ten years."

"But he had submitted his written apologies!"

"Apparently, Forgan threatened to introduce new information regarding Riley's IRA activities."

"Then how did he get readmitted?"

"Sir Thomas extracted a condition from committee that Riley would be allowed to compete at St. Andrews only if they agreed never to vote him onto the Walker Cup team."

"But winning the British Isles Cup always carried an automatic berth onto the Walker Cup team!"

"In the circles of power, nothing is automatic. The only rule is there are no rules."

"So Riley knew before he teed off in the final he wouldn't be chosen for the Walker Cup team, even if he won?"

"Sarah had told us as much."

"Knowing Riley, that would be enough to spur him to victory and force their hand."

"We see it that way, because we thought Riley could accomplish anything in golf, or in life, that he wanted. But he was only human. Trying too hard to press the issue was probably his undoing."

"What happened between Riley and Sarah and you?"

"It's late," replied Angus, cupping his pocket watch and adjusting the fob. "Nearly two, and tomorrow will be a long day. Let's get some sleep and talk about it in the morning."

"You're probably just worn out from replaying your match with Riley," Mick joked as they walked down the passageway to their compartments.

"And I expect you'll want caddie fees for listening to it," laughed Angus.

"I'd pay dearly just to see it again," Mick said wistfully. "There's very little that touches me like the days of our youth. You and Riley were so much a part of those times. It's comforting to relive them with you."

"Likewise, Mick. G'night."

"Tomorrow, then."

Chapter 5

*A*ngus tossed restlessly in his berth as the train braked to a crawl through Glasgow. The more slowly the train moved, the more pronounced became the clanking of steel wheels against the rails. He thought of the country-side that lay ahead before they would reach Stranraer. Images of the towns and terrain would soon give way to visions of the golf courses nearby. Drifting in and out of consciousness, Angus visited Western Gailes, then Troon and Prestwick. Some of his most memorable days of golf had been spent playing these revered links, and it was comforting to retrace the route of these courses he knew by rote. Having completed rounds at Western Gailes and Troon, Angus was finally overcome by sleep as he made the turn at Turnberry. All too soon, the screeching of wheels announced their arrival in the blustery seaport of Stranraer.

Mick had disembarked before Angus could finish a tepid cup of tea and a day-old scone. The ferry, Fitzhume, was docked a few dozen metres away, barely visible through the fog. The day was dull and drizzly, and the wind had freshened, churning bay waters into a froth. Thankful for his mackin-tosh and cap, Angus moved about comfortably as Mick shivered, head bare, wearing only a sweater. A weather-beaten porter expressed gratitude for the generosity of their tips, but nevertheless chomped into the coins with his few remaining teeth, just to be certain it was legal tender.

The men climbed the gangplank of the Fitzhume for the forty mile crossing to Larne, Northern Ireland, and looked out from the upper deck at whitecaps billowing beyond the mouth of the bay. They poured cups of thick, black coffee and settled onto a hard, wooden bench where Mick asked Angus to resume his story on what was certain to be a typical Irish Sea crossing . . . rough.

"We were sorting out St. Andrews," Mick reminded.

"Yes, well, two months after the British Isles Cup," Angus began, "I received a telegram from Riley. In it, he told me Sarah had missed her monthly and was with child. He was occupied with IRA business and couldn't get to St. Andrews straight away. He asked if I would go to her."

"A bit callous for someone in love, isn't it?"

"I thought so at first, until I spoke with Sarah."

"Really . . ." Mick offered, his voice trailing off into a tone that seemed at once incredulous and cynical.

"Oh, she was distraught, to be sure. But Sarah knew from the beginning that Riley was dedicated to Ireland. She told me the life of an IRA man was no way to raise a family."

"Her sentiments, or Riley's?"

"Mutual voices of reason, I suppose. When it came to Riley, Ireland was Sarah's only rival. She knew it would not be easily overcome. They planned to meet and work it out, but I could tell she was already preparing herself for life without him."

"What about giving up the child for adoption . . . or . . .

"Abortion? Never! She wanted the child."

"Under any circumstances?"

"Of course."

"But without the child, she could have had Riley."

"Don't you see, Mick? Sarah was one with the child. And Riley was one with Ireland."

"Cold . . . the way he turned her out."

"Mmm, so it might seem, but we can't imagine their pain."

"But what about your pain?"

"Trifling compared to theirs."

"It was almost as though Riley knew you'd be there to pick up the pieces."

"Not almost, that was precisely his thinking. If he and Sarah couldn't marry . . . Riley saw me as the safe choice."

"But surely he knew you loved Sarah."

"Of course he knew. But he also knew Sarah didn't love me. Love unreturned, seldom lasts. I doubted I'd ever see hers. And I think, so did he."

"How on earth did the three of you work it out?"

"In the end, quite directly . . . almost businesslike."

Is that really how it had been? Or was this version his way of coming to terms with the final arrangement? Angus thought back on that afternoon at Russacks Hotel. He had been stationed just off stage in the adjacent lounge, awaiting his cue, while Riley and Sarah sat on a divan in the lobby, knees touching, her hands buried into his, like fragile porcelain in a leather pouch. Angus could see their expressions in the mirror above the bar, but could not hear the words. He sat sipping tea, trying to decipher their lines.

At some point, he was sure Riley had argued the dangerous reality of being an IRA man . . . the *'no life for a family'* speech. And, he was equally certain Sarah had not willingly acquiesced to his logic. It was not her way to nod in easy agreement. A *short life with honour* may not have been her first choice, but Sarah would have taken Riley's life as she found it . . . the IRA . . . Catholicism . . . all of it. He had only to ask. Angus knew the discussion had been anything but business-like. In the mirror, he had seen her tears, but time had suppressed her emotions from his memory. After the tears, Riley had brokered his friend as the safe choice for everyone, and Angus was all-too-ready to accept his supporting role. They had only to ask.

But the safe choice . . . was that all he had been? Thinking about it made Angus feel even more inadequate now than it had then. How had Sarah reached such a place in her life . . . a woman of English high privilege choosing between a lowly Irish rebel and a working-class Scot? She might have selected from a legion of titled and propertied men, able to provide every comfort befitting her station. No matrimonial match was beyond reach for the daughter of Lord James Neville Shiells, Earl of Ainsworth, and Lady Constance Delano . . . so long as proper arrangements were made.

It was, perhaps, these stilted pretenses of British society that caused Sarah to break from tradition, to resist the practice of someone else making lifetime choices on her behalf. Attending private school at Pembroke had shaped her outlook toward British men. She had met the likes of Collier

Ames and Larry Dirleton at the Cambridge cotillions. Their attitude toward women was one of entitlement, not respect, and it took root in their politics. India and Africa and, especially, Ireland, were, to an Englishman, mere chattels, comprised not of thinking, feeling people, deserving of dignity and respect, but of resources and labour, to be used as a means to personal wealth . . . not unlike women, who were mere objects of personal gratification, adornments to their husband's estates, a means to a male heir . . . or so it seemed to Sarah.

All of this might have drawn the sympathy of an independent Englishwoman who favoured the underdog, but it didn't explain the attraction. Sarah simply wasn't interested in superficial men lacking wit and a well-developed sense of romance. But, above all, she needed commitment, the kind of devotion that leads to contentment. Between them, they may have mustered some of these credentials. Neither, however, had the complete bill of fare.

As youth is wont to do, Sarah reasoned with heart and loins. The physical appeal and easy-going charm of Riley became a ready substitute for all the other attributes she was seeking. Not that she was promiscuous or self-indulgent, merely a woman with real feelings and real needs. Most of the consorts Lord and Lady Ainsworth had arranged to court their daughter were utterly inept in the art of pleasuring a woman. They had such a clinical approach to the opposite sex that one had to assume their view of love-making was based more on science and engineering. Riley didn't suffer these shortcomings. And it didn't matter to Sarah that he came by his dexterity through the expert tutelage of the ladies of Dublin's back streets. Female arousal was not some figment of Victorian novels as some of her companions seemed to think. Sarah knew the difference between dress rehearsal and the play itself. The former offered all of the lines with little of the passion. She preferred the genuine performance.

Angus had long tried to repress the memory of Sarah and Riley at St. Andrews . . . to no avail. The comfortable ease of their touch that first night together at the ceilidh always brought to him a sense of lacking. The way Riley placed his hand in the small of Sarah's back and drew her to him, once again gnawed at him. The way she pressed against Riley, as he gently stroked her neck, produced the same numbness in his fingers that he had experienced then. The way Riley paused to caress the tiny cleft just beneath her shoulder made Angus wonder anew how he ever could have thought his own touch might receive that same contented gaze. But, knowing all of this was merely the prelude to a more complete surrender, left Angus the hopeless task of contriving some semblance of grace to combat the rush of a more debilitating emotion . . . envy. Sarah in the arms of his friend, the perfect couple, joined as one, as if sculpted from a single cast of clay, leaving no doubt of their love. Yes, Sarah would become his wife, yet the image Angus had lugged around for fifty years was the one of Sarah and Riley, together.

"How did she know you would accept the arrangement?" Mick said, interrupting the memory that more than any other had come to define the relationship between Angus and Sarah and Riley.

"Pardon?" replied Angus, still lost in the past. "Oh, the arrangement was much more difficult for Sarah than me," Angus said modestly. "If you were referring to the child, I had no problem with fatherhood so long as it was with Sarah."

"Your love of her is easy enough to understand, but it's quite another matter to raise someone else's child as your own."

"My love for Sarah was unconditional."

"As was your respect for Riley."

"I suppose so. It was painful to witness their love for each other, and to see the impossible decisions being made affecting all our lives. But, looking back, only Riley could have made those decisions. It must have been agonizing for him to give up Sarah and Patrick."

"The boy's name is Patrick?"

"After Riley Padraig O'Neill, but Anglicized."

"Whatever became of you and Sarah?"

"I think she came to appreciate me. I always hoped, but never expected to replace Riley in her heart. For most of those years, our love was more comfort and companionship than passion."

"And the boy, were you close?"

"Until the war," replied Angus, eyes moistening.

"What happened during the war?"

The waters were becoming more agitated. Whitecaps broke over the bow of the Fitzhume, the sea now heaving in twenty foot swells. Angus wrapped both hands around the coffee cup, eyes closing to quell the tears he felt rising like the seas. Mick insisted he not continue. Angus refused, asking but a brief indulgence.

"Patrick blamed me . . . for Sarah's death."

"For pity sake."

"Patrick's eighteenth birthday was March 17, 1944. He was in the last round of recruits before the war ended. Sarah was heartsick over his leaving home so young. I urged her to travel to London and visit him before he shipped out to the continent."

"But . . ." Mick tried to protest.

"Sarah never reached London," Angus continued, dabbing his eyes.

"What do you mean?"

"A rogue Gerry bomber hit the train at Lancaster. All passengers perished."

"My good God, man!"

"A freak catastrophe of war. God's will, I suppose."

"I am so sorry, Angus. But why was that your fault?!"

"I suppose Patrick felt I was wrong to send her away from Edinburgh during the war."

"But she was going to see him!"

"That made it even more difficult. You know how young men are . . . invincible at age eighteen . . . in no need of a visit from their mother. To him, it was a purposeless act from the beginning. He felt I should have seen it as such, and prevented her from leaving, much less encouraging the trip."

"Rubbish."

"It was a long time ago, Mick. I wish she hadn't gone. I've tried to accept her loss as something other than a foolish decision by me. Nothing I could have done . . . right?" Angus said, repeating the question he had asked himself each day for thirty years. "Patrick still blames me, though. And, well, who can blame him for that?"

"Have you seen Patrick, or heard from him?"

"Just once . . . the day he returned from the service and launched into a hateful tirade over the loss of his mother. Vowed never to speak to me again."

"How fate does turn. Losing Sarah and Patrick in the prime of your lives. As sorrowful as we feel today about Riley's passing, we've reached the end, and accept the inevitability of death. But you were only beginning back then."

Angus stared blankly at Mick. He was as numb at the telling as when he'd lost them. Some pain is not meant to subside.

"Where is Patrick now?"

"He's a reporter for the *Irish Independent* in Dublin . . . a much better journalist than I ever was. Writes mostly about Sinn Fein and republicanism. Reading his work mostly helps salve the hurt, but sometimes it just peels off the scabs."

Mick shook his head in disbelief. "Patrick finds his way to his blood father's passion through the profession of his surrogate father. Did he know anything at all about Riley?"

"We told Patrick that Riley was his godfather," said Angus, "so I assume Patrick stayed in touch and knows of his passing."

"Do you think he'll be at the funeral?"

"I've been hoping so ever since I read of Riley's death."

"You'll tell him everything, of course."

"Oh my, yes. I should have told him long ago. It's my deepest regret."

"There are no regrets, old friend, just people trying to do their best with the choices before them."

"That's a useful view, Mick. But then, you've always struck me as quite a sensible bloke."

"Not always. I used to regret not having done more with my training in the law to further the efforts of the Republic. But I know it's a waste of time and energy to worry about the past. I guess we should just try to let go of things we can't control."

"This is the first time I've ever heard you express a position one way or the other about the fate of Ireland, Mick. Ever since that incident at

Muirfield, I suspected you were sympathetic to the Republic, but just what was it you felt you might have done, and didn't?"

"My field was constitutional law," said Mick, returning the coffee cups to their hooks as the seas continued to churn. "The legislation that created home rule is flawed, and the partition of Ireland, unconstitutional. But the cases I tried, were in English courts of dubious equity. After twelve years, I concluded nothing would come of it."

"That's no cause for regret."

"I gave in to the bastards. Riley never did."

"No, but I think you'll agree Riley had more of a personal stake in the fight."

"Actually, I don't see it that way at all. I'm an Irishman, first, and always. I believe, as did Riley, that having the English in Ulster has prevented healing between Protestants and Catholics."

Mick was becoming emotional and, as he often did in moments of agitation, rose to vent his feelings, gesturing as he paced, raising his voice for emphasis.

"Their occupation merely reinforces the old resentments. Get the English out of Ulster, and the natural inclination of people toward peace and reconciliation will prevail. For that reason, every Irishman, regardless of religious belief, has the same stake in the fight as Riley did. Giving up is unforgivable! And I just . . . gave up."

Angus managed a thin smile and, from a consciousness indelibly scarred by life's pain, began to recite a verse he had long ago committed to memory:

> *We never give up.*
> *We may take leave of the battle, but we're forever engaged in the fray.*
> *We've fought the good fight and earned our respite.*
> *But now, as always, we must summon our reserves and plod ever onward.*

"Who said that . . . Churchill?" asked Mick, who took great pride in recognizing most quotations that, through the ages, had been deemed profound. This one, however, eluded him.

Angus said nothing, but stood and made his way down the corridor to his sleeping compartment. He returned and handed his friend a small quaich, a shallow drinking cup featuring lug handles that protruded from either side of the rim in a Celtic knot design. This particular vessel, like those made popular by the ancient Gaels, was constructed of alternating wedge-shaped segments, two species of hardwood, arranged like staves of a barrel, to give a randomly oaken-mahogany appearance. It was a cup of fellowship, used in serving guests a welcoming dram or two of whiskey and, upon departing, a dram or two more, just to ensure safe passage home.

Adjusting his bifocals in the dim light, Mick could see that a small, rectangular plaque had been attached to the underside of the basin. On the silver plate was engraved the refrain Angus had just recited. Mick squinted to make out the stanza and the inscription beneath it. The words of attribution were tarnished by time but not yet obscured. And, if ever they were to become obscured, never would they be forgotten.

From Riley to Angus in Loving Memory of Sarah. 1944.

Chapter 6

A thirty foot breaker crashed over the bow of the Fitzhume, sending chairs tumbling down the aisle of the passenger deck. Angus and Mick clutched the brass railing near their table, clinging to it for dear life. Both had made the crossing many times and knew this stretch of the Irish Sea to be most treacherous. They stared at each other, searching for some mutual reassurance the squall would soon pass, wondering what could have possessed perfectly sane Scotsmen to venture across these treacherous waters, centuries ago, in craft so ill-suited for the endeavor. It could not have been that their future in Ireland seemed so promising. It must have been that their existence in Scotland was so dismal.

When, at last, the turbulence had subsided, a sliver of light shone with faint paleness against the jagged coastline of Ireland. A short distance from where the Fitzhume would dock, lay the capital city of Belfast, and, beyond it, the Mountains of Mourne in County Down. The sunlight glistened against the blue-green outline of the Mournes, revealing the next leg of their trip . . . from Larne by train, along the coast through Belfast, then Newcastle, and Drougheda, and finally, Dublin.

Angus summoned an attendant to transfer their luggage from the ferry to the Great Northern Railway, a train comprised mainly of freight cars. Assigned to adjoining compartments in the second of only three passenger coaches, they watched in amusement as an officious conductor fussed with his watch, muttering of Irish ferries that don't run on time, and British trains that do. While the last passengers from the Fitzhume straggled onto the train under the impatient eyes of this self-important ticket-taker, Mick and Angus stowed their luggage and agreed to meet later for lunch, hoping a short rest might calm their sea-swirled stomachs.

The tumult of the Irish Sea followed Angus to his berth. He tried to fix his eyes on a portrait of Belfast's skyline hanging above the dresser, but couldn't. The compartment was gyrating like a child's top, and the spinning was unlikely to stop while he was lying down. Angus eased off the berth and staggered back to the observation car as if inebriated. Sifting through the morning papers, he located the *Irish Independent* and paged through the editorials until he found a piece titled *Ireland's Last Hope*, written by, what was this, Padraig Angus MacKenzie?

Angus was dumbfounded. Patrick had always written under the name Patrick MacKenzie, never using either Padraig or Angus to describe himself. Seeing both names pleased Angus. He was sure Riley would approve of Patrick's Gaelic spelling, just as Angus was proud to see his name as part of Patrick's new identity. And though he was familiar with Patrick's writings on the subject of Anglo-Irish relations, today's effort was much different.

IRELAND'S LAST HOPE

by Padraig Angus MacKenzie

A grand old Gael died today. He came to us from a long line of Gaels. He was a son of Ireland, a great, great, grandson of Finn MacCumhail, a distant nephew of Cuchulainn, cousin to Wolfe Tone and Daniel O'Connell and Charles Stewart Parnell; and the younger brother of Padraic Pearse and Michael Collins. He came to us through the echoes of these kindred spirits, and his plea for one Ireland rang out as loudly as theirs. He sang their psalms of freedom with the same clear voice, and passes with the same clear conscience, knowing he, too, devoted his life to the Eire he loved. And we mourn, knowing others like him shall rarely pass this way again. But his hopefulness remains, undiminished, and this hope is the sacred gift he bequeaths to us, as an ancestry of patriots did him. He was Riley Padraig O'Neill, a father to all patriotic Gaels, and an inspiration to those Gaelic sons following in his path . . . sons who must not forget their fathers . . . and must not forget to hope.

"Sons who must not forget their fathers," Angus repeated silently, "and must not forget to hope."

He knew then, the healing had begun. There is a good bit of me and Riley in Patrick, thought Angus. He pounds away at the typewriter for me, and he pounds away at the Brits for Riley. Joining Padraig and Angus together in his by-line must have been his way of beginning to salvage his own hope. This piece was not written by a bitter man. It was conciliatory and wistful. Maybe he's trying to come to terms with Sarah's loss, and the loss of others in his life. Maybe he's trying to accept me.

Hope and despair had been contending for Angus' heart these past thirty years, with despair gaining the upper hand. But had he given hope the nourishment it needed? Instead of confronting his demons, instead of reaching out for Patrick and seeking ways to reconnect with him, Angus had slipped into the dark void of depression that finds its own nourishment. Left unattended, it had become the deadliest of carnivores, devouring the soul, shutting out promise, until all faith is lost, and the last shred of optimism consumed. But now, this heinous black creature had been met by a glimmer of the possible, a radiance to combat the pall of forlorning that, year after year, had enshrouded his heart. And the light had come from a most unexpected source, Patrick himself. Maybe hope was still out there . . . just beyond the gloaming . . . pounding away at the door of darkness.

Angus glanced up to see a boy of ten or so, tearing down the aisle in front of Mick. The lad reminded Angus of his newsboy, Bobby Fenwick. If wee Bobby can summon the courage to struggle up Gullane Hill in wind, and rain, and dark of night, then I must also. Angus quickly brushed his cheek and folded the newspaper. Perhaps the article could be shared later with Mick . . . after he had read it again.

"Couldn't sleep," Mick said tersely. "Didn't want to miss Belfast or Colby."

"I had no idea this route passed through Sir Thomas Forgan's estate."

"I thought you'd be interested. I knocked on your door, but there was no answer, so I figured you were already up . . . or dead from that damned Irish Sea. We'll be coming to Colby soon after we pass through Belfast."

*   *   *

The cars clanked along the Irish Sea, through the village of Carrickfergus on their way to the capital of Ulster. The beauty of Belfast belied its violent history and concealed more sobering images of the horrific loss of human life in these environs during centuries of conflict. The fallen could have repopulated the city. From Stormont, the magnificent home of Ulster's parliament since the partition of 1921, to the neo-Baroque city hall, Belfast, despite all its gore, was drenched in grandeur. So much promise . . . so many for whom to pray.

They stopped to refuel at Queen's Quay Station, situated next to the River Lagan. The red sandstone of the station's façade had figured prominently in much of Belfast's architecture, and, today, seemed a metaphor of the blood that had been shed in Ulster. They rolled out of the city from the south side and began to wend their way into County Down. Far removed from the smokestacks of the city, the scenery soon receded into the pastoral . . . first, small hills known as drumlins, then dense woodlands dotted with tiny lochs.

"What made you think of Colby?" asked Angus.

"Actually, I was thinking of Sir Thomas Forgan," replied Mick.

"You must think of him on occasion as well."

"Hardly a day passes without some thought of Sir Thomas."

"What do you think happened to him?"

"I'm not sure anyone will ever find the whole truth about Forgan. I do know he was under investigation by the Royal & Ancient."

"Investigation for what, pray tell?"

"Violating the strictures on amateurism, just as we suspected at Muirfield when we saw Ames and his cronies stuffing money into their wallets."

"I thought you were on the take as well, Angus. You had more than a few quid in your envelope!"

"Oh that. It was just a payment from *The Scotsman* for services rendered. Turned out to be my severance pay," he joked.

"What exactly were the particulars of Forgan's offenses?" Mick asked in lawyerly curiosity.

"The fine print contained in the definition of amateur requires any contestant over the age of eighteen to personally pay all expenses attendant to competition . . . room, board, clubs, balls, clothes, et cetera. Sir Thomas was subsidizing Ames and Somersby and Dirleton, and God knows who else."

"But Forgan always seemed such a stickler for the rules. It isn't at all consistent with the way he preached to us about the virtues of amateurism."

"The evangelist often strays from his own preaching."

"You worked for the man. Did you ever suspect him of any misbehaviour?"

"Oh my, yes! It seemed to me he played fast and loose with all rules . . . applied them only if they served his purposes."

"But even if the R & A had uncovered any wrong-doing, surely it would have only resulted in a private reprimand. After all, these were not capital offenses."

"No, but the elite have a way of humbling their own. Remember, Forgan had risen to a position of considerable power. There are always others more powerful who may resent the advances of a man with such common breeding. He may have overreached."

"Are you suggesting he was a victim of his own ambition?"

"Perhaps . . . though I think he was more a victim of his own moral liabilities. He used his position and wealth to injure others, and in the end, his so-called peers were prepared to skewer him on his own petard. He may have been the Laird of Colby, but he was not to be the Laird of St. Andrews."

"Violating a code of conduct, and vulgar behavior toward his fellow gentlemen, may be revealing of Forgan's character, but it doesn't explain his mysterious disappearance a few years later."

"No, it most certainly does not. That is still the subject of considerable speculation."

Chapter 7

Colby comprised over ten thousand acres of the most scenic real estate in all of Ireland. As the train neared the northern boundary of the original estate, the two men gazed out at lush forests and verdant hills, once the domain of Gaelic earls. What forces had conspired to bring about the demise of this ancient system of clans and serfdom? Was their culture as romantic and grand as the poets had made it out to be? All the accounts Angus had read of the plantation of Ulster in the 1600s bore out the brutality of it all. But was the common man worse off under the Scottish gentry than he had been under the Gaelic chieftains? Perhaps not, but a way of life had been uprooted, and with it, the rhythms, those reassuring cadences of custom and friendship and religion.

Angus imagined a family like the Monahans striving to cope with the new order, scraping out an existence in the poorest of lands, while the intruders took the best. And he tried to envision a clan chieftain like Ui' Naill of Tyrone taking flight from his homeland with the promise of safety in some far off place while his lands were seized by the English and given away to Scots like the Forgans. These were not Gods, as portrayed by Irish mythology, but men. And they were no different than men will always be . . . courageous, to be sure, but also fearful. They knew when the odds were long, when it was time to cut and run. They knew how to barter for the best arrangement they could get from invading forces. While it was not wrong to glorify the deeds of these clan chieftains in an attempt to restore pride in the Gaelic past, neither was it right to use them as a guidepost to the future. In the Irish mist, reality and myth had melded into myopia.

Gradually, Colby Manor and its village of outbuildings came into view over a soft rise, flattening out into a broad plain from which the master of the demense could survey all that was his. The main house appeared far more majestic than the term manor depicted . . . more nearly Balmoral than Greywalls . . . more castle than country house. Yes, indeed, the lowly Forgans of Scotland had fared well at the expense of the native Irish.

"What do you think happened to Sir Thomas Forgan, Angus? I remember reading that, in October of 1929, the IRA burned Colby Manor to ashes and Forgan's body was never found."

"You probably know more about what may have happened to Sir Thomas than I do. After all, I'd left the employment of *The Scotsman* by that time. What little I knew, came from Hamish MacClanahan. We met each month for drinks and lies at the *Thistle & Rose* on the lower level of the Caledonian Hotel."

"He must have known a good deal about the comings and goings of Forgan. What did he tell you?"

"Well, he indicated Sir Thomas was feeling continued pressure from the Royal & Ancient, and was planning to take leave to his estate in Ireland."

"I would have thought by then, the R & A might have cornered Forgan on those rules violations."

"Hamish was vague about the reasons for his flight to Colby. But he did say he was surprised Forgan would return to the scene of his crimes."

Angus stared carefully into Mick's eyes to determine whether this was yet another long-buried secret to be shared with his friend. "You *do* know about Forgan and Sinead Monahan O'Neill, don't you, Mick?"

"Yes, of course. As Riley's lawyer, he told me everything. But, even today, I have a difficult time thinking of Riley and Collier as half-brothers."

"I know what you mean," replied Angus. "If ever there were two opposites, they were. In any event, the servants at Colby were friends of Sinead's and knew of Forgan's offenses. My guess is they were none too anxious to see him return to Colby."

"No doubt. I seem to recall the IRA being active in County Down during those times as well."

"I remember Hamish telling me the Orange Lodges had engaged in an unusually violent marching season in July of '29, taking the lives of dozens of Catholics in its annual purge of Ulster's demons of Popery."

"The most inviting targets for IRA reprisal would have been country estates of Protestant gentry."

"Hamish told me Colby was at the top of their list."

"If Colby wasn't safe, then the R & A must have been hard on his trail. What else did Hamish tell you?"

"Not much, really. Only that Forgan was to meet with his trusted caretaker, Mr. Trimble Savage on arrival in Colby. And, that he was determined to locate Sinead Monahan."

"You don't think Riley was involved in Forgan's disappearance, do you?"

"There are more versions of Forgan's departure than of John Fitzgerald Kennedy's assassination. Some say the sacking of Colby was a random act of reprisal by the IRA which resulted in the unplanned death of Forgan. Other's contend Forgan's bigotry toward the Irish caught up with him, and the IRA executed him."

Angus walked over to the condiments niche at the far end of the observation car to refill his teapot with hot water and to add a lump of sugar. Returning to his seat, he stirred the tea thoughtfully, and continued to speculate about Riley's connection to the disappearance of Sir Thomas Forgan.

"Some maintain the whole matter was masterminded by Riley himself, as personal revenge for his family. And, still others have speculated Forgan didn't die at all that night, but staged the entire scene in order to escape the embarrassment of an R & A inquiry."

Mick stood and stretched and paced about the observation car, becoming more animated, hands clasped over the lapels of his jacket as if he were addressing a jury.

"The first two theories are the most plausible. I know Riley killed for Ireland, but I don't think he would resort to murder, even if Sir Thomas deserved it. And I don't believe Forgan survived, though he was said to have been sighted in Australia years later."

"That begs the critical question, Mick. Assuming Riley wasn't present that night in Colby, did he nevertheless have a hand in ordering Colby sacked, and Sir Thomas killed?"

"Well, if we're to believe your conversation with Riley at the British Isles Cup in 1926, he had abandoned violence as a means of achieving a united Ireland."

"True enough, but just as he believed an Irish republic was a work in progress, he also had to deal with the daily outbreaks of violence by the Protestants in the north. Maybe he just threw up his hands at all the bloodshed and said *foock* the Prods!"

"Oh, Riley said that, all too often! But I don't think he believed in killing them."

"It must have been impossible for any reasonable Irishman to chart a sane course in the midst of all that insanity."

"Still is, I'd venture."

"Collier Ames might have the answer, if he's still alive."

"Collier Ames, It's been a long time since I've thought of him. If he is alive, he'd be seventy-nine, a year older than Riley and me. What makes you think he might know about Forgan's disappearance?"

"I read where he became the 15th Baronet of Colby."

"As the firstborn male child and, presumably, the only heir, that would certainly have been his birthright under the English system of inheritance."

"He might have been at Colby in 1929."

"Oh? Sounds like you know more than you're letting on."

"Well, the *Sentinel* spared no expense in its investigation of Forgan's unexplained departure. After all, he was the publisher of our rival, *The Scotsman.* Anytime your competitor is involved in something as unsavory as this, it's newsworthy."

"Were you assigned to the inquiry?"

"Not directly. I kept my appointments with Hamish, but he was tight-lipped by that time, no doubt pressured by *The Scotsman* to keep quiet. I did speak with the *Sentinel's* detective . . . Farmingham was his name. He told me only of Collier's ticket to Larne and balked at telling more."

"I recall the whole matter being hushed rather abruptly."

"The chairman of the *Sentinel's* board of governors, Lord Ashley, made it clear to our staff that nothing would be done to publicize any of our findings. Then, I was contacted by the solicitor representing the Royal & Ancient, a Mr. Selby Wexford from London, who advised me it would be best for all concerned if the matter was dropped."

"That only complicates the puzzle."

"Maybe we're making too much of it. *The Scotsman* and the R & A are both highly respected organisations that would go to any length to avoid a scandal. Regardless of how Forgan may have met his end, I'm quite certain they didn't want the world to dwell on it, for fear their reputations might be stained."

"I'd still like to know what happened."

"So would I. Interestingly, I also read where one of Collier's first acts as the 15th Baronet was to deed the majority of Colby's land back to the Irish Catholic families who had owned it before the English transferred it to the Forgans. In fact, I recall the largest tract was deeded to Sinead Monahan O'Neill, some 1500 acres. I think Ames retained only 500 acres immediately surrounding the demense."

"That seems so out of character from the Collier Ames we knew. If anything, he seemed more ruthless than Sir Thomas when it came to any dealings with the Irish. It makes one wonder what could have happened in his life to bring about such a change."

"Which, of course, assumes that Ames *has* changed," Mick quickly noted.

*   *   *

The train continued to weave its way through the grounds of Colby, and the two weary travelers were seated to a late lunch. The ferry crossing had been arduous, and now both were famished. To complement the ensemble of mixed greens, Irish salmon and new potatoes, they shared a delightful burgundy that displayed a personality as complex as Riley's. Conversation ranged widely during their leisurely meal, but attempts to steer it toward lighter topics were unsuccessful. The more they had explored the many dimensions of the Anglo-Irish dispute, the less apparent answers had become. Angus still had not the slightest notion why Protestants and Catholics in other parts of the world could co-exist without the all-consuming hatred and violence that persists in Ulster. Mick reminded him that both sides had been conditioned by generations of tales about past injustices which are regularly reenacted as an admonition for those who might wish to forget.

"Tell me about your cottage in Gullane," said Mick, veering far afield from Ulster.

"Well, centuries ago, the Dutch had a strong influence in Scotland due to the short distance across the North Sea from the Netherlands. Each Spring, Dutch traders would sail into various ports along the Firth of Forth and swap wares with the Scots."

"It's unfortunate that relations between the Irish, Scots, and English haven't been as cordial as those with the Dutch."

"Aye, the Irish could benefit from having a Dutchman negotiate with the British. They drive a hard bargain, but one that usually serves the interests of both sides."

"The Dutch must have settled along parts of the Firth."

"Yes, in fact, Wilhelm Van Luytens, a Dutch trader who visited ports along the Firth for years, decided he'd prefer to winter in Gullane, where weather is less severe. So, he built the little cottage I now own on Gullane Hill in 1734, giving him a winter retreat and an incomparable view of the Firth and the North Sea."

"The Dutch played a game much like our golf, you know."

"The game they played was called *kolfen*. But, yes, the rules and object of the game were very similar to golf . . . if you ignore the fact that it was played on ice."

"I've heard stories of how the game originated, but given the frequent visits of traders such as Van Luytens, and the similarity of the kolfen format, it seems likely they introduced it to the Scots . . . with the exception of the ice, of course."

"As good a theory as most, I suppose, though most Scots would take issue. Anyway, as I was saying, Van Luytens' descendants lived in the cottage for generations until the 1940's when they forfeited it to back taxes. I came along looking for property after the war and was instantly taken by the place."

"There must have been some divine power at work to bring you to the cottage when you most needed a diversion from your pain."

"For the remainder of my time at the *Sentinel*, I spent nearly every week-end doing carpentry, or masonry, or plumbing, in order to keep myself plodding onward."

"Speaking of masonry, Angus, did you ever enter the realm of Freemasonry?"

"No, the rituals of freemasonry never really interested me. What about you?"

"Oh, I entered the lodge as a young man . . . and rejected it in middle age."

"Sounds as though you became disillusioned."

"I learned the rituals of Catholicism that are forever condemned by the Protestants, are just as prevalent in Freemasonry. Their view is that the Catholic Church claims authority not only over spiritual matters, but over the secular as well. It does so by selling God's indulgences."

"Wasn't that the cornerstone of the Reformation?"

This weak attempt at humor provided Mick with a perfect segue to the remainder of his explanation. "Yes, and Martin Luther postulated the forgiveness of sins was a free gift from God's grace alone. Not only was the Pope's bartering of anyone's salvation unnecessary, it was improper. The Freemasons would argue that once the Church had become afflicted with its material possessions, its spiritual authority was forfeit."

"The Protestants have a point, Mick. But apparently, you have doubts."

"The most telling flaw in Freemasonry, is that Protestants pretend to separate the spiritual under the guise of the church, and the temporal under the Masonic Lodge. The result is the same hypocrisy they complain of in the Catholic church."

"There may be another way to look at it, Mick."

"How so?"

"Sin . . . confession . . . absolution. I never really thought about it until now, but the rituals of Catholicism *do* provide some clarity in life. I remember after Riley went to confession, he came out a new man, with a fresh outlook."

"But his priest had no real power to forgive Riley's sins."

"We may think so because we've been taught as Protestants to give our lives over to good deeds in the hope that at the end of the day the good will outweigh the bad."

"What's wrong with that?"

"Nothing. Except that we can never be certain the scales are tipped in our favor. We slog through life wondering whether our self-determination has been enough. Riley, at least, came away from confession with the feeling that his past sins had been washed away, and he could start with a clean slate."

"So priests are like placebos in medicine. They may have no real healing power over the soul or the body, but as long as the penitent or the patient believes they do, all is well."

"It's not that farfetched, is it?"

"Perhaps not, but I still contend that nowhere is religion more hypocritical than in Ulster."

"I wouldn't argue with you there."

"We were talking about your cottage before I got us into another religious discussion."

"You must visit the cottage after we've laid Riley to rest."

"I'd be honored. Maybe we could even play a round or two at Muirfield. It's one of my favourite courses."

"Aye, she's a beaut', maybe the best ever," Angus said, recalling Riley's description so long ago.

"We'll always have our golf, Angus."

"Our constant and unchanging companion," Angus agreed, "urging us to place one foot in front of the other, and march ever onward."

"Not just in the playing," said Mick, "but in its venues, where we are reminded who we once were . . . and who we've become."

"Regardless how our skills may diminish," said Angus, "they are the links to our past . . . the standards against which we measure our greatest success."

"Not to mention our most dismal failures," laughed Mick.

"Yes, but as I think on those times now, it's not the victors or the vanquished that I recall," said Angus, "it's the camaraderie and the competition."

"You're right, you know. There really were no winners or losers . . . just friendly rivals trying to do the best they could with the skills they had."

"Tell me, Mick, do you ever feel old and unnecessary . . . just used up? You strike me as someone who never really gets down."

"Everyone has their dark days, Angus. Churchill, you know, called his melancholia the *'black dog'*. He was fond of quoting the famous Russian poet Pushkin."

> I've lived too long, I'm in a ruck.
> I've drunk too deeply from the cup.
> I cannot fight, I cannot fuck.
> I'm down and out, I'm buggered up.

Angus sighed. Not the triumphant exhale that marks completion of the task at hand, this was more a moan, the sort one heaves in search of the will to carry on.

"Aye, Mick, that's the perfect lament for those of us who are getting long in the tooth. But down *and* out? Down, I can accept . . . out, never."

Chapter 8

*T*he train approached Newcastle, County Down, and, over the village arched a rainbow, betraying the recent departure of a thundershower. Beyond this colorful prism loomed the Mountains of Mourne, forever transmuting under broken sunlight, flooding the valley with a peaceful backdrop of purple and cobalt. A small gathering of passengers waited on the platform as the train stuttered to a stop beneath the red slate roof that was cantilevered above the white clapboard depot. Some of the freight cars were to be uncoupled, and three passenger coaches added, for the trip to Dublin. Angus and Mick disembarked to inquire about Ames.

"Would you be familiar with Mr. Collier Ames?" Angus asked the withered man sitting behind an iron-barred ticket window.

Inside the booth, the frail-looking fellow didn't budge beneath his official Great Northern Railway cap, seemingly engrossed in the counting of money and ticket stubs.

"Ev'ryone knuws Ames," the ticketmaster replied, at last, smiling through an incomplete set of tobacco-stained teeth. "Joost bought a seat t' Dooblin, 'e did. 'spect 'e'll be back soon enough," he said in an accent that was neither Irish or British but some strange amalgamation of the two, with a bit of cockney mixed in.

"An hour 'til we depart?" asked Mick.

"Roight you are, goov'ner," replied the drawn but spry, little man as he spat a thick stream of tobacco sluice into the spitoon beneath his counter.

"Let's take a walk over to the Slieve Donard," suggested Angus, "to see if Collier is in the vicinity."

The men strolled through town until reaching Down Street, where a red brick structure boasting ornate turrets rose before them. It was

Newcastle's most important lodging house, whose name, Slieve Donard, derived from the highest peak in the Mournes, looming as a constant vigil over the valley. They entered the lobby and found that it possessed the savoir faire of an earlier era. But like the femme fatale past her prime, the Slieve Donard's best days were behind it. The joints of her wooden floors creaked like bones in old age, a bit less strong from the trampling of humanity, and far less supple from the passage of time. Her once-glamorous façade now revealed dark circles under the eyes, creases so deep that even coats of rouge could not conceal what lay beneath. Though there were runs in her stockings, and her slip was showing, the Slieve Donard was quite dignified . . . in decline, perhaps, yet very much a proper lady.

The concierge, Mr. Caxton, set about imparting far more information than they had expected to receive or could put to good use. According to Caxton, Mr. Ames had checked out early to play golf at nearby Royal County Down. It was often Ames' custom to travel from Colby to Newcastle, spend a few days at the Slieve Donard, enjoy golf and friends at his club, then return to Colby. He seldom visited Dublin, but when he did, his chauffeur usually drove him. The concierge was surprised to learn that, this time, Ames would travel by train. The men thanked Caxton and returned to the station. Still no Ames.

Just as the conductor called for all to board, a black Duesenberg sedan came barreling around the corner and down the street. Not since the 1920s had either man seen such an impressive automobile, conditioned as if it might have just been driven off the showroom floor. The vehicle slid to a stop in front of the station platform, and the driver, wearing the uniform of a chauffeur, climbed out. It was Rawahli.

A pair of jodhpurs, flaring above knee-high Wellington boots, had replaced kaftan and sandals and, in lieu of the turban, a snap-brimmed cap. He eased into his ethereal gait, gliding to the rear of the automobile to open Ames' door. The men did a double-take to make certain it really was the Pakistani in that get-up. Angus and Mick eagerly watched as a tall, gaunt man swung one leg then the other out of the car and stood beside it. Though a bit stoop-shouldered from the gravity of his extended frame, his manner had a certain vitality. It was Collier Colby Ames, and his attire was just as they might have imagined . . . impeccable.

Grey worsted slacks with triple forward pleats were worn in subtle contrast to a white, polo-collared shirt, buttoned to the top. A navy blue cashmere sweater, emblazoned with the crest of Royal County Down, gave the elderly man a more youthful appearance. In serious tones, Ames was imparting last-minute instructions to his man as the two walked up the stairway to the platform. Collier carried a thin, black, leather valise, while Rawahli effortlessly hoisted a large portmanteau above his head with one hand and dangled a leather golf bag filled with hickory-shafted clubs from the other. As he prepared to board the train, Ames paused to glance at the two old codgers seated on a wooden-slatted bench beside the ticketmaster's window. In an instant, a crooked smile flashed over his pallid face that sagged beneath a completely bald dome.

"MacKenzie! Callahan! What on earth are the two of you doing in Newcastle . . . trying to incite an Irish insurrection?"

There was a time when such a comment, coming from Collier Ames, might have been taken as an insult, but not today. He was clearly making light of his past disposition and, in his old age, trying to make amends. No offense intended . . . and none taken.

"Collier Ames," the two men said in unison.

"You look as if you can still play to par," Angus complimented.

"The mind is willing. The flesh is not. I'm sure you both know the feeling."

Collier extended his right hand toward Angus. It was as limp as wilted lettuce. Some things weren't meant to change.

"You wouldn't be going to Riley O'Neill's funeral, would you?" Mick asked.

"And why would I not?" Ames protested.

"All the hard feelings between the two of you over the years," said Mick. "I just assumed the chances of reconciling were too remote."

"I suppose we did behave as typical English and Irish during the many encounters of our youth. People *are* capable of change, however."

"So, you've been the Baronet of Colby all these years," said Angus, "since Sir Thomas' passing, that is."

Startled by this reference to Forgan's death, Collier's face took on an even more ashen pallor. In clumsy silence, broken suddenly by the conductor's final boarding whistle, the three men eased up the retractable stairs to the pullman car and entered the shadowy corridor.

"We'll have more time to talk later," said Angus.

"Oh, most assuredly," replied Collier. "Let me get settled. I'll meet you in the observation car."

Chapter 9

*A*ngus and Mick lounged in the observation car, sipping tea and munching raspberry-filled pastries. It could not have been easy being Collier. Sir Thomas Forgan had been a most despicable fellow for whom to work, and Angus could not imagine how he might have behaved as a father. He didn't know quite what to make of this seemingly new Ames. The competitiveness and petty jealousies of youth seemed to be receding, giving way to the respect and tolerance of old age. His old rival somehow seemed transformed, with an entirely new personality and an altogether more pleasing disposition.

Collier entered the far end of the car and navigated through an obstacle course of passengers legs splaying out into the aisle. He had changed from his golfing attire into a double-breasted blazer worn over a heavily-starched white shirt with *CCA* monogrammed on the cuffs. A Royal County Down club tie, knotted snugly against his prominent Adam's apple, revealed the crest of an Irish harp and crossed golf clubs. As English protocol would forever dictate, the harp and clubs were situated exactly where they must always be, directly *beneath* the ubiquitous crown of Great Britain.

"I never imagined you two old sots drinking tea at this late hour," said Collier, grinning through a set of teeth that were obviously not originals.

A portly steward stumbled through the sea of limbs to reach Collier and take his order.

"Kummel, neat, wedge of lime," Ames said crisply, ordering his favorite clear, sweet, caraway-flavored liqueur.

When it arrived, Collier remarked, "The Irish aren't much on this stuff," hoisting his glass toward the two men as if preparing a toast. "It's popular in England as aiming fluid for putting. Been my secret for years. Well, here's to Riley . . . may he be up!"

The three men charged cups and glass at the obvious double entendre of their friend's pitiful putting, and his prospects for reaching heaven.

"May he be up!" repeated Angus and Mick.

"Collier, you've softened in your old age," Angus remarked.

"It's never too late to become the person you're meant to be. Besides, I grew weary of trying to live up to someone else's expectations."

"And are you the person you were meant to be?" asked Angus, trying to draw Collier out.

"Others must judge that."

"Whose expectations?" asked Angus. "Your father's? I mean, Sir Thomas Forgan's?"

"He was determined to mold me into his image. But when did you learn Sir Thomas was my father?"

"In 1921," confessed Angus. "After Muirfield."

"I was the consummate cad in that event."

"We had another description for you back then," Mick interjected with a smirk.

"I'm sure I had many more detractors than admirers in those days."

"And now?" asked Angus.

"I hope the score has improved. But it's often said the misjudgments of our youth follow us forever. I am curious though, how you learned that Sir Thomas was my father. We were always so careful not to publicly acknowledge one another."

"Actually," replied Angus, "his pride in you was obvious at the 1921 British Isles Cup. The words of praise at the banquet . . . the way he ran to your side when Riley cold-cocked you . . . I suspected there was a connection between the two of you even before hearing it from Hamish MacClanahan."

"Ah, the managing editor of the *The Scotsman*, of course! I'm certain he meant well."

"Why do you say that?" asked Angus.

"Sir Thomas Forgan lived a tormented life. He took Hamish MacClanahan into his circle of trust. Apparently, he felt the need to confide in someone, and that turned out to be Hamish. Odd, isn't it, this man of great power . . . able to amass a vast fortune . . . but incapable of acquiring even one true friend."

"I hope no confidence was broken," said Angus, deciding it best not to mention MacClanahan's clandestine reading of Forgan's personal diary.

"Heavens no! Sir Thomas forfeited any claims to secrecy by harming anyone who stood in his way."

"And just when did *you* learn Sir Thomas was your father?" asked Angus.

"1920, actually. Sir Thomas informed me of our ties while recruiting me to become a member of the elite squad of amateur golfers he was backing."

"You mean Forgan was providing financial support to British amateurs as early as 1920?" exclaimed Mick.

"It began harmlessly enough. I hoped working with my father would bring us close. But I soon discovered it was just another business deal for him. When I was called before a panel of R & A members to answer questions relating to amateurism, they revealed to me the details of Sir Thomas' behavior. I felt as if I were a common criminal, aiding and abetting a master felon."

"You must have had mixed emotions," said Mick. "On the one hand, Sir Thomas had been generous in his support, and on the other, most deceitful."

"His generosity was purely financial and squarely against the rules. Despite what you saw of his charade at Muirfield, I can assure you none of his affection fell to me."

"What were his motives then?" asked Angus.

"Only he could answer that. All I saw was a love of money and a bitter hatred of the Irish. He was determined to do everything in his power to keep them off the Walker Cup team. To him, the Walker Cup represented all those exalted ideals he so often espoused, but never practiced. The *mere*

Irish, as he called them, were inferior in every way to the English and would never be worthy of the stature conferred by the Walker Cup."

"You sound bitter toward him," Mick said.

"I was angry to be sure, and deeply hurt by this smug panel of inquisitors who took great pleasure in relating the sordid details of Sir Thomas' past. But, in the end, I pitied him more than hated him."

"Why was that?" asked Angus.

"He was a man who had known failure only once in life. I believe Sir Thomas was infatuated by my mother, in spite of his despicable behaviour. Her rejection of him was an obstacle with which he was ill-prepared to deal. When someone is conditioned to having life go their way at every step, they are often overwhelmed by a single reversal."

"If so," said Angus, "he carried the rage around for nearly thirty years . . . a long time to keep such debilitating sentiments alive."

"And that, my good man, sums up Sir Thomas about as well as one can, given such a monstrous disposition. His will was colossal. He had the choice to use it in a beneficial manner. Instead, he allowed the anger of his youth to consume him like a cancer. It festered in him to the very end."

"You sound disappointed at not being able to help him," Angus said.

"It would be presumptuous to think I could have made a difference after all those years, but a little forgiveness can go a long way toward helping to heal even the deepest wounds."

"A recipe for the Protestants and Catholics of Ulster," Mick added philosophically.

"Quite so. Living with the conflict for nearly fifty years has given me a far different perspective on the barbarity of it all. Your comparison is apt, Mick. But it's much more complicated when thousands are required to extend the hand of forgiveness in unison, and thousands more are needed to accept the offering. It seems there are always a few who have the will of a Sir Thomas to keep the hatred alive."

"What prompted your change of heart toward the Irish?" Mick asked.

"The trip to Colby in 1929. It changed my life in so many ways."

"Your mother, perhaps . . .?" Angus continued hopefully.

Collier did not respond and turned away, eyes glistening. As the train slowed to make the turn into Drogheda, County Louth, and the three men stared in silence at the enormous stanchions of railway trestle. Several moments passed before Collier spoke.

"I met my mother only once. The circumstances of that night were dreadful."

This was met with more silence.

"October 25, 1929," Collier continued, "is a night about which I have never spoken."

PART III

▼

ROYAL COUNTY DOWN

Chapter 1

$\mathcal{T}$he men stared out at Drogheda under skies made dismal by pewter smoke belching from smelters nearby. Angus was lost in thought. From the moment of their first meeting at Muirfield, he had been fascinated by Riley's colorful accounts of Irish history. Years after hearing tales of Finn MacCool, and other stories of Gaelic lore, Angus found he would often read Joyce or Synge or Gregory, and transport himself back to those ancient times that had captivated Riley as a lad. And, as he had grown older, his interest grew stronger.

Angus scanned the itinerary and realized they would be passing quite near the battlegrounds of Boyne, the historic engagement Riley once had depicted as *the watershed of misery for all Gaels*. This graphic description now returned in all its gruesome clarity. Angus imagined the year 1690, and the great Protestant armies of William of Orange, well-armored and in command of the high ground, taking dead aim at the out-manned Catholic troops of James II, mired in the mud of the Boyne Valley. This bloody battle was to become the seminal event of Protestant and Catholic relations in Ulster for generations.

Sadly, for the offspring of the defeated Catholics it would become an eternal cry of despair, portending future deprivations. And, for the descendants of the victorious Protestants, it would become an annual celebration, a drumbeat of dominance to be thumped resoundingly into the heads of those who might wish to challenge the Order of Orange. As Lady Gregory put it; *Hatred answering hatred; death answering death; through the generations like clerks at the Mass*. Their whole existence seemed locked in terrorism as if their very being depended on it.

Equally memorable was Riley's grim but ironic version of the financial support the Pope had given William of Orange. Louis XIV, the Catholic King of France, whose troops fought on the side of James II, had challenged the Pope's authority, and was seen as a threat to the Vatican. Angus supposed it was in keeping with the hypocrisy of both religions for the Papacy to surrender to sectarian politics. But why help finance the Protestants against one of the strongest outposts of Catholicism? As with the entire chronology of this war without end, it defied all reason. Indeed, as Riley had once pointed out in a fit of rage, the course of Irish history and the balance of power in Europe had been changed forever at Boyne, when William of Orange regained the English throne due, in no small part, to the role of the Pope.

Today, however, these three old rivals weren't interested in revisiting historic battlegrounds. They were sorting out personal conflicts of a more recent past. Angus still was mystified at this change in Collier. Perhaps it was his reluctance to erase from memory the animosity he had harbored against Ames in their youth. At best, Angus was ambivalent toward the new Collier. The skepticism of a reporter still filtered information before he accepted it as fact. He was not yet convinced that someone who had behaved so abominably as Collier Ames could have undergone such a dramatic change. But, for now, he would suspend judgment.

"I noticed you brought your old hickories," said Mick.

"It's the set I used in the 1930 British Isles Cup," replied Collier . . . "a reminder of Riley on the way to his funeral."

"That tournament was played at Royal County Down, wasn't it?" asked Angus.

"Yes, it was. And it may have been my most memorable championship, even though I was beaten by O'Neill."

"I'm sure Riley was still driven by a desire to make the Walker Cup team," said Angus.

"After all those years of extraordinary play, he'd been written off the amateur golf scene by a group of old men who couldn't break a hundred if they picked up at the 16th. They were, however, quite keen on putting the mere Irish in their place . . . behind the English."

"That's a much different tune than you used to sing, Collier," said Mick. "You now seem resentful of Sir Thomas and his crowd. Back then, you were the ultimate snob."

"To think I once aspired to be one of them. It's more than I can bear at times."

"Surely, you wouldn't indict the behaviour of all the members of the Royal & Ancient," said Angus.

"Of course not. But on balance, the organisation is an extension of the so-called ruling class. Those who make the rules, must rule. Their arrogance . . . their self-righteous pronouncements . . . standing in judgment of those beneath them . . . all so very typical of imperial Britain."

"Careful, Ames, you're beginning to sound like a socialist," said Mick, chuckling.

"Hardly. Just pro-republican and anti-monarchist. Our system of deifying royalty has been outdated for more than a century. Progress demands that Great Britain stop worshiping a ruling family whose blood, like all the rest of us, is red, not blue. The Irish nationalists were right to resist the oath of loyalty to the King of England during the 1920 treaty talks."

"That high and mighty resistance ultimately led to a civil war in Ireland," Angus reminded Collier.

"Yes, well, it is undoubtedly easier for those of us who have stayed above the fray to judge which sacrifices should be made in order to secure freedom. I often wonder how courageous we'd be if put to the ultimate test."

"Like Riley O'Neill?" asked Mick.

"He, at least, lived his convictions, rather than just talk about them, like the rest of us cowards."

"Tell us about the tournament, Collier," said Angus. "I'd stopped competing by then and only read about it."

"I usually bore my audience to death by first describing the course. But I'll gladly make an exception in your case, since you've both played it."

"We don't mind being bored by you, Ames," said Angus. "You perfected the art years ago. Don't stop now on our account. Right Mick?"

"What else can we do? Collier has us right where he wants us, trapped on a train, a captive audience. Besides, it's been years since I played there,"

Mick replied. "As I recall, Old Tom Morris laid it out in 1889 for the princely sum of four pounds, twenty."

"About what you'd pay for a double shot of Jameson's Irish Whiskey today, Mick," Collier replied, coolly ignoring their swipes at his behaviour "One of the many bargains bestowed upon the game of golf by its first true patron, Old Mr. Morris."

"I remember reading somewhere that the 9th is the most photographed hole in the world," said Angus.

"Undoubtedly," said Collier. "It's a stern par four of over 420 metres, requiring your best tee ball to carry that colossal sand dune guarding the right side and reach a thin ribbon of fairway situated in the valley some eighty feet below."

Nothing more needed saying. Angus and Mick once had played there, and Collier's description of the 9th brought it all back. Each had experienced the blue-green crescent of Dundrum Bay at their backs, the majestic Mountains of Mourne in their faces, and the carmine spire of the Slieve Donard Hotel as the target. Few sights in golf were more captivating. Both agreed the 9th was the signature hole of Royal County Down, but stunning vistas from any point on the course earned it the rank of *first among equals* to the other holes.

"It has an unusual number of blind shots, similar to Lahinch," Angus remarked. "Not that blind shots detract from the quality of a course. Camouflage is the art of golf course design. Whether the target is completely, or partially obscured, the masters introduce an element of doubt in order to identify the best players."

"That's certainly true of Royal County Down," continued Mick. "It has a mixture of smallish greens and narrow fairways . . . diabolical bunkers and massive sandhills."

"In Spring, the entire grounds are laced with yellow blooms of gorse and, in Autumn, blanketed with the lavender of heather," added Angus. The melody of Royal County Down had returned to them, complete with lyrics.

"You most certainly have been there," said Collier, knowing any description he might conjure would be no match for the image they had just painted.

"Riley must have been very much at home at Royal County Down, given the many blind shots required at his home course of Lahinch," Angus said.

"I suppose," said Mick. "But it's one thing to play the blind shots offered by your own course, and quite another to face those of an unfamiliar one."

"I couldn't agree more," said Collier. "Riley was mentally prepared to play the blind shots at Royal County Down. And, rather than complain about them as most golfers do, he accepted the unseen as part of the examination. But only by playing those shots over and over can one become even moderately comfortable playing them. That's where I had an edge."

"What happened in the final? asked Angus.

"We were both damned lucky to get through to the final."

"You outlasted Sean O'Sullivan 2 and 1 in the semis," said Mick. "And I believe Riley held off Jamie Ferguson 1 up on the 45th hole."

"An exceptional memory for someone in his dotage, Mick," Collier joked. "O'Sullivan was also a member of County Down, and in far better form than I. But, he found the dreaded whins, as we say, on the 14th and 15th, to hand me the match."

"The marvel of the tournament, though, had to be Riley's victory over Ferguson," continued Collier. "It may have been the best stretch of amateur golf ever played. They were both twelve better than the card on the day. Riley holed all the odd six footers in overtime to keep his chances alive. It was as if he were willing his way back to the brutal 9th, so he could take advantage of his length."

"Ferguson was no slouch off the tee either," noted Angus.

"No, he surely was not. When they reached the 9th, their 45th hole, it was pitch dark, black as a coal miner's arse. The spire of the Slieve Donard was nowhere to be seen. Now faced with the ultimate blind shot, Riley blasted a drive so immense that, years later, the members imbedded a plaque in his honor at the spot where his ball came to rest. Many times, nowadays, my goal is to pass Riley's plaque with my second shot."

"Riley went on to birdie the 9th," said Mick.

"Indeed he did. And, if you ask anyone in Newcastle over the age of fifty, they'll say they saw *The Drive*, and the niblick second he laid stone dead. Of course, there were no more than half a dozen spectators that day."

"How did either of you find the energy to play well in the final?" asked Mick.

"Thankfully, the weather changed, and the ninety degree temperatures were replaced overnight by rain and cool breezes."

"Playing each other once again must have brought out the best in you," said Angus.

"There was a time when our matches brought out the best of my golf and the worst of my behavior. But I received the ultimate lesson in sportsmanship from Riley that day. It changed my outlook on many aspects of life."

"As I recall, you went extra holes," said Mick.

"Yes, but Riley had the match won on the 36th."

"How so?" asked Angus.

"Well, in those days, you will recall we played stymies," said Collier. "If your opponent's ball came to rest between your ball and the hole, your opponent was not required to mark his ball. You are required to play around it, or chip over it."

"Golf finally came to its senses when it changed that silly rule," said Mick, disgustedly. "Playing stymies wasn't golf, it was tiddly-winks."

"More often than not, the result was an extra stroke and loss of the hole. On the 4th hole of our match, I stymied Riley, and made him try to chip over my ball for the halve. He failed, made bogey, and I won the hole."

"That's the Collier we know," said Mick jokingly.

"We reached the last all square," said Collier, ignoring Mick's jab, "Riley putted first and left me stymied for my par putt. After he marked, I had an easy two-footer to tie."

"If he'd chosen to make you play the stymie, as was his right under the rules," Angus interjected, "you probably would have lost the hole and the match."

"Instead, we played on."

"That may have been his way of showing how unfairly the Brits applied their rules to control the Irish," said Angus.

"Whatever his motives, knowing how I had treated him in the past, and on that very day, caused me to rethink my views of both Riley and the Irish."

"After your unexpected break, you probably just gave in and let him win," said Mick, winking at Angus..

"Not at all," laughed Collier, "my conscience hadn't kicked in quite that fast. No, he won by being the better player. On our 40th hole, he flagged a driving iron some 215 metres through a crosswind that damn near blew us off the tee . . . a fitting way to close out the match."

"Just as you had closed Riley out on the 40th at Muirfield in '21," Angus recalled.

"Justice had been served," sighed Collier.

Since when had Collier become interested in justice? Angus had never seen Ames concerned with anything but winning, and his own self interests. So, he asked the inevitable. "Where was Rawahli during the match?"

"What on earth do you mean by that?" Ames demanded.

"Well, every time I watched you compete with Riley, your man Rawahli seemed to show up and change the momentum your way," Angus said. "I was just wondering why he wasn't with you at Royal County Down?"

"You don't know the first thing about Rawahli."

"No, I don't," agreed Angus. "But surely you can understand our curiosity. He seemed to be so important to your game."

"Rawahli is none of your concern," snapped Ames.

"We always assumed he was some sort of guru," said Mick, "odd fellow . . . remarkable, really."

"The only thing remarkable about Rawahli was his will to survive. He had no interest in golf. To him, golf was a petty pursuit, nothing more than pampered adults trying to escape humdrum lives. The daily grind may be monotonous, but certainly is not dangerous. He always wondered how golfers could take seriously the predicaments they faced on the links, when he had escaped circumstances far more grim. Once I understood what it must have meant for him to cope with genuine peril, golf became easy."

"You mean when he rubbed that talisman and mumbled those incantations, he wasn't imparting some special power to you, or casting a spell over your opponents?" asked Angus.

"Of course not," Collier replied coolly.

"Well, it certainly seemed so," said Mick.

"What Rawahli imparted to me was perspective. Golf just isn't very important in the grand scheme. Now, the fact that my opponents found his rituals mysterious, and his presence intimidating, was their problem, not mine."

"I suppose you did nothing to cultivate that image," said Mick.

"I didn't have to. He was merely being himself."

"Just what did Rawahli endure that was so terrible?" asked Angus.

Pressed by his old colleagues for details, the harrowing story of Rawahli was revealed, bit by bit, beginning with his mother, Mohasha Kundun. Collier explained that Mohasha had served as an interpreter for a minor British diplomat, who, prior to his appointment to the embassy, had been a soldier of the Crown, best known for his killing of Islamic fundamentalists in a skirmish at the Kyber Pass in 1901, roughly on today's border of India and Pakistan.

When the radical Muslims discovered this foreigner had fathered a son by Mohasha, they were determined to take their revenge. After several failed attempts to assassinate the man, these fanatics settled for retribution against mother and son, reasoning, Ames supposed, that it was vital to impress upon Muslims as well as non-Muslims, that the all-powerful Allah would extract penalties in the extreme for such betrayals. The boy and his mother were kidnapped from the British embassy in Karachi by the extremists and taken to Bombay.

Before they disemboweled Mohasha in full view of her son, they cut out the boy's tongue, a gratuitous act of brutality intended to illustrate to the Christian infidels the dire consequences of occupying their country and defiling their culture. Inexplicably, when the barbaric deeds were complete, these self-appointed avengers released the boy, presumably to suffer in silence, a life of heart-wrenching memories. But Rawahli, explained

Ames, slipped down to the docks of Bombay, stowed away a steamer trunk, and arrived in London by British liner three months later.

"My . . . good . . . God!" exclaimed Mick.

Angus was struck dumb. He had no idea Rawahli had suffered so. He always thought of him as a mystic and a manservant. None of that mattered now, but it didn't keep him from prying.

"How did he become your valet?" Angus wheedled.

Rawahli was one topic on which Collier had no intention of telling the whole truth. He was ashamed of his real motives in taking the Pakistani under his wing. They were both cruel and calculating. During his University days, Ames was intoxicated by British imperialism. Why did the English own things and countries and people? Because they could. Back then, that was reason enough. Collier thought it clever and sophisticated to have at his beck and call, a servant, especially a half-breed Scottish-Pakistani mix. It was exotic, and it mirrored the state of British domination. But the version he gave Angus and Mick was plain vanilla.

"We met at Cambridge during my first year. He was doing odd jobs at the University during the day and reading books under street lamps by night. Where he got the books, we never knew, but it was always the teachings of Buddha or the Dalai Lama. He developed his own beliefs and rituals, and trust me, they weren't Islamic. He couldn't speak, of course, but I had no trouble understanding him. At first, he caddied for me, but had little interest in the game of golf. It was the spiritual that he cared about, cleansing the mind and soul of imperfections."

"Something to be said for that," sighed Angus.

"We thought he might be a creature of the occult," said Mick, "putting the hex on Riley when he played against you."

Collier's snigger seemed far too smug. The act was well-rehearsed and performed to perfection. Ames had seen the possibilities early on . . . the power in those eyes, the mystery in the garb and the sapphire and the rites. He showed Rawahli how to dress, and how to behave, and when to show up for the greatest effect. Ames would never admit it, even now, but what Angus and Mick and, most of all, Riley, had seen so long ago, was precisely what he had wanted them to see . . . a shaman capable of producing the unexpected. And what a production it had been, giving confidence to Ames, and depriving his opponents of theirs. The edge was his.

"I have no idea how you could think that," he lied. "Rawahli Kundun was nothing more than my valet. He took only a passing interest in my golf. It is true that he practiced his religious beliefs openly, and dressed as he pleased. My most sincere apologies if any of that gave you the wrong impression."

"There may be someone from the old days who would believe that rubbish, Collier," said Mick, "but we're not among them."

"You, sir, are entitled to believe as you wish," Collier sniffed, putting aside the topic of Rawahli once and for all, and imposing a ten minute hiatus in their conversation.

"After he won, Riley was finally named to the Walker Cup team for the 1932 matches at The Country Club in Brookline, Massachusetts," said Mick, volunteering a change of topics.

"Forgan could no longer blackball him," said Collier, as if to unburden his conscience.

Another curious observation, coming from Ames, but Mick chose to ease around it. "Odd, don't you think, that Riley chose not to participate in the '32 Walker Cup."

"No, he retired instead," said Angus. "Since Jones played his last Walker Cup in 1930 after winning the Grand Slam, Riley probably felt there was no reason to play."

"I think Riley was quite disappointed at not getting the chance to play Bobby Jones," said Collier.

"In the end, I think it was enough for Riley to finally win the British Isles Cup and be named to the Walker Cup team," said Angus. "He had nothing more to prove in the game of golf, except to beat Bobby Jones. And, with Jones' retirement, that wasn't going to happen. It was as good a time for Riley to retire from golf as it was for his idol."

"Too bad they didn't play against one another. I'd have put my money on Riley," said Mick.

"As would I," Collier seconded.

"Me too," added Angus.

"*I*," corrected Collier. "*I would too*, not *me too*."

"Good God, man. You haven't really changed at all," groaned Angus, recalling the grammar lesson he had received from Ames at Muirfield over fifty years ago.

"Just trying to get a rise out of you Angus," chuckled Collier. "I thought that might do it. Besides, I'm Cambridge trained. It's what we do, you know . . . correct others, that is."

"And here I thought being obnoxious came naturally to you," laughed Angus. "I had no idea there was formal training for that sort of behaviour. In any event, I think you'll find that *'me too'* is acceptable usage."

"Acceptable though it may have become, never will it be proper," replied Collier.

"Sort of like the Irish, then, accepted, but never quite proper?" Angus parried.

"Touche," laughed Collier.

"Score one for the Scotsman," added Mick.

Chapter 2

They passed through the township of Dundalk, and Angus could no longer contain his fascination with all things Irish. How had a Scotsman like him come to admire Erin's proud but ill-fated struggle for freedom? Riley was partly to blame, to be sure. But it had gone beyond that. He and Riley hadn't spoken for years, separated by time and space and circumstance. Yet, Angus was forever reading the *Irish Independent*, and the poetry and prose of Ireland's great fraternity of authors.

He had always admired those who were able to consign their lives so completely to their cause. Riley had done that. Oh, his Irish friend was by no means without fault. There were many aspects of O'Neill's nature that did not wear well with Angus, but his single-minded pursuit of a free and unified Ireland was not one of those shortcomings. And so, from afar, Angus had adopted the Irish crusade against England as his own, cheering its successes and lamenting its failures. But, rooting for the Irish was a bit like pulling for Riley against Collier in the British Isles Cup . . . there always seemed to be far more bemoaning of defeat than celebration of victory.

Surely Mick, an avowed Irishman, would indulge Angus. And, given his self-professed change of heart toward the Irish, even Collier might suffer this curiosity over an Ireland not easily understood.

"When do we reach The Pale of Dublin?" Angus asked absently.

"We just passed into it," replied Collier.

"You know the story, then," said Mick. "When England began its more serious domination of Ireland in the 1600's, *The Pale* was the region surrounding Dublin over which English control seemed relatively secure."

"As the Brits were fond of saying," added Collier, "*beyond the Pale, lay the wild and untamed Irish.*"

"Aye, they were regarded by the Brits as little more than savages," Mick added, "speaking Gaelic and living a wretched life of nomadic squalor under the Irish clan chieftains."

"Ah, Dublin," intoned Collier, "one of the world's great cities . . . founded by the Vikings in 841, but it's name comes from the Gaelic words *dubh*, meaning black, and *linn*, for pool, a reference to the pool of black water in the River Liffey that runs through it."

Ever the journalist, Angus turned a phrase describing Dublin the others assumed he must have lifted from one of those great Irish writers about whom he always spoke; "one can imagine the Liffey then, as now, flowed from Kildare to the Irish Sea as would Guinness from brewing vats into wooden casks."

"Curious city," Collier opined. "Class warfare has been foisted upon the Irish since the beginning of English dominance. But nowhere in Ireland are the distinctions between the native-born Irish Gaels and those repotted Brits we call the Anglo-Irish more pronounced than in Dublin."

"And nowhere," replied Mick, "can one find a better illustration of the prevailing state of Anglo-Irish attitudes toward the Gaels than the remarks of the Duke of Wellington, whose family had its roots in England, but flourished in Ireland for more than three centuries."

"What exactly was it Wellington said, Mick?" Collier asked, tongue in cheek, confident the Ulsterman would know.

"The Duke is rumored to have said that, '*merely being born in a stable, does not make one a horse*'."

"Well, Dubliners changed the name of the Wellington Bridge to *Ha'Penny Bridge*," replied Angus. "Probably their way of thumbing their noses at the Duke's insults."

*   *   *

The sun slid behind a bank of menacing clouds, and the men began to consider a refreshment before their arrival in Dublin. Just a wee dram, perhaps, to steel them against what was sure to be a typical May evening in Dublin . . . raw. The bar steward returned with three Kummels in chilled glasses and a platter of fried oyster canapes. Angus and Mick were now as anxious to learn of Sinead and Sir Thomas as Collier had been reluctant to talk of them, and his reticence had only aroused their interest.

To pass the time, Angus did what old newsmen do best, observing others, searching for the story in their midst, giving free rein to an always fertile imagination. He watched as a lanky man in a tweed suit and felt fedora made his way down the aisle to sit across from them. The man lit a long-stemmed pipe and cradled the bowl in fingers made leathery by the elements. His moustache was untrimmed and drooped over his lower lip. He removed his hat and crossed his legs, placing an elbow on his knee and peering out the window until joined by another, taller gentlemen, also in tweed. The second fellow's clothing was better kept, and the shoes more polished. Despite their subtle difference in appearance, these men seemed more alike than not, as if cut from the same bolt of cloth. They nodded introductions and spoke to each other in muffled tones, quiet and cryptic.

What sort of story might Angus develop merely by studying the behavior of these two men? That they were acquaintances was evident from the ease each displayed in the other's presence. But as he eavesdropped, it was difficult for Angus to determine whether they were also friends. The deference each afforded the other seemed too wide a berth between chums. Perhaps they were rivals. If so, it would explain the wariness that seemed to exist between them, as though each had a secret, something personal to be withheld one from the other, a ploy to gain a competitive edge.

Discarding the mysterious, Angus turned to a familiar angle . . . golf. Struck by the resemblance of these two men to Harry Vardon and James Braid, two-thirds of the golfing triumvirate of the '20s, he whispered this uncanny similarity to his traveling companions. Collier and Mick were not as taken by the likeness, but humored Angus by discussing Vardon's record six Open victories, and, of course, his invention of the overlapping grip, the staple of modern golfing fundamentals. They paid tribute to Braid's prowess as a golfer, but agreed his most significant contribution to the game was his brilliance as a designer . . . the Kings Course at Gleneagles being lauded as one of his best. If only J. H. Taylor, the last of this storied trio could have been present, Angus thought, his rapture continuing to evolve, the six of them might have concocted a golfing competition between amateurs and professionals.

That's it! Now he had a scoop. A championship to rival the Ryder and Walker Cups. It would pit the best pros, twelve men, like Vardon and Braid and Taylor, against the twelve finest of amateur golf, including Ames and Callahan and . . . yes, perhaps even MacKenzie. Such were the musings of a man now viewing life from the caboose instead of the engine, someone whose dreams of glory had become more dream than glory.

But whose name would it bear? Angus persisted in this pointless abstraction. Vardon had already been honored by a trophy given in his name to the professional with the low scoring average for a season. But Braid or Taylor? Had they distinguished themselves for the ages as had Sarazen or Hagen? And what about an amateur whose skills were unbounded by time? *The O'Neill Cup* for instance. Enough nonsense, he scoffed. Nowadays, such a competition and its trophy would undoubtedly be named for some stodgy business tycoon or slick politician. Besides, it had been decades since golf's top amateurs were a match for the best professionals. Just as the halcyon days of the amateur had disappeared with Bobby Jones, the idyllic notions of nostalgia and altruism were yesterday's news. Today, the front page was reserved for glitz and greed. Angus finally abandoned his musings and ventured a question only someone with a reporter's temerity could have posed.

"What *did* happen on October 25, 1929, Collier?"

"Sir Thomas Forgan met his unfortunate demise," Ames replied curtly.

"I've noticed you always refer to him as Sir Thomas," said Mick, "and never as your father."

"That's because, to me, he was Sir Thomas Forgan, M.P.," Collier replied, stiffly. "My father was Sinclair Ames."

For years, this had been Collier's stock response. Early on, he discovered it was easier to denounce Sir Thomas Forgan's relationship and take refuge in the anonymity of his adoptive parents, Sinclair and Millicent Ames. But, deep down, the memories of his foster home brought him pain of a much different sort. The Ames had been anything but kind to Collier. In fact, they had been quite callous, enthusiastically pocketing Forgan's support checks, while bestowing upon Collier little, if any, affection. His strongest memory of his step-parents was that they had barely tolerated him. Collier had always felt their indifference was more humiliating than hostility might have been. It took so little effort to be ambivalent. Even hatred requires work. Their relationship had been sort of like melba toast . . . too real to deny . . . too bland to be considered sustenance.

From the moment Forgan brought Collier to live with them, the arrangement had been nothing more than a business transaction, a second source of income. Had Sir Thomas not insisted at the outset that the cost of Collier's attending Eton and Cambridge be paid from Forgan's monthly stipend to the Ames, the money, most assuredly, would have been diverted toward the purchase of a country cottage in Sussex, or a new sedan. At the very least, the Ames would have extended their annual vacations in the Cotswolds, while sentencing Collier to do time at some out-of-the-way boarding school.

And so, it had just come down to a matter of convenience for Collier. Whenever anyone ascribed to him a father-son tie with the disreputable Sir Thomas Forgan, he simply referred to the lesser of two evils, his less loathsome, but equally uncaring foster parents, Sinclair and Millicent Ames. It was easier to explain and much less painful.

"If you don't wish to relive that night, just say so," said Angus, "and we won't broach the subject again."

"There is really no reason to dodge the event any longer. After all, it occurred fifty years ago. All those involved have passed on, or will soon."

"I know you took the Stranraer ferry to Larne in August of '29, along with Sir Thomas," said Angus. "But why was the R & A's solicitor, Selby O'Bannion, involved in the matter?"

"Well, the affairs of Sir Thomas were of great concern to the Royal & Ancient."

"Something beyond the amateur rules violations?" asked Mick.

"Oh my, yes! The business of amateurism paled in comparison to the much larger muddle he had created."

"What sort of mischief was he up to this time?" asked Mick.

"For several years, Sir Thomas had been in business with Lawrence Dirleton. I'm sure you remember Dirleton from Muirfield."

Angus shuddered at the memory of the forty foot snake Dirleton had holed to oust him from the British Isles Cup Championship at Muirfield. Though he hadn't thought of it for years, the image of the putt hovering in mid-air before disappearing into the cup was as vivid now as it had been in 1921.

"He came to Sir Thomas with an idea for an investment company that would buy equities listed on the surging New York Stock Exchange, sort of a forerunner to today's mutual funds."

Reaching for another canape, Collier shook it gently into a napkin to free any loose crumbs from the crust before continuing.

"The post-war boom was seductive for many of the Royal & Ancient patricians. The company formed by Dirleton, known as Bruntsfield Securities, Ltd., was portrayed by Sir Thomas as a perfect vehicle for parlaying family fortunes into Carnegie-like wealth."

"I've heard of Bruntsfield Securities," said Mick. "There's nothing corrupt about operating an investment company."

"Of course not. If it's done with integrity," he cautioned. "I don't know if Sir Thomas was aware of Dirleton's every deception, but he had used his position at the R & A to convince the members they were certain to make millions. When the stock market crashed in October of '29, the investors in Bruntsfield Securities were ruined. But by that time, Dirleton and Sir Thomas had managed to skim considerable fortunes from their clients accounts."

"So that's why Forgan left so hastily," exclaimed Angus. "He saw the whole scheme coming unraveled."

"But why did you leave Scotland at the same time, Collier?" Mick interrogated.

"I was threatened by a client of Bruntsfield's. The R & A told him Sir Thomas was my father, and that I must have had some involvement. He thought I'd repay some of his losses."

"You weren't involved, were you?" Angus asked pointedly.

"Not in the slightest. I thought I could follow Sir Thomas to Colby and convince him to make restitution to his clients, rather than face prosecution."

"Was he receptive?" asked Angus.

"Not in the least. He believed these dupes got their due, since it was greed that turned them to him in the first place."

"Heartless bastard," Mick muttered.

"But something terrible must have happened for you to be silent about it all these years," pressed Angus.

"Was it the IRA that killed Forgan, or was he done in by disgruntled investors seeking their revenge?" asked Mick.

"Nothing so sinister as all that. And yet, in a way, what did happen was much worse. The night of the 25th was terribly chaotic. The senseless murders of innocent Catholics by the Orange Lodges during the July marching season had brought a series of reprisals onto Protestants in County Down by the IRA. We had been forewarned Colby Manor would be their next target."

"Is there no law and order in Ulster?" groaned Angus.

"Vigilantes on both sides of the conflict have controlled the fate of the Irish forever. Unfortunately, Sir Thomas responded to the threat by inviting the Ulster Special Constabulary, or B Specials, as these Protestant ruffians were known, to encamp at Colby as a deterrent to the IRA."

"Sounds like your home became a battleground," said Mick.

"It was well-fortified and guarded by men who thrived on violence. The prospect of killing members of the IRA had these thugs drooling all over themselves."

"Dangerous circumstances," said Angus.

"As hazardous as the situation had become at Colby, I've chosen to believe it was his own vanity that led to the death of Sir Thomas," said Collier, motioning for another round of Kummel.

"Oh, he might have eventually perished at the hands of the IRA," Collier continued. "And, there may have been investors desperate enough to take justice into their own hands. Sir Thomas certainly received many threats. But those he bilked were gentlemen, more inclined to end their own lives than his. In fact, some did, rather than face the humiliation of losing the family fortune."

"I find it hard to believe anyone would have wanted Forgan dead more than the IRA, or more than those he had bilked . . . unless . . ." Mick stopped, cold.

A pall fell over the conversation. Angus and Mick stared at Collier, then at each other. They knew where logic was taking them. Neither wanted to follow this line of reasoning, but since Mick had started down this path, it was up to him to complete the inquiry.

"Surely Sinead didn't . . ." he began, clumsily, "someone else must have . . ."

Collier interrupted. "As I said, I've chosen to believe Sir Thomas himself set in motion the cause of his own death. In the months prior to our arrival at Colby, Sinead had written the estate's caretaker, Mr. Trimble Savage, seeking employment for her eighteen year old daughter, Kathleen."

Collier brushed both palms down the creases of his slacks to remove any crumbs. He emptied the last drop of Kummel from his glass and stared thoughtfully out the window at the Irish countryside rushing past. It was obvious Ames was still loath to speak of these events, distant though they were.

"Savage accommodated Sinead. After all, she had been a faithful servant of the estate. So, he had given Kathleen a position as chambermaid. Tragically, in the short time Sir Thomas had been at Colby, it was apparent he had designs on Kathleen of . . . well . . ."

"He had no shame?" Angus muttered.

"Savage had contacted Sinead in Lahinch to warn her of Forgan's behaviour," Collier continued. "She arrived on the 25th to retrieve Kathleen from harm's way. That's when all the worst collided."

"Don't tell us Forgan had already forced himself onto the poor lass by this time!" Mick exclaimed.

"We hoped not, but knew it was only a matter of time. I met Sinead at the entrance to the estate. She explained to me the unspeakable particulars between her and Sir Thomas so long ago."

Collier paused to gather his emotions. "She told me how sorry she was for having abandoned me, but in the urgency of the moment, we had no time to reflect on her ordeal. We simply had to distance them from Sir Thomas. Then the wrath of Catholics and Protestants complicated everything."

"You mean the IRA attacked while you and Sinead and Kathleen were fleeing the premises?" asked Mick.

"Precisely. The IRA had planted a firebomb in one of the B Special vehicles. When the ignition was switched on, the van exploded. It was filled with munitions that spontaneously detonated in every direction. It was as though the entire compound was under siege."

"Holy Jesus!" shouted Mick. "It's a wonder you were able to escape."

"We all began to run down a forested lane to the south side of the manor. The B Specials had secured it for us as a safe route in the event of an all-out attack. As Sinead and Kathleen and I were running, we could make out Sir Thomas just ahead, also making his escape on the moonlit lane. Apparently, he believed we were IRA men giving chase, because he suddenly veered off the gravel path and into the heath. That's when he met disaster."

"Shrapnel from the explosives?" asked Angus.

"A fate far worse for all of us. I immediately recognized his diversion as the peat bog. By the time we reached him, he was waist deep in the muck and sinking rapidly. The three of us just stood and watched as his life was drawn, inch by inch, into the black, bottomless pit."

"Nothing you could have done," said Mick, with a smug look of satisfaction, borne of knowing Forgan had gotten his due.

"We'll never know, because we never tried. We just waited in those fatal few moments, listening to his dismal cries for help . . . so repentant . . . so powerless . . . so in need of our aid as others had been in need of his. We simply did as he had done . . . turned our backs on his pleas."

"You might have joined him in the mire had you attempted a rescue," said Angus, "or taken a bullet from the gunfire at the manor."

"Our only thought at the time was to get to safety. It was after Sinead and Kathleen were on their way back to Lahinch, and the panic had subsided, that remorse began to set in. To this day, I hear his screams."

Chapter 3

$\mathcal{A}$ngus and Mick sat in dazed quiet on the scorched old sofa of the observation car, their solitude interrupted only by the clacking of the train clicking off sections of rail. A mist fell over the seaside hamlet of Malahide in dingy layers of gray as gloomy as the mood inside the car. Approaching from Dublin's north side, Portmarnock Golf Links lay just beyond the strand of dunes erupting to form a craggy coastline along Howth Harbor. Though the links were not visible through the leaden drizzle, they could sense the presence of Portmarnock just as surely as they could sense Collier's sorrow.

"I gather that was the last you saw of Sinead," said Angus.

"Those were troubled times. Sir Thomas' investment scam victims were suing his estate to recover any assets they could. I was inundated with claims, so it left little time to contact Sinead. In any event, I understood her discomfort with the horrifying memories. My presence may have served to remind her of Sir Thomas' brutality. It seems we can never reclaim the past."

"But you were able to protect Colby from Forgan's creditors," said Mick.

"Much to my surprise, Sir Thomas had not yet spent all his spoils. The money had been deposited into the Bank of Ireland. I returned all the cash on hand. Then, I disposed of Sir Thomas' properties in England and Scotland and Portugal, and auctioned off his automobile collection, except, of course, the Deusey."

"And you apparently managed to retain the manor and some acreage," noted Angus.

"The original demense of 500 acres was exempt from creditor's claims, protected by the terms of a grant from the king. I deeded the remainder of the estate to its rightful owners, the native Irish that had owned it before the Forgans."

"But when we passed through the estate this morning, the manor appeared to be in its original condition," said Mick.

"I raised enough cash to satisfy the creditors' claims and had a bit left over to rebuild Colby. Unexpectedly, the Irish to whom I returned the land offered their labor . . . a gesture most kind."

"You must feel some sense of vindication at the way things turned out," said Mick.

"I hope I've done something to help make up for the pain so many have suffered at the hand of Sir Thomas."

"Odd, how justice works," said Angus. "First, Forgan receives his due, swallowed up by the very ancestral lands he and the British had stolen from the Irish. Then, the victims of the investment scam get their restitution. You've done well by doing good, Collier. But what about the rest of your life . . . have the blind lady's scales been kind to you?"

"I suspect I'm no different than either of you, a product of my experiences. It's been agreeable for the most part, marred only by the betrayal of Sir Thomas, and the absence of any real family. Yet, in the striving, I think I've become a better person. The scales may have begun to tip in my favor."

"And that, my friends, is all we can take from this life," sighed Mick, "the comfort of knowing we've done all we can each day to improve."

Angus' doubt now seemed misplaced. Ames *had* changed. Trying to rectify Sir Thomas Forgan's misdeeds had been an impossible burden to bear. His empathy for the man was as deep now as his resentment had been in their youth, the prickliness between them blunted by Collier's painful contrition, as if barbs of Scottish thistle and thorns of English rose had been plucked at last from their proud flesh. Just as there had been no words to comfort Angus for the loss of Sarah and Patrick, there was no way, now, to console Collier.

"What about Kathleen?" asked Mick. "Have you tried to bridge the past with her? After all, she's what . . . your half-sister?"

"And Riley is my half-brother. No, sharing a womb wasn't enough to bind us. We were separated by the gulf as wide as the one that has forever divided Ulster . . . religious differences between Catholic and Protestant . . . cultural differences between Irish and English."

"But you had given the O'Neills 1500 acres of land," Angus countered. "Surely they appreciated your generosity."

"I don't know how they felt. Sinead died of diphtheria in 1934 without ever setting foot on the property. Riley and Kathleen were joint heirs to the land, but they also avoided visiting. It's been leased to the family O'Shaunessy all these years."

"You never spoke to Sinead or Riley or Kathleen after October of '29?" asked Mick.

"Not once," said Collier. "I took their attitude to be a statement of pride. They resented the theft of their lands by the English, and the plantation of Scots like the Forgans. But when they got it back, they were too proud to thank me."

Collier reached for the last of the canapes and tucked it carefully into his mouth, disguising his ravenous hunger with refinement, as only the cultured are able to do. The bar steward bussed their table and announced the train's arrival in Dublin. The vitality Collier had shown at Newcastle was now gone. He was tired and, in the last light of day, his face resembled the rumpled folds of an unmade bed, disheveled by the stress of old age, very much in need of smoothing.

"I don't think they were ungrateful, just conditioned not to trust the motives of any Prod, including me. Maybe, especially me, given the acts of Sir Thomas. They didn't want to give the impression they needed the land. The whole matter was awkward. Perhaps they felt I was trying to purchase their affection."

"Weren't you, in a way?" asked Mick.

"Have you ever tried to buy someone's friendship, Mick? No, I merely hoped they might see me in a more favorable light. I wanted no part of false affection."

"But, I am surprised you saw no sign of gratitude whatsoever," said Angus.

"Oh, Riley did send an invitation to compete with him in the 1932 West of Ireland Foursomes Championship at Lahinch. But I didn't respond. I just couldn't believe he meant it."

"Seems to me you were both wrong," said Angus. "You expected the O'Neills to fall all over you with thanks, and when Riley reached out, you rejected him as insincere. I suspect they were as mistaken about your desire to become part of the family as you were about the extent of their gratitude. Feelings are hard to express."

"Angus, that's my greatest fear. It's sad to think all these years have been wasted worrying about how we all felt toward each other and never bothering to simply ask. It would be sadder still to attend Riley's funeral and not talk to Kathleen."

"Is she still living in Lahinch?" asked Mick.

"She is. I rang her yesterday to tell her of my plans to attend Riley's services."

"Nothing more?" asked Angus. "Just notice of your trip?"

"She sounded tired. I'm sure she had a lot on her mind. I didn't want to impose by prattling on."

"Does she have any family besides you, now that Riley is gone?" asked Mick.

"I really know nothing of Kathleen's life these past decades. After Riley's service, I hope we can share the many detours our lives have taken."

"Aye, 'tis a dull road, indeed, that has no turns," Angus said, reminded at that moment of the old adage he had often heard Riley share during a philosophical moment, or when he was at a loss for words. "I expect Kathleen is just as anxious to share her life's travels as you are to share yours, Collier."

Chapter 4

*T*he train coasted into Pearse Station over a bridge spanning the River Liffey. Seeing Padraic Pearse's name reminded Angus of the many stories Riley had shared of his mentor. Perhaps the highest tribute Ireland could pay this patriotic bard, it seemed to Angus, was to fasten his name to a train station through which most visitors into Dublin would pass. As head-master of St. Edna's School until executed by the Crown for his role in the 1916 Easter Rising, Pearse had become an icon of dissent against England, as had his protégé Riley O'Neill.

Angus recalled the devotion in Riley's voice that time he had described Pearse's dream for St. Edna's. Riley was convinced this bilingual prep school for boys would spark a revival of the Gaelic culture among Irish Catholic youth. Its students, he said, would learn to speak their native Irish tongue to restore pride in Ireland and to rectify the British slant on history being taught in public schools. Riley often quoted the immortal words of the mythical warrior, Cuchulainn, etched onto one of the walls at St. Edna's . . . *I care not though I were to live but one day and night, if only my fame and my deeds live after me.* These words would become the hall-mark of Pearse's commitment to the Irish rebellion. They should have been his epitaph.

Angus arranged for the luggage to be delivered to the Shelbourne Hotel for their overnight stay. Tomorrow, they would board the train to Lahinch at the westbound terminal, Kingsbridge Station. Today, however, before heading to the hotel, the three men would explore the historic streets of Dublin that Riley and his fellow insurgents had fought to reclaim from the British in 1916.

They departed the station platform and strolled down Pearse Street toward O'Connell, crossing the Liffey to the Eden Quay where the massive statue of Daniel O'Connell loomed before them. *The Liberator*, thought Angus, stepping closer to admire the monument that had taken nearly twenty years to construct.

"The Irish couldn't have picked a better man to get them out from under the brutal Act of Union passed by the Brits in 1800," he remarked.

"I don't suppose there's ever been a law so misnamed," Mick replied.

Angus recounted for his companions, the history lecture in which Riley had proudly described how very close Wolfe Tone had come in 1798 to uniting Irish Protestants and Catholics against England. And in the aftermath of that brief glimpse of the possibilities of freedom, Riley had gone on to describe how England had stripped the Catholics of all human dignities . . . the *Act of Disunion*, he called it.

Taking a full thirty years to undo, Catholics were forbidden to speak Irish, or hold public office, or practice their religion. *'Gave 'em the buckle end o' the strap, y' know,'* was how Riley had described it.

"Just a few minor deprivations," Collier sighed.

"Tone was one of those rare visionaries in Irish history who was able, if only for a moment, to unite Protestants and Catholics alike in a common cause . . . the removal of the English from Ireland," Mick noted.

"His statue stands at St. Stephen's Green," said Angus. "We should visit him later."

"In light of all that had transpired on this island over the past four centuries, it seems only fitting for the Irish to honor Wolfe Tone as their *Prophet of Independence*," added Collier.

The three men walked north on O'Connell Street until they reached the General Post Office, or GPO, as it was better known by Dubliners. This magnificent Italianate structure, built in 1818, had become one of the most compelling symbols of the Easter Rising. Members of the Irish Citizen Army under the leadership of James Connolly seized the building on Easter Sunday, 1916 and, from its steps, Pearse read the *Proclamation of the Irish Republic*.

"How did that excerpt go?" asked Angus, searching for the words. "You know Mick, the one Riley would always quote during heated arguments."

"*The Irish Republic is entitled to the allegiance of every Irishman and Irishwoman*," Mick recited from memory . . ."*oblivious of the differences carefully fostered by an alien government which has divided a minority from the majority . . .*"

"Differences carefully fostered by England to divide Protestants and Catholics is more like it," Angus restated. "The rebels were on the mark with that grievance. The Brits always prop up their occupation of Ireland by emphasizing religious differences."

The trio stood examining the still-visible markings left by British bullets on the GPO's enormous portico columns. Artillery shells had forced these determined but doomed insurgents from their stronghold after only a week of fighting. It was an effort inspired entirely by passion, an outlandish grab for freedom to be equally admired and pitied.

"Riley was here," whispered Angus. "No wonder he never spoke of the experience. It must have been traumatic to face the overwhelming forces of England, then endure the summary execution of the rebellion's sixteen leaders."

"Not to mention the ridicule they received from an unsympathetic Dublin populace which acted put upon by the inconvenience!" Mick added cynically.

They entered the GPO, and a sculpture of the legendary Cuchulainn came into view. It seemed appropriate that the rebels' impetuous act of bravery would be memorialized by this immortal figure of Irish folklore. History would record their story with the same improbable proportions it had Cuchulainn's.

"Well, I see Lord Nelson is still absent without leave," Mick noted, as they stepped out of the GPO and into the intersection of North Earl and Henry Streets. "When I used to visit Dublin, I could count on him being right there," he said, pointing to the spot where the 135 foot pillar, topped by a statue of famed British Admiral Horatio Nelson had stood since the early 1800s.

Angus had long seen the method of the Brits. The statue of Lord Nelson, a compelling symbol of British military might, had been erected in the center of Dublin as a constant reminder to the Irish that the power of England was but a boat ride away. But in 1966, to commemorate the 50th anniversary of the 1916 Easter Rising, the IRA blew up Lord Nelson.

"His head is all that remains of the statue," Angus remarked with satisfaction. "It's kept on display in Dublin's Civic Museum."

"So very typical of both sides of the conflict," said Collier. "The destruction of human life and precious landmarks seems to be the favorite pastime here."

"Perhaps," replied Angus. "But, just as it served British purposes to remind Ireland of their military prowess, the IRA removed Lord Nelson to demonstrate he was not a hero to the Irish, and didn't belong in their pantheon of immortals."

"On the lighter side," intoned Mick, "it *was* a fleet of Spanish and French ships that Nelson had defeated in the Battle of Trafalgar. If the Admiral had lost, England and Ireland might be ruled today by the Catholics of France or Spain."

"Perish the thought," said Collier.

"I hadn't considered that possibility, Mick," said Angus. "Maybe the Irish should have left Nelson standing guard."

Continuing up O'Connell they crossed Cathal Brugha Street. Brugha, whose Anglicized name was Charles Burgess, had been one of the leaders of the 1916 Rising and had died during the Irish Civil War. Though he had accompanied Michael Collins and Arthur Griffith to the treaty talks, in the end, he had sided with Eamon de Valera and helped lead the hardliners into civil war. de Valera's defection, along with Brugha's, had always troubled Angus. Were it not for their refusal to swear allegiance to the Crown, he reasoned, Ireland might have been spared its bloody civil war. The mantle of leading Ireland might have fallen to Collins, a man with the broad appeal needed to unify the country. Instead, he was killed by followers of de Valera and Brugha, and the country's leadership became even more fragmented.

They had arrived at Charles Stewart Parnell's memorial. Angus examined the obelisk-shaped monument, and launched into a discussion of yet another tragic leader who almost changed the course of Irish history.

"Parnell was one of the few Irishmen who nearly did *out-Brit* the British," he said. "With a passion that was all Irish, his wit was as polished as any of the career politicians in London. But, in the clinches, the British outmaneuvered him as they had all the other Irish leaders."

"As a Protestant, like Wolfe Tone, and a member of the Ascendancy from County Wicklow," Collier continued, "he might have succeeded in obtaining Home Rule for all of Ireland, had he not been sabotaged by the Brits."

"Don't forget the Catholic Bishopry," added Mick.

"Only Katy O'Shea stood in his way," sighed Angus. "Sadly for Ireland, Parnell's tryst with the unhappily married Mrs. O'Shea became the subject of a crusade by his opponents."

"Unhappily married, as they say, but married she was," said Mick. "When the Catholic church publicly placed its scarlet letter on the affair, Parnell was finished . . . and along with him, Home Rule for Ireland."

"Another near miss for Eire," Collier replied.

The cool dampness of evening hastened the pace of their strides. Crossing back to the south side of the Liffey over the steeply arched Ha'penny Bridge, they passed through the Temple Bar district and entered onto Dame Street. Before them stood Dublin Castle, the preeminent symbol of English oppression in Ireland for over seven centuries. From this seat of government power, had been dispensed all of England's acts of domination over the Irish, and all the unspeakable atrocities.

Wending down College Green and onto College Street, they crossed onto Nassau and came to the entrance of Trinity College. An exclusive bastion of higher learning for Protestants since it was founded in 1592 by Queen Elizabeth I, over four centuries passed before Catholics were finally permitted to attend in 1970.

Huddling together, arms locked for added warmth, they turned at last onto Kildare Street and St. Stephen's Green. This magnificent park, encompassing some twenty acres of trees and ponds and grassy space at

the center of the city, had been preserved for the enjoyment of Dubliners by a grant from Sir Arthur Guinness. Onto the Green, faced the landmark Shelbourne Hotel, its entryway flanked by statues of Nubian princesses . . . two bronze goddesses with torchlike lamps held aloft, showering the sidewalk with a soft, warm light. The three men, now weary from touring the haunts of their dear, departed friend, made their way under the awning, past the top-hatted doorman, and into the foyer of the splendid old hotel.

It had been a long day. The ferry ride had sapped their strength, but it was the adulation with which Dublin had enshrined its martyrs that left Angus drained. Riley had been a part of all this. How extraordinary yet tragic it must have been. The rebellion of 1916, which had seemed so remote to Angus as a lad, had come alive during their walk. Angus was not much younger than Riley, who, at 19, had joined the Irish Volunteers after his only year at St. Edna's. If Riley had seemed so mature when they first met, it was because he had already risked his life for Ireland, and, if so boyish, that too, came from serving his country. The spectre of death had hardened him against life's perils and had summoned the lighthearted frivolity of his youth. *We've earned our respite*, he had said. With religion at the heart of Ireland's battles, golf had become a form of faith all its own, and had served as his respite. There was nothing cowardly about seeking temporary refuge from the rigors of duty. The serious business of striving to achieve freedom for Ireland must have been terribly taxing. And yet, Riley had summoned his reserves and trudged onward.

*   *   *

Collier and Mick had already secured a table in the Shelbourne Bar next to an inviting peat fire in full glow. The room was filled to capacity with guests of the hotel, and by local Dubliners who had been drawn to the warmth of the fire for a dram or a pint on this chillingly moist May evening. Angus entered near the long, granite-topped bar adorned by miniature versions of the Egyptian goddesses of the Nile stationed at

the hotel's entry. Similarly sculpted of bronze, these statues featured coiled cobras fashioned into outlandish tiaras above their sensuous profiles. As he approached, the two old men seated at the cramped corner table did not look up from their spirited discussion. And when Angus sat, Mick addressed him as if he had been part of the conversation from its onset.

"Eamon de Valera doesn't deserve a statue. That's why he doesn't have one."

"Do you suppose I might get a drink before we debate the merits of Mr. de Valera?" joked Angus.

"I took the liberty of ordering you a Guinness," said Mick, sipping from his own pint of tar and depositing a thick foamy residue on his moustache.

"When in Rome . . .," Angus joked, invoking the Catholicity of this enclave that was Dublin. "Besides, it gives you strength," he said, hoping the Guinness advertisments that claimed as much were accurate.

"What do you make of the legacy of Eamon de Valera, Angus?" asked Collier.

"As mystifying in death as he was in life," replied Angus. "I've never known quite how the Irish felt about him. The absence of a memorial does speak volumes, but he served for such a long time, he must have had his supporters."

"The paradox began early," said Collier. "Born in New York City in 1882 to an Irish mother and Spanish father, de Valera was shipped off to live with relatives in County Limerick as a child."

"All I know, is that he opposed the treaty of 1921, single-handedly set off the Irish Civil War, and he may have been behind the assassination of Michael Collins," Mick said.

"I suppose a case can be made for all of that," said Collier. "But he did end the civil war in '23. And he resigned from Sinn Fein. So he seemed to be opposed to violence . . . another contradiction."

"He was *the* political leader in Ireland for the better part of fifty years," conceded Angus.

"Despite policies that were consistently out of step with the will of the Irish people, on and on he went, until age 90," said Collier. "A remarkable run of political mastery by one of Ireland's most ambiguous leaders."

"Maybe some of the Irish aren't fond of the fact he was the only prominent participant of the Easter Rising to escape execution by the British," Mick noted.

"It does add to the puzzle, doesn't it?" said Angus. "de Valera was certainly of high rank among the rebels and was slated for execution, but for some reason he was spared."

"Still no statue," said Mick smugly. "In a country that remembers, he's been forgotten."

"Or simply ignored," said Collier. "But, since Collins and de Valera reached an important crossroads in Irish history at the same time, and the National Museum at Collins Barracks is named in memory of Michael Collins, it's probably fair to conclude Collins was more loved by the Irish than de Valera."

"That settles it!" exclaimed Mick, tugging his pocket watch by its fob and checking the hour. "Besides, I'm famished."

The three companions marched shoulder to shoulder across the marbled foyer to the maitre'd's podium at the entrance to No. 27 on The Green. They were shown to their table near a window looking onto St. Stephen's Green by a French waiter in white tie and tails. The quiet elegance of the restaurant offered an agreeable contrast to the steamy raucousness of the lounge. The menu was splendid, with entrees to please everyone, and a wine list fully stocked with the best that France and Spain had to offer. Conversation was sparse as they dined. Outside, an eerie incandescence from the torch lamps shimmered across rain-dampened pavement. Fatigue from the day's events had begun to invade their limbs, but an invigorating jolt of Irish coffee seemed likely to revive their flagging energy.

The Frenchman, Beauclaire, pushed to their table, a cart containing the most delectable array of ingredients. The aroma of rich, freshly-brewed coffee filled their nostrils, while a bottle of Bushmills stood nearby, spigot inserted. Beauclaire ignited a slender stream of whiskey, simultaneously pouring both coffee and flaming spirits into three glass steins. With fiery liquor and hot coffee colliding into the mugs, he held a tablespoon, rounded side up, and above it from eye level, poured a cascade of cream that floated over each mixture like an ivory oilslick, forming a whitecap of sweetness atop an ebony bed of whiskeyed coffee. The concoction was well worth the wait, and the production, an art form. They sat and sipped and smelled the delightfully decadent drink while a horse-drawn jaunting cart clip-clopped slowly past the window. It might have been 1916.

"Some of Dublin's leading citizens sat in this very room during the Rising and marveled at the rebels clashing with the English, but did nothing to come to the aid of the brave men and women who were fighting to free Ireland," said Mick.

"Most of the Anglo-Irish Protestants, or the Ascendency, as they were known, were perfectly content to remain under British rule," replied Collier. "The city of Dublin was then, almost as British as London."

"Since the beginning, Dublin has probably been more British and less Irish than the rest of the country," Angus noted.

"The only time the Gaels really held control of Dublin was a thousand years ago, when the Irish High King, Brian Boru, drove the Vikings out of these parts," said Mick.

"Even then, infighting amongst the Irish clans caused them to seek aid from the English against rival clans," added Collier. "Dublin has been under the British thumb for a long, long time."

"At least until 1949", said Angus, "when the South left the Commonwealth and formed its Republic."

"What about Northern Ireland," Mick interrupted, "they've been held hostage ad infinitum."

"Maybe Yeats was right," said Collier. "Maybe only Irish blood can wash the Brits from this island . . . as in *The Rose Tree*."

"Ah yes," said Mick, once again dredging up the verse, presumably catalogued with all the others in the dark recesses of his mind;

'O, words are lightly spoken,'
Said Pearse to Connolly,

'Maybe a breath of politic words
Has withered our Rose Tree;
Or maybe but a wind that blows
Across the bitter sea.'

'It needs to be but watered,'
James Connolly replied,
'To make the green come out again
And spread on every side,
And to shake the blossom from the bud
To be the garden's pride.'

'But where can we draw water,'
Said Pearse to Connolly,
'When all the wells are parched away?
O' plain as plain can be
There's nothing but our own red blood
Can make a right Rose Tree.'

"I'd wager you could recite chapter and verse from *Ulysses* if we asked you to," Angus remarked, admiring Mick's memory for even the most obscure passages.

"William Butler Yeats was most insightful in *The Rose Tree*," said Mick, "but not all his work was sympathetic to the cause."

"No country has had such a diverse cast of characters vying for a seat at the table of ideas as has Ireland," said Angus. "Academia was never quite sure whether to support or to satirize its brave crusaders."

"It might have been easy for learned Irishmen to rail against England. After all, it was Irish monks, not the English, that helped lead the world out of the Dark Ages," said Mick.

"Sometimes, passion must be allowed to rule reason," Angus countered. "The rebels yielded to their emotion, while Irish society and academia stepped back into clinical analysis. The call to action was heeded only by the unselfish, those few who knew the sacrifices required to unshackle their country. The rest were just too comfortable to care for the inconvenience caused by the pursuit of freedom."

"Keep up that line of oratory, Angus, and the Irish will be erect a statue in memory of you!" laughed Mick.

"In fairness," argued Collier, "Yeats and Joyce and Synge and the other leaders of the Irish literary renaissance at the turn of the century were faithful observers of the events of history. Surely, not everyone in Ireland could be expected to commit their lives to revolution with the utter completeness of a Pearse or a Connolly or even a Riley O'Neill."

"If everyone had committed utterly, perhaps England would be on the other side of the Irish Sea where she belongs," argued Angus.

"Or, perhaps Ireland would now be entirely repopulated by the English," Collier countered.

"We'll never know," Mick sighed wearily. "But I do know it's time for me to bid you both a good evening."

"Aye, and a fine ev'nin' she's been," replied Angus in a contrived Irish lilt.

"There was a time when we considered eleven o'clock to be the shank of the evening," said Collier.

"I'm afraid the shank has been foreshortened by old age," replied Mick with more grimace than grin.

"If I'd known I was going to live so long, I'd have taken better care of myself," laughed Angus.

"Come on, Angus," insisted Collier. "Let's go dissipate what's left of our lives, while Mick gets his beauty sleep!"

Chapter 5

*W*armth from the coals of the peat fire billowed into the hotel lobby, its radiance enveloping Angus and Collier in a cloak of comfort, drawing them back into the pub, still lively with patrons on a dreary night. At a table near the embers, they spoke little but peered about the room with the curiosity of visitors in a culture not their own. They observed in this particular crowd, a gaiety unlike any they had seen in Edinburgh or London. While Dubliners may have a long lineage from England, their sense of celebration, at least tonight, was unmistakably Irish.

"You seldom see the Brits or the Scots enjoying such spontaneity of song," Collier noted, as he watched four middle-aged men, arms draped over shoulders, swaying to the sounds of their own unrefined voices, valiantly straining to match lyrics to the haunting melody of *Galway Bay*.

"How the people of Ireland maintain such mirth in the face of their tragic past is a marvel," agreed Angus.

"A testament to the notion that good humour is the universal antidote to the poisons of the world."

"When he wasn't using his fists or his rifle to rectify wrongs, Riley always had a quip at hand to ease the tension."

"And just what wrongs needed to be rectified with his fists?" asked Collier rubbing his jaw. "I wish he'd made a joke out of my poor behaviour at Muirfield instead of bashing me with that mallet he called a fist. I don't think it ever healed."

"He could have told you his tale about the Irish Catholic playing golf with the parish priest and the English atheist. Let's see if I can remember how it goes . . ."

A Catholic priest, his Irish parishioner, and an English atheist, arrive at the eighteenth with their match all square.

The Irish Catholic sinks a fifty-foot putt for par and shouts, God loves an Irishman! The English atheist misses his ten-footer for birdie and curses, Goddammit!

The priest walks over, picks up his ball lying six feet from the hole for birdie and says; Now boys, God had nothing to do with either of those poots. He doesn't take sides in sportin' events unless it's to further His good work.

But why did you pick up, Father? asks the Englishman. That putt could have won you the match.

Oh, but I did win the match, replies the priest. God told me 'twas good. And the two o' you owe me one punt each.

I didn't hear Him, Father, says the Englishman. Noo, and you won't hear Him either, says the priest. You don't believe in Him, and you address Him only in vain. He wouldn't be speakin' to you, now would He, lad?

But Father, I'm a good Catholic and I didn't hear Him give you the poot either, says the Irishman.

Aye lad, and if you could hear Him, you wouldn't be needin' me, now would you, says the priest. So pay up, the both o' ye!

"I trust he told that story tongue in cheek," said Collier. "It strikes very close to the heart of the troubles in Ireland."

"It *does* make a point," said Angus. "There's more than an ounce of truth in those characters."

"One would hope all the parties to this ceaseless conflict between the Catholics and Protestants, and Irish and English, could be resolved with the same self-deprecation."

"Aye, the Irish Catholics seem able to laugh at themselves. But when others tease about similar topics, they bristle."

"I suppose it's a trait we all share."

"Recognizing our own shortcomings is the first step to bridging the divide in any dispute," said Angus, wistfully, "whether its Catholics and Protestants, English and Irish, or father and son."

"Angus, the man at the end of the bar looks oddly familiar. I've watched him for the past few minutes, and I could swear he looks just like . . ."

"Riley O'Neill?"

"Yes. Riley O'Neill. That man looks just how I would expect Riley to look if he were fifty."

"That man . . . is my son."

"Come now!" sputtered a disbelieving Collier. "How is it he has the identical appearance and bearing of Riley."

"He was fathered by Riley. But I was his father."

"Why do you say *was?*"

"He disowned me thirty years ago."

As he revealed to Collier the painful details of his past, Angus' discomfort was made even more intense by Patrick's proximity. He longed to embrace his son in a way that would make up for all the lost time, but the urge soon passed. Angus was reminded he hardly knew Patrick, and the rift that long ago had separated the two had not yet been repaired. Hopeful as Patrick's article had been, hugs were unlikely, so long as reconciliation was incomplete.

"He seems unaware of your presence."

"There is no reason for him to recognize me. Many days I don't even recognize myself."

"It goes beyond physical recognition. Patrick seems detached from his surroundings."

"I see what you mean. He does appear to be cut off from the world."

"I'll leave you to your thoughts, but if I were you, I'd speak to him now. What is there to lose? You haven't had Patrick in your life for thirty years. If he doesn't care to mend the past, you're alone again. You've been alone for a long time."

"It's just so final. While we're apart and haven't confronted our differences, there is always the chance that we might reconcile. If I try now and fail, it's finished."

"Hope is a powerful motivator, but even hope must give way to action when time is short. You're running out of time. I suspect he's as apprehensive about your differences as you. It's up to one of you to extend the hand of forgiveness. Don't emulate Ulster and end at an impasse with your son."

"You're right, Collier. I'm quick to suggest solutions for others, but can't seem to right my own shortcomings."

"Good night, Angus, and good luck."

*   *   *

Angus sat alone, his thoughts turning to happier times of Patrick's youth, times when he and Patrick and Sarah had been a family. He could not help contemplating the destiny that had brought them all together, the unlikely coupling that brought Patrick into the world. Riley still seemed the very antithesis of Sarah . . . the coarse Irish commoner and the sleek London debutante. He, street-smart and crude . . . she, erudite and elegant. Riley, the spirited Catholic Gael . . . Sarah, the genteel Anglo Protestant. What made this odd pairing possible? Where was the slender thread knitting these lives together? It could be summed up in a single word . . . passion. But theirs was not the sort of fire that burns steadily for a lifetime. Like the meteorite, it was too intense to last, flaming out all too soon. Angus had little doubt how the spark between Riley and Sarah had occurred, for he had seen it first hand at St. Andrews fifty years ago, and knew well their emotion. It was standing right before him in the person of Patrick. He must try now, as he did then, to forget the pain he felt when Sarah had chosen Riley instead of him. All that mattered was this one last chance to reconcile with his son.

The warmth of the fire was of little solace in these lonely moments, watching as Patrick stood at the end of the bar, sipping his Guinness, looking at no one, lost in his own solitude. Patrick Angus MacKenzie often came to the Shelbourne. When Riley had visited Dublin, it had always been at the Shelbourne that they would meet. And now, Riley was gone. Patrick already missed his stories and his companionship. But there were others he missed as much, his mother, Sarah, most of all. Her devotion to him had been Patrick's touchstone over the past thirty years. It was just a feeling now, a kind of spiritual sensation that she was with him, always. No substitute for seeing her, of course, but a stronger impression than the one he had of Angus, whose absence had begun to leave an equally vacant scar on his life.

Patrick's recollection of Angus was more ephemeral, never lasting more than a few moments. The only real connection with him had come from a collection of short stories Angus had authored after the war. Patrick had recently stumbled onto a tattered copy of *The Lost Souls of Edinburgh* at a used book store that specialized in long-out- of-print publications. After reading the book, Patrick found a renewed interest in seeing Angus, and in talking to him, not just from an appreciation of his writing, but from the poignant, if somewhat sad, stories of the desperate characters whose lives Angus had depicted. They had given Patrick some much-needed insight into Angus' soul, and perhaps more meaningfully, a glimpse into his own.

For such a long time, he had denied Angus' importance, even his existence, choosing instead, to gravitate toward Riley. He not only had condemned Angus for his mother's death, but had gone so far as to blame him for the Admiralty's refusal to allow Patrick to attend her funeral. At the time, Patrick thought it just as well. He hadn't wanted to see Angus anyway, even if it was at his own mother's memorial. But all those feelings had long ago vanished. Now, he simply felt ashamed to have cut his ties. It was time to heal the wounds. They were the worst kind . . . self-inflicted.

Rising from his chair, Angus began to walk stiffly toward Patrick. As he came nearer this once familiar, but now unknown man, he wondered what words he would speak. Then, as if he had been expecting all along to see his father, Patrick looked up from his pint. Angus stood before him, silent, seeing both the boy he once knew and the man he did not. Patrick stared back, knowing he held the power to remove regret from his past, the ability to wipe the slate clean. In that brief instant, they were both traveling through time, across the rocky shoals of their endless rift. And they had arrived together at the Shelbourne bar at just the right moment . . . just in time to salvage their relationship from its wreckage.

"Angus . . .!" Patrick exclaimed with both joy and relief. "Dad." He spread his arms and encircled his father with the very embrace that, moments earlier, Angus had imagined giving Patrick.

"Patrick," Angus replied tearfully, hugging back, "dear God, how I've missed you."

"I've missed you too, dad. I've been so foolish all these years. Can you ever forgive me?"

"Of course, son," said Angus without hesitation, holding both of Patrick's hands in his. "I didn't have the courage to reach out. You must have thought I'd written you off after all the years of silence."

"Come sit down, Angus," said Patrick, leading him to a table. "We've made a hash of it. There's a lifetime of bits and pieces to sort out."

They ordered Guinness and made their way back to the table where Collier and Angus had been seated. The fire felt pleasant now, as it penetrated the chill Angus had experienced during his uncertain walk toward Patrick. It was warm and comforting, and, somehow, he knew everything was going to be alright between Patrick and him.

"I remember once when I was just a lad," Patrick said, "you counseled me on this very subject."

"I don't remember. What did I say?"

"I wanted to be friends with a boy in school, but thought he didn't like me. You told me to be careful not to make rash judgments of others. He might just be shy, you said."

"A lesson often imparted and, just as often, ignored."

"Shame on both of us. We both thought the wrong things of each other."

"Are you going to Riley's funeral?"

"Aye," said Patrick, downing the last of the Guinness. "I came here to drown my sorrows. I lost my father and mother thirty years ago, and now my godfather has died."

"Riley O'Neill was not your godfather, Patrick. He . . ."

"I know, dad. But all that was before I was born. You're my father. You gave me my bearings. I know I'm Riley's son, but you are my father."

"Did he tell you?"

"No, he was always true to your friendship. Mother told me before I left for the service. Knowing you were not my real father made it easy for an immature boy to cast you aside. I needed a reason for her passing. You became a convenient choice. I thought I could get from Riley all the love you and mother had given me. Somehow all I had to do was to be rid of you, and Riley would replace both of you. I was so wrong."

"But surely Riley accepted you as his son."

"I just didn't comprehend anything mother and Riley told me. She revealed Riley's real identity to me, not so I would abandon you, but so I would love you as she did. And Riley's refusal to embrace me as his son was not from his lack of love for me, but out of his sense of loyalty to you."

"I don't quite understand."

"Mother once loved Riley, but her love for you had grown beyond any feelings she had for him. She wanted me to know, in case anything happened to her. It was as if she had sensed her own death."

"She told you she loved me?"

"Mother loved you more than she ever said. It was her one regret. She had spent most of her marriage wondering how life might have been with Riley, never admitting to herself or to you, how much you meant to her."

"What else did she say?" asked Angus, wanting more than ever to hear the words from Sarah herself.

"Everything. She shared with me all the conflicting emotions she felt for you and Riley . . . her physical attraction to him . . . her spiritual bond with you. I'm certain she did all she could to rationally sort out her feelings. In the end, she was content with her life. Surely, you must have known how she felt toward you, dad."

"I did see her change over the years," replied Angus, brushing his cheek. "Once . . . when we were at Glen . . ." he started, then stopped.

Composing himself, Angus continued, "She became less preoccupied and seemed to embrace our life together, rather than just endure it. I tried never to judge. After all, I knew how much Riley had meant to her."

"You made her very happy. The choices the three of you had made together so long ago was their guiding light. It would have been easy for them to reason you out of their lives. Riley's circumstances had become less dangerous, and it had been the risk to mother and me they wanted to avoid. But having chosen you to be father and husband and friend, neither broke faith."

"And Riley, was he all right with all this?"

"Riley had entrusted his life to you when he asked you to care for Sarah and me as your own. You had been true to Riley, and it was unthinkable for him to replace you in my life simply because I asked. Riley knew the sacrifices you had made and the loving home you had provided. He had made his choice to be a servant to Ireland, and wasn't about to undo that choice at your expense, just because I made it convenient for him."

"How did you deal with the confusion in your life, Patrick?"

"Not well, obviously. Mother and Riley tried to direct me down the path of love and forgiveness. I chose self-pity and resentment instead. I should have seen that you were no more to blame for mother's death than the monster of Loch Ness. I just couldn't come to terms with it. I've been so stupid all these years to keep us apart with my self-righteousness."

"But you seem at ease now. I read your article, *Ireland's Last Hope*, this morning, and felt you were speaking to both Riley and me."

"It took Riley's passing to make me appreciate you. While he lived, it was easier to blame you for my pain and cling to the hope my real father would rescue me. But you were my real father all along."

"We didn't take your feelings into account when I became your father. The only consideration was Riley's concern for Sarah's safety. None of us could predict the future."

"The three of you behaved so selflessly. I, on the other hand, was concerned only with me. Reading your collection of short stories, *The Lost Souls of Edinburgh*, helped me to understand how silly it is to wallow in self-pity."

"How'd you ever find a copy? There can't be many in print."

"The *Nom De Plume*, over in the Temple Bar district had one. I found it filled with fascinating tales on how the downtrodden are able to cope with misery. My circumstances were trivial compared to theirs, and I began to change my outlook. Besides, it gave me a sense of who you are, dad, and what I'd missed by not seeing you all these years."

"We must begin again, Patrick. I'm so glad we've found each other. No more regrets about the past . . . let's look ahead."

"I love you, Angus," said Patrick, once again encircling the older man's shoulders.

"I love you too, Patrick," said Angus squeezing back. "Let's go honor the memory of Riley together, as a family."

Chapter 6

Saturday dawned with bright blue skies and the freshness of last night's rain. Angus was awakened from a sound sleep by the blare of police sirens, but nuisances like these now seemed trivial. His days would now begin with a sense of purpose rather than dread. The reunion with Patrick had sparked renewed interest in a life that, only yesterday, had seemed so moribund. Though it would not be possible for them to simply pick up where they had left off thirty years ago, he looked forward to the prospect of a close relationship with his son for the remainder of his days.

Angus had completed his daily tour of the obituary page and was on his second cup of tea when his eye caught the image of a young woman seated across the room. He hadn't really even looked up from his newspaper. It was more a sense of form and movement that had attracted his attention. He noticed, at first glance, that her hair was black, and that she was fussing with it, trying to recompress her bun with just the right placement of a bobby pin. These movements were so familiar to Angus that he lowered the newspaper slightly to allow a better view. Though she was facing away, a mirror on the wall opposite her reflected all that Angus wanted to see. At this distance, and at this angle, and in this light, she was Sarah.

The contour of her cheeks, her delicate complexion, even the shade she now applied to her full lips, called up Sarah. Her manner, so proper, yet sensuous, cried out Sarah. Her suit, cut from fine fabric and tailored to perfection, was the latest in women's fashion, just what Sarah would have worn. Then, as the woman glanced into the mirror, she engaged Angus with eyes that were blue, yes, but not Sarah's blue. And she offered the smile often afforded old men caught in the act of admiring younger women, most definitely not Sarah's. The enchantment had been broken, but not in sadness. Angus was frequently overcome by these interludes. They brought Sarah back to him, if only for a moment. And it was the memory of her that kept him alive.

By the time Mick and Collier entered the hotel dining room for breakfast, Angus had finished reading the sports page. Some chap from County Kildare named O'Flaherty was favored to win this year's British Isles Cup at Muirfield. Apparently, some things *were* meant to change. Angus checked the time. They would depart within the hour and were scheduled to arrive in Lahinch at noon, just in time for Riley's wake and funeral. He greeted Mick and Collier jovially. Beads of perspiration were beginning to form on his brow, and he noted that the day promised to be unusual for Ireland in May . . . hot.

"How did your evening turn out, Angus?" Collier asked.

"Better than I could ever have imagined. Thanks for bolstering my courage."

"You needed courage to survive the night?" asked Mick. "What happened after I left the two of you?"

"Patrick was here last night, Mick. We went a long way toward putting things right."

"A happy turn of events, Angus. You've suffered enough. And I'm sure Patrick has too. Your reconciliation was long overdue."

"It's sad that Riley's death was the reason for our coming together. But maybe it was meant to be. As long as he was living, Patrick might not have reached out, and I would not have come to Dublin."

"I doubt Riley arranged his death, so you and Patrick could be reunited," said Collier.

"Don't be so certain," Angus replied. "Much of what Riley did in life was done in the best interests of others."

"Will Patrick be joining us on the trip to Lahinch?" asked Mick.

"Those were his plans last night. I hope he hasn't changed his mind," said Angus, looking anxiously at his watch.

"He'll be there," insisted Collier. "And we'd better be moving in that direction as well," he added, studying his own pocket watch.

*   *   *

Kingsbridge Station had been patterned after an Italian palazzo, cleverly designed to conceal all trains from public view by a central block of nine bays. Corinthian columns and Ionic balustrades of carved swags and urns, harkened back to the 1800s, when Victorian opulence gave rise to public buildings that were rather more artistic than utilitarian. Domed campaniles on either side of the main entryway suggested a theological, rather than sectarian theme. Once inside the station, Angus eagerly began to look for Patrick.

"He'll be here," Collier reassured.

"Oh, I know he will. I just want to continue our discussion from last night. There's so much I've missed over the years about Patrick and Sarah . . . and Riley."

"Dad!" Patrick called from fifty metres down the brick-lined platform, "Angus!"

"There he is!" exclaimed Angus. "Let me introduce you."

The middle-aged man striding toward them was not the bright-faced boy Angus had sent off to war thirty years before. The freshly-scrubbed cheeks had been replaced by a sallow complexion beneath two days of scruffy black beard, flecked with grey. The once ramrod-straight posture was now slightly bent, giving Patrick the appearance of being even smaller than he had been in his youth. One thing had not changed . . . he was Riley. The chiseled features of a matinee idol had not yet conceded to time or intemperance. The hair, slicked back from his forehead, was thick and black and in need of cutting . . . all Riley. But the eyes were Sarah's . . . warmer, more accepting. And the smile was a blend of both parents . . . Sarah's pouting lips, parting to reveal Riley's slightly lopsided, impish grin. He and Angus hugged as if it were the first time.

"Patrick, I want you to meet two dear friends, Mick Callahan of Edinburgh, and Collier Ames of County Down."

"Yes, of course. Riley spoke often of both of you. It's a pleasure to finally make your acquaintance."

"For us as well," said Mick, extending his hand.

"And, I guess you would be *Uncle* Collier," said Patrick as he grasped the softness of Collier's hand.

"Well, I hadn't thought about it, since I only learned last night of your existence, but yes, I'm proud to be your uncle, or half uncle. Whatever I am, I'm damn proud of it."

"What's all that?" Angus asked Patrick, pointing toward a large carrying case with some sort of pipes protruding from its opening.

"Oh, those are the drones to my bagpipes," Patrick replied. "The bellows and chatter are inside. I thought I might play a dirge or two at Riley's wake. But you must promise to be kind, I haven't played the thing since I piped for the Royal Scots Greys."

In the midst of introductions, the conductor trilled the boarding whistle. They climbed onto the train and settled into the observation car. Onlookers who had lined the platform to see other passengers off to Limerick or Ennis or Lahinch or other destinations to the west of Ireland were waving excitedly, and the men waved back. Sunlight streamed into the car, prompting Angus and the others to remove their jackets. Strains of Louis Armstrong's *West End Blues* drifted through the car from the train's loudspeakers, providing an air of retrospection to the four companions. They might have been traveling in the 1930s.

"Angus tells us you've been writing for the *Irish Independent* for many years," said Mick.

"Aye, the paper has given me a good deal of latitude to explore *The Troubles*."

"His writing has a certain resonance rarely found in journalism these days," Angus interjected proudly. "Sort of like the pure notes an accomplished trumpeter articulates from his horn," he added, referring to the sorrowful riffs Satchmo sent wafting through the speakers.

"You're entirely too kind," said Patrick, lowering his gaze in modesty, "and more than a little biased, I might add. But, I do enjoy trying to make sense of a conflict that continues to be senseless."

"What do you think it will take to remove the British from Ulster?" Mick asked bluntly.

"I honestly don't know. There was a time when I believed jabbing John Bull in the eye was the only way to proceed. My revolutionary rhetoric peaked in 1966, about the time of the 50th anniversary of the Easter

Rising. One of my articles was credited, or blamed, depending on your perspective, for inciting the IRA demonstration which ended in the destruction of Lord Nelson's memorial"

"Surely you didn't advocate the demolition of public property," Collier teased sarcastically.

"I didn't make a direct reference to Admiral Nelson. But I did say something to the effect that symbols of British tyranny were strewn about the city of Dublin, and that our good citizens were being subjected each day to the subliminal messages of English oppression so long as those emblems were allowed to stand."

"Nothing too subtle about that call to action," said Angus. "I'm sure that you endeared yourself to those great scholars like Pearse and Plunkett, whose writings spawned the 1916 revolt."

"I doubt the IRA needed any blast from my journalistic bugle. The Irish have always been romantic followers of their past. They magnify the achievements of their martyrs, and they exaggerate the significance of ancient events. It may be their obsession with looking backward that undermines their ability to forge an orderly future. In any event, the tone of my editorials has become less radical."

"I'm sure Riley must have influenced your writing," Angus remarked, with a twinge of envy.

"Well, Riley was committed to gradualism. And in the 50s and '60s, I wasn't. I guess the anarchist mentality of the '66 riots finally opened my eyes to his point of view."

"I believe the Irish Civil War was a turning point for him," said Angus. "Because he, too, once advocated force as a means to achieve a united republic."

"He always said there's nothing like aiming your rifle at friends and neighbors to make you question the wisdom of your cause," replied Patrick. "He wasn't prepared for the slaughter of his own people, even the Protestants."

"Where will it all end?" asked Collier.

"That's sort of like asking whether the world will ever see another Messiah. It happened once, nearly two thousand years ago. The troubles in the North have existed for over four hundred years, and it may take an Irish equivalent of the Messiah to provide the light."

"It always comes down to leadership," sighed Angus. "Even Riley conceded the voices of Ireland were too fragmented. There's been no unifying message around which to coalesce."

"And there may never be, so long as the most strident voices are the loudest," Patrick noted.

"Maybe you should enter politics, Patrick," Collier observed. "You sound like a thoughtful moderate. You have the diversity of Irish and Scottish fathers, an English mother, and a Protestant upbringing. You just might be able to provide the objectivity needed to move all Irish people toward peace."

"Politics is such a tawdry business. I think I can be more effective from my current platform. Maybe my writing will influence the right leader to incorporate some of my ideas into a new vision for Ireland."

"Isn't that your theory, Collier?" Angus asked. "The quill is more potent than the blade?"

"We must hope," replied Collier. "We must always hope," he repeated, whispering.

Chapter 7

*T*he train slowed to a stop outside the village of Ballymackey. Fifty-deep across the tracks stood a flock of sheep, while their grizzled shepherd of seventy-odd stood nearby, leaning on his crook, a hand-rolled cigarette sagging from his lips, his Donegal tam rakishly askew. These wooly charges seemed to sense they were the beneficiaries of Ireland's local rules of the road. They, *by God*, had the right-of-way, and were now bleating emphatically that it be honored at their leisure. An hour-long delay meant dining on the train instead of in Lahinch as planned. But barring further delays of the ovine variety, they might yet arrive in time for Riley's services.

After an excruciating crawl through Limerick, they were now clattering at full speed alongside the River Shannon on their way to Ennis, a village whose name derived from the Gaelic *'inis'*, for island. It was an important stop, the three older men recalled fondly, on the now-defunct West Clare Railway. The system of narrow gauge lines and peat-fired engines had once connected Dublin with the rest of Ireland, bringing back pleasant memories of more leisurely travel. For all their appreciation of a less hurried past, today, they were thankful for a faster mode of transportation.

The train eased through Ennis and the men lunched on trout filets from the River Shannon, vegetables from the fields of Clare, and Irish biscuits, better known as soda farls, washed down with tankards of Smithwick's ale. They passed the *Eamon de Valera Public Library* housed, ironically, in a converted 19th century Presbyterian church, and Angus made note of it for Mick with gentle humor. Now within thirty miles of Lahinch, Angus longed to talk of Sarah with Patrick, but such intimacies were surely to be reserved for private discussion. Instead, he asked of Riley.

"Did you see much of Riley over the years?"

"Oh, my yes," replied Patrick. "He was a regular visitor to Dublin. I'd say we met half a dozen times a year for tea or a pint. He always spoke of the three of you. No matter how pressing the business of Sinn Fein, it was always the golf and the esprit de corps he had shared with you that came first."

"Riley did have a knack for celebrating life," said Collier, shaking his head. "I was just thinking about the men serenading at the pub last night, Angus. It brought back memories of Riley's singing at the Slieve Donard after he won the British Isles Cup in 1930."

"I haven't heard this story," said Patrick. "What happened?"

"Well, after the tournament, Riley went to the hotel bar to commemorate the occasion. It was the first time the Cup had ever been contested in Ireland, so there was much celebrating to do."

"It became the *only* time it was held in Ireland if I remember correctly," added Mick. "Something to do with the celebration getting out of hand."

"That's right, Mick. Will the wonder of your memory never cease?"

"I seem to recall Riley getting into a tiff with some Brits that night," replied Mick, ignoring Collier.

"Right again!" exclaimed Collier.

"Well," urged Angus, "go on."

"As you might imagine, County Down was a tinderbox of Catholic-Protestant struggles in 1930, and tensions were heightened by the presence of a dozen or so members of an old Black and Tan unit."

"Those barbarous mercenaries did more to disturb the peace than keep it," said Mick. "The British were dead wrong to send them in to stir up trouble."

"Probably so. And Riley picked a bad time to cross swords with them. They were all gathered in the Oak Room of the Slieve Donard, singing patriotic British hymns when Riley arrived carrying the British Isles trophy."

Collier pulled his sweater over his bald head and placed it next to his blazer as though he were expecting the observation car to become even more stuffy during the telling of this story. His voice began to rise.

"In the midst of the refrain of *Rule Britannia* which goes; '*Rule Britannia, Britannia rule the waves, Britons never never never shall be slaves,*'

Riley broke into the Irish ballad, *A Nation Once Again*. His raspy tenor belted out the chorus, 'A *nation once again, A nation once again, And Ireland long a province, be a nation once again.*' When he finished, the Black and Tans had gone stone silent, stunned by the brass of this wee man holding the enormous silver cup."

"It's a wonder he escaped with his life that night!" exclaimed Patrick.

"The leader of the squad was a brute named Billy Leeds. And apparently, Leeds was prepared to chalk the whole thing up to the misjudgment of an overzealous golfer who had just won a big tournament. He said something like, '*If you'll shut your Fenian gob on this fine Saturday eve, wee man, we'll leave you be*'."

"I'm sure Riley couldn't walk away from a scrap with the British regardless of being heavily out-manned," said Angus.

"You know him well. So, he said something like, '*You Brits are all the same. You sing of Britons never bein' slaves, but you don't mind makin' us lowly Irish yer indentured servants*'."

"Being from the South of Ireland, he wasn't likely to have any supporters in a County Down pub," said Patrick.

"Nary a soul. All the patrons were Presbyterians. Even Riley knew he couldn't fight the room single-handedly, but he wasn't about to swallow his pride. He simply asked Leeds, who outweighed him by a hundred pounds and stood ten inches taller, whether he was the toughest sonofabitch in the Black and Tans."

"To which, Leeds blared, '*You can bet your black Irish heart on that!*'"

"He had a face even a mother couldn't love. Bloated from years of overconsumption, it was a mass of white pustules which wept like open sores beneath the closely-cropped bristles of his hairline. His porcine appearance would have been laughable on someone less ferocious."

"Riley asked, '*Will y' be tellin' yer bullies t' stand down if I whip y', now?*'"

"To which the Brit replied; '*If you can whip me, I'll have my men kiss your bare Fenian arse, and we'll stand you all the Guinness you can drink!*'"

Collier's pride gushed forth as he related the story of Riley's encounter with the British hired goon.

"Eyes squinting into tiny slits, Leeds removed his khaki jacket to reveal biceps, gnarled as if they had been hewn from oak. His fists were curled into a pugilistic pose reminiscent of the bare-knuckled boxers of John L. Sullivan's era."

Standing to demonstrate his half-brother's boxing strategy, Collier continued, ever more animated.

"Riley began to circle this giant of a man as a predator might stalk its quarry, crouching low, looking for an opening. Suddenly, without warning, he kicked his right leg like a Gaelic footballer, planting his spikes into Leeds' crotch. The fists that had been proudly positioned to protect Leeds' abcessed face dropped quickly to his groin. Knees buckling, and body doubling over at the waist, Leeds gave a low groan of agony as his pig eyes now became bulging saucers of white, rimmed in red."

Building to a graphic conclusion, Collier roared as any enthusiast of the sweet science of boxing would.

"Riley charged into the breach, peppering the Brit's greasy face with rapier-like punches until blood flowed freely into the pus. The bout was over before it had started. While the other Black and Tans tended to their leader, Riley pointed at Leeds and said, *'Y' can save yer ass kissin' fer him . . . the toughest sonofabitch in the Black 'n Tans.'*"

"Cradling the Cup under his arm, he strolled over to an empty table blithely humming *Bold Fenian Men*. The Prods in the pub gave him a standing ovation when he refused to accept the Guinness bought by the Brits, calling instead to the barman that it was his shout."

Finally catching his breath, Ames whispered, as if in tribute to a legend.

"To this day, you can stop off at the Oak Room of the Slieve Donard and hear various versions of the story, some more embellished than others, of course, but the theme is the same. Riley won the Prods' respect that night."

The men sat in quiet meditation, savoring the memory of Riley's pluck. It was an incident none but Collier had known, yet reminiscent of any number of events which defined Riley's commitment to his beliefs. His valor in the face of danger had been the hallmark of a life spent in service of an idea . . . a united Ireland. And those who had witnessed Riley's battle of 1930 with Billy Leeds and his band of Black and Tans in the Oak Room of the Sleive Donard would not soon forget his mettle, nor would their children, for whom this oft-repeated tale would become lore.

"I have nothing to top that," said Patrick, finally breaking the silence.

"Surely Riley told you some golfing yarns we may have missed," implored Mick.

"Well, let me think," said Patrick, pausing to take a sip of ale. Then, with his reflective frown flashing into a lopsided grin, he piped, "You might remember how keen Riley was to play a round of golf with Bobby Jones. But you probably didn't know that he got his wish."

"Surely you jest," said Collier. "Who won? Why didn't we hear about it?"

"Slow down, Collier," Angus interrupted. "I'm sure Patrick will get to all that. Where was it played? Did they draw a big crowd?"

"You're worse than schoolboys," Patrick laughed. "For several years, Jones would return to Scotland or England as a spectator of The Open Championship. He loved linksland golf, especially at St. Andrews, having won there in 1927. So, when the Open returned to The Old Course in 1933, Jones came to watch."

"I don't recall Riley spending any time in Scotland or England after 1926," said Angus.

"They met in Ireland. Jones had long been interested in playing some of the top courses here. Following the Open, he arranged to tour various courses, including Royal Portrush, Royal County Down, Portmarnock, Ballybunion, and Lahinch."

"But why didn't the public know of his tour?" asked Mick. "People would have turned out in droves to see Jones play golf in Ireland, even if he was past his prime."

"Bobby Jones, past his prime, was still better than all but a handful of players," said Collier.

"I'd wager Riley O'Neill was one of those precious few," added Angus.

"Jones was a very private man," Patrick continued. "He didn't enjoy the crowds. He'd had enough adulation to last him a lifetime. He simply enjoyed good golf with dear friends and old rivals on great courses."

"How did Riley manage to get Jones to play?" asked Angus.

"Actually, it was Jones who requested the honor of playing with Riley. But he wasn't in Ireland to play competitive matches. Bobby Jones was a strong proponent of the Scottish custom of playing foursomes."

Angus thought back on his own experience with this format where two golfers collaborate to post a medal score with only one ball. To him, it was the most difficult game in golf, requiring one player drive on the odd numbered holes and his partner the even ones, alternating shots until the ball is holed.

"I remember reading in Jones' autobiography, *Golf is My Game*, that he favored foursomes, because each player was given added psychological pressure," said Collier. "No one likes to hit his own shots into disagreeable spots, but if you do it in foursomes, then your partner is the one to play it, not you. He used to say the measure of how well two players combine to shoot one medal score depends entirely upon the trust and patience fostered between them."

"Jones' tour consisted of finding the best local amateur at each course, and requesting the privilege of joining him in a game of foursomes. Riley told me the story so often, I sometimes think I was there. Even the conversations he had with Jones come freely to mind when I think of their day together."

"Tell us the story as Riley would have," said Angus.

"Well, Jones arrived at Lahinch with no fanfare. It was just past six o'clock on one of those fine Irish summer eves when daylight continues well into the wee hours. Lahinch was nearly vacant when Jones asked the local pro, Jimmy O'Brien, whether he could tell him who was the best amateur in town."

Chapter 8

*P*atrick slid easily into the pleasing accent of County Clare as he mimicked Riley's Irish lilt. When he began to speak, the men saw their old friend reincarnated. Even the voices of Jones and other members of the supporting cast came to life under Patrick's gift of imitation.

"Mr. O'Brien," Patrick began, mimicking Bobby Jones, "who would you say is the best golfer in Lahinch?"

"That'd be Mr. Riley O'Neill, sir," replied Jimmy, not quite able to place this oddly familiar stranger. "Y' ain't never seen a gowfer like Riley O'Neill."

"Do you think he'd care to play a round of golf on short notice?"

"Never know'd Riley to tarn down a chance to play gowf."

"If ah wait over there on the practice green, do you think you might be able to tell Mr. O'Neill that Robert Jones of America is here, and that ah'd be obliged if he'd join me for a game of foursomes?" Jones drawled politely. "On second thought, it'll just be twosomes, since we won't have opponents."

Jimmy O'Brien was numbed by the realization he was in the presence of the greatest player in golf, and couldn't believe he'd just advised Jones that Riley was a golfer unlike anyone he had ever seen. Jimmy quickly reconsidered. By damn, Riley was one of a kind! No need for Riley O'Neill to take a lower rung on anyone's ladder, even the one occupied by the Emperor of Golf Himself.

"Of coorse, Bobby, er . . Mr. Jones. I'll joost climb on me bike, pedal over to Riley's, and fetch 'im back here . . . before you and ol' Calamity Jane get overheated," stammered Jimmy, referring to the popular pet name for Jones' putter.

"Thank you, Mr. O'Brien. Ah'll be waiting."

When Jimmy reached Riley's cottage and explained the situation, Riley thought his friends were shining him on. They never missed an opportunity for pranks, and this seemed a likely candidate.

"Jimmy O'Brien, if this is you and the boyos gettin' in yer cups, and makin' sport of me, there'll be hell to pay! Y' know damn well I'd give anything to play with Bobby Jones. 'Tis a cruel and heartless thing you're doin'. You'd best be certain you can handle the consequences of your shameful deed."

"I swear on the grave of me dear, dead Mum," said poor Jimmy, "Bobby Jones is pootin' on our practice green. Now don't y' dare keep the great man waitin'!"

They returned to Lahinch and there he was . . . Bobby Jones in the flesh and spikes and plus fours. Riley had imagined the moment so often it now seemed beyond belief.

"Mr. Robert Tyre Jones, Jr.," said Jimmy, "meet Mr. Riley Padraig O'Neill."

"Mah pleasure, Mr. O'Neill," said Jones, clenching his teeth as Riley crushed his hand.

"Riley, or R.P., if y' please. Mr. O'Neill was me Pap. 'Tis me great privilege t' make yer acquaintance, Mr. Jones."

"Ah've heard a good bit about your golf, Riley. And please, call me Bob. Only my adoring fans and the press call me Bobby," he said modestly.

"I hear you've got some gemme yourself, Bob," replied Riley, his everpresent puckish grin spreading across his face. "Jimmy here, tells me you want to play one ball. We usually play ev'ry man for himself, but I could make an exception . . . just for you."

"Splendid! Would you prefer to drive on the odd or the even numbered holes?"

"Lahinch's got balance. We'll both git our fair share of predicaments regardless of who hits where. Why don't I take ol' number one. She's a fierce opener," he added, removing the J. Braddell from his bag with the customary flair of Flynn.

"Would you care to warm up a bit before we tee off?"

"Noo, I've got me rhythm for today, lad. Wouldn't want to upset the balance of power, now would we?"

"Then by all means, lead on," said Jones.

The first at Lahinch measured 360 metres, but played much longer. From the lowest point on the course, the fairway rose some fifty feet on its journey to the green. Sloping sharply from left to right, it demanded a solidly struck shot with a high, hooking ball flight. A mishit drive, or one with slicing spin, would leave an uninviting second shot to a green perched like the aerie of an eagle on a wind-swept shelf.

Riley teed the ball a bit higher than usual and moved it slightly forward in his stance. His familiar three-quarter backswing sent the opening drive howling up the center of the steep fairway in a tight draw that hugged the contour of the slope, coming to rest a mere hundred metres from the green. Jones' jaw dropped ever so slightly.

"I'm glad you chose to lead off, Riley. That was one helluva blow. Let's go see if we can make a birdie. By the way, what are they doin' here?" he asked, pointing to the goats that had congregated by the clubhouse.

"Barometers! If you see 'em out on the course, it'll be a grand, dry day. But if you find 'em near the clubhouse, you're liable to get wet."

"So weather's movin' in?"

"Mor'n likely. Better pack your waterproofs."

To his dismay, Jones discovered Riley's perfect drive had left him with an imperfect lie, the ball hanging several inches below his stance. Allowing for the tendency of this sort of lie to produce a fade, he cut a niblick to just above the hole, ten feet away. The moment the shot left Jones' club, Riley could see it would be past the pin. He also knew it was a much easier putt from below the cup, even if at twice the distance, but said nothing.

"Damn," said Jones, as they reached the putting surface, "I should've guessed this green would be canted toward the front. Sorry about the leave, Riley."

"I might've supplied that information. 'Tis me home course, after all. Not to worry though, Bob. No hill for a high-stepper. I'll just ease 'er down nice and gentle . . . like a fine Irish mist."

Riley knew the putt must be made, for if it were missed, the speed and steepness of the green would cause the ball to tumble past the cup to a point further away than it was now. The prospect of turning a potential birdie into a difficult par was something all golfers must face, but this was his one chance to play with Bobby Jones . . . no time for one of his twitching jabs.

What would Angus do, he asked himself? Riley summoned the lasting image of his friend's silken putting stroke, then stood frozen over the ball, grappling for quiet in both mind and muscle . . . that inner calm, as Angus MacKenzie, grand master of the short game, would say. The whole process took so long Jones thought Riley might have fallen asleep. When he finally did putt, there was so little daylight between ball and putterface it was difficult to tell whether he had made a stroke at all. A mere nudge sent the ball swiftly down the glassy surface, gathering speed, and heading off the green, when a late swerve to the right caused the ball to slam into the back of the cup and disappear.

"Never a doubt!" Jones exclaimed, winking at Riley. "You could have made that putt with your eyes closed."

"Me eyes *were* closed!" Riley admitted, finally exhaling.

Jones' mammoth drive on the short, downhill par five second left Riley with a spoon that he knocked onto the front edge of the green. After Jones slid the thirty-foot eagle putt by the cup, Riley tapped in for another birdie.

The third was parred when Riley tugged a mashie niblick into the greenside bunker, and Jones saved their three by splashing from the sand to within inches. The partnership was two under par through three holes.

"This may be the toughest hole on the course," said Riley, as they reached the fourth tee. "Your drive must carry that monster," he added, pointing to the sixty-foot promontory of sand that loomed before them. "It's a carry of about 200 metres to a tiny crowned landing on top. That rock's your best line."

"Any other advice you can give me?" Jones asked, laughing as he chose his brassie for added loft.

"Just LFF," Riley deadpanned.

"LFF?" Jones asked with eyebrows raised.

"*Let 'er Foockin' Fly!*" Riley blurted, grinning impishly.

"That must be a local swing thought," laughed Jones. "Ah'll give it a try."

With a lazy backswing that took the club well past parallel, Jones cocked his wrists into a powerful vee and pivoted into the ball so effortlessly it seemed unlikely any clubhead speed could be generated. The ball leapt off the clubface in a thunderclap and screamed through the heavy seaside air, easily clearing the crest of the sand dune before landing in the center of the hog-backed fairway 250 metres away.

"Seriously, Bob, what do you think about when you hit a shot like that?" asked Riley, as they hiked up the face of the sandhill like sherpas in the Himalayas.

"Absolutely nothing! I've already played the shot in my mind before I actually swing. The mind is the most powerful force in golf. It can inspire a player to do the impossible, or paralyze him into the ordinary."

"For me, linksland courses have always offered the most thorough examination of the mind. Like Lahinch, you must keep your eye on the process of playin' the game, instead of the results. Not ev'ry well-struck shot gets its due. And the poor, feeble mind can't take much punishment before it begins to question the mechanics of the swing."

"I couldn't agree more, Riley. When you hit the shot you've imagined, and it winds up in a spot of trouble, it can wear you down. But players who complain about bad bounces are apt to bemoan the unfairness of life. All we can ever do is put forth our best effort and accept the rub of the green."

"Looks like the old rub got us this time, Bob."

They had reached the summit of the mountainous sand dune only to find the ball had caromed off a knobby knoll in the fairway and skidded into the left-hand rough.

"Whenever I get a bad result from a good shot, I always try to find something positive. Looks to me like we've got a little better angle to the green from this side. And, even though we're not on the short grass, the lie is pretty flat. Besides, I hit it right where you told me!"

"No wonder you won the Grand Slam, thinkin' the way y' do. I never dreamed you were going to hit it so far you'd bring the knobs into play. I shoulda had you hit the spoon!"

With acres of untamed seascape rolling like tidal waves between his ball and the putting surface, Riley's second shot to the 4th green was every bit as intimidating as Jone's drive had been. It appeared in the distance as a tiny speck of smoothness, an unreachable safe harbor enshrouded in peril on all sides. Riley's mashie niblick cut through the beach grass like a scythe, striking the ball cleanly, and sending it sailing onto this lonely haven of bentgrass, sheltered amid the sedge. Jones' short, jabby prod with Calamity Jane took a victory lap around the cup, but fell in for their third birdie.

They had arrived at Klondyke, the quaint 5th, hard by the Atlantic Ocean, its fairway rising between tumultuous sand heaves like a path less taken, before dead-ending into a colossal dune at 270 metres. The green for this peculiar par five lay beyond the peak and down a grade at least as steep as the one that now confronted them. With the wind freshening at their back, Riley considered his options.

"The further I drive it up the slope, the steeper it gets. We won't be findin' any flat lies unless I aim for that shelf in the left rough. But it's no bargain in that tangle of grass."

"Sounds like a layup of about 220 metres is in order."

Riley followed Jones' instructions to the letter, playing a spoon that rode the sharp tailwind. Carrying 208 metres and rolling twelve, it stopped abruptly against the incline of Klondyke. Though the steep upslope created an awkward stance for Jones, it would add much-needed loft to his spoon. As he addressed the ball, Riley stopped him.

"Hold on, Bob. I'll take a peek to see if she's clear."

One of the many oddities of Lahinch was the unusual configuration of tees and greens in this congested corner of the course. The 18th fairway was routed across the 5th and the 6th fairways, and anyone playing the last was given the right of way. With the monstrous dune in the center of Klondyke obscuring everything from view, it was imperative that players on the 5th exercise caution.

"All clear!" Riley shouted from the summit.

Jones swept the ball into the air in a graceful arc, sending it toward the apex of the enormous sand dune on a trajectory scarcely adequate to traverse the peak. Landing near the base of the downslope, it pitched forward in a direct line with the pin, trundled briskly along the firm turf and skittered through the green, before coming to rest against the fieldstone wall which formed the boundary of Lahinch. Riley had no backswing.

"What if you were to take your cleek and deflect the ball off that wall, back in the direction of the green? asked Jones, as he surveyed their dilemma.

"'Tis the only shot I've got. I won't be takin' any blasted unplayable."

Pulling his favorite utility club from the bag, Riley studied the angles of the wall and inspected each individual stone. They were all jagged and uneven, making the shot dicey at best, and at worst, disastrous. He gripped down the hickory shaft below the leather wrapping on the handle, drew back his cleek, and struck the ball so that sparks flew as the clubhead clanked into the wall on its follow-through. It ricocheted off a flattish stone and caromed toward the green, settling into a low undulation just six feet below the hole. With an air of authority reserved only for champions, Jones calmly knocked the putt into the back of the cup. Four under.

"Well done, Mr. Jones!" blared Riley, whacking him on the shoulder.

"That rock shot turned six into four," Jones said with a wry grin. "Sorry about the way my spoon ran on."

"Nothing we can do about those uncontrollables. Could just as well gone in for a two," Riley said, hands still reverberating from the contact of his cleek against the wall.

"Or," Jones counseled, "that ricochet might have hit you and gone out of bounds on its way to an eight!"

As they moved the few steps from Klondyke's green to the tee of the quirky 6th, a group of locals began teeing off the 18th. The percussion of their drives cracked and hissed quite near the heads of Jones and O'Neill. Riley exchanged pleasantries with the men as they crossed in front, but declined to reveal his companion's identity when the foursome remarked how closely he resembled the great American golfer, Bobby Jones.

"You'll enjoy the *Dell*," said Riley, referring to the name of the 6th. "She sits hidden behind those drumlins," he added, pointing to a pair of rounded sand hills some 140 metres away.

"Where's the flag?"

"Ahh, you'll not be seein' the flag, laddie. Over the white rock is your best line."

"I don't think I've ever played a par three where I couldn't at least see part of the flag."

"Farst time for ev'rythin'. This is links golf at its best. The green is just beyond the mound, and she won't be movin'. Just trust in your swing now."

Riley's instruction came more from a golfer's common book of wisdom than as a suggestion that Jones might need his, or anyone's, advice. And the great man of golf accepted this reminder in the spirit given, knowing all-too-well the anxiety of a blind shot is often accompanied by an indecisive swing.

Jones selected his mashie niblick and lofted a towering shot into the teeth of a wind whose velocity had grown ever stronger during their conference. Flying straight and true over the white rock, the ball disappeared from view behind the sandy mounds.

"She's in the hands o' the Dell's leprechauns! Can't be too bad. Just a matter of how good she is."

They approached the green through the gap to the right of the mound. No ball in sight. Jones looked on the hillside past the white rock, in case he had been short.

"I can see now, why the goats like Lahinch," Jones said, nearly toppling off the steep hillside. "They're in their element here."

Riley checked behind the green to see if it had been overshot. Still no ball. Then, years of witnessing shots played with unerring exactness, of gauging just how far and how straight the ball was traveling in relation to its target, drew their eyes toward the pin. A chunk of turf was missing from the lip of the cup. Jone's shot had gone in on the fly. Six under.

"Who said you need to see the pin to hit it!?"

"Your leprechuans were smilin' on me that time, Riley!"

"I 'spect you make your own luck, Bobby! Glad you holed it though, 'cause I can't poot a whit on Dell. And don't be upset with me for callin' you Bobby. I am one of your adorin' fans, after all."

Another blind tee shot now faced Riley. A series of unkempt hummocks defended the corner of the dogleg at the 7th, dense thickets commandeering the dunes, daring Riley to cut a slab off the sharp left turn. But failure to carry the corner meant an overgrown lie in knee-deep undergrowth. Bogeys, or worse, lurked in this maelstrom of marram. And too far right would bring into play a crevasse of sand sixty feet wide and twenty feet deep . . . no place for Jones. Safety meant laying up. Riley laid up.

Unsure of the yardage into a biting headwind, Jones' slight fade of a mashie niblick landed short, and well to the right of the narrow green. When Riley chipped tidily to a foot, they were six under through seven holes.

The diminutive 8th, at first glance a pushover of only 320 metres, posed its own set of challenges. Lying parallel to the Atlantic, it was exposed to the most disagreeable sort of wind for the right-handed golfer . . . one crossing sharply from left to right. Unruffled by the elements, Jones turned down the toe of his spoon to deloft the club. Fabricating a low hook designed to stay beneath even the most resolute of the cross-cutting blasts, it carried up to a plateau of fairway not visible from the tee below.

Shielded from the wind by a corridor of sand dunes some 120 metres from the green, Riley felt a false sense of calm. The distance, though ideally suited for his niblick, would require more club than normal to offset the 20 metres of added resistance the ball was sure to encounter above the ceiling of the dunes. Selecting his mashie niblick, he punched a three-quarter shot that cut through the wind like a beam of light on a moonless night. It landed near the pin, then spun back down the tilted surface of the green, forty-five feet away.

"Nothin' too brilliant 'bout that," Riley snorted.

"Tough pin placement," Jones consoled. "You go at that back left tier too hard and the ball will fly the green. I wouldn't want to chip down that hill to a spot no bigger than my kerchief. No, Riley, you played the only shot you could. The wind kept it short of the top level, but at least we're putting uphill."

Jones was beginning to develop a feel for these coarse, seaside greens. The short stabs of the first few holes had been replaced by a confident, flowing stroke. Gauging the speed perfectly, his attempt at the forty footer grazed the cup and stopped inches away. Riley kept them at six under by brushing in the gimme leave.

The twosome climbed a steep slope to the 9th tee and had now reached the highest point on the course. From this knoll, the fabled limestone Cliffs of Moher could be seen rising sharply from the Atlantic, sheer crags, forming a valiant defense against the angry seas crashing into Ireland's coastline some seven hundred feet below. The village of Lahinch was blurred by a misty fogbank blown in by the gathering storm. They were now squarely in the midst of weather predicted by the goats . . . most foul.

In this moment they seemed as two old tars, squinting through pea soup at flagsticks strewn across a tempestuous ocean of linksland. Like miz'n masts listing leeward in a sou'wester, the slender spars of Lahinch arched and strained in defiance of the storm, their tiny cloth spinnakers fluttering unbattened.

"My favourite spot on all of God's earth," Riley shouted above the roar as he prepared to play his tee shot on the 360 metre hole. "Someday my ashes'll be scattered on this hillside."

"I can't imagine a lovelier place, Riley. From here, you can see your home and your golf course. And your soul will draw from the energy of the sea and the wind for all eternity."

With a favoring wind and an elevated tee, the 9th was a deceptively simple-looking hole that gave one the sensation of being able to drive the green. But of course, one cannot. A fairway that pitched fiendishly right to left, and a green tucked into tiny hillside, made it nearly impossible to approach from the right. And, with a steep declivity at the left side of the slender green resembling a miniature version of the Cliffs of Moher, it was imperative the drive be placed at the correct angle. Riley did just that.

Pounding the J. Braddell down the right half of the fairway in a powerful draw, aided by wind and terrain, it traveled over 300 metres, stopping inches shy of the left rough. With a pitch of less than 60 metres, Jones nipped his niblick crisply off the tight, seaside turf. It flew head-high at a velocity that seemed far too swift, checked twice as it skidded toward the pin, and stopped stone dead. They had turned the outward nine in 29 strokes.

"We tied my course record!" Riley said gleefully.

"Not bad for a coupla retired has-beens," said Jones.

"Better than being a coupla never-weres!" quipped Riley.

"I wouldn't have bet on a score like that in this gale," replied Jones. "The ball begins to have a mind of its own in a stout blow."

"Aye, but you know what the Scots would say to that, Bob. *Nae wind . . . nae gowf.*"

"Well, wind and all, I love your links here at Lahinch! This is the way golf was meant to be played. I'm trying to create a similar challenge on my new course in America."

"You're buildin' a golf course in the States?"

"It's carved out of an old orchard in Augusta, Georgia. We call it Augusta National Golf Links. In fact, the architect is Dr. Alister MacKenzie. I think he did some fine tuning of Lahinch back in '27."

"Aye, that he did. But he found most of the original work of Old Tom Morris to be farst rate. Didn't touch Klondyke or Dell. Said they were curiosities, but natural and memorable."

"That's why I chose MacKenzie to design Augusta. It's a parkland layout, so he won't be able to replicate the linksland qualities of Lahinch or St. Andrews. But he will include the same natural design features, shot value, and memorablility, on what we hope will be one of America's finest courses."

"Lahinch is known as the St. Andrews of Ireland, and MacKenzie tried to retain a few of the Old Courses's oddities here. We're grateful for his ability to update Old Tom's early genius. By the way, my dear friend Angus MacKenzie is a shirt-tail cousin of Dr. MacKenzie."

"You don't say. Does he play golf?"

"Angus is a fine player."

"But not up to your calibre?"

"He doesn't think so. And that's often the best gauge of a golfer's ability."

"It usually separates those who win from those who don't. But winning at golf may not be as important to him as it is to you. Golf is a pursuit that brings enjoyment to people for a variety of reasons. Your friend MacKenzie may get more pleasure from your company on the course than from defeating you."

"If I didn't know better, I'd think you've played golf with Angus!"

"Angus MacKenzie by any other name is a man who plays the game for the joy of its mysteries, and for the enrichment of the friendships it inspires."

"Well said, Bobby."

"What's your record on the inward nine, Riley?"

"31. Shall we take 'er a notch lower?"

"By all means. Lead on."

Chapter 9

*W*aterproofs that once seemed impervious to the rain now allowed it to enter freely through every pore. Umbrellas, though useful in deflecting the downpour, had the lift of a kite and threatened to soar off into the dreary sky if not held tightly. Turning up the collar of his jacket to shield his neck from the storm, Jones toweled off his hands and the grip of his driver, then, in defiance of the unruly elements, held his tee shot against a vicious crosswind, propelling it some 240 metres down a slender furrow of fairway that, for the faint of heart, would have inspired sheer terror.

Riley watched in quiet admiration as Jones posed in his signature finish. It was yet another shot deftly played, further cementing the bond of friendship and respect that had begun to form, unspoken, between the two men. Though worlds apart, separated by continents and cultures, it was their command of the game that served as the medium of expression. They took delight in their own well-struck shots, of course. But, just as those who revel in golf as art, each found particular pleasure in his colleague's brushstrokes of genius, painted onto this canvas of fescue precisely as the artist had intended. The joy they derived from sharing these rare gifts must have been a phenomenon felt only by such masters as Michelangelo discussing sculpture with da Vinci, or Bach comparing notes with Beethoven.

From just beneath a sand blown embankment, Riley rifled a cleek toward the tiny parapet masquerading as a green amongst a squadron of dunes and, like Dublin Castle in 1916, nearly impregnable for all but the most expert of marksman. Riley's ball, perhaps unluckily, struck the pin and bounded forty feet away. When Jones lagged his slippery downhiller near the hole to secure their par, Riley admitted;

"I'll take four at the 10th ev'ry time, 'specially in this slop."

"Ah'm with you, Riley. That fortress they call a green is a bugger to find, and damn near impossible to putt."

The 11th was a bantam-weight three par nestled in among sandy hillocks, its right flank defended by a nasty little pot bunker. The green leaned so abruptly that ten feet off line would land the team in the tiny coffer, and fifteen feet to the left would leave them on top of the lean with little chance of a two-putt. Moving the ball off the brass toe-plate of his right shoe, Riley swung his mashie niblick steeply, and squeezed a shot under the wind to a spot just beneath the cleft. The ball hesitated for a moment before beginning its descent and was trickling off the green when the pin blocked its path.

"Ah, what a game golf is!" Riley exclaimed, plucking his ball from between the flagstick and the lip of the cup. "That pin turned a sure three or maybe even four, into an ace!" he yelped, kissing the ball as if it were the Blarney Stone itself.

"One of the best shots I've ever seen!" said Jones, who'd seen just about everything in golf. "No room to land the ball and get it close when the pin is in that far right location."

"No better time for the luck o' the Irish!"

"I suspect you make your own luck, Riley."

Though considered the most difficult hole at Lahinch, downwind, the 12th played much shorter than its 440 metres. With the Atlantic skirting the left side, and the contour sloping toward it, Jones hit a powerful fade to counteract the magnetic force of the ocean. When Riley laced a mashie into the center of the green, they held par. Two under.

"What do you Yanks think of the Irish situation?" Riley asked Jones, curious as to how the rest of the world viewed the Irish *Troubles*. "Is our aim any diff'rent than your War of Independence?"

"If you mean the partition of Ireland into North and South, then no, the Irish have their gripe. By splitting your country in two, the British seem to endorse religious bigotry. Our system of government, at least in theory, is blind to religious differences. It's one of the reasons we fought."

"Then why shouldn't we declare war on England?"

"I suppose anyone can declare anything they want, but when it comes to a fight for freedom, I'd say Ireland is overmatched. Even our war against the Brits succeeded as much out of the difficult logistics of fighting far from England as it did from our persistence, or our military genius."

"What do you mean? You routed the bastards!"

"Thanks in no small part to France's navy, and British supply lines that stretched across the Atlantic Ocean. No, the conditions for the British fighting the colonists in America were much more demanding then, than fighting Ireland in their own back yard is now. You have about as much of a chance of beating the Brits as an eighteen handicapper has playing straight up against a plus two."

"What about guerilla warfare? You know, the IRA."

"Isn't that another name for the assassination of political officials? Or the random killing of Protestant citizens? Or the destruction of public property? I just can't see Ireland becoming united by those means. All that can come of terrorism is more reprisals by the Protestants and the British against the Irish Catholics. The hatred gets dug in deeper and the cycle gets repeated."

"A lot of the IRA's funding comes from Americans."

"Yeah, I've heard of the *Clan na Gael* in the U.S. Seems normal for Irish families in America to want their homeland, the *Auld Sod*, as they call it, united. It's a noble cause. But sending money to the IRA isn't the answer. Not if the IRA is going to continue the violence. Irish-Americans would be better served backing leadership in Ireland that could speak to the many economic and social merits of a united republic."

Jones placed his right hand on Riley's shoulder to steady himself while dislodging an accumulation of mud and grass from between his spikes and continued; "That way, maybe the Protestants in Northern Ireland who are on the fence would vote for the republic. The only solution is for the peaceable removal of the British. They'll never leave of their own accord. The voters in Northern Ireland will have to ask them to leave."

"And the voters in the narth won't be askin' the Brits to leave unless it's in their best interests."

"Precisely. Respect the system. In the end, it's the laws, not the men, that prevail."

The 250 metre par four 13th was birdied when Riley drove the green. As the course routing took them further inland, this spectacular marriage of land and sea known as Lahinch had begun to recede into the sheltered breakwater of the 14th. These more tranquil contours allowed the men to maneuver safely between two soaring dunes that guarded a tiny spit of green. On in two . . . down in two . . . another birdie.

Jones paused to savor this rare linksland, heaving savagely along the coast, enveloping him in a cocoon of sand and grass and sagging gray sky. It was obvious this was the work of some higher authority. Man could never replicate these rugged dunes. Wind and ocean, under the guiding hands of God, had carved the sand into shapes that architect and machine simply could not. And into this medium He had sown only those grasses that flourish in adversity. A golfer might do well to emulate the fescue and marram of Lahinch, Jones thought, for they embrace the elements and dig deep for their sustenance, never yielding to hardship.

Even more now than earlier in the day the two seemed as salts, buffeted by this angry squall opposing their safe passage home. They sailed by the difficult 15th in par, but nearly capsized their round at the short 16th when Riley's approach putt veered ten feet off its charted course. Jones managed to right the ship by tacking toward the cup, away from the eye of the storm. Only after Riley's drive had taken them far to starboard, and Jones' second had come about too strongly to port, were they able to dock for par at the treacherous 17th. As Jones prepared to shove off on the 18th, a par five reachable in two, these ancient mariners had navigated the inward nine in four better than par.

"Bobby, I can't remember when I've had such fun. I'll be a bucket o' tears if we don't tie my record of 60. We'll be needin' a birdie here, to do it."

"59 has a better ring to it. It's been my great pleasure to play with you today, Riley. I can see you'd have given us Americans fits if you had played in the Walker Cup matches."

"Ah, that's sore spot fer me, Bobby, but your words are kind. It's been a blessin' to play with you t'day and contribute a wee bit to our fine round."

"We've got quite a score on our ball. And, how about those aces?"

"Rare as dry eye at an Irish wake. Now, put one out where I can reach the green."

A frigid wind continued to whistle through the waterlogged twilight. The sudden drop in temperature had turned rain into needles of ice. Shivering beneath his rainslicks and drawing his cap tight to his eyes, Jones retrieved a spare ball from the pocket of his trousers and placed it onto the tee in hopes that warmer ammunition would compress better and fly farther. Then, summoning a focus deep from within, he launched a drive through the determined crosswind. Over the fairways of Dell and Klondyke it flew, bounding across the dune-pocked terrain until it was spent, a mere 200 metres from home.

"Jaysus, Bobby, now there's a cracker!"

"Time to give your home crowd a thrill," said Jones, pointing to the throng behind the last green.

"Jimmy O'Brien's been to town," said Riley. "Too much loudmouth soup."

"We've had a nice, quiet go of it, Riley. They could have come out earlier, but didn't, probably because of Jimmy. It's time to show our appreciation."

"How did you deal with all the crowds during your career as a competitive golfer, Bobby?"

"It was grand in the beginning. But it was one of the reasons I retired early. The crowds always expected me to win. I had high hopes for myself on the golf course, too. But knew I couldn't win every tournament. Trying to live up to the public's unreachable goals tore me up inside. I had to get away from it for my own health. This show of affection by your fellow townfolk, however, is most welcome."

"It's a smooth brassie, or a mighty spoon," said Riley, inspecting his lie and calculating the distance to the green.

"I like the brassie," replied Jones. "It'll stay under the wind and may even cut a bit to hold it against that crosswind. Looks like the green has a false front, so you'll want a shot that'll release through the swale."

"You've never set foot on the course," Riley said, shaking his head in amazement, "and you can still figger each shot like you've been playin' here for years. I was thinkin' the brassie all along."

"Get on with it then, lad," Jones said, grinning, as rain ran off his umbrella in rivulets. "Those folks are getting' wet as a duck's ass waitin' for us."

With wind and rain pounding sideways in sodden sheets, Riley removed the head cover from his brassie and toweled off the grip. From a tight, hanging lie, he caught the ball flush on the ivory insert and sent it shrieking through the curtain of sleet. They watched as the tiny white speck pierced the veil of darkness like an Irish bullet through British armor, penetrating the rain-soaked horizon and landing just short of the green, directly on line with the pin.

"Go in!" Jones blurted, not out of wishful thinking, but with the insight of a golfer who knows when a shot has been struck perfectly and may indeed have a chance of being holed. The ball raced through the swale fronting the 18th and scooted up the slope toward the flag. Roars rolled down the fairway toward the golfers as, with a loud clank, it struck the pin dead center, rattled, and spun out. Expectant cheers slipped into disappointed groans, and the golfers knew their albatross had narrowly escaped.

"Too much club," complained Riley, winking.

"The wind must have shifted a skosh," Jones, kidded, inserting an already-soaked index finger into his mouth and holding it up as if to check the direction of the wind.

Jones and O'Neill were given a rousing ovation as they strode up the fairway and onto the green. The eagle was captured and an inward nine of 30 posted. It was an inconceivable alternate shot 59 on a day that had been anything but soft and balmy.

When the excitement had subsided, and the locals had returned to their favourite alehouse, the new comrades savored a quiet moment before Jones began his journey home.

"I filled out a scorecard and signed it for you, Riley," said Jones. "I'd be grateful if you'd do the same for me. It's been a day I will always cherish, not just for the golf, but for the companionship."

"Aye, our trophies will all soon tarnish," Riley replied, "but our friendships will remain forever bright and shiny."

PART IV

▼

LAHINCH

Chapter 1

$\mathcal{A}$ cobblestone path slithered past the edge of Lahinch Golf Links. To one side stood a fieldstone wall, and beyond it lay the sea. Opposite the wall were rows of simple Irish cottages built of cheerfully whitewashed stone. Roofs in dire need of new thatch lent stark contrast to front doors freshly painted in bright, bold colors of red or blue or green. The four men ambled down the gently curving lane past the 18th fairway to a cottage overlooking the tee of Dell. Tendrils of blue-grey smoke drifted skyward from the chimney, and a chorus of music filled the air through an open doorway.

Angus had donned the traditional formal wear of a Scotsman. A black and white horse-hair sporran hung from his waist, smartly accenting his MacKenzie tartan kilt. His Prince Charlie jacket fit snugly over a wing-collared shirt, leaving twenty, or so, unwanted pounds nowhere to hide. Cable-knit knee highs were set off by tartan flashes and, tucked rakishly into the stocking band of his right calf was a dirk, the dagger of a high-lander. His ghillies had been burnished to a bright shine, with laces wound in several revolutions around his thick ankles, ending in perfect bows above the shoe-tops.

Patrick, wearing the dress military tartan of the Royal Scots Greys, and Collier and Mick in their most mournful suits, gave the quartet an oddly mismatched, but respectful appearance. Angus ducked his head to avoid the low crossbeam of the door and stepped inside. The music stopped.

"Would that be Angus MacKenzie?" a soft voice called from the kitchen of the three room cottage.

"It is," replied Angus. "We've come to pay respects to our dear friend Riley O'Neill," he added, gesturing with open palm to his three companions.

"And we've been expectin' y', Angus," said the woman, wiping her flour-coated hands on a linen apron and stepping into the living room. "I'm Kathleen McAndrew. Riley's sister."

The white embroidery of her apron contrasted sharply with the black of her floor-length mourning dress. Kathleen appeared a decade younger than her fifty-nine years, face flushed by wind, and raven hair beginning to intersperse grey strands in equal number. Her ample tresses, pulled back tightly into a French bun, revealed the fine features of an O'Neill and a warm, welcoming smile. But, as she turned to face the men, a jagged scar, running the full length of her cheek from her left eye to the corner of her mouth, marred what otherwise was perfect skin.

"And you must be Mick," said Kathleen, extending her hand toward the big Scotch-Irishman. "We'll have to bust out the doorway to get you in!" she blared, flashing Riley's grin.

"Deepest condolences, mum," Mick replied, folding his hands and bowing his head. "God bless this house and all those in it."

"Bless you, Mick," she replied.

"Collier, I'm so glad you made the trip," she said, turning to Ames. "Our meeting was long overdue."

"Thank you, Kathleen, for allowing me to be part of the services. I was so sorry to learn of Riley's passing. May we speak later?"

"Riley would have been pleased to see you in his home. There's never a convenient time for death," she sighed, "but, yes, of course, we'll talk. We must catch up."

"And Patrick," she said, as the music resumed, "'tis good to see you again after all these years."

"Aye, Kathleen," said Patrick, shouting over the din, "I 'spect you've been slavin' over soda bread and lamb stew."

"And I'd best be gettin' back to it so you can all fill your bellies," she teased, returning to the kitchen through a passel of musicians who, with great enthusiasm, were blowing their hornpipes, and bowing their fiddles.

"We put Riley in his bedroom to allow for the dancin'," Kathleen shouted over her shoulder. "Go on now," she said, motioning with the back of her hand. "Give 'im your best."

Angus stepped to the bedroom door and peered in. Candles flickered beside Riley's wasted frame, casting eerie shadows about the small room. He lay prostrate on what appeared to be an old door, supported at each corner by wooden, straight-backed chairs. Moving closer, the four companions edged into the room. A plain, white linen shroud was draped over his emaciated body, covering all but head and shoulders. Bony arms were folded across his chest, and from around his neck hung a crucifix with its rosary beads laced between his fingers. A midsection so spare that hip bones protruded from beneath the sheet like tent pegs, it was as if Riley was melting away before their very eyes. All color had vanished from his face, so wax-like only the merest film of ashen skin remained. With vacant eyes left open to observe the rites, there remained a familiar curl at the corner of his mouth, suggesting he might know something the rest of the world did not.

Two old women, with scarves tied beneath their chins and shawls wrapped around their shoulders, huddled together on the far side of the room, keening low, mournful wails, not just for Riley, but for all souls long ago lost. Out in the living room a young tenor began to sing the plaintive notes of Londonderry Air.

"What was it G. K. Chesterton wrote in his *Toast to the Gaels?*" asked Collier.

On cue, Mick drew from his reservoir of adages . . .

> "... *the great Gaels of Ireland are the people God made mad.*
> *For all their wars are merry, and all their songs are sad."*

"So this is what it's come to, Riley," Angus said remorsefully. "All the hopes and dreams of a lifetime laid out on an old door."

"Ah, but not just any old door," Kathleen interjected, as she joined Riley's friends in their time of sorrow. "My late husband, Duff, owned the *Sea Hag Pub* for thirty years before he drowned at high tide last summer . . . God rest his soul," she sighed, crossing herself and pursing St. Christopher to her lips. "Duff had that door made special for the Hag, and it had a certain significance for Riley."

"Kathleen closed the *Hag* after Duff's passing," said Patrick, "but Riley insisted on keepin' the door. As Duff's best customer for three decades, seems he thought he'd paid for it."

"The door commemorates the poetic story of *Baile and Aillinn* as told by W. B. Yeats," Kathleen continued. "The two young lovers hailed from different cultures . . . Protestant and Catholic, Irish and English, Northern Ireland and Southern Ireland. Pick one, any will do for purposes of this sad old fable."

Kathleen ran her hand along an exposed edge of the door next to the cadaver and continued; "They were forbidden to marry and died alone of broken hearts. My late husband, God rest his soul, dearly loved the story and commissioned a woodcarver from County Cork to fashion the unrequited lovers on either side of this magnificent slab of bog oak."

"You can't see the carvings for Riley's corpse," said Patrick, "but trust me, a finer piece of work was never done."

"Riley's last request was to be laid out on the door," said Kathleen. "It's ours to reckon what he might be tryin' to say."

"I'm sure that everyone who loved Riley has their own interpretation of the message," said Angus. "There is always something unsaid or undone in our lives. Barriers . . . like the door separating *Baile and Aillinn*."

Angus' gaze shifted from Riley's remains to the roll-top desk situated against the wall. Stepping around the carved door, he spied Riley's old hickory shafted clubs lying on the floor next to a shag bag filled with gutta percha balls. Removing the crusty leather headcover marked *JB* to reveal the J. Braddell driver, Angus paused to examine the details of the club. Eyes closed, he caressed the grip, imagining all the colossal shots he had seen Riley smash off the rock-hard leather insert. On the top shelf of Riley's desk sat the 1930 British Isles Cup, tarnished black as the inside of a firebox. Angus spat on the corner of his handkerchief and vigorously rubbed the inscription until Riley's name returned to its original luster.

Raising the desk's cambered door, Riley's collection of books and papers were piled high as space would permit and covered with a thin film of dust. A large, leather-bound volume sat to one side of the writing surface, its brass clasp unlocked. Angus brushed dust from the cover, opened it, and, as he did, several envelopes placed inside fluttered to the floor. Stooping to pick them up, he noticed Riley's handwriting scrawled on each. Names were prominently printed on four of the envelopes and, on the fifth appeared the notation, *Will.*

"I guess Riley had to have the last word," said Angus, holding the envelopes above his head.

"What are those?" asked Patrick.

"Personal letters to each of us, and his *Last Will and Testament*," replied Angus.

"Do you think we should read the *Will?*" he asked Kathleen, distributing Riley's letters.

"And why not? Most of the townfolk have headed up to St. Theresa's. Let's have Father O'Shea do the honors. Father," Kathleen called into the living room to the parish priest, "would you be so kind as to do the readin' of Riley's *Will?*"

"'Twould be me privilege, Kate."

The portly clergyman arose from his seat near the fire, waddled into the bedroom, and took the document from Kathleen. Wheezing from his recent exertion, he began to read in a loud, deliberate voice.

Dear Friends and Family,

What on earth are you doing inside, when you could be enjoyin' a grand game of golf? Well, since you're all here, I may as well share my final wishes.

Firstly, I want to be cremated. I don't like close quarters, so a coffin won't do. Of course, Lahinch has no crematorium, so I've made arrangements for the burning to be done over at Burke's Timber Yard. Sean Burke has promised me he can fire their kiln to a temperature suitable to do the job. You can scatter my remains on the hill above the 9th tee.

I give my interest in the Colby property to my sister, Kathleen, for the rest of her life, may it be long and filled with joy. And at her death, it'll go to each of her three children. At her age, Kethleen isn't likely to add to her brood, but if she does, any I don't know of should get their share.

I leave my cottage to Kathleen, but if she cares not to live in the poor hovel, then I ask that she rent it to my dear friend, Jimmy O'Brien, PGE (Professional Golfer Extraordinare). Jimmy's getting on in years and feeling the gout. It's a merciless trip from his home to the office, so he'll enjoy the short walk to the links from my cottage. Should a bargain be struck, I set the rent at one pint per week, to be poured on the site of my ashes by Jimmy himself.

To my Godson, Patrick MacKenzie, I leave my leather-bound journal. It contains all my thoughts on the events of my life since I began to record such things in 1916. Patrick, I know you'll take my ramblings with the appropriate dose of salt, especially those that relate to the pursuit of our Republic. You will find tucked inside the crease of the front cover, my favorite photographs of people and places that were dear to me, and the scorecard signed by Bobby Jones. It's not for sale to the blasted autograph collectors at any price.

I give to my dear friend, Mick Callahan, my copy of **Ulysses***, signed by the great James Joyce himself. Mick, you're one of the few of my friends who might just understand it.*

To my half-brother Collier Ames, I give the pearl brooch of our mother, Sinead. Collier, she wore it every day of her life. May it bring you as close to her as she was to me.

And, to my dear friend, Angus MacKenzie, I give my J. Braddell driver, and my collection of W. B. Yeats poetry. Their importance is of a most personal nature, Angus, as I'm quite certain you are aware.

Finally, I give to my home of Lahinch, the 1930 British Isles Cup trophy. I'd be honored if it were displayed over the mantle of the fireplace in our clubhouse, as a constant reminder to the lads who follow, that, we too, could play the game of golf.

Riley Padraig 'Parbuster' O'Neill

"Well," said Kathleen, drying her eyes with the corner of a tea towel, "we'd best be gettin' to St Theresa's. Father O'Shea has prepared a fine service for Riley as he makes his lasting peace with The Lord God, Himself."

"I'll bring the Cup," said Patrick. "All shined up, she'll make a grand toasting chalice at the cremation."

Outside the cottage, a mangy bay mare stood harnessed to a low-slung lumber wagon, hooves blackened with soot out of respect for the deceased. The driver, Sean Burke, wore the black suit of an undertaker and a black bowler hat, reminiscent of the 1920s. With Angus and Patrick lifting the door at Riley's head, and Mick and Collier raising his feet, they carried body and door out of the cottage, placing both onto the bed of the wagon. Down Links Lane they marched, pipers and fiddlers breaking into ballads of Ireland's mournful past. Riley's favorites, *Bold Fenian Men* and *A Nation Once Again*, were played, as family and friends marched slowly behind, heads bowed. The more celebratory mood at the cottage was replaced by the somber realization that no amount of making light of Riley's predicament would bring him back to them.

Friends and acquaintances lined the sidewalks as the procession made its way down Main Street past the Atlantic Hotel where it was met at St. Theresa's by Father O'Shea, whose clerical collar was now soaked through with perspiration from trying in vain to stay one step ahead of the day's events. Hoisting body and door above their shoulders, the four pallbearers marched down the aisle of the chapel toward the altar. They knelt before the likeness of Christ nailed to a cross beneath stained glass windows depicting his birth and resurrection, then settled into the front pew, waiting in reflective silence for the apoplectic priest to ascend his pulpit.

Traditional Catholic rites soon gave way to the more secular urgings of Father O'Shea for friends and relatives to join in the homage. A life incapable of being distilled by just one person would be eulogized by committee. One by one, it seemed, the entire village had an anecdote about their favorite son, each slightly more embellished than the previous.

Jimmy O'Brien, at least one pint past equilibrium, recalled his days as a young amateur golfer competing against Riley in the South of Ireland Championships.

"I could beat damn . . ." he started. Then, realizing he was in the Lord's house, crossed himself profusely and revised his remarks to say, "I could beat *darn* near anyone in any tarnamint, 'cept Riley in the South."

Jimmy puffed up his chest and continued in a thick slur. "When he beat me eight straight years, like me Maude beatin' mud from our doormat, I turned pru!"

"Aye, Jimmy, y' showed 'im now, didn't you!" a fellow mourner called from the congregation, drawing loud laughter from everyone, including his wife, Maude, who blushed with pride and shook her head from side to side in mock embarrassment.

And so it went, until the people of Lahinch had remembered Riley in the way that only small towns and villages remember those who are a daily ingredient in their lives. It wouldn't be the last of the recollections. The stories told before God's altar would be repeated and refined in the local public houses for generations to come. When the last of the eulogists had descended from the pulpit, Mick whispered to Angus.

"The man in the last pew on the right reminds me of Sir Thomas Forgan fifty years ago."

"I thought I'd seen an apparition," Angus replied. "The hair isn't as white, but all other features are Forgan's, right down to the way he carries himself."

"Collier, do you recognize the man in the back pew"? asked Angus, elbowing Ames.

"Why, it's . . . Sir . . .," Collier exclaimed, cupping his hand to his mouth as he realized how loudly he had spoken in the quiet of the church.

Chapter 2

*T*he scruffy mare stood in front of the church, right rear fetlock suspended, sway-backed from a lifetime of hard labor and indifferent care.
She looked like Angus felt. Riley and door were carried reverently down
the steep steps of the chapel and placed into the wagon for the short trip to
the kiln. Well-wishers and mourners had adjourned to the pub for a reprise
of the day's affairs, while close friends and family accompanied the funeral
carriage to Burke's Timber Yard.

Flames in the furnace were stoked to maximum intensity and, in its
proximity, Angus and the others were beginning to sweat like Father
O'Shea. Sean Burke had fashioned a ramp of metal rollers in front of the
oven door, as if they would be tendering green lumber to the kiln.

"And what'll we be doin' with the door, Kathleen?" yelled Sean.

"Ah, she's a beaut' ain't she, Sean," Kathleen replied. "And it meant
more to Riley than anyone, except Duff. But they're long gone, God rest
their souls. No, I'll keep the door. Put Riley on another platform."

"Got just the thing, Katie," replied Sean. "Gimme a hand, boys!" Angus
and the others hoisted Riley onto a side panel of pine crating that had
housed the new boiler for the hospital.

"Much better burnin' material than oak, pine is," Sean announced
authoritatively. "Might've taken a coupla days to consume the door. Well,
boys, anything to add, before we render our dear friend here into the ashes
from which he came?"

"Just one last remembrance," Angus said, walking toward the kiln in the
company of Mick and Collier. Carrying their hickory shafted putters to
the pyre, the three men laid them, one by one, on Riley's chest like kin-
dling on a campfire.

"May he be up!" they shouted in unison, as Sean rolled crate, cadaver, and clubs into the blaze.

"He'll be done in twenty minutes," Sean said to the procession. "Just enough time for a pint at *O'Doolan's.*

*   *   *

"Fill 'er with the black ooze," Patrick shouted at the barkeep, who placed the silver cup beneath a tap of Guinness and ran a river of the dark stout into the two litre vessel.

Time and again the Cup made its rounds. The crowd exalted Riley, then glorified the Republic, regaled Ireland's martyrs, and came full circle to once again praise Riley. The refilling intervals grew shorter, the exaltations grew louder, and twenty minutes grew into an hour and a half. Finally, the four men retrieved the Cup and returned to Burke's Timber Yard.

"What took y' so long?" asked Sean, knowing full well the men had succumbed to spirits and salutations. "I've separated iron from ash," he said, handing them the three non-combustible clubheads.

"And what'll we be puttin' ol' Riley into, now that he's burnt?" Sean asked, pointing to the cubic foot of ashes cooling on the hearth.

"Guess we hadn't thought about a container for Riley's remains," Angus replied

"The Cup'll do just fine," Patrick interjected, visually sizing up the pile of ashes and the capacity of the Cup.

"What won't fit in the Cup, we can deposit into his shag bag," joked Angus. "We'll just remove all the old gutties to make room for Riley."

"I guess that'd be all right," Mick said, "after all, he won't be staying confined too long. We'll be taking him to his favourite spot come evening."

Carefully removing the ashes from the hearth using coal shovel and broom, the Cup proved adequate storage for Riley's remains. To prevent the contents from spilling, Sean fashioned a cover from a densely woven burlap nail sack, fastening it under the brim by a loop of heavy wire. Cup and golf clubs in hand, the men returned to Riley's cottage for a taste of Kathleen's cooking and a continuation of the wake.

*   *   *

Angus and Patrick sat on the fieldstone wall that ran along Links Lane with Riley carefully situated between them in his Cup. They watched, as both sky and Lahinch were transformed through feathery clouds into a canvas of pastels. The dunes were adorned with grasses, dappled in olive and tinged with sienna, forever changing under the sun's vigilant eye. And, just beyond the untamed terrain, the sea spoke in hushed syllables.

"It's easy to see why Riley loved this place," said Patrick. "The simple splendor of Lahinch reminds me of mother."

"Her beauty went well beyond what the eye could see," sighed Angus. "I can see how the calm of this moment would remind you of Sarah."

"Remember the holiday you took just before I went off to the war?"

"1944 . . . Gleneagles . . . you were seventeen." His eyes moistened. "It remains my fondest memory of your mother. But why would you remember the trip?"

"Those days the two of you spent at Gleneagles were a turning point in her life. She finally allowed herself to love you completely, and to part with Riley. She told me how much it meant to her."

Angus stared at Patrick in search of the truth. He wanted to believe Gleneagles had meant as much to Sarah as it had to him. But, she had died so soon afterward, he never heard the words. Their moments together at Gleneagles had completed him, but he wasn't sure how Sarah felt. Angus always wondered whether she had made the trip to console Patrick, to send him off to war with a sense of family unity . . . a mother comforting her son during a time of danger, providing a touchstone of harmony in an age of uncertainty. And, he wondered, despite all that he and Sarah had shared, whether Riley would always remain at the center of her soul. After all, the images of Riley and Sarah at St. Andrews somehow seemed more real to Angus than those of Sarah and him at Gleneagles. For all these years, he had tucked Gleneagles into the anteroom of his mind, a place he dare not visit. Wishing something, didn't make it true. So, when Patrick had spoken for Sarah and confirmed those dust-covered wishes, it would have been easy for Angus to fall back into denial and to rebuild his barricade of despair. But hope was pounding away at the walls. Instead, he just closed his eyes with a sense of relief and returned with Sarah to Gleneagles.

For some time, the two of them had known their awkward charade couldn't continue. Riley had grown less militant over the years, and the threat to his safety had diminished. Early in their marriage, it seemed to Angus that Sarah was looking for a signal to reunite her with Riley. And, of course, there was Patrick. Angus felt no resentment toward him, but he had become the very image of Riley. His wit and manner, even his voice and laugh were Riley's. It was a daily reminder to Sarah of the feelings that had brought Patrick into the world, one more reason to leave Angus and return to Riley.

But, just when their lives together seemed so tenuous, Sarah suggested the trip to Gleneagles. Only an hour by train from Edinburgh, they shared a fondness for this grand retreat, isolated from the worries of the world. And yet, Angus was surprised. With more thought, he might have seen it as her way of deciding their future. She must have reasoned if she couldn't love Angus at Gleneagles, then surely, love with him was not meant to be.

Since St. Andrews, Angus had bottled up his feelings. He could no longer pretend. Sarah would have to choose, again. Riley or him, once and for all. No longer could he be a husband to someone whose love lay elsewhere. It wasn't at all clear whether Gleneagles would be their final farewell, or their forever more. But Sarah must have had some doubt of her love for Riley or she would have headed to Lahinch long ago. Her staying had given him hope.

It was raining when they departed Waverly Station on that most elegant of all trains, the Royal Scotsman. And, throughout the afternoon, the weather appeared to be socked in, until just before they reached the high plateau of Perthshire, where the magnificent Gleneagles Hotel was revealed in bright sunlight. An attentive staff doted on the couple as if they were newlyweds. From their suite overlooking the King's Course, they could view the alluvial plain cut by glaciers centuries before, its esker ridges heaving sharply to form crowned corridors into which James Braid had cleverly tucked the fairways of his Kings Course. And, as far as the eye could see, were ancient copper beech trees, splashing the landscape with burgundy leaves, as if great casks of wine had been overturned amidst green needles of fir and pine.

Sarah opened the windows to let all this rush into their room on the wings of a warm and gentle afternoon breeze. Then, she turned to Angus with the gaze he had wanted for eighteen years, the one she had always reserved for Riley. It was like the gaze Sarah had given him on the 17th tee of the Old Course in his match with Riley, but said so much more. It was the gaze that said, *I know you can*, but added, *I want you to*. And that made all the difference. He now knew he'd been right to believe her gaze had moved past respect, to love. And, even seventeen years too late, the knowing made him tremble.

Every so often, her scent of lilac and rose returned as it did now, and they were together again. The dream was always the same . . . the tender ebb of exhilaration enjoyed only by those whose love is true, her head nestled on his chest, their limbs gently intertwined, breathing as one. All the feelings through all the years, of sharing everything in life, except those moments which are most intimate, had, at last, come to them at Gleneagles. And now, everything was right between Sarah and Angus and Riley.

Patrick saw this in the eyes of his father. Nothing more needed saying. He slipped down from the wall and took Angus into his arms.

Chapter 3

*I*nside the cottage, the air was teeming with a familiar aroma of cabbage and leeks being mashed into the potatoes. Lamb stew had been ladled onto pewter plates, along with generous dollops of colcannon, balanced by massive wedges of soda bread. Tins of whiskey cake sat cooling on the kitchen cupboard, while a kettle of coffee steamed to a boil on the wood-burning stove. Several strands of greying hair had worked loose from just above each of Kathleen's ears and were now pasted with sweat to her reddened cheeks. With everyone served, and invitations extended for cake and coffee, she slumped, at last, into Riley's over-stuffed leather chair in the corner of his bedroom. Kathleen had begun to drift off to sleep when Collier's croaky voice intruded.

"Kathleen? Is this a bad time?"

"Oh, . . . Collier . . . no, I was just tryin' to collect myself a bit. It's been a hectic few days."

"How did he pass?"

"Right out there on Dell. Every evenin' he'd go out and play his Wee Loup, the 6th, the 10th, and the 14th. Found him keeled over on the green, we did. Only had a six footer. S'pose it was for birdie?"

"It was probably the putt that killed him! You know how he labored over those tiddlers."

"Have you read his letter yet?"

"I haven't found a quiet moment, but I must admit I'm a bit apprehensive."

"Don't be. I think you'll find Riley compassionate in our times of suffering."

"Sir Thomas saw to it we all had our share of suffering. What about you and Sinead? What became of your lives after you escaped Colby in '29?"

"Right off, Mother fell ill. She fought the croup, then pneumonia, and finally was consumed by diphtheria. Her last days were dreadful. All of her strength was needed to resist the infections. Very little thought was given to . . . well, you know."

"What about your life? When do I get to meet your children?"

"All three are grown and scattered to the winds. The first daughter, Mary, lives in Belfast, married to an ironworker in the shipyard. Three wee babes they have and couldn't make the funeral. The second, Sinead, is still unwed and working as a seamstress in Dublin. She came yesterday to pay her respects, but couldn't stay longer. The slave drivers in the garment trade wouldn't allow mor'n a day off."

"And the third child?"

"Riley . . . me eldest. We call 'im Lee, to label him apart from our brother Riley. You may have seen him at the funeral t'day. Came and went quickly, as he always does. Never speaks to anyone, especially me. Lives in London, I think. He was sittin' in the last pew on the right at St Theresa's."

Collier went slack-jawed. "You mean the middle-aged chap who looks like . . ."

"Your father?" She couldn't bring herself to call the man by name. To her he would always be some shadowy creature.

"Why . . . yes," Collier mumbled, mouth still agape.

"Don't look so shocked. Surely you knew."

"We feared . . . but hoped not," said Collier.

Kathleen filled her lungs in a deep, uneven breath, and spoke as if in a confessional. "The night before you and mother helped me escape Colby, that . . . that . . . beast cornered me in the wine cellar. My screams were of no use twelve feet underground."

She exhaled with the same uneven breathing, but did not cry. "He took me . . . just as he had taken mother. And through the filthy ordeal, he repeated Sinead's name . . . as if I were her,"

She ran the back of her hand along the scar where Forgan had slammed her face into a glass case during his assault. Though it had healed, the one that ran the length of her soul had not. The memory was recent enough to bring pain, too distant to draw tears. Over the years, Kathleen had carefully annulled all remnants of that October night in Colby. Oddly, it was seeing Sinead consumed by the humiliation of being violated by Sir Thomas Forgan that had helped her cope. She simply wasn't going to allow a single event, degrading as it was, to destroy her life as it had her mother's. But, all too often, the strength of her will to block out Forgan's crime had prevented her from feeling the tenderness of Duff's touch. There was a part of her that just couldn't deal with the intimacy of love after experiencing the brutality of Forgan. The horror of his forceful advances had ebbed in time, and Kathleen had resumed a life filled with all the joys of marriage and motherhood. But in the company of Collier, the only person left alive from that fateful night, the anguish that had been in remission for such a long time, now returned in full force.

"We were too late," Collier murmured emptily. "I feared as much. It's little wonder you and Sinead wanted nothing to do with me after what you suffered at the hand of Sir Thomas. You must have been devastated. I am . . . so sorry."

"You did all you could, Collier. I just didn't know how to deal with my shame. Mother didn't know either. It contributed to her premature death. I was determined not to let my health fail as hers had."

"Surely Sinead must have counseled you on the pain she endured with me. Why would you want to go through that?"

"The choices weren't any better for me than they had been for her. Abortion was not an option."

"I don't know how you managed through it all."

"I have my faith, with all its blessings, and its curses. And, like mother, I had a good man who loved me unconditionally. Padraig never judged Sinead, and Duff never judged me. Sadly, it's my son who's been unable to deal with the particulars. Branded a bastard early in life, he hasn't been able to move past that self-image. To him, he has a rapist father, and a mother who couldn't possibly love him, because he wasn't conceived in love."

"You do love him though, don't you, Kathleen?"

"Just as Sinead loved you, Collier. A mother always loves her son. What happened to you and Lee was beyond your control. A mother doesn't transfer to her child, either her loathing of the culprit, or her personal shame. I suspect it took you a long time to get over your feelings of inadequacy."

"I still haven't. But I didn't have the opportunity to speak with Sinead as Lee does you. It may take an overture from you to change his perspective. He probably feels as I did. For our mothers to be rid of their painful memories, they had to be rid of us."

"I'm sure you're right, Collier. I'll try once again to reach out to him. I'm glad you came. I haven't been able to confide in anyone since Sinead died. It was hard to discuss my feelings with Riley. He struggled to find peace with his own tortured views of Forgan, and had to first stifle his anger before he could even say the man's name. The cretin did us all a favor by drowning in the peat bog. Had he survived, I'm afraid Riley might have killed him to avenge our family honor."

"I doubt Riley would have killed Sir Thomas. He may have felt a powerful urge to set things right, but I think he would have let nature take its course. If it hadn't been *that* peat bog, there would have been another. Bad deeds don't go unpunished. Riley believed that."

"Maybe you could talk with Lee. After all, you are his half-brother and have an insight he can't ignore."

"I guess I'm also his half-uncle," Collier added, sorting out the convoluted family ties wrought by Forgan's misdeeds.

"I'd be pleased to discuss the matter with him. But we both know the love he craves has to come from you. Let him feel the love you felt from Duff. His love sustained you. Yours will sustain Lee."

"What a family this is."

"Yes, but we do keep striving to be a family."

Kathleen rose and cupped Collier's gaunt face in her hand, brushing his cheek with her thumb. "Please read Riley's letter before you return to Colby. You'll find your apprehension misplaced."

Chapter 4

$\mathcal{M}$ick Callahan rinsed his plate under the kitchen faucet and walked out the back door of Riley's cottage for a smoke. Next to the privy stood a rusty bicycle missing its seat and most of its spokes. A musty burlap sack, partly filled with potatoes gone to sprout, lay rotting beneath a makeshift clothesline, and the remainder of the pratties were strewn haphazardly about the bare, dirt yard. Mick sat on an oaken ale keg, weathered beyond grey to near black, with mildew and moss flourishing on its staves. Lighting a cigar, he reached inside his sweater to retrieve the letter Riley had written him. He slid the blade of his pocket knife beneath the flap of the envelope and began to examine the handwriting. Riley's hand was steady and strong, if a bit unkempt . . . sort of like his life, thought Mick, glancing about the disorderly back yard. Possessions and appearances didn't matter to Riley, friends and fellowship did.

Dear Mick,

I must be headed to the hereafter, old friend, or you wouldn't be reading my last farewell. It's been a long and lively road since we first met as schoolboys in the Irish Junior Golf Championship at Ballybunion in 1913.

Who would have thought a Prod from County Down, and a Fenn from County Clare, could strike up a bond that would survive all the bloodshed between Catholics and Protestants these past sixty years? More than likely, some of the Prods'll be making the trip to Lahinch just to dance a jig on my grave and be certain I'm gone. They'll be disappointed to learn I've been burned instead of buried . . . or maybe just sorry they missed the big blaze.

Mick, you've always had a keen sense of right and wrong. That much was clear, when, as a Protestant barrister from Ulster, you championed the cause of Irish landowners in English courts. I know you feel you failed, but victory isn't always swift. It took centuries for the Brits to plant their dominance onto Irish soil. It may well take centuries to be rid of them.

You've made such a difference, Mick. And, I don't just mean in the effort to unite Ireland, but in our friendship. You didn't have to publicly display your Irishness, but you always did. At times when it would have been easier and safer to become a British bootlicker, you were always your own man. It'll take thousands like you to tip the balance of power in Ulster, but you showed the way.

I am eternally grateful, and forever,

Your Friend,

Riley

Mick folded the letter and tucked it inside his sweater. Many more Protestants would be mourning Riley's passing than rejoicing over it . . . of that, you could be certain, he thought. The sense of humor Riley had brought to the dialogue between Catholics and Protestants would be sorely missed . . . as would his patience. Mick snorted. Patience? There had been a time when nearly everyone viewed Riley as a quick-tempered Irishman. He had always been mischievous and fun-loving, but it had taken a life-time to dampen that short fuse.

Mick thought back to the day of their first meeting. Paired at age fifteen in the 1913 Irish Junior Golf Championship held at Ballybunion, neither had formed a strong opinion of Ireland's future, but each had a bias cultivated by

Riley's Catholic upbringing and Mick's Protestant heritage. What happened during the course of their round together had forever altered Mick's outlook. The third player in the group at Ballybunion was an Anglo-Irish lad from Dublin, a member of the Protestant Ascendancy, named Samuel Langston. Deference to the English and disdain for the Irish had been instilled in young Langston from birth. His treatment of Riley had been contemptible, but it was his presumed collegiality with a fellow Prod that had caused Mick to re-examine the underpinnings of the conflict between Catholics and Protestants.

The son of a linen mill foreman, during his early years in Belfast, Mick had accepted the liturgies of family and friends recounting the evil designs of the Pope and his Catholic disciples. But, he had also witnessed the tendency of young Prods and Fenns to befriend one another despite this daily bombardment of hateful teachings. Mick found Riley likeable, and that was all that mattered to him. He refused to label any Catholic untrustworthy, simply on the basis of faith.

Samuel Langston, however, was accustomed to ethnic branding as his guide to friends and foes. Mick was Protestant, therefore friend. Riley was Catholic, therefore, foe. During their round of golf together, he treated each accordingly. When both Mick and Riley refused to accommodate young Langston's bigotry and sent him off the eighteenth green in a snit, he protested to officials that a conspiracy was afoot. And, when tournament supervisors dismissed Langston's complaints as the sniveling of a spoiled brat, Riley and Mick basked in their first triumph of common sense over prejudice. Their collusion had endured for more than half a century.

"Mick," Angus called from the doorway of the kitchen, "are you all right?"

"Yes, of course. I was just finishing Riley's letter."

"Did he cover everything you thought he would?"

"He was as gracious in his passing as he was in life."

"You seem troubled, though."

"Well, there was an episode in our lives I thought he might have mentioned. It's a matter over which we were both ashamed. Perhaps embarrassed, would be a better description."

"Do you want to share it with me?"

"In the early years, when Riley was active in the Irish Volunteers, and they were preparing for the 1916 rising, we became involved in a desperate scheme."

"I didn't know you were active in the rebellion."

"Oh I wasn't, really. I was studying law at the time. But Riley was my friend, and anything I could do to help him, I did. Within reason, of course."

"Sounds like this may have gone beyond the bounds of reason."

"The Volunteers were dangerously short of arms and munitions for any sort of insurgence against the Brits. But with the Great War being fought between the powers of Europe, the leaders of the rebellion saw England's preoccupation with the Germans as an opportune time to claim independence for Ireland."

"I know the Irish rebels were hoping to capitalize on the Brit's distraction, but how did that affect you?"

"Pearse and other leaders reasoned the war was a family squabble between two of Queen Victoria's grandsons, Kaiser Wilhelm II of Germany and King George V of England," said Mick. "You may recall loyalties in certain corners of Ireland lay not with the King, but with the Kaiser."

"Some nationalists *did* have the notion Germany would be less oppressive toward Ireland than England had been. The feeling seemed to be a sort of cavalier, why not throw in with Germany. She may win the war anyway, so let's be on the winning side, and, while we're at it, be rid of the Brits."

"The moderates in that camp would argue they were just trying to leverage Germany's sympathies to Ireland's advantage, but not become her ally. You remember Sir Roger Casement?"

"Irish nationalist . . . British consul . . . knighted by the Queen for his humanitarianism in the Boer War. Seems to me he tried to broker arms from Germany to Ireland just prior to the Easter Rising."

"Close enough. Riley asked me to deliver a special communiqué to Casement on the day of the arms shipment."

"But why you?"

"Because Riley trusted me, I suppose. In any event, I tried to locate Casement with a message that the British had uncovered the plot, and that he should abandon the mission."

"Is that when the German freighter *Aud* was sunk and Casement captured?"

"Yes. I was unable to find Casement in Tralee. Apparently, he sensed something was amiss and changed his position. The whole matter was wayward in my opinion. But I wasn't nearly as concerned about failing to deliver my message to Casement as I was about our overtures to Germany."

"Must've been quite a dilemma. When a country has been so dominated as Ireland by England, it's tempting to resort to any port in a storm."

"The larger issue was one of good versus evil. As disagreeable as England has been, I didn't want to be speaking German. They intended to rule Europe, for God's sake!"

"In the realm of world affairs, I'm certain most Irish felt as you did. If it had been known the leaders of the rebellion were selling Ireland's soul to Germany in order to gain freedom from England, in all likelihood, they would have admonished; '*the divil you know, is better than the divil you don't*'."

"That's why I felt so ashamed to have been in any way connected with such a scheme. I had friends and relatives from Ulster who were dying in trenches to keep Germany from conquering Europe. And here we were, consorting with the Huns. The Irish in the south were exempt from conscription into the British army, but there were many men who had enlisted to fight against Germany. Our actions were a slap in the faces of those brave men."

"That's probably why Riley didn't mention it in his letter. He was even more ashamed than you. He had traded on his friendship to get you to help him. I'm sure, upon reflection, he saw the attempted alliance with Germany to be just as misguided as you had. He took his shame with him to the hereafter, and probably expects you to do so as well."

"You're right, of course. I've been wanting to free my conscience for such a long time. I just assumed it would be with Riley. I feel better having spoken to you, Angus. But what was it Collier said? The misjudgments of our youth follow us forever? I won't be free of this disgrace until I've returned to ashes . . . like Riley."

"It's over, Mick. Let it go. Come on inside, now. Kathleen's serving whiskey cake."

Chapter 5

Slouching his six-foot, four-inch frame beneath the six-foot header of Riley's front door, Collier Ames crossed Links Lane, surveying the sandy blowouts of Lahinch as he went. Putter and ball in hand, he stepped his gangly legs over the stile arching across the fieldstone wall and strolled onto the 5th green. Dropping the ball twenty feet or so from the cup, he stroked it firmly, rolling it down a slight undulation and over a rise where it came to a momentary halt on the left lip, then toppled in. Still have the old touch, he thought.

Although the Atlantic lay more than five hundred metres away, the scent of the sea filled the air. At least a dozen of Ireland's forty shades of green were plainly visible across the dunes. So this is where Riley developed his game and his guile, mused Collier . . . an ideal setting from which to do both. He could see how this union of irregular terrain and capricious weather might collaborate to form a sturdy examination of golfing skill and emotional stamina.

As Collier crouched over another putt, his concentration was broken by a cry of *fore*, ringing out from behind the mountainous dune of Klondyke. He snatched his ball from the green and, in a bandy-legged gait, wobbled unsteadily toward the stone wall. The unmistakable thud of a golf ball could be heard striking the rock-hard turf in front of the green. A white streak sped across the putting surface and came to rest near the wall just a few feet from where Collier had taken refuge. Down the steep slope strode an enormous man, a bag of hickory-shafted clubs slung nonchalantly over one shoulder. Against the backdrop of a dimly-lit horizon, he formed an outline reminiscent of Sir Thomas Forgan, and sauntered as would Forgan himself.

"Sorry to hit into you like that," said the hulk, extending his hand. "I'm Lee McAndrew, Kathleen's son. I saw you at Riley's service. You must be a friend."

"Collier Ames. Both friend and relative, in manner of speaking, I suppose."

"Collier Ames?! Pardon my ignorance. I should have known you would attend the service."

"There's no call for an apology, Lee. You had no way of recognizing me."

"No. Unlike me, you look very little like Sir Thomas Forgan," Lee said gloomily, as if he were describing the anguish of his life sentence to a co-conspirator who had received a more lenient penalty.

"I got Sir Thomas' size, but none of his grace . . . Sinead's features, but none of her beauty," remarked Collier. "Like a stork who's the offspring of an eagle and an egret."

Collier's self-effacing description made Lee laugh. He was already beginning to feel more comfortable with his uncanny resemblance to Sir Thomas.

"Well, what do a couple of bastards like us talk about?" Lee asked, voice dripping with cynicism.

"We can start by changing your woeful, self-pitying, weight-of-the-world-on-my-shoulders, attitude. Who cares but us, that we're bastards? The people we meet care only how we behave in their presence, and what we contribute to matters at hand."

"But I've always felt a certain tendency in others to view me as beneath them due to my background. Especially those who know me to be the illegitimate son of a scoundrel."

"I suppose we all feel the need to redeem ourselves in the eyes of those who judge us most harshly. But the circumstances of our birth don't make us inferior to anyone. It's just our familiarity with the shame of Sir Thomas that forces us to compensate for his acts."

"I don't want to spend my life paying for the vile deeds of someone I didn't even know."

"Nor should you. But it's been said that virtue is its own reward. Knowing you're the son of a degenerate will always make you want to be a better person. Trust me, there's nothing better than shedding one's own improprieties."

"You're beginning to sound like Father O'Shea! Old age and Catholicism must prompt repentance, not only for our own sins, but for the sins of anyone who has ever perpetrated an evil act."

"Well, I'm certainly old, and you are Catholic. Maybe between us we can lend some conscience to this unconscionable world."

"Let's deal with one lost soul at a time."

"You're right, Lee. There's as much false piety in the world as there is evil."

"How true. Were you out here to play a few holes?"

"No, I was practicing my putting. I had just finished reading Riley's last letter, and wanted to reflect on it. He has some thoughts I think would benefit you. Here, read what he has to say."

Dear Collier,

We can't control who brings us into the world any more than we can control how our golf ball behaves on the links. We may strike the perfect shot and still suffer the odd bounce into the gorse, or the misfortune of landing in someone else's divot. The damned uncontrollables. How unfair they can be. Like having a father who doesn't inspire pride, or respect, or from whom you receive no love.

I know there was a time when you felt everything in your life was subject to your will and control. But I saw from your personal amends that you changed. Once we accept life's little whims, it seems easier to deal with the turns of fate it parcels out. I watched how you became a caricature of Sir Thomas Forgan, condescending toward people in general, and hateful toward the Irish in particular. Then, as you saw through Forgan's corrupt ways, you became his opposite, kind and generous to everyone. Your generosity to the Irish has become a guidepost of humanity in Northern Ireland. I'm sure you've noticed the Irish don't forget. Your sacrifices won't be forgotten. The O'Neills will be forever grateful for your kind gift of

1500 acres at Colby. Words can't express how meaningful it is to have our ancestral lands returned to the family legacy. My only regret is not showing my gratitude by including you in our family. Too late wise . . . too soon dead.

Still, you should have accepted my invitation to partner together in the '32 West of Ireland Foursomes Championship. We would have demolished the field like blight on potatoes. You could always play the game, Collier. I must admit, you came closer to imposing your will on a golf ball than any golfer I've known, (except Bobby Jones, of course). You had no weaknesses. And no one could come up with the crucial shot when a match hung in the balance like you. My nightmare of that shot you holed from the Road Hole Bunker at St. Andrews in '26 will most likely follow me to the beyond.

It's taken me a lifetime to come to terms with our relationship, Collier. Watching the tension build, day after day, between Kathleen and Lee, finally allowed me to appreciate just how difficult your ordeal must have been. No mother to love you. A father you despised. You've overcome so much, alone. If only Lee could understand he need not be alone in battling his demons. Kathleen loves him dearly, but he can't accept anyone's love at face value. The burden of his shame won't allow anyone into his life. Perhaps seeing you were able to plod ever onward, will help him to reach out to those who love him. I know it's unfair of me to ask you to help Lee navigate through his personal challenges, but life's most difficult assignments go to those who are able. You are able.

I will forever be your friend, and

Your Brother,

Riley

"Need I say more?" asked Collier.

"Riley had that talk with me once before. But somehow, it takes on greater meaning when I hear it told to someone like you. I can see now, that my efforts to buck up have been puny compared to what you had to deal with."

"I suppose we all tend to do just enough to suit our situation. We play up to better competition on the golf course, or down to lesser opponents. Life's no different. I just don't see any sense of urgency from you to get over the disgraces of Sir Thomas."

"I've always known I could count on mother and Duff. I see now, that since my resentment toward Forgan couldn't be vented on him, I unleashed my bitterness on my family. They endured it because they loved me, and wanted me to be rid of my hatred."

"As long as it's more important to you to be angry than to be caring, anger will prevail."

"It's all so clear, now. I've used my loathing of this nonexistent and irrelevant man as a crutch to perpetuate the disappointments in my life. The only victims have been those who love me."

"That about sums it up. Kathleen awaits, my good man. Shall we begin anew?"

"Yes. And, Collier . . . thank you."

"Don't thank me. I'm still trying to sort out my own emotions. All we can do is try, each day, to improve. Sometimes it helps to get a nudge in the right direction. Riley did that for both of us."

Chapter 6

$\mathcal{T}$he stench of death lingered in Riley's bedroom as Patrick slipped, unnoticed, past Kathleen. She looked uncomfortable, sleeping curled up and contorted in Riley's favorite leather chair. A small shaft of light shone through the four-paned window above her head, its rays filtering through limp, lacy curtains that hung from a rod, bowed in the center. Sunshine flooded onto the bare, wooden floor, projecting the square-shaped pattern of the pane divider, and, in its wake, floated a channel of dust particles, a dense sunbeam, defying the laws of gravity.

Tiptoeing over to Riley's desk, Patrick switched on the green-shaded accountant's lamp, slid the clutter of books and papers to one side, and opened Riley's leather-bound journal to the first page. Sepia toned photographs, lying unfastened inside the cover, cascaded into Patrick's lap. Many were of Riley in uniform beside unidentified officials of the Irish Republican Army. Thumbing through the faded pictures, he occasionally recognized someone notable . . . Riley with Michael Collins in front of the General Post Office in Dublin . . . Riley posing with Padraic Pearse at St. Edna's School for Boys. Most, however, were of family or friends, or of Riley's golfing exploits. One small, particularly clear photograph showed Riley holding the 1930 British Isles Cup. It fit nicely into Patrick's wallet. Much sorting to do, he thought, stacking the memories into a neat pile at the side of the desktop.

The first entry was dated June 2, 1915, the day Riley had graduated from St. Edna's. As he read Riley's most intimate thoughts, it seemed to Patrick that summaries of the memorable events of the week had been recorded each Sunday, presumably following Mass, after Riley had cleared his conscience. Turning to the passage dated June, 1921, he read Riley's enthusiastic account of his new friend, Angus MacKenzie. Hardly a word had been written about the golf tournament, except to detail how powerfully he had driven his fist into Collier Ames' jaw. In the margin was scribbled something about fragmented Irish leadership, an allusion to the discussion he'd had with Angus over Irish politics.

Patrick paged ahead to June, 1926, and the week of the British Isles Cup Championship at St. Andrews. The notes in this section were much more expansive. Riley detailed just how lucky he'd been to beat Angus in the semi-final match and the disappointment he had felt at, once again, having been defeated by the Brit, Collier Ames, in the final. His entry, one week before the tournament, referred pointedly to his goal of making the Walker Cup team and playing against Bobby Jones. Given the space he devoted to recounting the week, and the detail of his descriptions, it was obvious that the experience had been dear to him.

Patrick blushed at the lyrical entry Riley had devoted to Sarah. They were not the words one would expect from a coarse and irreverent Riley O'Neill. They were words of a poet . . . the thoughts of a romantic . . . the voice of a St. Edna's scholar. They spoke of his soul.

> *I gaze at you, Sarah Delano Shiells, and repeat your name. The sound of it leaves me spellbound. Your elegance, unrivaled. Your grace, most rare. Your spirit, unbridled. Your presence, calming. Your beauty, humbling. Sarah Delano Sheills. I repeat your name, and . . . I am.*

Riley's description of what had happened between him and Sarah at the ceilidh seemed carefully chosen. His personal anguish over the inevitable conflict between friendship and love reverberated in each sentence. Riley's love of Sarah, and his friendship with Angus, which had lain fallow between the lines of his journal for decades, were once again, alive.

> *Angus, dear friend, we have fallen from the Cliffs of Moher, side by each. It is a blissful descent as we are still in mid-air, but only one of us will be warmly embraced into the breast of Aphrodite, while the cold and suffocating seas of Poseidon await the other. I fear for our*

friendship. We seem bound for a collision of colossal proportions. Even simple mathematics reveals that three into two is an irregular sum. One of us will be odd man out, for it seems unlikely either of us is prepared for life without Sarah.

The tormented soliloquy continued, but Patrick could not. For the moment, at least, it was too painful to experience through Riley's words the depth of emotion that had passed between the three people he loved most. He needed the comforting lecture Riley had regularly supplied when Patrick was mourning his mother's death, resentful of Angus, clinging to the hope Riley would fill the void. He reached into the back pocket of his trousers and tore open Riley's letter. Patrick needed to hear from him, now.

Dear Patrick,

My life is an open book. When you read my journal, I'm certain you'll find contradictions on various subjects I've written about over the years. But it needs no revision. First impressions, it is said, are often the most reliable. So, what you read, is who I am, or perhaps, who I have been, as I've undergone many changes in my life.

You are my son. You are not my son. You were my son. You were never my son. Which is it? Choosing so long ago to serve my country, and to forsake the personal pleasures bestowed by family, I cannot now have it both ways. It wrenches my heart to have kept our relationship at arms length, but I must. My most solemn wish is to have been true to those I have loved. To Sarah. To you. To Angus. I take comfort in knowing I've done right by them. I'm not so certain where I stand with you. Nothing would have pleased me more than to have been a real father to you. All the hours we spent together. You reaching out. Me holding back. Sarah gone. Angus far away. You could not see then, why it had to be that way. Can you now?

And The Republic. There was always The Republic. I've pursued it for such a long time I sometimes lose sight of what it means. My life is now spent for The Republic, to the exclusion of much that may have mattered more. I've often asked . . . was it worth the trouble? The fever of an Ireland, free and united, is contagious. I fear you've been infected. But you, too, must ask, is it worth the trouble? Whether Ireland is more to you than an inanimate substitute for people? Whether you are drawn to Her because I was drawn to Her? Whether She serves simply to deflect the pain of Sarah's loss? Be certain, before you forsake all else that matters, that She is so all-important. I am beginning to sound regretful. I'm not. We are the sum of our choices. I chose well. You are not my son. But once . . . you were my son. I am proud to have been,

A Father,

Riley

Patrick folded the letter and returned it to Riley's journal next to the passages of June, 1926. The words Riley had spoken so often, as Patrick had grappled with just how he fit into the lives of his three parents, now took on greater meaning against the backdrop of the journal. Listening to Riley's advice in the midst of his own turmoil, somehow made it easier to accept all that had happened. Patrick's healing had begun when he and Angus met in Dublin, but these parting words from Riley would speed the process. Switching off the lamp, he closed the journal. Kathleen stirred at the sound of the click. Yawning, she stretched into the halo of light that now encircled her head. The vision was angelic.

"Patrick?" she asked, straining to see into the darkness from the shaft of sunlight. "Is that you?"

"Aye, Kathleen, it is."

"And what would you be doin', all in the dark?"

"I was reading Riley's journal. And his letter."

"He spoke of you often, you know."

"I know. I'll miss his visits to Dublin."

"There was a time when he thought you'd settle here in Lahinch. He did so love it when you came to visit. Even went so far as to try and arrange a match with Jimmy and Maude O'Brien's daughter, Marta."

"Marta told me all about it," laughed Patrick. "She lives in Dublin now, you know. Married to Jamie O'Bannion. Four boys they have."

"What'll you do, lad?"

"Back to the *Independent*, at least for now. Someday, though, I might return to Lahinch, and try my hand at publishin' a weekly. Might be nice to be the voice of a village, down country. The city isn't the seat of all wisdom, you know."

"You'd be most welcome in County Clare. It'd be nice to have a familiar face playin' Riley's Wee Loup."

"Kathleen, there'll never be another Riley. I'm Patrick, not Riley. I need, more than ever, to be my own man."

"You're right. He was always concerned your attachment to Ireland's cause was his doin', not your own."

"There's a bit of truth to that. But journalism is my first love, and I got that from Angus."

"What you're sayin' is you could choose to write on any subject. Maybe it's time to take on another crusade."

"Could be. But the fever of a free and united Ireland is contagious, Kate. I fear I'm infected."

Chapter 7

*J*immy O'Brien returned to Riley's cottage with the members of Sunday School in tow. Now that Riley was gone, only Sean Burke and Jackie O'Doolan and Jimmy remained of the original group of eight that had played golf together most Sunday afternoons since 1935. They sat in Riley's cramped living room swapping stories with Angus and Mick and Collier. If these three visitors provided the link to Riley's competitive golfing past, then Jimmy and Jackie and Sean were the bridge to his casual golfing past.

"In the beginnin'," said Jimmy, "we threw our names into the British Isles Cup, and drew for partners. Riley used t' keep the Cup in me pru shop."

"After Bobby Jones came to Lahinch, we all thought we could equal the 59 he and Riley posted in alternate shot," said Jackie. "So foursomes was our game from the git go."

"We were all low handicappers, 'cept for Putter DeFrieze. He was Riley's permanent handicap," added Sean. "We needed some way to keep Riley from winnin' ev'ry match. Pairin' him with Putter was just the ticket."

"How did the group get it's name?" asked Angus.

"From the lesson Sean and Jackie conducted for the rest of us in our very farst match," replied Jimmy. "Shot 62 in a monsoon, they did. Nobody else broke par. The bet was always a one punt Nassau, with mandatory two down nudges. Had to give up me Guinness for a week, just to pay the tuition!"

"When we got back to the clubhouse to settle up, Riley said he'd been *schooled*," said Sean. "From that day on, we became known as the *Sunday School*."

"If I hadn't seen it meself, I would'na believed the round the two of you shot!" complained Jimmy. "62 swings got Blinky and me to the 16th tee. Never been a match since that was decided by mor'n a single stroke."

"Who were the other members of Sunday School?" asked Mick.

"Duff McAndrew, Blinky Moran, Putter DeFrieze, and Donk MacLeod," replied Jackie.

"Just thinkin' about ol' Blinky doubles me over," snickered Sean. "Jimmy once told 'im he was peekin' on his shots. So Blinky goes to the livery and buys some horse blinders. Has Shoe Jameson sew those blinders onto a leather cap. Wore that cap 'n blinders fer thirty years, to keep from lookin' up."

"It warked, by damn!" Jimmy exclaimed. "Blinky played his best golf after he got those blinders."

"Shoulda taken the cap off to cross the street, though," sighed Jackie, shaking his head. "Might'a seen that truckload o' peat comin' at him."

"Aye, the blinders had their drawbacks, they did," agreed Sean. "But the truck woulda hit him anyway. Goin' too fast, it was. Laid ol' Blinky to rest in '68, blinkers 'n all," he added, looking skyward.

"'Twas the partnership of Riley and Pooter that gave me the shivers," said Jimmy. "Riley couldn't putt a lick. Got to where we couldn't give 'im anything. Might three-tap it from inside the leather."

"Aye, 'til Putter fixed it for 'im," said Jackie. "One day we were in the *Sea Hag* pitchin' pence fer pints," said Sean. "Riley could pitch pence bet-ter'n anybody, so Putter gits an epiphany."

"Now, Putter was no golfer, y' see," Jimmy continued. "But he was a keen student of the game. Blacksmith by trade, always tinkerin' with clubs. Invented a long-handled putter fer Riley made from the counter-weight of a double-hung window. Ol' Putter cut out a four inch section of th' cylinder and soldered it to the tie rod of an old wagon. Had Riley tuck the butt-end under his chin like so," Jimmy said, demonstrating the technique, "And then stood him facing the hole, like so. Had a special grip fer his right hand 'bout half-way down the column. Used the butt-end as a fulcrum, and pistoned his right hand down the line of the putt. Joost like pitchin' pence. Never missed, once he got the hang of it."

"Way ahead of it's time, 'twas," said Sean. "That section of counterweight was heavy 'nd rounded. Easy to keep on line, and got the ball rollin' end over end. Don't know why we all didn't have one."

"I'll tell y' why," Jimmy replied, testily. "Donk wouldn't allow it! Always grousin' 'bout the unfairness of the Beast, as he called it. Like it had a life all its own. Threatened to petition the R & A for a rulin'."

"Donk was right as rain, there," said Jackie. "No more legal or proper than a golf ball that flies ferever, and spins like a dervish. The R & A woulda outlawed the brute, sure enough."

"We were always takin' something up with the Royal & Ancient," said Jimmy. "Joost our way of remindin' Riley what a royal foockin' they'd given him."

"Ach, you just couldn't operate the Beast, O'Doolan," Sean teased. "If you'd made a poot or two with it, you'd have tarn up all the windows in your cottage to find a counter-weight."

"Donk had trouble usin' the Beast too," chimed Jackie. "'Twas as long as he was tall, and heavier, too. Donk only stood a metre and a half with his spikes on, and weighed but eight stone after a double helpin' of stew and colcannon."

"Ah, but what a player the wee man was," sighed Jimmy. "Pound for pound, he could hit it further than Riley, and nobody gobbled more often than Donk. At least once a round, or he'd had an off day."

"How'd he come by the name, Donk?" asked Mick.

"Kept a few donkeys on his farm to help pack the pratties," replied Jackie. "He'd ride the creatures ev'rywhere. Saw him all over Lahinch, ye did, packin' his golf clubs on his back. Poor wee man fell off his favorite, Ginny, a few years back, after hoistin' a few at the *Hag*. Busted his skull. Buried 'im in '71. Guess y' just shouldn't drink and donk."

"What about Duff McAndrew?" asked Collier.

"Duff was the youngest member of Sunday School," replied Sean, "and a more playful scalawag you've never seen. Eyes darting toward the kitchen to see if Kathleen was about, he whispered,

"Duff had more solutions for the love life of an old married couple than the Book of Kells has pages."

"I can hear yer ev'ry word, Sean Burke," Kathleen called from Riley's bedroom. "Be mindful what you say 'bout the dearly departed."

"Aye, Katie," he said contritely, lowering his voice. "One day we get to the farst tee, and Donk sees one of the old goats has a horn missin'. Without hesitatin', Duff says he's ground it up, and mixed it with a chunk of ewe's hoof for an aphrodisiac. Course, Donk needs to know just how it works. So, Duff gives him a wee leather bag of what he claims is the potion. Tells Donk to sprinkle a pinch into Molly's colcannon that night and prepare for the fireworks."

"What happened?" Mick asked excitedly. "Did it work?"

"Donk follows Duff's directions, but figures a pinch won't do the job. Quite a full-figured woman, Molly was. So he dumps the whole bag into her colcannon," said Sean. "She takes a big bite and spews leeks and potatoes right into poor Donk's face. *'Michael MacLeod!* she says. *What have y' done to me colcannon?'* 'Course Donk is struck dumb by this unexpected turn of events. *'There's crushed chili peppers in me colcannon!'* says Molly. Donk tastes the concoction, and knows straight away he's been done in by Duff. Needless to say, there was no activity in the ol' boudoir that night. Donk told us later that Molly made him sleep with his donkeys."

"'Twas temptin' to call Donk, *'Chili'* MacLeod after that fiasco," said Jackie. "But how 'bout the time Duff and Jimmy put Riley into a tailspin over the J. Braddell?"

"You mighta known how persnickity Riley was with his golf clubs," said Jimmy.

"Only too well," replied Angus. "He slept with his clubs at Muirfield in '21. Always thought someone might sabotage them."

"Riley never changed," said Jimmy. "The Sunday School all left their clubs in storage with me, 'cept Riley. Packed 'em home ev'ry night, he did."

"One Saturday night in '37, Duff kept Riley occupied at the *Sea Hag*, while Jimmy snuck over to Riley's cottage," said Jackie. "Ol' Jimmy reshafted the J. Braddell with a slightly cracked hickory shaft."

"How'd you get a match for the shaft and grip so he wouldn't be suspicious?" asked Mick.

"I'd been workin' on it for a month, tryin' to find just the right one," said Jimmy.

"Sunday afternoon, we all held our breath as Riley got set to drive off the farst tee with the J. Braddell," said Sean. "He laid into one with a little extry oomph, and keerack! That aluminium clubhead went whirrin' off into space, and there stood Riley, holdin' half a hickory shaft."

"Looked as if he'd lost his last friend," said Jimmy. "Held on to that broken shaft all the way down the farst. He'd had the J. Braddell since '21. Always told us that the shaft was special selected fer that aluminum head. If the shaft ever broke, he claimed the club would be useless. Told us he could never find another piece of ring hickory that would handle the torque. Thought seriously of not playin' that afternoon, grievin' as he was for the J. Braddell."

"By '37, he could have reshafted it with steel," Mick interjected, looking for a more practical solution.

"Not Riley," said Jimmy. "He loved the way the hickory would load up the club on the backswing, and catapult through on the downswing. Spent thirty years developin' just the right technique fer hickory. No, Riley wasn't about to change to steel."

"When did you tell him about the ruse?" asked Collier.

"On the next tee," said Jimmy. "We let 'im stew over it fer one hole. Knew he'd be sick if he couldn't hit driver on the par five second. I had the repair kit in me bag, and I reinstalled his old shaft right on the spot. Thought he was goin' to kiss me, so relieved he was."

"So thankful to have the club back in one piece," said Jackie, "didn't even raise his voice. Just hammered a drive and fussed with the J. Braddell all the way round the course. Had to make certain 'twas put t'gether all proper like."

"Aah, what a touchin' sight, to see poor Riley reunited with his favorite weapon," sighed Sean. "We knew it had been a cruel and heartless joke. Dismantlin' the J. Braddell was like severin' a limb."

"We were about to take Riley's ashes to their final resting place," said Angus. "What would you lads think of a Saturday evening session of Sunday School? If the three of you could persuade Lee McAndrew to join your foursome, then Mick, Collier, Patrick, and I would round out the field of eight."

"That'd be grand, Angus!" exclaimed Jimmy. "It'll be our great pleasure to have one last session. Besides, I'll need to get a fix on the spot where I'm to pour his weekly rent."

Chapter 8

$\mathcal{S}$unday School convened on the tee of Dell at precisely 7:35 p.m. Saturday, May 8, 1975. Jimmy O'Brien decreed the format to be a most cordial alternate shot, with score being kept only out of respect for the traditions of the game. The score that mattered most, they were reminded, was one of companionship and bereavement. Kathleen had been invited to serve as honorary referee and stood holding Riley, safely ensconced in the British Isles Cup, quietly presiding over the spirit of the match.

With Riley's Wee Loup designated as the honorary course, Angus and Patrick were chosen to lead off. The men milled about the tee, comparing their old clubs and limbering up their old bones. Armed with the hickory shafted clubs used so long ago in rounds with Riley, Angus offered to caddie for his team while Patrick toted his bagpipes. Earlier, having somehow located Duff's old set in a lean-to next the defunct *Sea Hag*, Lee now beamed with pride as he displayed his heirlooms to the others.

A great hue and cry for the Beast was met by Angus' unexpected announcement that he'd found the Beast hidden under Riley's bed.

Holding the putter over his head like a barbell, he said, "Patrick and I thought we all might need some help in the putting department."

"I figgered the Beast was long gone!" Jimmy exclaimed. "She's a damned heavy instrument, y' know. When Riley got along in years, he calculated the wear and tear on his back wasn't worth the strokes he saved, so he went back to his old putter."

"Shoulda known Riley kept the contraption," muttered Jackie. "Looks like he used the damn thing to stoke his peat fire. Soot's coverin' ev'ry inch of the monster."

"I'm glad he decommissioned the Beast," said Sean. "After years of stokin' our ire, it was better suited fer stokin' his fire."

"C'mon then, lads, let's get on with the match," announced Jimmy. "Now on the farst tee from Edinburra . . . Angus MacKenzie. Play away, Mr. MacKenzie, sar."

Stepping confidently to the tee of the 142 metre par three, Angus plunged a wooden peg into the turf and placed one of Riley's old Slazengers onto it. With a more mature and methodical version of the swashbuckler's flourish he had seen Riley perform at Muirfield, Angus unsheathed the J. Braddell from the tattered leather bag and surveyed his opening shot. Once, a mashie niblick would have been the correct club, but not today, not at age seventy-five. Today, he would need a cleanly struck driver to cover the distance.

What Angus wanted was the power of youth, the trajectory of a mashie niblick, and the luck of the Irish. The mind was willing. The flesh was not. Aiming slightly to the right of the gigantic sandhill, where a low-flying shot might bounce through the narrow aperture of dunes, Angus swung smoothly. Somehow the contact between J. Braddell and ball was crisp and precise. The shot came off just as Angus had imagined, leaving Patrick a short chip of some forty feet from a flat, firm lie. Sunday School was in session.

The evening was cool but comfortable as the sun swooped below the feathery clouds, its rays shooting rose beams across the sky, casting long shadows over the sandscape. Dell was played with the good-natured goading of comrades who share a love of the game of golf and understand its humbling powers.

"Have you always had that hitch in yer backswing?" Jimmy asked Mick, who had stubbed his spoon, sending the ball a mere 20 metres toward its target. "You should have that looked at before it gets any worse."

"I laid up for my partner," Mick laughed. "Collier has always been good from 120 metres."

Jimmy teed off with his mashie, determined not to give Mick any ammunition to reciprocate the gibes he had just shot in his direction. "I got 'er airborne!" Jimmy exclaimed, thrilled to have gotten his ball halfway to the green. "Jackie might just pitch it in from there."

"Donk might have," Jackie quipped. "I'll be pleased just to advance it." Lee took the tee and was hooted down.

"Not so fast. We won't be havin' the youngsters hittin' farst," Jimmy blared. "Sean, you'll be teein' off here."

Shrugging with indifference, Sean Burke replaced Lee on the tee. His brassie-driven shot struggled to gain altitude, coming to within a few feet of clearing the top of the enormous dune, then sadly, its energy dissipated, dove instead into a stand of grass just short of the summit.

"Take yer sycthe with you, Lee," joked Jackie. "It'll be knee-deep in there. We used to let Donk go in, but only on a tether, so we wouldn't lose him."

"Don't fret Sean," replied the six foot four inch Lee, "I'll gouge it out of the rushes."

They marched off into the gathering dusk, Patrick carrying the Cup on this first leg of the Loup. Trophy under one arm, bagpipes slung over the other, he took his turn transporting Riley, as would each of the others, on this last trek across the links to his panoramic plot high atop Lahinch. Locking arms with Lee and joining Riley's cohorts in song, Kathleen led their off-key yet poignant voices through the Scottish ballad, *Will Ye Nae Come Back Again*.

Each partnership holed out using the Beast. To a man, the uniquely contorted stances provided ample amusement as they experimented with various styles, all calculated to achieve the most effective pendulum motion. Angus and Patrick managed to save par, as did Jimmy and Jackie. Mick and Collier suffered a bogey, along with Sean and Lee. Climbing in solemn procession to the 10th tee, the company of mourners launched drives into the darkening horizon.

"What is it the Scots say?" asked Jackie.

"It'll take three, t' get home in two t'day, laddie," replied Angus.

"Aye," said Mick. "But not so much from resistance of the elements, as from reluctance of the flesh."

Though a score was not their objective, the instincts of these old war horses to always put forth their best efforts provided great theatre. Lee rifled a drive that drew high marks. And Patrick matched it with the J. Braddell, prompting comparisons to Riley's powerfully compact swing.

"Ahh, to have the strength of the young," sighed Jimmy, wishfully.

"But would y' swap the wisdom of old age for it, Jimmy?" asked Sean.

"Straight away, Sean," countered Jimmy, "And throw in me mature good looks fer good measure!"

The partnership of Lee and Sean hit the green in regulation, two putting for par. Collier and Mick also saved par, when Collier holed a thirty footer.

"Still have the old touch," beamed Collier.

"Didn't I see you practicing earlier, on Klondyke?" asked Sean. "Katie, we need a rulin'!"

"Since when is practicing not allowed?" Collier asked with surprise.

"Since Sean here decided he needed an edge," joked Jackie.

"There'll be no practicin' on the course during the day of the competition," Sean deadpanned, as if he were reading from the rulebook.

"There'll be no penalty to the team of Mick and Collier," Kathleen interjected. "Collier didn't practice on any of the holes of the Wee Loup. Klondyke's green is out of play."

With a sweep of her hand, Kathleen cleared the men from the green and announced in her most official voice that all teams were now tied at one over par.

"We'll resume the match on the 14th tee after we've had our last rites for Riley."

As the troupe made its steep ascent up the grassy embankment from the 10th green to the knoll behind the 9th tee, Kathleen carried the Cup these last few steps to Riley's chosen place of rest. Standing on the fescued enclave, they scanned the vista in silence. The lights of Lahinch sparkled in the distance, and the beacon of Leithinsi swept its beam across the entire peninsula. The ocean roared, but the wind had ceased altogether, casting an eerie calm over the ceremony. With daylight waning, the sun now shone more up from the sea than down from the sky. A slender thread of smoke could be seen smoldering from the chimney of Riley's cottage, barely visible above the shaggy hills.

Angus took the Cup from Kathleen and climbed alone to the top of the knoll. He stood in waist-high marram and turned a slow pirouette, admiring this heavenly site. Clutching Riley close to his chest, he murmured, "you've chosen well, old friend."

Removing the burlap sack from the top of the Cup, he held it high over his head, reciting from W. B. Yeats', *The Four Ages of Man*:

> *He with body waged a fight,*
> *But body won; it walks upright.*
>
> *Then he struggled with the heart;*
> *Innocence and peace depart.*
>
> *Then he struggled with the mind;*
> *His proud heart he left behind.*
>
> *Now his wars on God begin;*
> *At stroke of midnight God shall win.*

"God speed, Riley!" Angus shouted.

Just then, in unearthly stillness, with the others invoking *'God speed'* as one, the ghostly calm was broken by a chill gust of wind. Before Angus could release the ashes and christen the sacred site, a whirl of wind abruptly whisked Riley from his vessel, as if some supernatural force had unexpectedly entered their midst. Riley hovered in a cloud over Angus' head, momentarily suspended by the zephyr. Transfixed by this scene from the occult, Angus slowly backed his way down to the level of the others. As swiftly as it had come, the breeze subsided. Riley's ashes floated an instant longer, then fluttered gently to earth, mingling with the grasses on the knoll . . . *Riley's Knoll*.

Patrick inflated the bellows of his bagpipe and stood as a silhouette against darkening skies, the skirl of the pipes filling the air with the sorrowful yet comforting strains of *Amazing Grace*. Though he had not piped for years, Patrick's notes seemed blown in from the heavens, as if God Himself was joining the tribute. Cloaked in the haunting sounds of this ancient instrument, the eightsome and Kathleen bade their final farewells to Riley.

The journey down to the 14th tee was made in reflective silence. They might have declared the match over at that point, but that isn't what Riley would have wanted.

"Riley would have urged us to plod ever onward," said Angus.

"Aye, said Jimmy, "we'll be walkin' down the 14th anyway, we may as well be chasin' a golf ball."

"Who's up?" asked Patrick.

"Who cares," boomed Jackie. "Ready golf. If yer ready, play away. There's no honor . . . not amongst thieves or old rascals."

Down the fairway they came, daylight fast fading, each of the eight sensing the presence of the force that had appeared on Riley's Knoll. It was as if they had, in this moment of mourning, regained the lost powers of their youth. Three of the partnerships had birdied the par five 14th, and only Angus and Patrick were yet to putt out.

Facing a tricky ten footer to end the match in a four-way tie at even par for the Wee Loup, Angus now wished he hadn't thrown his old putter into the kiln with Riley. The Beast was for nervous putters with jabby strokes. Angus had always considered himself an able putter, but now faced a ten footer in the gloaming for the most dear of all stakes in golf . . . pride.

"C'mon boys, give 'im some light," said Sean, lighting a match and holding it above the hole.

With matches lit, they stood, flames flickering, on either side of Angus' line. Adopting Riley's sidesaddle style of facing the hole and anchoring the handle of the Beast under his chin, Angus took a practice stroke, pushing his right hand toward the hole. Stepping in before the matches could expire, he pistoned the bulky cylinder into the ball, sending it up the slope. Just when it left the blade, as if from unseen lips, a breath of wind extinguished the matches. Pitch black. Silence. The hush was broken by the unmistakable metallic rattle of the ball falling to the bottom of the cup. The eightsome and Kathleen whooped in unison.

"I knew you could do it, dad!" said Patrick, clapping his hand onto Angus' shoulder.

"Good thing y' made it, MacKenzie," Jackie said seriously. "Losers buy the farst round."

"Using my referee's prerogative, I proclaim the farst round compliments of *O'Doolan's*," Kathleen exclaimed. "Jackie's got a corner on the pub trade now that the *Hag's* closed. Dividend back a wee bit of our hard earned wages, Jackie."

"Fair enough, Katie," replied Jackie. "Bring the Cup. We'll fill 'er 'til no one's left standin'. It's O'Doolan's shout tonight!"

Chapter 9

The crowd spilling out of *O'Doolan's* doorway onto Main Street was, at once, boisterous and solemn, the mirror image of a day marked by revelry and reflection. The clear night sky shone with such brilliance it was as if a new constellation had been summoned for the occasion. In a corner booth, Angus and Patrick and Mick sat with Jimmy and Sean, recounting some of the lighter moments of Riley's life, adding to the collection of anecdotes that had already enriched their memories of him. Behind the bar, Jackie was feverishly filling and refilling the British Isles Cup, as 'round and 'round the room it went, quenching everyone's thirst for one final communion with Riley. Outside, Kathleen and Lee were drinking in a fresh-aired reprieve from the bar's fogbank of smoke. Joined by Collier, the three of them gazed skyward at the dazzling display of stars.

"I'm glad you're staying over, Lee," said Kathleen. "We have much to talk about."

"No one wanted Riley to leave us," Lee replied, "but his passing did bring us all together. I might have been able to figure out my course alone, but talking to Collier, and hearing from Riley, has helped considerably."

"Have you given any thought to where you'll go from here?" Kathleen asked.

"Not really," replied Lee. "I've been in the pub trade for the past ten years, so I'll probably continue. But I would like to be closer to the two of you. London has been just another of the many crutches I've used to stay away from you, Mother. It no longer appeals to me. I'd sooner come home."

"What would you think of reopenin' the *Sea Hag*?" she asked, hopefully.

"I'd be honored to follow in Duff's footsteps," Lee quickly replied. "Would you help me?"

"I rescued the door of *Baile and Aillinn* from the fire in hopes you might someday come home and rebuild the *Hag*," said Kathleen. "She'd make a fine entryway again."

"Maybe we should rename the pub," said Lee. "The *Sea Hag* was Duff's pride and joy. There'll never be another Duff or another *Hag*."

"What about honoring Duff by naming it after him?" asked Collier. "Or better still, call it *McAndrew's*, for a family that, like *Baile and Aillinn*, has come together at last."

"I like that," said Kathleen, beaming. "What do you think, Lee?"

"*McAndrew's* it'll be," replied Lee. "I can't wait to give O'Doolan a run for his money."

"What about you, Collier?" asked Kathleen. "Back to Colby?"

"Yes, Colby will always be my home," Collier replied. "But I'll visit Lahinch again."

"You'll always be welcome," Kathleen said softly. "And we'll come to see you as well. A stop in County Down will be included anytime we go north to visit Mary in Belfast."

"I'm so pleased to be part of this family, at last," said Collier. "It's a moment I've waited for most of my life. God bless you, both."

"God bless you, Collier," said Kathleen.

"And be well," added Lee.

*   *   *

Bidding good night to the night's festivities destined to continue well into the wee hours, Angus headed off to the Atlantic Hotel, alone. Tomorrow, he and Patrick and Mick would board the train for Dublin, while Collier would stay on in Lahinch for a few days before returning to Newcastle. Pausing in the street and peering out toward Riley's Knoll where only hours before the baleful notes of Patrick's bagpipe had sent his friend to eternal peace, he murmured . . . *"you've earned your respite, Riley O'Neill."*

Angus sank onto the couch in his room at the Atlantic, drained by the day's emotion. Switching on the lamp, he noticed the book of Yeats' poetry lying on the end table. Opening its cover, he found a photograph of Sarah and Riley and Angus tucked inside. The faded snapshot captured the dashing young trio standing outside the entrance of the Royal & Ancient. Like a rose between two thorns, Sarah's arms were interlocked with Riley on her left and Angus on her right, her head tilted ever so slightly toward Angus, her eyes stealing a sideways glance in his direction. Though he hadn't seen the photo in over fifty years, Angus realized at once what Riley had intended. He was urging Angus to see Sarah in a light he might have been over-looked or, perhaps, ignored. Angus took Riley's letter from the pocket of his shirt, smoothed the crumpled corner of the envelope, and inserted his thumb under the flap to break the seal.

Dear Angus,

Nothing calls up the truth like a few pints, or the closeness of death. Since I'm not long for this world, you can be sure of these parting words. Ours has always been a friendship based on a bond of simple understanding, but at times like these, it is comforting not only to receive reassurances, but to give them.

Angus, you have my solemn word of honor that it was you, not me, that Sarah loved during all the years of your marriage. I must confess, there were times when I was torn in my choice between Ireland and Sarah. And, my decision was not always made from the appeal of country over heart.

The lines of Yeats' **Never Give All the Heart** *would often run through my mind. I selfishly believed that you, deaf and dumb and blind with love, had given all your heart to Sarah, and would lose her as a result. Not that I wished for any divide between the two of you. It was more from being incapable of the absolute dedication you had for Sarah. I envied that.*

It is apparent from the photograph of the three of us at St. Andrews, that Sarah had given her heart outright to you. I had confidence. You had commitment. For a fleeting moment, confidence had its day. Over the duration, commitment always prevails.

I could sense Sarah's true feelings on the 17th tee of our match on the Old Course. Though we had shared our passion in the days preceding the match, her love for you was revealed in that instant. When you saw her encouraging glance, you were no longer concerned with things so trivial as a game.

She saw your complete capitulation at that moment, not as weakness, but as a testament to your strength of caring for her. There were times when I chided you for not believing in your abilities on the golf course. I now realize that you were simply being true to your own character. You are kind. Only once did you defeat me in a match . . . our practice round at Muirfield in '21. Your reaction was to apologize and to make excuses for my failures. You are generous.

We couldn't have known at St. Andrews what the future held. I knew only that your kindness and your caring and your generosity would last forever. I am so grateful we followed our hearts. Sarah and Patrick were blessed to have you as husband and father. I was blessed to have you as my friend.

And so, Angus, we come to the end. I have given to you all the foolish and passionate trappings of my youth . . . the J. Braddell driver, a source of strength in competition . . . the Yeats collection of poetry, a source of inspiration in times of conflict . . . and the photograph of Sarah and you and me, a symbol of eternal and uncompromising love and friendship.

Finally, Angus, it is to you that I give my most dear possession of all . . . my heartfelt thanks for showing me the qualities in life worth cherishing.

I am forever grateful and will always be . . .

Your Friend,

Riley

Angus placed the letter onto the end table and cradled Yeats' book of poetry on his lap, thumbing through the pages until he located *Never Give All the Heart*.

> *Never give all the heart, for love*
> *Will hardly seem worth thinking of*
> *To passionate women if it seem*
> *Certain, and they never dream*
> *That it fades out from kiss to kiss;*
> *For everything that's lovely is*
> *But a brief, dreamy, kind of delight.*
> *O never give the heart outright,*
> *For they, for all smooth lips can say,*
> *Have given their hearts up to the play,*
> *And who could play it well enough*
> *If deaf and dumb and blind with love?*
> *He that made this knows all the cost,*
> *For he gave all his heart and lost.*

He closed the book and rubbed his tired eyes. Tears that had so often welled up on this sorrowful day, now would not. Padding across the room in his stockings, Angus removed the J. Braddell from his bag, hoping, as so often had been the case in life that, once again, his best thinking might be done golf club in hand. Like the game of golf, relationships were endlessly complex, he mused, gripping and regripping the J. Braddell, waggling it thoughtfully, so as to feel the aluminum head torque in perfect harmony with the hickory shaft. If relationships were all simple and straight-for-ward, everyone would have only those that are harmonious. No, there is always the human element . . . the damned uncontrollables. And, when the lives of three people are intertwined, the variables are countless.

Patrick had shared with Angus the passage from Riley's journal in which he had struggled mightily between his love of Sarah, and his friendship with Angus, not wishing to part with either. In the end, he had chosen to keep both intact, thought Angus. Riley's love, and his friendship, had simply been reshaped into a form more suitable to all three. The book of poetry had fallen open to a page so often visited by Riley that its spine was split permanently apart.

The friends that have it I do wrong
When ever I remake a song,
Should know what issue is at stake:
It is myself that I remake.

Easing onto the bed, Yeats clutched tightly to his chest, Angus gazed at the hickory-shafted clubs as if they held the lost treasures of his youth, and soon, he was adrift once again in the Spring of 1921.

EPILOGUE

*G*ullane Hill was concealed from view by a patch of gray clouds hovering off the Firth. At the foot of the hill, Dr. Robert Fenwick stood staring up at the dunes he had once climbed to reach the MacKenzie cottage. The grade didn't seem as steep and the grasses didn't appear nearly as impenetrable as when he was a young newsboy. The cottage was empty now, vacant these past twelve years. Had it already been twelve years since Angus passed on . . . and twenty five since Bobby Fenwick had delivered papers to him? It didn't seem possible. Wasn't it only last week that Angus had congratulated him on receiving the Angus MacKenzie grant in aid of journalism at Edinburgh University? And hadn't they celebrated his graduation just days ago, before Angus taken his final leave? Today, Angus would be delighted to learn that Dr. Robert Fenwick had been named to the MacKenzie Chair of Journalism at their alma mater. Twelve years ago Bobby Fenwick had promised to return to Gullane and purchase the MacKenzie cottage. That day had finally come.

*   *   *

When Angus died at age ninety, none of his friends survived him. Collier Ames had returned to Newcastle after Riley's funeral and donated the Colby estate to the Irish Preservation Society for use as an historical display of a typical Scotch-Irish gentry. He took a permanent room at the Slieve Donard and played golf nearly every day at Royal County Down.

On the fiftieth anniversary of his last match with Riley in the British Isles Cup, he passed away. At age eighty-four, Collier had decided to play the same forty holes he and Riley had played in 1930. While climbing a steep sand dune to reach the tee of the par three fourth, his final hole, Collier's heart gave out. Or maybe he just decided to shut it down, given the will and control he seemed to possess.

Posting 81 and 83 that day, he bested his age for the twenty-seventh and twenty-eighth times. Right to the end, Collier Colby Ames could still play. His ashes were scattered by Rawahli on the hillside of the 4th, where the blooms of heather and gorse stand watch over Dundrum Bay. In the sand dune where he came to rest, Angus and Patrick and Mick and Kathleen placed a memorial which read: *Collier Colby Ames. An Irishman.* Of all the tributes that could have been conferred, this is the one Collier wanted most. He was no longer merely proper. He had been accepted. He belonged.

*   *   *

Mick Callahan died at St. Andrews one month before Angus passed on. In his last years, he could be seen wandering the Old Course, playing shots from various angles as if still studying the subtle mysteries of the auld sod. One early morning, thick with haar, he fell into Hell Bunker while trying to play from an awkward lie near its right-hand lip. The first foursome of the day found Callahan lying face down in the sand, clutching an old hickory-shafted cleek forged by J. W. Grainger of Belfast.

It took all four caddies and two of the players to hoist Mick's two-hundred sixty pounds of dead weight out of the bunker and carry him down the last four holes. The other two golfers alternated shots on the way in out of respect for the tradition that Mick had shared with his cronies at the *Jigger Inn,* hard by The Road Hole. His stories of Riley O'Neill and Angus MacKenzie and Collier Ames were mainstays for the motley collection of caddies and golfers that frequented this cozy little tavern near the Road Hole.

When Angus and Patrick MacKenzie arrived for the funeral, Mick's drinking companions knew just what to do with his ashes, though he died without a Will. The service was as public as The Old Course itself, with hundreds of onlookers lining the green and white rail fence. As Patrick piped *Amazing Grace* from the center of the eighteenth green, Angus stood on the front apron scattering Mick Callahan's ashes into the Valley of Sin. It was the last visit Angus made to St. Andrews and, in the twilight, he peered through the window of the Royal & Ancient Clubhouse where, in 1926, Sarah had sat as registrar for the British Isle Cup. He remembered, but didn't go in.

＊   ＊   ＊

His purpose in life had ceased the day Sarah died. Oh, Angus had gone through the motions of living until he had reconciled with Patrick. And if they hadn't found each other, the light may have gone out long ago, perhaps when Riley had died. As it was, his final days were quite content. He and Patrick corresponded often, and he was pleased hear his son talk of moving from Dublin to Lahinch to publish a weekly satire of British politics he proposed to name *The Parliamentarian*.

Angus filled his last days with reading newspapers from London and Edinburgh and Dublin. He would occasionally venture to *The Cleek and Brassie*, but that, too, ended when Malcom Campbell finally gave in to the vicissitudes of life. Even the effervescent Campbell couldn't ward off fate when his own linchpin snapped. While playing Gullane No. 1, the hickory shaft of his brassie cracked just above the hosel. Malcom lost his balance, toppled over into its exposed jagged edge, skewering himself in the process. It was a dramatic exit by a character from whom nothing less would be expected.

And so, in the late afternoons, when the last light of day raised long shadows on the hills and hummocks of Muirfield, Angus would traipse down to the course with just two clubs . . . Riley's J. Braddell driver and his own Dreadnought niblick. Crossing the stile over the stone wall along the second hole, he would play his own loop . . . the third, fifteenth, and first, before making his way back up Gullane Hill to the cottage. If any members were playing at dusk, they knew to give way to Angus MacKenzie.

The afternoon of his passing was a perfect replica to the one in June of 1921 when he and Riley had played their first round together . . . a breeze freshening off the Firth, sun spilling onto the slate of Muirfield's roof, fescue crunching beneath his spikes. Angus always chose the first hole to finish because of its difficulty. If only he could bogey number one, he felt that he had accomplished something special. Angus had become a surprisingly good putter with the J. Braddell and that day holed a thirty footer at the first for par. Two over for the loop, it was as well as he had played in a decade.

He crossed the stile and started up the hill, knowing full well he couldn't finish the steep climb. But he was headed home, and wouldn't bring himself to quit. Halfway up, out of breath and wheezing, a pain shot across his chest. In the gloaming, and plodding ever onward, Angus turned toward Muirfield one last time, settled back into the warmth of sand and rustling of marram, and closed his eyes.

*   *   *

The services for Angus were quiet and private, attended only by Patrick MacKenzie, Kathleen and Lee McAndrew and Bobby Fenwick. After the funeral, the ashes of Angus Alexander MacKenzie were released from the top of Gullane Hill, carried down the slope by a gentle evening breeze. Patrick piped the mournful refrains of *Will Ye Nae Come Back Again* and far away, in the village of North Berwick, the five o'clock train to Edinburgh piped back a plaintive whistle, lamenting the passing of an old friend. Against the echo of bagpipes, Bobby recited *A Prayer for Old Age* from the tattered book of Yeats.

God guard me from those thoughts men think
In the mind alone;
He that sings a lasting song
Thinks in a marrow-bone;

From all that makes a wise old man
That can be praised of all;
O what am I that I should not seem
For the song's sake a fool?

I pray—for fashion's word is out
And prayer comes round again—
That I may seem, though I die old,
A foolish, passionate man.

The foursome meditated on their favourite memories of the man as they made their way back into the cottage for the reading of Angus' *Will*, where Patrick cleared his throat and began:

> *I give to Kathleen McAndrew the Yeats Book of Poetry. May it provide as much inspiration to you, Kathleen, as it did Riley and me.*

> *I give to Lee McAndrew, Riley's J. Braddell driver. May you someday purchase the patent on the club from the defunct J. Braddell Co. in Belfast so that golfers of today may enjoy the wonders of technology that Riley enjoyed.*

> *I grant to Bobby Fenwick, the first right of refusal to purchase my cottage on Gullane Hill. I know it means as much to you, Bobby, as it did to me. And I know you'll pay Patrick a fair price for it.*

> *I give to Patrick, my son, the remainder of my worldly possessions, including the proceeds from the sale of my cottage. Patrick, you might take the profit and start a weekly newspaper in Lahinch. I know how much that would mean to you, and to Kathleen. Your voice can be heard just as clearly from there as from Dublin.*

> *Lastly, I would like to share with all of you, the genealogy chart that I found taped inside the front cover of Yeats' book of poetry, after Riley willed it to me.*

> *Angus Alexander MacKenzie*

Kathleen handed the book of poetry to Patrick. Carefully removing the chart, he spread it onto the kitchen table for all to see. The history of the Clan O'Neill was laid out from the time of Hugh Ui 'Naill, chieftain of Tyrone in 1547, through fifteen generations of O'Neills, down to Padraig, born 1872, whose marriage to Sinead produced a son, Riley Padraig O'Neill, born 1898. But, curiously, next to the name of Riley's grandfather, Liam, appeared the name of Sean, a brother, whose surname was shown as *Neel*. Married to Sioban, they produced a daughter, Nettie, born 1875, wed to a Scotsman, Alexander, and in the year 1900, they brought into the world a son . . . Angus Alexander MacKenzie.

0-595-66623-X

Printed in the United States
22554LVS00002B/103-180

9 780595 666232